THE PRESIDENT'S DAUGHTER

THE PRESIDENT'S DAUGHTER

ELLEN EMERSON WHITE

Feiwel and Friends New York

For my mother. Naturally.

A Feiwel and Friends Book
An Imprint of Macmillan

Library of Congress Cataloging-in-Publication Data Available

ISBN-13: 978-0-312-37488-4
ISBN-10: 0-312-37488-7

Feiwel and Friends logo designed by Filomena Tuosto

Originally published in the United States by Scholastic Press

First Feiwel and Friends Edition: August 2008

10 9 8 7 6 5 4 3 2 1

www.feiwelandfriends.com

THE PRESIDENT'S DAUGHTER

1

MEG WAS TEN minutes early. It was her mother's opinion that three minutes were more than sufficient, but Meg liked to play it safe. Less pressure that way.

She slouched into the country club, wearing old blue sweatpants, a baggy V-neck tennis sweater, and a faded green Lacoste shirt. The receptionist at the front desk nodded, and Meg nodded back. It was Friday afternoon, so the place was pretty quiet, although commuters would probably start showing up any minute now for after-work drinks. Which meant that her mother would have to shake hands all over the place. Pretty embarrassing.

She sat down in an uncomfortable upholstered chair, checking to make sure that no one was watching before swinging her legs up onto the coffee table. There were a bunch of tennis and golf magazines stacked there, along with the latest copies of *Travel & Leisure, Architectural Digest, The New Yorker*, and *Vanity Fair*. She had a tremendous urge to go up to the desk and ask if they could get her a couple of tabloids, but repressed it. Sometimes people didn't have a sense of humor about things like that.

She glanced over at the clock. Seven minutes of five. That meant she had four minutes to go—unless her mother's plane was late, or she was tied up in Boston traffic. Some Fridays, that happened.

To occupy herself, Meg unwrapped the blue bandanna from her racquet handle, not sure whether to tie it around her head as a sweatband or just hide it inside her tennis bag. She could never decide if bandannas were cool or trendy—it was impossible to be both.

The front door of the club opened, and she heard a familiar voice: Glen, her mother's top aide.

"—at eight-thirty," he was saying. "And then, at nine—"

Her mother nodded, looking both dignified—and tired—in a grey silk dress and her London Fog raincoat. She saw Meg, and her face changed, the fatigue and political smile replaced by a grin. She crossed the hall with swift grace, and Meg stood up to receive an enthusiastic hug, smelling bold but understated perfume.

"I hope I'm not late," her mother said, glancing at her watch.

"No," Meg said. "I was just kind of early."

"Well, I'm sorry you had to wait." Her mother held her away. "Smile."

Meg smiled obediently.

"Oh, you look beautiful," her mother said. "Much older." She turned to Glen, and her press secretary, Linda. "Doesn't Meg look beautiful without her braces?"

Linda and Glen nodded. They weren't what you'd call effusive types. More like what you'd call grumps.

"Well." Her mother checked her watch again. "We'd better get moving." She looked at Glen and Linda. "I'll anticipate seeing you shortly before eight."

Glen scanned whatever message had just come in—he always carried the newest and most flashy handheld gadgets; cost be damned—and then shook his head. "I think seven would be more—"

"I haven't seen my family since Monday," her mother said, somewhat sharply. "Eight will be quite sufficient."

He sighed, but nodded.

"Thank you," her mother said. "I'll see you in a few hours." She took the tennis bag yet another one of her aides had just brought inside. "Thanks, Frank." Then, she put her free arm around Meg. "Come on, let's not waste any court time."

"See you later," Meg said to Glen and Linda and Frank, then followed her mother down to the womens' locker room. Watching her, Meg decided that her mother was the kind of person who made her wish that she had on pumps. Not that Meg could walk in pumps.

Not that she really *wanted* to walk in pumps. Put-together, that's how her mother looked. As if she'd never had a grey hair. Except, forty-four was kind of old for that.

"Mom?" she asked.

Her mother unzipped her tennis bag. "What?"

It was maybe tactless, but—"Do you color your hair?" she asked.

Her mother instantly shook her head. "No."

Hmmm. Meg considered that. "Never?"

"Occasionally." Her mother turned to looked at her. "Why?"

"Just curious," Meg said.

Her mother lifted an eyebrow, but didn't pursue that.

Meg sat in the lounge part of the locker room, slouched low enough to avoid the many mirrors. She wasn't heavily into mirrors.

In short order, her mother came out in a designer pleated skirt/striped shirt ensemble, walking over to the largest mirror to put up her hair, doing so with three deft bobby-pin jabs. She frowned at the mirror, retouched her makeup, then shook her head to loosen some of the hair in the bun. The Senator prepares to enter the public eye. She saw Meg watching, and smiled.

"I only color it when it starts greying strangely," she said.

Meg put on her best solemn expression. "I guess only your hairdresser knows for sure."

"What, are you kidding? I do it late at night," her mother said.

"Do you turn the lights out first?" Meg asked.

Her mother laughed. "Always." Leaving the locker room, she glanced down at Meg's outfit. "What happened to all of those nice clothes you got for your birthday?"

"I don't know," Meg said, a little self-conscious about the contrast between them. The Senator and the slovenly daughter. "I feel like I'm not supposed to perspire in them."

Her mother nodded. "No point in ruining good clothes by wearing them."

Meg looked at her uncertainly, not sure if that was a joke.

"How's your ankle?" her mother asked.

Christ, not that again. "That was *months* ago, Mom," Meg said. "I'm fine." She had rolled it pretty badly during the quarter-finals of the North Sectionals, and even though she was still able to win the match, she had been diagnosed with such a severe sprain that her parents made her withdraw from the tournament, and she'd had to gimp around on stupid crutches for a few weeks.

Her mother nodded, a little bit defensively. "Okay. I was just asking."

They continued towards the courts in silence.

"I was going to win," Meg said, "and go on to the MIAA." Which was the tournament to determine the high school state champions.

Her mother nodded—except that it wasn't very convincing.

"I was," Meg said, although, privately, she wasn't too damn sure of that.

Her mother nodded again.

"You don't think I was going to win?" Meg asked.

Her mother sighed. "Meg, I know you wish we had let you play, but you were injured, and you weren't going to get past that kid—what's-her-name?—from Concord-Carlisle, anyway."

Well, okay, probably not. Especially since she—her name was Janice Yates—was three years older, ranked 7th in the New England USTA 18-and-under division, and had ultimately ended up winning the individual state title.

But, still.

"Next season, though," her mother said, as they took their court. "*Next* season, I'm picking you."

She was probably just saying that to be nice, but it *was* nice, and Meg nodded, slightly mollified.

"Rally for a while?" her mother asked, already on the other side of the net.

"Um, yeah, sure," Meg said, starting to take her Babolat racquet out of her bag—she had only brought two along—but then, changing her mind and pulling out the Volkl, instead. Her mother was like, a phenomenal tennis player, and Meg generally felt lucky to get more than a few games off her, although she would play as hard as she could. Over the last year or so, more and more games had gone to deuce, and sometimes Meg even won a set.

Not often enough, but sometimes.

They kept the court for almost an hour, her mother winning 6–4, 7–6. When she lost the last point, Meg wanted to swear very loudly, but she let out a hard breath, instead, looking down at her racquet and wondering whether she should have gone with the Babolat. Or maybe, she should have brought her Yonex. Yeah, she might have won with the Yonex.

Meeting her up at the net, Meg noticed that her mother was flushed and trying to hide the fact that she was out of breath.

"Are you okay?" Meg asked, just to be sure.

"Fine." Her mother blotted her face with a towel. "You've been playing a lot lately?"

Meg shrugged. "Pretty much."

Her mother nodded. "It shows."

"Hello, Senator," one of the women taking over the court said. "How's Washington?"

"Not bad," her mother said. "How's psychology?"

"Not bad," the woman said.

"Have a good match." Her mother draped a light sweater around her shoulders, then picked up her tennis bag.

"How do you remember all that stuff?" Meg held the door as they left the court area. "I mean, all the people you meet."

"Practice, I guess," her mother said. "I've never been one for mnemonics."

Meg nodded intelligently, rather than asking, "What are mnemonics?"

"I mean," her mother's voice was very casual, "I personally find that memory devices complicate things even more."

Meg blushed. She would have to work on her intelligent nod.

"Hey." Her mother paused near the club's bar. "Feel like going into the Grille to get something to drink?"

Meg shrugged and followed her, trying to get her sweater to drape just as sportily around her shoulders. Or at least *half* as sportily.

The bar was crowded, and it took a few minutes for her mother to finish shaking hands and exchanging pleasantries with various people. Then, they sat at a table in the corner, a waiter instantly hurrying over.

"What can I get you, Senator?" he asked.

"Orange juice, thank you." She grinned. "It's not just for breakfast anymore."

"I know the chef would love to send out a tasting menu for you," the waiter said, "if—"

Her mother shook her head. "Thank you, that's very thoughtful, but we'll be having supper at home very soon."

With—judging from the time—Glen and Linda, and probably Frank.

"I believe," Meg said, "that I'll have a martini."

"That's what you think," her mother said. "How's orange juice sound?"

"Not as good as Coke," Meg said.

Her mother nodded at the waiter, who nodded back and scurried off to get their drinks. When he returned, her mother took a sip of juice, glanced around at the other people in the bar, and leaned forward.

"How can you play tennis, or golf, and be terribly healthy, and then come in here and drink?" she asked.

Good question. Meg gulped some Coke. "Are you sure I can't have a martini?"

"What do you know about martinis?" her mother asked.

Another good question. "Lots," Meg said.

"Right." Her mother finished half the juice, still flushed from playing. She lowered her glass, looking at Meg thoughtfully. "Since it's just the two of us, I thought we could have a—"

"Senator Powers." One of the men who had been standing at the bar was suddenly at their table. "I wanted to congratulate you on the work you did on the chemical dumping bill."

"Oh, well, thank you," her mother said. "How've things been going for you?"

He shrugged. "Not bad, not bad."

"Oh, I'm sorry." Her mother turned. "This is my daughter, Meghan. Meg, this is Mr. Garvey."

"How do you do," Meg said.

"Hi," Mr. Garvey said briefly. "Senator, what I wanted to ask you was, the wife and kids and I are going down to D.C. for a week. What's the chances of us being able to get some gallery passes?"

Her mother nodded. "Call the Boston office, and talk to Harriet. She'll arrange everything for you."

"Okay, thank you. Thank you very much," he said, and went back to the bar.

"Another day, another vote," Meg said.

Her mother grimaced.

"You know, there's a pothole on Hammond Street that's *really* bugging me," Meg said.

Her mother grinned wryly. "Call the Boston office. Be sure to use my name."

Right. "How come you have to go out and give speeches tonight?" Meg asked. "I thought you were going to be home."

"Well." Her mother looked uncomfortable. "It's only two. I should be back by ten-thirty, at the latest."

Meg nodded. It wasn't as though this was the first time.

"Anyway," her mother said. "I thought since it's just—" She glanced around to make sure. "Since it *is* just the two of us, I thought we could have a talk."

Meg stiffened. "Am I in trouble?"

Her mother shook her head. "No, of course not."

That still didn't sound good. "I wasn't limping before," Meg said. "I just tripped." Which was actually true.

"I know. I just want to talk to you," her mother said.

Meg relaxed. "If it's about sex, I already know," she said, sitting back in her chair.

"Since we went over it about six years ago, I should hope it's sunk in by now. At any rate," her mother went on, "your father and I have been discussing this at length, and—"

"What," Meg said, "sex?"

Her mother looked impatient. "Meg, come on, I'm being serious."

Recognizing the irritation in her mother's voice, Meg was quiet.

Her mother took a deep breath. "I guess I wanted to talk to you before your brothers, because—well, it's about the next election."

Whoa. Meg sat up straighter. "You mean, you're not running?"

"I'm not running for Senate," her mother conceded.

How completely excellent. "You mean, you'll like, live at home all the time?" Meg could almost feel her eyes lighting up, or whatever it was that eyes did.

"Meg, I want to run for President," her mother said.

Meg choked, losing half her mouthful of soda on the table. She shoved her napkin onto the liquid, still coughing. "Are you kidding?"

Her mother shook her head.

"Oh my God," Meg said.

"A lot of party people have been approaching me. And, quite frankly, a lot of the big donors," her mother said. "They think the country's ready for—well, what do you think?"

At the moment, she kind of thought it would be nice if Mr. Garvey came back over and ignored her some more. "Isn't it kind of early?" Meg asked, because she couldn't come up with anything else to say. "In the, you know, election cycle?"

"It's kind of *late*, Meg," her mother said. "Almost everyone else already has organizations on the ground, and the greybeards are signing on, and—well, I don't have much time left to decide."

Her mother had always been pretty well known—she had already been in Congress when Meg was born—but after she had given an incredibly well-received keynote address at the last Democratic Convention, she had turned into the kind of high-profile politician who regularly appeared on the Sunday morning talk shows, and who made national news on a not irregular basis.

"Is this because of the speech?" Meg asked.

"Well, I like to think there's more to it than that," her mother said.

Yeah, but, *President*? Meg frowned. "Will you be in the primaries and everything?"

Her mother nodded. "At least the early ones. And—well, I would be planning for considerably more than that."

This whole conversation felt like a really bad dream. Or, anyway, a really *weird* dream. "Will you be able to be home at all?" Meg asked.

"Not much," her mother admitted.

Great. "What's Dad think?" she asked.

"I want your opinion," her mother said. "Not his."

Meg studied her, healthy and alert, the thin neck and face quite tanned against the white sweater. "You look like a President."

Her mother's eyebrows went up. "*Now?*"

"Yeah," Meg said. "You dress right. And you're tall enough."

"Well, thank you." Her mother laughed. "Think we can work 'five eight' into a slogan somewhere?"

Meg twirled her straw, thinking about all of this. "You're not—I mean—what happens if you win?"

"I guess that would mean I'd be President," her mother said.

Perish the thought. "My God." Meg shuddered, dropping the straw. "You think you'll win?"

"I'll be happy if I make a good showing in New Hampshire," her mother said, "forget anything else."

"My God." Meg shuddered again.

Her mother looked at her uneasily. "Well, what do you think?"

"Can I have a martini?" Meg asked.

GETTING HOME HALF an hour later, they found Meg's little brothers Steven and Neal on one side of the kitchen table, making a salad—while Meg's father sat on the other side, drinking a Sam Adams and frowning at the newspaper.

Steven was eleven, thin and pugnacious, with their mother's dark hair and blue eyes—which, all things being equal, was pretty much the way Meg looked herself. Neal, who was six and still hanging on to somewhat blondish hair, took more after their father.

"Hey!" Neal scrambled up. "It's Mom!"

"Hi." She caught him in a hug, dropping her tennis bag.

Steven shoved the carrots away and moved in for his turn. Their mother hugged him, and then Meg's father, which was a different kind of hug. Longer. They looked at each other, and Meg's father brought his hand up to her mother's cheek.

"You look tired," he said.

"Well"—she kissed him lightly—"I've been playing tennis."

"Mom, Mom, look!" Neal rushed out of the room, then back in with a handful of school papers. "I got a hundred in spelling and everything!"

"Well, let's see." She sat down, and Neal climbed up on her lap, grass-stained and disheveled from soccer practice. "Wow, a ninety-five in math. Oh, that's great."

"Hi," Meg said to her father.

"How was school?" he asked.

"Okay," she said. "How was work? Get lots of new clients today?"

"Hundreds." He smiled at her. "How was *tennis*?"

Yes, that was the more important question. "I got her to a tie-breaker," Meg said.

"Good for you," he said, and then winked at her mother. "Need some Advil?"

Her mother, who had actually been limping a little herself when they got out of the car, shook her head—but grinned sheepishly and took a couple when he went over to one of the cupboards and handed the bottle to her.

"Bet Mom'll make you get a haircut tomorrow," Meg said to Steven, just to get him going.

He threw some carrot peelings at her as the phone rang, and they both jumped for it, Steven getting there first.

"Hello? Oh, just a minute, please." He covered the receiver. "Mom, it's what's-his-name from Texas. Mr. Palmer."

Otherwise known as the Senate Minority Leader. Her mother picked up the phone. "Brian, hi," she said, and went off into a conversation about some Select Committee hearing or something.

"Party business," Steven said, trying to make his voice deeper.

"Party?" Meg said. "Who's having a party?"

"Boy, do we have a dumb sister," Steven said to Neal, who laughed.

Half an hour and six phone calls later, they were sitting down to dinner, observing her father's very strict no-electronic-or-telephonic-devices-during-mealtimes rule as they ate the stew that Trudy, their housekeeper, had made and the salad Meg had had to finish making. On weekends, Trudy usually went home to her house over in Brighton.

Their father frowned, which made him look like the stern, businesslike tax attorney version of himself. His smile, on the other hand, usually made him look more like a jolly lumberjack. "Steven, we'd better see about getting that hair cut tomorrow."

Steven groaned, and Meg laughed.

"You'll probably be even better at basketball if it isn't in your eyes all the time," their mother said, reasonably.

"Me, too?" Neal asked.

"You, too." Their mother leaned over to cut his meat.

He watched her, his elbows on the table. "Were you important today?"

She made four quick horizontal slices. "Not really."

"Did you talk in front of everyone?" he asked.

"I guess I always do, don't I?" She handed him his plate, indicating with her eyebrows for him to move his elbows.

"Boy." He reached in front of Steven for the bread basket, saw his father's expression, and sat back. "Would you please pass me the bread, please?" he asked politely.

Steven grabbed two pieces, then shoved the basket along.

"Boy," Neal said, taking two pieces of his own. "I bet all those Senators listen to you."

Their mother smiled. "Some days more so than others."

"Boy," he said. "You should be President."

She glanced at Meg, who had to fight off yet another shudder.

"Meg, be a good munchkin and pass me the salt, will you?" she asked.

2

AFTER THE USUAL fight with Steven over the dishes—the fight they always had when Trudy wasn't around either to officiate or do them herself—Meg escaped upstairs with the excuse of homework, although mostly she just answered email, goofed around on the Internet, and called her best friend, Beth Shulman, to bring her up to date on the latest turn of events, getting a lot of "*Seriously*?" and "Wow, that sucks" remarks in return.

Which were, of course, the exact responses she wanted.

But, homework actually would not have been all that terrible an idea, since the next night there was a dance at school, and she and Beth and Sarah Weinberger and a few other people were planning to go and collectively stare at Rick Hamilton, which would undoubtedly be fruitless, but entertaining. Then, Sunday night was out, because her parents were having a dinner party for an ambassador and his wife, along with the governor, and a bunch of other political types. Party business, as Steven would say. Anyway, that would mean that they'd have to make appearances, be properly well-mannered and articulate children, and maybe pass hors d'oeuves. At least there would be maids and butlers and caterers around to serve dinner. Even with Trudy's extensive tutelage, she and Steven would definitely have made a mess with dinner.

"Looks like no homework this weekend," she said to her cat, Vanessa, who was sitting on the side of her desk, washing.

Vanessa purred, rubbing her head against Meg's hand, and then, gave her a healthy swat with her right paw—which was pretty much the way life was with Vanessa.

They had five animals, and technically, that meant each member of the family should have one, but it hadn't worked out that way. Vanessa was hers, and had been ever since the day Meg found her, a tiny grey kitten wandering around outside the Chestnut Hill Mall, and brought her home. Adlai and Sidney, the two Siamese, were her parents' cats and rarely deigned to leave their bedroom. Humphrey, the lumbering, arrogant tiger cat, didn't belong to anyone. He had shown up on their patio a couple of summers before and decided to move in, no matter what anyone else said about it. He took turns sleeping in everyone's rooms—"sleeping around," her father said.

Then, there was Kirby, their dog. They had gotten him at the pound right after Neal was born—so Neal could have a twin, was Steven's explanation—and no one could agree on what breed he was. He had grown up into a large shaggy brown-and-white dog with floppy ears and a shepherd head. The kind of dog whose loved ones were the only ones who thought he was beautiful. Anyway, Kirby belonged to all of them, although mostly, he would sack out on Steven's bed at night. For that matter, he napped there almost all day, every day, too.

"I think"—Meg looked at her cat and then opened the music library on her computer—"that it's time for a musical interlude."

Vanessa stretched out her front paws, back arching, then jumped over to the bed and settled down to sleep.

Meg's favorite song in life was Joan Jett's "I Love Rock and Roll," but that was too rowdy for sitting down and being fretful—which was her plan. Something soothing would be preferable, so she went with *The Sound of Music*, since, secretly, she was a major fan of musicals.

Or, okay, maybe not at *all* secretly.

During the overture, she went over to her bed to lie down and be pensive. President. Good God. As far back as she could remember, her mother's life—and, as a result, the rest of the family's lives—had revolved around Washington; it was a given. First, the House of Representatives, then the Senate. Nothing like moving up the old ranks.

Her mother had taken maybe six weeks off when Steven was born, and they'd lived in Washington for almost two years when Neal showed up, but basically, it had always been like this—the family here in Chestnut Hill, outside Boston, and her mother living in an apartment in Georgetown, flying in on weekends and whenever else she could. They were all used to it, and as her mother put it, "tried to make the days they *were* together count." Those days always seemed to be hectic.

It was hard even to imagine what it would be like if her mother was a lawyer in her father's firm, or a teacher or something, and lived at home all the time. Not that Meg didn't wish it were that way. Whenever Congress recessed and her mother didn't have to be out among her constituents—possibly Meg's least favorite word in the English language—it was so nice. Kind of a luxury. Waking up and hearing those quick footsteps on the stairs made her feel complete inside, that everything was as it should be. When her mother was home, the footsteps never seemed to stop, as though she was trying to make up for every single day that she hadn't been there.

No one at school thought it was much of a big deal, thank God. They were used to it. In fact, a lot of her friends were always saying they wished *their* mothers didn't have to be around all the time and yelling at them or whatever. Meg would have chosen the yelling any day.

She ruffled up Vanessa's fur, then smoothed it down again, except for the fur on and around her head, creating an ugly, out-of-proportion beast. Quite the stray cat look.

It was funny—it had gotten so that no one even thought about it twice when her mother was on CNN or someplace. And it was an odd day if she wasn't prominently mentioned in the paper and all over the Internet. For a while, Meg had saved all of the articles, but it just got ridiculous. There were magazine write-ups, too, like the one a couple of months earlier in the *New York Times Magazine*—a story about "The Leader of That Growing Minority: Women in

Washington." With that one, she'd even had her picture on the cover—which several national publications had also done, in the wake of her speech at the Democratic Convention.

"A Minority of One," she said to Vanessa. "Female Presidents."

Enough of being pensive. She went over to her computer, turned her speakers all the way up, and clicked on an ancient Ramones song, "Cretin Hop"—she was nothing if not retro; in fact, Beth occasionally accused her of being downright *antediluvian*—so that she could dance around the room with Vanessa for a few minutes. Dancing amused Vanessa.

She was singing along and hopping on one foot, when the door opened, and she stopped, in mid-gyration, to blush. "Don't you knock?"

"Well, I—" Her mother was trying, unsuccessfully, not to grin. "I—the music was so loud."

Meg put Vanessa down and clicked the song off, her face very hot. "Did you want anything?" she asked stiffly.

"Well, I—" Her mother's eyes were bright, and she seemed to be shaking from keeping the laughter inside. "The music was so loud," she said again.

"Yeah, well"—Meg coughed—"what can I do for you?"

"How about 'Slaughter on Tenth Avenue'?" her mother suggested, and broke up completely.

Meg scowled.

"I'm sorry," her mother said, controlling herself. "I didn't—I'm really sorry."

Meg didn't say anything, arms tightly folded.

"Come on," her mother said, "where's your sense of humor?"

"I don't have one," Meg said, trying to stay grouchy, but unable to keep back a small grin. It was probably pretty funny to come across an energetic hopping cretin. She looked at her mother, who was extremely soignée in a light grey wool dress. "How'd the speeches go?"

"Not bad," her mother said. "A little tiring, maybe."

Meg nodded, smoothing the fur on Vanessa's head. Her mother spent most weekends being exhausted.

"Well." Her mother moved towards the door. "I'm sorry I disturbed you."

Which maybe wasn't the best way for them to end the night. "You, uh, going to bed or something?" Meg asked.

Her mother turned instantly. "No. I just thought—well." She came back in. "So. How are you feeling about things?"

"Which things?" Meg asked, to be difficult.

Her mother just looked at her.

"Oh, that," Meg said.

"Mmm, that." Her mother picked up the copy of *All the President's Men* that was on the bedside table, automatically smoothing the binding and putting in a piece of paper as a bookmark. "Were you reading this before, or did you start it tonight?"

Because—not that she would go around admitting it—she did kind of like reading about politics. Novels were good, too, but her parents had a pretty amazing collection of political non-fiction, and she had been raiding it regularly for the past couple of years. And it was a lot easier to talk to a lot of the guests who came over if she knew a little about the subject. Besides, she had gotten tired of reading book after book about Iraq, and stuff like that, and it was sort of relaxing to go back in history a little. "Book report," she said, then thought about that. "You going to call yours *All the President's People*?"

Her mother winced. "God forbid."

Yeah. "I'll, uh, probably have to watch saying things like that," Meg said.

"Probably definitely." Her mother glanced over. "You're feeling a little better about the idea?"

"I don't know." Meg stroked Vanessa's fur down, making her face very serpentine. "I mean, it doesn't seem real."

"No, it doesn't," her mother said, and Meg watched her pace, wondering if she would do that someday—or be more like her father, who just tightened up and didn't move. "It really doesn't."

"What's it going to be like?" Meg asked.

Her mother shrugged. "I don't know. Undoubtedly full of media assaults, ugly rumors, and depressing defeats."

Swell. "Sounds fun," Meg said.

Her mother stopped pacing. "I'm sorry. I'm not answering your question, am I?" She sat down at the end of the bed. "There's going to be a great deal of publicity, much of it probably very unfavorable and unkind. And your father will have to be away with me, or traveling on his own, a certain amount of the time."

"What about us?" Meg asked, uneasily.

Her mother shrugged. "I'm not going to *make* you campaign, if that's what you mean."

"So," Meg said, "I could, like, back another candidate?"

Her mother nodded, looking amused. "If you're so inclined."

Well, she'd have to examine everyone else's positions on the issues, first. "Will it mostly be leafleting, or standing around having our pictures taken, or what?" Meg asked.

"Probably a little of both," her mother said.

Terrific. "Gross," Meg said. "I hate having my picture taken."

Her mother laughed. "I do like you, Meg." She reached over to touch her face, and move some of her hair away from her eyes. "I feel like—you're growing up, and I'm missing it."

Well—yeah. That was more or less what was happening. "You're not missing it," Meg said, awkwardly.

Her mother nodded dismissively, and then looked at her for a long minute. "You know, there must be a lot of crushes over at that school."

"Yeah," Meg said. "And I have all of them."

Her mother smiled. "Be thankful. When I was your age, I was at an all-girls school, and I was absolutely terrified of boys."

Her mother? Afraid of men? Inconceivable. "Really?" Meg asked.

Her mother nodded. "Really. And I was tall. Height was the bane of my existence."

"Rough life," Meg said.

Her mother's expression was hard to read. "Well, I know I thought so."

Neither of them spoke, listening to Vanessa purr.

"Was it hard?" Meg asked.

Her mother looked over. "Was what hard?"

Could she ask this, without starting trouble? "N-not having a mother around," Meg said.

"Yes, it was." Her mother laughed shortly. "Not that I have to tell *you.*"

She never should have brought up this particular subject at all. "Mom."

"Well, it's not as if I'm around," her mother said.

No, but—"It's different," Meg said.

Her mother nodded, obviously not agreeing.

"It was a riding accident?" Meg both asked and said. This wasn't something they ever discussed.

Her mother nodded again. "My mother wasn't a person who knew her limitations. She—" Her hand clenched tightly. "I don't know, it's hard to remember. I was so small."

Meg looked at the thin, tense hand in her mother's lap, and moved closer. "I always thought you were mean when you wouldn't let me take riding lessons."

"I suppose I was," her mother said, with very little expression on her face.

"I don't mean I think so anymore." She touched the hand for a fraction of a second and saw it relax. "Mom?"

Her mother glanced over.

"Do you know your limitations?" Meg asked.

"No," her mother said. "No, I don't guess I do."

"I kind of figured." Meg tilted her head up to look at her, noticing the laugh lines around her mouth and eyes. Unexpected lines. Lines no one would ever see from a distance. "Are you going to win?"

Her mother shook her head. "I very much doubt it."

Well, maybe, but her mother had never exactly been the type to embrace futility—or lost causes. "Then, how come you're running?" Meg asked.

"I don't know." Her mother's laugh lines deepened suddenly. "I guess I think I can win."

HER MOTHER ANNOUNCED her candidacy in front of a huge crowd in front of Faneuil Hall in downtown Boston, the whole family standing behind her, the event covered by so many different media outlets that it was more than a little mind-numbing. Also, Meg thought that she, personally, looked sort of nervous and haunted on camera—which was embarrassing. Regardless, the level of media saturation was so intense, that she kept expecting to see her mother show up on the cover of *Popular Mechanics* or *Ranger Rick* next.

Within a couple of weeks, the campaign became a routine like everything else. Her mother was home even less often, traveling around the country whenever she wasn't in Washington, calling at some point every night to talk to them all. Lots of weekends, Meg's father would fly out to be with her, while Trudy took care of Meg and her brothers. Sometimes—not very often—her mother would make it home for a day or two, and once, for just a few hours, so she could see Neal on his birthday.

When her mother was home, Meg got accustomed to the house being full of campaign people, a few of whom she knew from her mother's Senate staff, but most of them were strangers. Hired-guns. Seasoned hands. Gurus. Glen—who had been christened *The Boy Wonder* by the press—was the official campaign manager, and had become more high-strung and intense than ever, as a result. Very jittery guy. Linda, her mother's press secretary, had only been working for her for about ten months, and Meg realized now that she must have been brought in specifically to help prepare for the planned Presidential campaign. So, the whole thing must have been in the works for a long time. Linda was obsessed with "images"—as opposed to Glen, who mostly cared about "sending messages"—and Meg didn't like her much. Smooth California blond, combined with aloof Smith College poise. Meg suspected that Linda had been brought on because she was able to be tough in ways that her mother wasn't—cutting off press conferences, dodging questions, withholding information until the appropriate moment. With the press, Meg's mother was apt to be either very candid or very funny—both of which made Glen and Linda nervous.

The rest of the top-level campaign people were an incongruous bunch. There were quite a few more men than women, and the vast majority of them reminded her of bespectacled, intellectual versions of some of the professional athletes to whom she'd been introduced over the years at various political events—extremely competitive, and even more cocky.

And, although nothing much would really happen—other than a few meaningless, crowded debates—until the Iowa Caucus, her mother was getting more and more publicity, a decent percentage of it positive, although some of the coverage was so vicious and invasive that, even though her parents had warned the three of them in advance that the campaign was bound to get ugly, she couldn't help being a little shocked by, say, a total stranger who would surface, claiming to have had a long-time, extra-marital affair with her mother and that sort of thing. New polls of the "would you vote for so-and-so, if Candidate A joined the race; and what if Candidate B joined the race, too?" variety seemed to come out almost every day, and her mother generally placed second or third among the eight or nine candidates who were currently officially in the race.

Naturally, ultraconservative types were making all sorts of noise about a woman's place being at home with her children, and the country's need for a Strong Leader in such perilous times—which, Meg assumed, meant a *male* leader—but her mother was so well-respected as a Senator, that the negative publicity didn't seem to be doing very much damage. So far, anyway. She had been a prominent member of the Senate Foreign Relations and Armed Services Committees for years, and was the chairperson of the Emerging Threats and Capabilities subcommittee, and she also served on the Health, Education, Labor and Pensions Committee, and the Select Committee on Intelligence. And, of course, it went without saying that she had successfully sponsored, and co-sponsored, legislation across the spectrum, going back to her first term as a House Representative. A pretty fair political package, as Linda would say.

Meg and her brothers had decided early on that their favorite campaign person was Preston Fielding. He was this young, incredibly cool black guy who had been a top aide to the Speaker of the House, and was now a full-time media relations and legislative outreach consultant for her mother. Titles aside, Meg had noticed that Preston just sort of did whatever needed doing. When other people had lost or forgotten demographic sheets or expenditure lists or whatever, Preston invariably had copies handy. He would show up with pizza and a case of Heineken when everyone was getting uptight and grouchy; he seemed to know about six important people in every government agency—all of whom owed him favors; he was great at fund-raising. Important as all of that was, Meg liked him because he was so funny. And, okay, unbelievably *handsome*.

Every day, their lives seemed to change a little more, as a direct result of the campaign. Like the telephone company showing up to install multiple extra land-lines in the house. Or the Secret Service all over the place, studying their neighborhood and interviewing people, because her mother was going to start receiving protection soon—an idea too scary to even *think* about yet. Since—as far as she knew—none of the other candidates were being protected yet, she assumed it meant that her mother was already getting significant threats. The post office was delivering so much mail that they came to the door with sacks, instead of trying to use the mailbox, and the mail was being carefully *examined* first, before any of them were allowed to touch it.

The concept of which was also very god-damn unsettling.

Maybe the hardest part of all was that her father was now out of town frequently, too. The house felt so empty. Steven would slouch around, pretending not to miss them, and Neal would have ten times as many bad dreams as usual. And Meg never knew what to do for either of them. Thank God for Trudy.

One Sunday night, when her parents were in Pennsylvania or someplace, Steven and Neal wandered off after dinner, while Meg hung around in the kitchen to help Trudy with the dishes.

"I can take care of this," Trudy said, smiling at her over grandmotherly glasses. "You should do your homework."

"I don't have any," Meg said. Which was a flat-out lie.

"A sophomore in high school, and you don't have any homework?" Trudy clicked her tongue with disapproval.

"Nope," Meg said, drying the spaghetti sauce pan.

Trudy looked at her *through* her glasses this time.

It wasn't all that hard to get away with things around her mother—but Trudy had a much more suspicious nature.

Or else, she was just paying closer attention.

"Okay, I maybe have a little bit left," Meg said, and then looked at the clock. "Wonder what Mom and Dad are doing." Of course, she could probably turn on CNN, or check the Internet, and find out, in due course.

"They're probably at a church supper," Trudy said, washing the salad bowl. "And your mother's getting ready to make a speech."

"Probably," Meg said, and resisted the impulse to put the pan away harder than necessary.

Which Trudy, predictably, noticed.

"You know, Meg," she said, "if you need someone to—"

Meg shook her head. "I don't. I mean, thanks, anyway, but I really don't." She closed the cupboard. Very quietly. "You think I ought to go see what Steven and Neal are doing?"

Trudy nodded. "We're almost finished here, anyway."

Hearing the television, Meg went into the den, where Steven was sprawled on the couch, a New England Patriots notebook next to him.

"You do your homework?" she asked—and immediately regretted it.

"Nope," he said.

Oh. "Are you going to?" she asked.

"Nope," he said.

Well, okay. Not much she could do about that. So, she sat down next to him. "What is this?" she asked, as she watched two cars crash, rolling down an embankment and exploding into fire.

"It's boring," he said.

They sat there quietly for a minute, as two of the police cars responding to the violent crash also slammed into each other, although only one of them blew up.

"Where's Neal?" she asked.

"Dunno," he said. "He went upstairs."

Hmmm. "Is he okay?" Meg asked.

Steven shrugged. "Guess so. Didn't ask."

"Well, maybe I'll go see what he's doing." She reached over to rumple his hair. "Why don't you watch something more cheerful?"

Steven shrugged again.

Jesus. Did her parents realize that two of their children were spending a good chunk of their time moping around these days? "Okay. Be back in a while," she said.

She went upstairs and found Neal's bedroom door closed—which, since her family was big on privacy, wasn't shocking, but it still bothered her, in this particular case. The light was on, so she knocked.

"What," Neal said.

Make that *three* children moping. "Can I come in?" she asked.

He mumbled something, and she opened the door to see him sitting up on the bed, looking very small and very sad.

"What's wrong?" she asked. Which was stupid, since she knew quite well what was wrong. "Are you okay?"

He shook his head.

"Are you sick?" she asked uneasily. When Neal was upset, it tended to have a bad effect on his stomach.

"No," he said.

"Okay. I mean, that's good." She started to put her hands in her pockets before remembering that she had on sweatpants. "Can I keep you company?"

He shrugged, and she climbed onto the bed, sitting up next to him.

"You've been pretty quiet tonight," she said. "You sure you aren't sick?"

He nodded.

"It's hard, having them away," she said.

He nodded, and moved closer, which was a signal for her to put her arm around him—which she did.

"He'll be home tomorrow," Meg said.

Neal nodded.

"And maybe she'll come home in a few days, too," she said.

"No, she won't." He burrowed closer. "She never does."

It was hard to argue with that. "Well, she can't help it," Meg said. "She has to campaign."

He shook his head, and she could tell by the trembling in his shoulders that he was crying.

"Come on, Neal, don't. Please, don't." She hated it when he cried—she never knew what to do. "Don't, okay?"

"How," he was trying to stop the tears, but not succeeding very well, "how can she be away if she loves us?"

An excellent question. "She's away *because* she loves us," Meg said. Oh, good. Very good. She couldn't even convince *herself* with that argument.

And it was clear that he wasn't buying it, either.

Okay, time to try and justify that—and she would grant him sixty seconds for rebuttal. "Neal, running's important to her," Meg said. "She feels like she has to do it. If she didn't, she'd be unhappy, and she doesn't want to be unhappy around us, because that would upset everyone. She's doing it now, so things will be better later."

"But—" He hesitated, so she must have made an impression with that. "I miss her."

Good, an easy one. Meg nodded. "I miss her, too. That's normal."

"I like it when she says good-night." He snuggled next to her, suddenly smiling. "She smells so nice."

Kind of an alarming mood-swing, but if he was happy again, that was fine with her. Actually, her mother always *did* smell good—and it wasn't just the ever-present perfume.

"And she holds me." He hugged himself, demonstrating. "And says that she loves me."

"Well, she does," Meg said. "You know she does."

He beamed up at her, and she smiled back. Child psychology. She had found her career.

"Daddy smells nice, too," he said.

She nodded—since, in fact, he did.

"But different." Neal squared his shoulders in imitation.

"You're right," she said. Observant little kid. Her mother smelled expensive. Unruffled. As if nothing she did required physical effort, and she could just flit about at will. Her father, on the other hand, smelled like flannel shirts. He smelled safe. Even in a dinner jacket, he smelled like flannel shirts. Comfortable.

"I like the way you smell, too," he said.

Hmmm. "How do I smell?" she asked.

He turned his head to sniff her hand on his shoulder. "Ivory Liquid."

Fair enough. She shrugged. "I was helping Trudy with the dishes."

"Sometimes like shampoo," he said.

That was probably true, too.

"And," he took a long time deciding, "like outside."

"Yeah," she agreed. "I fall down a lot."

"No!" He pushed her with giggling impatience. "Like raking leaves. Like *doing* things." He tilted his head to peer up at her. "Steven smells like new sweatshirts."

"Like baseball gloves," she said.

He nodded, and then looked at her expectantly. "What about me?"

"Well, I don't know." She traced his haircut with one hand. She loved Neal's hair. Her mother generally cut it, wrapping him up in a big towel and using a pair of black-handled scissors. His upper lip always seemed to be smiling, and she couldn't help hoping that he would never grow a mustache and cover it up. Except for milk mustaches. His milk mustaches cracked her up. "Like very old sneakers."

"I do not!" he said.

"Hmmm." She hugged him, pressing her face into his hair. "Marshmallows."

He laughed, shaking his head.

"Ski jackets," she said.

"That's no good!" He tried to get away from her, and she tightened her arm around his shoulders, tickling him. "Meggie!"

She held on, not releasing him until a few seconds before he would start getting mad.

"You're mean," he said, laughing weakly.

Kind of, yeah. "I am not," she said.

He tickled *her*, and she managed, through the utmost self-control, not to react.

"You're not ticklish?" he asked doubtfully, pausing.

"Sorry, kiddo." She grinned at him. "Want to go watch TV with Steven?"

"Will you make popcorn?" he asked.

They had eaten two huge bowls of popcorn that very afternoon, while watching one of her parents' favorite old movies, *What's Up, Doc?* "Again?" she said.

He nodded enthusiastically. "And use a real pan? And put in way too much, so we can watch the cover come off?"

She looked at him for a second, wondering vaguely why stupid little things always made people happy.

"Yeah," she said. "Sure."

3

A COUPLE OF weeks after Christmas, Meg went into Boston with her friend Beth. After the divorce, Beth's father had given her a bunch of charge cards, and she loved to go into the uptight, exclusive stores on Newbury Street, look disreputable enough to irritate salespeople, then whip them out and buy a bunch of stuff she didn't need—or even really *want.* Meg would often comment that this was extremely nouveau behavior, and Beth would sigh deeply, and say, in a very glum voice, not *everyone* can be old money. Apparently not, Meg would say, and they would laugh loudly enough for the salespeople to suggest that they think about going elsewhere. Immediately.

Actually, the concept of money kind of embarrassed Meg, and she would never make a crack like that in front of anyone other than Beth. Oh, come on, Beth would say, *flaunt* it; whereupon Meg would always answer, no, thanks.

"Where's your mother get her clothes?" Beth asked, as they looked through a display of rather tacky sweaters in one of the department stores near Downtown Crossing. Her mother often lamented the loss of the original Filene's Basement, but since Meg couldn't remember it, she had always figured that the current group of stores was just fine.

"I don't know." Meg held up a very ugly maroon crewneck. "Lots of places. New York, mostly." And Paris and Milan, all too often, despite the fact that the notion of not *unfailingly* buying American products had the potential to annoy an alarmingly high percentage of eligible voters. "Can you see anyone ever buying this thing?"

"And here I was, planning to get it for you." Beth held it up and shook her head. "I don't know. I like you better in salmon."

Meg nodded. "Most people do."

"Just the other night," Beth said, "before he climbed out my window, Rick Hamilton said, 'God, Beth, why doesn't Meg wear salmon? She wouldn't look nearly as ugly if she wore salmon.' "

"Which night?" Meg asked.

"Wednesday? Thursday?" Beth shrugged. "Who keeps track?"

"Well," Meg said, "the thing of it is, he's been at *my* house every night this week."

"It's all right," Beth said gently. "You can have your fantasies."

Meg grinned. "Likewise."

"That's for sure." Beth dropped the sweater. "This is kind of boring. Want to go hang out in the bookstore?"

Did she? Not really. "If you want," Meg said.

"What about some food?" Beth asked.

Meg shrugged.

"Do you feel all right?" Beth asked.

"Yeah." Meg glanced around restlessly. "Let's get out of here, okay?"

"Whatever." Beth followed her out of the store, Meg walking very quickly. "Hey, slow down already."

"Sorry." Meg stopped, putting her hands in her pockets to avoid the winter wind.

Beth frowned at her. "What's your problem, anyway? You're not a whole hell of a lot of fun to be around these days."

"Yeah, I know," Meg said. "I don't know."

"Well, what is it?" Beth asked.

"I'm sorry. I just—I don't know." Meg hunched her shoulders. "Cold out here."

Beth zipped her jacket up, also hunching. "Very."

"Yeah." Meg looked up and down Washington Street, seeing grey, slushy snow and hurrying commuters. "You mind going for a walk?"

"A walk," Beth said.

Yeah, heading over to the bookstore was probably a better bet. "It's not far," Meg said.

Beth sighed, very deeply. "Not everyone has such a kind and generous friend."

Meg grinned at her. "Guess I'm just lucky."

"Not," Beth said, "that I won't collect on the favor."

"What happened to generosity?" Meg asked.

Beth pulled out a pair of gloves. "When it's this cold out?"

"We'll walk fast." Meg started down Washington Street towards Government Center, veering down one fairly deserted side street, and then another.

"It's getting dark for this sort of thing," Beth said.

Meg looked up at the sky. "Yeah, kind of." She turned one more corner, stopping when she saw the building with the huge "Katharine Vaughn Powers for President" banner across the front window, along with lots of red, white, and blue bunting, and several large posters of her mother.

"Hunh," Beth said, also staring. "I didn't know there was one down here."

"This is the main one." Meg let out her breath. "I've, uh, never been here before."

Beth looked surprised. "There wasn't some kind of ceremony when it opened?"

"I don't know, maybe." More likely than not, actually. "We just went to the one in Coolidge Corner." Meg swallowed. "It's big."

Beth nodded.

"Really big." Since the ordinary-looking storefront hid the fact that the campaign had also signed a lease for the entire second floor, and was likely to expand to another floor soon. Meg stared at the posters, trying to relate the smiling candidate posing with the elderly, minorities, soldiers, students, and other voting blocs, to the woman who did things like burn toast and swear under her breath. The woman in the pictures—the *candidate* in the pictures—looked as if she were perfect. Friendly, kind, intelligent—but, it was scary. Sort of like the semiannual reports her mother's office sent out about what the Senator had accomplished lately—which, somehow, always gave Meg the creeps.

"Kind of weird," Beth said.

Major understatement. "Yeah." Meg looked at the photo of her standing in Iowa or someplace with some farmers, in the middle of a cornfield. "I haven't seen her since the day after Christmas."

"Well," Beth said awkwardly, "I guess she's pretty busy."

"Yeah." Meg started walking. "Anyway, let's get out of here."

"You aren't even going in?" Beth asked.

Meg stopped. "Why should I go in?"

Beth frowned at her. "You dragged me all the way down here, and now you're not even going to check it out?"

"Well—no," Meg said, uneasily.

"Come on." Beth headed across the street. "Don't be a jerk."

"No," Meg said, "I really don't want—"

"What about that favor you owe me?" Beth asked.

Oh, for Christ's sakes. "All right," Meg said—although she was very tempted to be surly, instead. Petulant, even. "Just pretend we're regular people, okay?"

"I *am* a regular person," Beth said.

"You know what I mean," Meg said.

"Yeah, I know what you mean." Beth flipped up her jacket collar. "We'll make them think we're spies from the enemy camp."

"Swell," Meg said, following her.

Beth opened the door, and warm air rushed out at them. They stepped inside, and Meg was surprised to see the maze of activity going on. Normally, at this stage of a campaign, she would expect things to be pretty quiet. But, the main room was crowded with people talking and laughing, phones were ringing, and two large televisions were tuned—loudly—to different stations. There was a strong smell of coffee, both old and new, and doughnuts. The walls were covered with posters, and tables were stacked with buttons, bumper stickers, and leaflets. The volunteers were different ages, but there were a lot of senior citizens, and college students. Some were stuffing envelopes, some were sorting stacks of papers, some were working on computers, and most of the rest were on the phones, either taking or making calls, Meg couldn't tell.

They stood there for a few seconds, Meg feeling more and more uncomfortable; then, a girl from one of the long tables near the front came over, smiling, her hair tied back in a loose ponytail.

"Hi," she said. "I'm Lily."

"I'm Beth," Beth said, shaking her hand.

"I'm—" Meg hesitated. "I mean, hi." She shook the hand the girl offered, not sure if she should have taken her glove off first. Her mother would have.

"Is this your first time here?" the girl asked.

Meg blushed, and Beth nodded.

"Well," the girl said, still smiling, "we have a lot of high school workers."

Were they about to be signed up for duty, or something? Meg shook her head. "No. We're just kind of here because—well, we were just curious."

"Then, let me show you around." Lily was very cheerful. "Do you know much about the candidate?"

"Uh, kind of," Meg said, not looking at Beth.

"Well, then." The girl began giving them some personal background on the candidate, as well as issue positions, while Meg tuned her out, wishing that she'd never had the stupid idea of coming down here.

She focused on a photograph of her mother talking with energy officials—they all had on hard hats and everything. Her mother looked concerned, interested, informed. Ridiculous in the hat. So this was what was coming out of all of those late-night conferences around the kitchen table. Probably no one would ever know that slogans like "The Way to Honest, Open Government" made her mother laugh. "Message, Kate, message," Glen would say. "Trite, Glen, trite," her mother would say.

As the girl explained the candidate's deep interest in education and women's issues, she couldn't help wondering if workers had a speech ready for every kind of person who might wander in. If they were older men with thick, calloused hands, would they get a speech about unions and Social Security?

"Have you met her?" Meg asked, interrupting.

"Well, not personally," the girl admitted. "But I've heard her speak. She's wonderful. You can just tell how honest she is."

She liked to think that her mother was honest, but, in her opinion, the Senator was also awfully god-damned *smooth* sometimes. "How?" Meg asked.

The girl blinked. "Well—it's her attitude, mostly, although everything I've read substantiates it. Have you ever heard her speak?"

"Yeah," Meg said.

"Me, too," Beth said. "Once, when I was little."

Meg elbowed her.

"Well, then, you know what I mean," the girl said, apparently regaining her confidence. "She doesn't hesitate when she answers questions, she doesn't have stacks of notes up there with her, she's not afraid to say what she thinks. I don't know—I guess it's sort of hard to pin down. But I know I could never support anyone I didn't trust."

"Is it true that she completely supports the doctrine of preemptive war?" Beth asked.

Meg shot her a look, which Beth returned innocently.

"My God, no," the girl said. "The Senator's positions are strongly—"

Meg looked around some more. Everyone in the room seemed enthusiastic and confident. Excited. It was pretty impressive to have so many people already working long hours—before the primaries had even started.

And now, Beth was asking whether the Senator planned to

appoint strict constructionist judges, and Meg wasn't sure whether to laugh her head off—or smack her.

The girl actually handled that follow-up curveball pretty well, but she was starting to look very tired.

"What about—" Beth started.

"Would you like a couple of buttons?" the girl asked.

Beth nodded, taking one, and Meg blushed and shook her head.

"We have a bunch at home," she muttered, shifting her weight.

"Is your family working on the campaign?" the girl asked.

"Sort of." Meg heard Beth choke back a laugh. "Is this place always so crowded?"

The girl nodded. "Every time I've been in here. Like, tonight's Tufts Night, and a lot of these kids are from there. Most of the colleges around here have Nights every couple of weeks. It's crazy in here on Harvard/Radcliffe Nights, because that's where she went. Plus, a lot of the unions have Nights, too. And church groups. She's pulling in a lot of the church groups."

Hard to believe. "I thought people were afraid she might be, um, too secular," Meg said. "And that her position on abortion was a problem." God knows her mother got enough hate mail about it.

The girl hesitated. "Well, I guess that it might be an issue, but we still get an awful lot of people in here. Oh, Bruce." She moved to intercept a man in chinos and a blue Oxford shirt who was coming out of the office in the back. "Come over here and talk to some people." The girl dragged him over, and Meg flushed, recognizing Bruce Gibson, who she'd met quite a few times.

"Meg, hi," he said. "What are you doing down here?"

She turned even redder. "I don't know. We were just kind of walking around and—"

"Well, great." He seemed very happy to see her. "You haven't been in before, have you?" He turned to the girl. "Lily, this is Meghan, the Senator's daughter, and—?"

"My friend Beth," Meg said.

Bruce smiled. "And her friend Beth."

"Really?" The girl's eyes got very big. "Wow. Why didn't you say anything?"

Meg shrugged. "I don't know. I guess I felt—" Like a jerk.

"Well, come on," the girl said. "We should introduce you to everyone."

"No, I—" Meg hung back. "I'd really rather not. It's getting late, and we—well, we just wanted to—"

Bruce rescued her. "It *is* dark out there. Do you two need a ride home?"

"Oh, no." Meg shook her head very hard. "We'll take the T."

"It's no problem for me to get a car for you," he said, "and—"

"Bruce, can you look at this, before we post it?" someone called from the back.

He nodded, and motioned for Meg and Beth to follow him through the maze of tables, boxes, and workers to the cluttered office, half-empty coffee cups and pizza boxes everywhere.

"How're things going?" Meg asked.

"Great," he said. "Our big worry was your mother's early fund-raising power, but the donations are pouring in. I think this quarter's going to be even more spectacular than the last one. And once she starts winning, we'll be up for the *really* big money."

"You're that sure she's going to win?" Beth asked.

He nodded. "Absolutely."

Her mother sure could inspire dedication. Unreal. Meg was about to say something polite—and noncommittal—when her "My Favorite Things" ring tone went off, and she dug her phone out of her jeans pocket.

"Where are you, Meg?" her father asked, sounding very annoyed, when she picked up. "We expected you to be home an hour ago."

"I'm still downtown," she said. "I got sort of held up."

"You're supposed to *call* when that happens," he said.

Yeah. In fact, her parents were absolutely adamant about that policy, and she had been grounded more than once for breaking it.

"Well, where are you?" he asked. "I'll have to come pick you up."

If he had to drive all the way into Boston, during rush-hour, he was going to be in an even worse mood. Meg sighed. "Dad, we can just—"

"Where are you?" he asked, less patiently.

"Mom's headquarters," she said. "Anyway, we can just get on the—"

"Really?" His voice was more pleased now. "What are you doing there?"

"Just looking around," she said.

"What do you think?" he asked.

"It's really busy," she said. "There's like, all kinds of people here."

"Well, maybe later on you can start doing some work down there," he said.

Ideally not—but this wasn't going to be the right time to bring that up. "Yeah, maybe," she said. "Look, we're going to go out and get on at Government Center, okay?"

"All right," he said. "I'll pick you up at the station."

After she hung up, she waited for Beth to finish her conversation with *her* mother—who was also cross—and then they went back out to the main room with Bruce. Everyone seemed to be looking at her, so Lily must have spread the word. Meg nodded at them, taking a button to pin on her jacket.

"So," Beth said, as they walked to Government Center.

"Preemptive war?" Meg asked.

"I was making conversation," Beth said.

Right.

They took the D Line train back towards Newton, Beth getting off at Reservoir, Meg getting off a stop later at Chestnut Hill. Her father was in the parking lot and started up the engine when he saw her. The *energy-efficient* engine, it went without saying.

"Where's Beth?" he asked as Meg climbed into the car.

"She got off at Reservoir," Meg said.

"Did she have a ride?" he asked.

"Her mother," Meg said.

He nodded, turning on the headlights. "Next time, I want you home when you're supposed to be."

"Yes, sir," she said.

He reached over to give her scarf a tweak. "And enough with the 'sirs.' "

She nodded. "Anything you say, sir."

He laughed, putting the car into reverse and driving out of the lot. "What did you think of the headquarters?"

"It was okay." Meg slouched against the seat. "I hate those pictures, though. She doesn't look—I don't know—real, in them." She glanced at him. "Are they all staged?"

"I don't think they're staged, so much as there are photographers following her everywhere she goes." He braked for a stop sign. "It's advertising, that's all. You have to win the election before you can do anything."

Meg frowned. "So, you do anything to win?"

"No, of course not. It's just—" He started to turn the corner, then put on his signal and pulled over. "Sorry. I can't talk and drive."

Meg grinned. "Kind of like walking and chewing gum?"

He smiled back. "Kind of. Anyway, you really shouldn't worry, Meg. Have you *ever* seen your mother do anything unethical?"

Well—no. She shook her head.

"Neither have I," he said. "And I don't expect her to change now."

How could she *not* change? "I don't know," Meg said. "I guess."

"Meg, all I can tell you is this: your mother is absolutely, totally, almost sickeningly honest," her father said. "She doesn't do anything she doesn't believe in. She humors them—"

"Them?" Meg asked.

"Glen, the staff, you know. She humors them," he went on, "but once she gets out there, she does what she wants. And she says what she wants. She doesn't do things because they 'look good.' "

Maybe. "So, how come what she does looks so good?" Meg asked.

"Because it's what people want to see." He let out a hard breath. "I don't know what to say, Meg. I can't believe that I'm sitting here telling you something you should already know."

"I guess." Meg jiggled her knee up and down, thinking. "Is she going to win?"

"I don't know," he said.

One thing she was sure about was that her *father* was honest. "Do you *think* she's going to win?" she asked.

"I don't know," he said. "But I think everyone's going to know she was in the race."

"Hmmm." Was she brave enough to ask the obvious question? "Do you want her to win?"

Her father didn't answer right away. "I don't know," he said finally. "I want her to be happy."

Which meant what, exactly? "Wouldn't being President make her happy?" Meg asked.

"I'm not sure," he said, both gloved hands resting on the steering wheel. "It's almost as if—she wants a woman to be President, she wants that desperately, and at this point, she knows she's the only one around who can genuinely pull it off."

Meg frowned again. "What about ambition and power and stuff like that?"

"I don't know, Meg." He shook his head. "I don't think your mother's obsessed with either—it's more of a challenge thing with her. She's a very complex woman. A very wonderful woman," he added more quietly.

If they were getting along right now—which wasn't always the case—she definitely wasn't going to get in the way of that, so she let a few respectful seconds pass. There had been too many times when her parents hadn't seemed to be quite so much in love—maybe not even in love at all. Maybe not even in *like*. It hadn't been that way recently, but that didn't stop her from worrying, especially with her mother being gone twice as much as usual.

She looked at her father, thinking about what a nice man he was. Probably the nicest man she knew. She remembered suddenly being the star of the Thanksgiving play when she was in third grade. The part had required pigtails and a little blue dress, both of which she had. The play was in the afternoon, and her father had come, one of the few men in the audience, sitting up front with Steven, who was in nursery school. After the play, he came backstage to get her, his smile very proud. He gave her some flowers—she couldn't remember what they were; daisies, maybe?—then picked her up in a big hug, and the three of them went all the way in to Harvard Square to have hot fudge sundaes at their favorite ice cream place. Then, Trudy stayed with Steven, and she and her father went to the movies—*at night*. He had always been able to make them feel special.

Seeing him next to her, his face healthy and wind-burned, as though he never sat behind a desk or read *The Wall Street Journal*, Meg obeyed an overpowering urge to hug him.

"What was that for?" he asked, as she pulled free before he could hug back, embarrassed.

"I don't know." She blushed, staring out through the windshield. She almost never gave in to urges to hug people. "I like you."

"Well, I like you, too," he said.

She hated conversations like this. "Steven's probably making Trudy crazy right now." Especially if he was hungry.

"Probably." He started the engine, then looked over at her, shaking his head. "You're very much like her."

Meg flushed. "I am not."

"When your grandfather was alive, he used to sit there for hours, watching you," her father said. "He said it was frightening."

"Well, I guess I *look* kind of like her," Meg said. "But I mean like, she's—and I'm—"

Her father just grinned, glancing over his shoulder to check for cars, then pulling out into the street.

4

RIGHT AFTER DINNER that night, the phone rang.

"I've got it!" Meg yelled from the kitchen. "Hello?"

"Hi," her mother said. "How are you?"

"Okay." Meg sat down at the table. "Where are you?" Which was always the first question any of them asked her these days.

"Detroit," her mother said.

Oh. Well, okay. Whatever. "I thought you were in Iowa," Meg said.

"I was." Her mother yawned, and Meg had a momentary disturbing flash of her sitting alone and exhausted in a hotel room somewhere. "I flew up because we ran into some luck today."

"What happened?" Meg asked.

"The UAW endorsed me," her mother said.

The autoworkers union. Which was a big deal. Meg wanted to gulp, since—well, her mother was getting *a lot* of endorsements. Already. "Um, wow. That's really good, isn't it?"

"It's *tremendous*," her mother said. "I really wasn't expecting it. Or, anyway, not yet." She yawned again. "What did you do today?"

Well, it was safe to say that no one had endorsed her. Meg shrugged. "Nothing much. Beth and I went in and kicked around downtown at Macy's and everything."

"Did you pick up anything?" her mother asked. "Aren't they still having Christmas sales?"

"Yeah. We were mostly just looking around, though." Meg mouthed the word "Mom" as Steven came in.

"Well, you really need a new ski jacket," her mother said. "That thing you're wearing around now is disgraceful."

Next, presumably, she would have to hear about how terrible her hair looked, too. "I like it." Even though it was ratty and beat-up, and covered with ancient, partially torn lift tickets.

"Then, get the same kind," her mother said.

"Yeah, but—" Meg pushed her brother's hand away from the phone. "Steven, wait a minute, will you?"

"Come on, let me talk," he said impatiently.

"I said, wait a minute." Meg pushed him harder. "When are you coming home again, Mom?"

"I think maybe next weekend," her mother said. "So, do me a favor, and get the jacket, and maybe we can all go up to Stowe for a couple of days."

"Wow, really?" Meg lowered the phone. "Mom says she's coming home, and we can maybe go skiing next weekend."

"Well, let me talk to her," Steven said.

"Okay already." Meg lifted the phone back up. "Steven's being a jerk, so I'd better let him talk to you. That's really good about the autoworkers."

"Thanks," her mother said. "Take care of yourself, okay? It sounds as if your cold is pretty much gone."

Meg nodded, dodging Steven's attempt to grab the phone again. "Mostly, yeah. Where are you going tomorrow?"

"South," her mother said.

"Just in general?" Meg asked.

"It feels that way. Actually, Atlanta, and Miami; then I have to head up to Washington by Monday." Her mother laughed. "It sounds as though you'd better put your brother on."

"Yeah, really." Meg scowled at him. "I'll talk to you tomorrow."

"Okay. I love you," her mother said.

"Um, yeah, me, too," Meg said quickly. "I, uh, went to your headquarters in Boston today; they were pretty neat. Here's Steven."

"God, about time." Steven grabbed the phone from her. "Hi, Mom, where are you?"

Meg got up, moving to the door. "Dad? Neal? Mom's on the phone!"

"Oh, good." Her father came in from the sitting room. "I thought it might be."

"Wow, let me talk!" Neal rushed in, trying to get the phone away from Steven. "Come on, it's my turn!"

"God, wait a minute, will you?" Steven pushed him.

Not that she and her brothers were predictable, or anything. "Neal, don't bug him," she said. "He just got on."

Neal scowled, and sat sulkily in a chair to wait.

"She still in Des Moines?" her father asked.

Meg shook her head. "Detroit."

He looked surprised. "What's she doing there?"

"She got the UAW," Meg said.

"Really? My God, she's cleaning up on the unions." He tapped Steven's shoulder, indicating for him to hurry up.

Once Steven and Neal had finished, and her father was on the phone, she and her brothers waited at the table.

"Guess what Mommy said?" Neal asked, leaning forward on his elbows. "She bought me a cowboy hat in Texas! A real one!"

"How dumb is that?" Steven snorted, his mouth full of Oreos he'd found on top of the refrigerator—since Trudy always hid unhealthy food from them.

"Yeah, well, she got you one, too." His face fell. "That's supposed to be a surprise."

"Yeah?" Steven looked eager. "What color are they?"

"If you really think it's stupid, we can have Dad tell her to take yours back." Meg helped herself to some Oreos, giving one to Kirby, who wagged his tail and retreated under the table to eat it.

"Meg, shut up, okay?" Steven said, blushing.

"Be careful, okay?" their father was saying. "Well, I have to worry, I can't help it." He listened. "Okay, I love you, too." He listened again, then hung up to see Meg grinning, Steven pretending to throw up, and Neal giggling. "Little brats." He picked up what was left of the package of cookies. "Come on, who wants to go watch the Celtics game?"

"Gross," Meg said. "I hate hockey."

"Cute," her father said.

SHE SPENT THE next couple of days looking forward to going skiing, but began to lose enthusiasm when she realized what it was going to be like. The first warning came on Monday night when her father remarked that "there would be some politics going on, and they all had to be prepared for that." What she had seen as a relaxing family weekend was going to be more of a marathon three-day campaign session. Glen was coming, Linda—who Meg had decided to call the Ice Queen—was coming, campaign coordinators and pollsters were coming—and Meg didn't feel like going.

She didn't communicate that to her brothers, both of whom were so excited that the weekend was all they talked about. She was anything *but* eager.

Wednesday night, hearing her father wandering around—he did that a lot when her mother wasn't home, especially after they were all in bed—she got up and went downstairs, finding him coming out of the den.

"What are you doing up?" he asked, automatically checking his watch.

She shrugged. "I don't know. I'm not tired."

"Terrific." His expression was wry. "It's going to be fun waking you up tomorrow."

Since she always stayed up as late as possible, it was probably *never* fun to wake her up.

He reached forward, touching her forehead with the back of his hand. "Do you feel okay? You're not coming down with anything, are you?"

Oh, good idea. If she was sick, she wouldn't have to go. "I don't know," she said. "I just can't sleep."

"Would you like me to make you some warm Coke?" her father asked.

She looked at him uncertainly. "Would that help?"

He laughed. "No." He sat down on the stairs, indicating for her to sit next to him. "What's wrong? Are you still upset about this weekend?"

Well—yeah. But, she shrugged. "I don't know. I thought it was going to be just us."

"She's running for President," he said. "There's no way it's going to be 'just us' for a long time."

Meg slouched down, not wanting to hear that.

"Oh, don't worry." He put his arm around her. "It's not going to be that bad."

If they had to do stupid politics the whole time, they weren't even going to get to *ski*. "Will people be taking our pictures all over the place and asking questions and everything?" she asked.

He nodded. "Probably."

"Sounds like fun," she said grumpily. "What am I supposed to say to reporters?"

He sighed. "We've gone over that, Meg. Just be polite and friendly. And don't worry about it. Your mother's staff will keep them out of the way—that's what they're there for."

Meg kicked at the bottom stair with her right foot.

"World champion fretful child," her father said.

Yeah. So? "Don't make fun of me," she said.

"I'm sorry. Look," he kissed the top of her head, "please don't worry. It's going to be fine. All you have to do is stand there and smile."

Right. "Look daft, you mean?" she asked.

"I'll buy that," he said, grinning. "But, it's really going to be fine."

Not likely, but she didn't want him to call her fretful again. "Do you promise?"

He nodded.

"Can I quote you on that?" she asked.

"Sure," he said.

THEY GOT TO Stowe right before dinner on Friday night. The place was packed with reporters and cameras, and her mother's staff was very excited. Her mother had a press conference, and then, there was a quick photo session, naturally. They ate at the Tavern at the Inn, a dinner which wasn't exactly restful, but they *were* together, as her father kept pointing out.

By the time they finished, it was too late to do much of anything else, although she and Steven and Neal—and an advisor named Nasira who had gotten her PhD when she was only about twenty-three, and was an expert on the Middle East, particularly issues relating to Iran—went down to the game room and played pool and air hockey for a while. Her parents had rented a townhouse for the family, and the campaign had taken over part of the nearby conference center, as well as a couple of condominiums and a block of rooms at the Inn itself for the ever-expanding staff. Her mother's formal Secret Service protection hadn't started quite yet, but she noticed that a bunch of agents and other security people seemed to be around the resort, too.

Steven and Neal ended up going to bed pretty early, so that they'd be wide awake for skiing in the morning. Meg wasn't tired, so she hung out down in the living room, watching the same kind of endless strategy session that she usually saw around the kitchen table or out on the patio. And, as usual, her father was making jokes that only her mother seemed to think were funny. Everyone else was too busy being serious, and she wished that Preston had been able to come, since everyone would be a lot more relaxed if he was there. Although, as far as Meg could tell, Glen and Linda *never* had a good time.

After about an hour, she gave up, deciding that the meeting was never going to end.

"Going to bed?" her father asked, as her mother flipped through a thick sheaf of reports and briefing books.

"Yeah." She nodded. "I'm pretty tired. Are you guys going to do this all night?"

"We're going to call all of the other candidates, see when they're going to bed, and stay up fifteen minutes longer," her father said, and her mother laughed, touching his shoulder with a caressing hand, without looking away from what she was reading.

"Well," Meg said, self-consciously. "Good night."

Her mother took out just enough time to smile at her. "Eight o'clock breakfast sound good?"

"Yeah." Meg shrugged. "Sure. Good night," she said to the room in general, getting a couple of nods, a couple of good nights, and a couple of grunts in response.

"Don't stay up too late," her father said, "okay?"

"But I'm expecting someone," Meg said, amused to see three sharp glances from campaign people.

Everyone seemed very busy and distracted, so she went upstairs, feeling a little lonely. She could watch some television, maybe, or go online—but, she didn't really feel like it. Since it wasn't going to be a family weekend, she should have asked if Beth or someone could come along. But, the five of them were *supposed* to be spending time together, so it wouldn't have seemed right to invite any of their friends. It would be a lot more fun if she had, though. She stood at the top of the stairs, listening as a man named Jim—who had worked on every Democratic Presidential campaign for the last thirty years—droned on and on about New Hampshire and the early primaries. Well, her leaving sure hadn't upset things much.

Steven and Neal must have had no trouble getting to sleep, because it was *extremely* quiet on the second floor. She changed into her nightgown, thinking about Vanessa. Missing her.

She was just about to turn the light off, when there was a small tap on the door. Her mother. For a confident person, her mother always knocked very shyly.

"Is that you, Arthur?" Meg said.

She heard her mother laugh, and then the door opened.

"Did you come to tuck me in?" Meg asked.

"I wanted to make sure you were all right." Her mother looked worried. "Are you?"

Meg shrugged. "Sure."

"Good." Her mother glanced at her watch.

"What," Meg said, "you have to get right back down there?"

Her mother shook her head. "No, I just wanted to make sure that you were going to get enough sleep."

Oh. Okay. Meg flushed. She had probably been a little quick to be hostile there. "So, uh, you going to read me a story?"

"Sure," her mother said. "*The Cat in the Hat* sound good?"

"Yeah," Meg said, and pulled up the covers in four-year-old anticipation.

Her mother automatically turned down the spread. "I used to love reading to you. You always got so excited."

"Yeah." Meg kept her arms around upraised knees, remembering those nights, the theatrical way her mother read, and how she'd always been able to tease her into reading two or three instead of just one. She pulled her knees in closer, almost wishing she were Neal's age again, and could still be cuddled. Parental cuddling was nice. She missed parental cuddling.

Her mother looked at her curiously. "Meg?"

Okay, she must *look* about six years old. Meg released her knees, sitting up straight. "I was just thinking."

"I'm sorry about this weekend." Her mother sat at the bottom of the bed. "I wish it could be just the family, too."

Meg shrugged affirmatively, bringing her knees back up.

"It's not bothering you too much, is it?" her mother asked.

"Not really," Meg said. "Some of your campaign people sure are grumpy, though. They don't even like Dad's jokes."

"And he's really terribly funny." Her mother laughed, and Meg wondered which one of his remarks she was remembering.

"How come you hired such grumps?" Meg asked.

"They aren't *all* grumps," her mother said.

Okay, there was at least one exception to that rule. "How come Preston is the only one who isn't a grump?" Meg asked.

"Because I need a team of highly organized, serious people." Her mother's face relaxed out of her political expression. "You're right, I like Preston, too. Although, my God, he's *young*."

Which was probably why he sometimes felt more like a pal, or almost even a peer. "Glen and Linda kind of bug me," Meg said.

Her mother shrugged. "He's a perfectionist, that's all. You just have to get used to him. And Linda is utterly competent."

"Ice Queen," Meg said disparagingly.

"Is that what you call her?" Her mother tried to look stern, but Meg could see the amusement in her eyes. "That's terrible."

Maybe, but it was still accurate. "She's like a robot," Meg said. "I swear I've never heard her say a sentence that didn't have the word 'image' in it."

Her mother frowned at her. "I might remind you that she's in a profession in which women have to work twice as hard."

"So are you," Meg said.

Her mother nodded. "Precisely. And for all we know, there's a country full of people who think I'm an Ice Queen." She smiled. "And worse."

"No, they don't," Meg said—although she had made the mistake of reading a few angry right-wing blogs, and had promised herself *never* to go near any of them again. Criticism was one thing; misogyny and graphic insults and not-at-all-veiled threats were another.

Her mother looked at her sharply. "What?"

"The, um," Meg didn't quite meet her eyes, "Internet. I mean, people say—well, there's some *really* bad stuff."

Her mother sighed. "Your father and I don't want you looking at any of that."

Yeah, that had been the parental edict, but since references to her mother were everywhere, the only way to accomplish said edict was to stay off the Internet *entirely*—which, obviously, wasn't going to happen. So, Meg just shrugged.

"It's easy for people to make up terrible rumors about someone they've never met, especially when they get to hide behind anonymity. So, it isn't anything to take seriously." Her mother glanced over. "Do you think your brother's coming across things like that, too?"

Meaning Steven, since, presumably, Neal was too young to be quite that computer savvy yet—although he was already developing a surprising knack for email, and some stupid interactive game he would happily play for three days straight, if his computer time wasn't strictly monitored. But, even by her family's unusually high standards, Steven was particularly private and uncommunicative. "I don't know," Meg said. "I think he mostly just watches really dumb videos and plays all those weird avatar games and all."

Her mother blushed slightly. "I guess I made a little splash last week."

Meg couldn't help grinning, since that particular civilian-filmed clip was one she'd watched herself—several times. Her mother had been giving a speech and started talking about various aspects of the Mile High City, and how much she enjoyed being there—to a crowd of quite baffled people in *Chicago*.

"I was very tired," her mother said, defensively.

"The view of Lake Michigan right out the window wasn't, you know, kind of a big clue?" Meg asked.

Her mother nodded. "Yes, when I noticed that, I began to suspect that something might be amiss."

Good thing she hadn't promptly remarked how pretty the ocean looked. Part of what also made the brief film funny was that when the Senator—in short order—figured out that she was yammering on about someplace else entirely, she'd immediately said something to the effect that as soon as she was finished speaking, she was very eager to go outside and tour the Alamo, and maybe take a ride up to the top of the Space Needle, after that. Fortunately, her audience seemed to find this amusing.

"The other day," her mother settled herself more comfortably, "I gave a speech at a Rotary Club luncheon and afterwards, at the reception, a very pleasant-looking man came over and told me that I was a harlot."

Whoa. "What did you do?" Meg asked.

"Well, you know me," her mother said. "Always quick on the uptake. So, I said, 'What?' He repeated himself, I said, 'Oh,' and he walked away."

"At least you told him off," Meg said.

Her mother shrugged. "There're a few in every crowd. Anyway, that's why Linda is the way she is. If you spend that much time with your defenses up, it gets to be a habit."

"But you're not like that," Meg said.

Her mother shrugged again. "To a degree, I am. You have to be."

Hmmm. "Has anyone ever called you a strumpet?" Meg asked.

Her mother nodded. "Trollop, too. I gather Preston has been keeping a running list of insults. He has a pool going for various words, too."

Which sounded like something Preston would do, both to amuse everyone—and to try and take the sting out of some of the considerably more unpleasant invective that had to be coming her mother's way on a daily basis.

"Floozy and hussy are long gone, of course," her mother said. "So, I took 'doxy' in the pool, and I believe your father went with 'slattern.' "

All too often, hanging around her mother made her want to run for the nearest dictionary.

"But, let's talk about something *other* than politics, okay?" her mother said.

It was hard to avoid, when it was the perpetual elephant—or, okay, *donkey*—in the room. "Do the other candidates have as many reporters following them around as you do?" Meg asked.

"Probably not," her mother admitted. "I don't think it means much, though. I may just be a novelty act."

Somehow, that didn't sound very convincing. "Who're you worried about the most?" Meg asked. "Governor Kruger?" Who was an avuncular, decorated military veteran from the South—and from what she could tell, he seemed to be so reasonable, and surprisingly progressive, that he was the only other candidate she found appealing.

The only one who struck her as a serious threat, too.

"Well." Her mother folded her arms, considering that. "He's certainly very impressive. Hawley's doing well, too. And you can never tell about Mertz. Every four years, he throws a scare into people. And Jarvis seems to have a little boomlet going."

Which seemed to be about the same way most of the pundits saw the race shaping up, so far. "What about Mr. Sampson?" Meg asked. Who was *proud* to describe himself as a gadfly, and played the role to the hilt.

"Oh," her mother brushed that aside, "no one takes him seriously. But, who knows? Maybe Clay Grundy will come from nowhere and take a lot of votes. He's been spending most of his time in New Hampshire, and he just might make some inroads there. But Lloyd, and Foster, and McGreer are all getting ready to drop out, I think."

Not that she watched C-Span—a lot—or, say, checked in on the *Washington Post* website—often—but, that sounded about right.

Her mother bent to tuck in the blankets, and then hugged her, long enough for Meg to feel awkward.

"You should go rescue Dad from the grumps," Meg said.

Her mother grinned. "You mean, rescue the grumps from *him*." She went over to the window, checking to make sure that it was locked, and then closing the curtains.

"No, don't do that," Meg said. "How will Arthur get in?"

"I'm sure he'll think of something," her mother said.

5

HEADING FOR THE life line for a third time the next morning, Meg felt someone glide up next to her, and turned to see Linda, stiff but well-groomed in her light blue ski suit, smiling that sterile smile.

"Would you like to share a chair up?" she asked.

"Sure," Meg said. Being trapped on a ski lift had to be the ultimate example of a captive audience.

"I thought we should get to know each other better," Linda said.

Oh, boy. Her mother had undoubtedly put Linda up to this. Meg smiled and nodded.

"H-how is it?" Linda gestured up the mountain.

Meg shrugged. "Great. Maybe a little icy."

Linda looked nervous. Scared, actually.

"It's not that bad," Meg said quickly. "Just stay away from the fall line."

Linda nodded. "Your mother tells me you're very good."

"I don't know." Meg leaned forward against her poles for a few seconds, stretching. "Steven's probably going to be the best out of the three of us."

"What about Neal?" Linda asked.

"Well," Meg straightened up, moving forward in line, "he's been doing it since he was three, so he's pretty good, but Dad doesn't like him skiing alone, so we take turns keeping him company." In fact, keeping Neal company was sometimes one of her favorite parts of skiing. She loved to watch him square his shoulders, push off down a slope—and laugh all the way down. She glanced at Linda. "Have you been skiing long?"

"Not particularly," Linda said. "I went a few times when I was in college. I prefer golf."

Which was only the most boring sport in the world, in Meg's opinion.

"And, of course, I go to the gym," Linda said.

Which was almost as boring as golf. Meg—who considered herself to be in pretty damned good shape—had once taken an exercise class with Beth and Sarah Weinberger, neither of whom did more than an occasional flight of stairs, and had found it so difficult that she had had to fake a sudden, extreme headache.

They didn't say much of anything else until they were in the chair on their way up the mountain.

"Eric told me he saw you talking to someone from the *Times* this morning," Linda said, shifting her poles to her right hand.

Maybe her mother hadn't initiated this, after all. "Oh, the *Times*," Meg said. She hadn't been sure where the man worked. "I knew he was from one of the papers."

Linda looked at her critically. "What did he ask you?"

Meg thought back. "I don't know. It was no big deal."

Now, Linda frowned. "Well, can you try to remember?"

"He wanted to know how the skiing was here, and I said that it was really good." Meg moved the zipper on her new jacket—her mother had insisted—up and down, thinking. "Then, he asked if I liked coming up here, and I said yes, and he said it must be nice to be spending time with my mother, and I said yes, and he said it must be hard to have her away so much, and I said that we missed her and everything, but that she was always there if we needed her." Meg glanced over. "Is that okay?"

"That's fine." Linda's smile was significantly less sterile. "I should have realized that you'd be pretty well politicized."

"But, it's true," Meg said. "I wouldn't have said it, if it wasn't true."

Linda just nodded, seeming very pleased by her performance.

"She always comes if we really need her," Meg said.

Linda nodded.

Maybe she was protesting too much, but—"Like on Neal's birthday," Meg said. "She flew home and everything."

"No one is saying that she didn't." Linda's voice was calm. "You just have to remember that your mother isn't running for school committee; she's running for President. There's a great deal at stake."

Wait, she was running for *President*? Of the country. Wow. Who knew?

"But, in the future," Linda said, "I'd rather that you didn't talk to the press unless I'm there, or someone from my staff is sitting in."

Great. More rules to follow. "Yeah," Meg said, "but—"

Linda immediately cut her off. "I'd like that to be the policy."

"But—" Meg released a slow, frozen breath, ordering herself not to lose her temper. "What if someone comes up and asks me a question? Do I say, I'm sorry, I can't answer that unless someone's with me?"

"We need to be very careful, that's all," Linda said. "People have an image—"

Meg grinned, in spite of herself.

"—very important that you and your brothers come across as happy, well-adjusted—"

"Fake it, you mean?" Meg asked.

Linda did not smile. "That's not what I said."

Meg grinned, then recognized two familiar shapes twisting down a steep slope below them: one small and darting in bright red, the other tall and graceful in royal blue. "There's Mom and Neal."

Linda looked down, wincing as the figure in blue took a jump over an uneven patch of snow and stayed airborne for several feet before landing effortlessly.

"Your mother is sometimes incautious," she said.

Yeah. "A few years ago, she broke her leg," Meg said, remembering how the incident had been both frightening and amusing—frightening because she and Steven had been skiing with her when it happened, but amusing because of all the pictures *Newsweek* and everyone printed of the Senator crutching her way around Capitol Hill.

"It's over if she breaks her leg," Linda said grimly. "A candidate, particularly a woman, is supposed to be invulnerable."

"Invincible," Meg said.

Linda was not amused.

They dismounted as the lift got to the top, Linda's descent unsteady.

"Which trail would you say is the least demanding?" Linda asked, sounding more nervous than she looked.

"Toll Road," Meg said, pointing to the right. "And take the Crossover."

Linda nodded her thanks. "Please try to be careful with reporters. Everyone will be glad to help you."

They separated, and Meg cruised over to Hayride. There was one particularly icy section, and she'd almost fallen on her first run down, so she wanted to try it again and see if she could get it right. She adjusted her sunglasses—blue Oakleys, and in her opinion, *very* cool—and paused at the top of the trail, studying the terrain to see how she could attack it differently this time.

Then, she took a deep breath and jammed her poles into the snow, shoving off. She made a few quick parallel turns, enjoying the speed and the challenge of the ice. Her father—who loved *projects*—always tuned and waxed all of their skis before trips, and she really liked whatever wax combination he had used this time. The edges had good bite, but the bases felt like they were floating, which was perfect.

Whipping along, carving short, neat turns, she considered slowing down before the difficult part, but decided not to, enjoying the rushing wind too much. She cut one of her turns a little late, and her right ski skidded unexpectedly, sending her down in a hard tangle of skis and legs. She lay on her back for a minute, staring at the cloudy sky, annoyed at her own stupidity in trying to take it too fast. Nothing like being incautious.

There was a spray of snow as someone stopped next to her and, focusing on dark curly hair and a tanned face, Meg decided that she believed in God.

"You okay?" the guy asked, his voice flippantly concerned.

"Yeah, thank you. Just hit some ice." Embarrassed, Meg used her poles to push herself up.

"Let me give you a hand." He moved a thick glove underneath her elbow.

"Thank you." She stepped back into her right ski, which had released when she crashed, and then knocked the snow off her jacket and jammed her Red Sox cap back on. Luckily, she had tied the cap to the loop on the inside of her jacket collar, so that while it flew off constantly when she was skiing fast, it would just flap behind her, instead of getting lost.

"My name's Dave." He brushed some snow off her back, and she blushed, the touch somehow intrusive. "What's yours?"

"Meg," she said.

He studied her for a second, his eyes going down. "How old are you?"

Unexpected, magical romance would have been too much to hope for. She sighed. "Almost sixteen." Well, more like fifteen and a half—but, that was a mere detail.

"Would have guessed older." His eyes moved again.

Great. She turned to avoid the scrutiny, reddening more. "How old are you?"

"Be nineteen in a couple of months. I go to Dartmouth." His voice was superior.

"Good school," she said.

"Yeah." He bent to adjust a buckle on his boot, balancing on one pole, and she wondered if she should seize the moment and make a quick escape. He straightened up. "You hear we've got a celebrity up here this weekend?"

"Oh?" Meg tried not to groan aloud.

He nodded. "Yeah. Presidential candidate. You ever hear of Senator Powers?"

Meg let herself look faintly puzzled. "She's the woman, right?"

"Yeah." This time, his nod was patronizing, and he spoke in the authoritative voice of a college freshman taking Political Science 101. "Of course, she'll never win."

Oh, really? "Why not?" she asked.

"We need a *man* in the position," he said. "Particularly these days."

What a jerk. "We do?" she asked pleasantly.

"Absolutely," he said, not even noticing that she'd stiffened. "Certainly, Powers is probably qualified, and she gives a good speech, but she wouldn't have the authority, especially in dealing with world leaders. If she's lucky, Kruger or someone'll ask her to be his running mate—that'd be a better place for her."

It would be fun to watch and see how much further he could get his foot into his mouth. She smiled very, very pleasantly. "Why?"

"No responsibility," he said.

Within seconds, she was going to have to perform the Heimlich maneuver on him.

Or, perhaps, *not* perform it on him.

"I mean," Dave shifted his weight to the other pole, "she'd probably be good at functions—she's poised, and God, no one can say she isn't good-looking. But, you have to have a man at the top."

It was too late for the Heimlich; they had now moved into emergency tracheotomy territory.

"But," he smiled at her, "I'm sorry to go on like that, I couldn't expect you to be interested."

"Why not?" Meg asked in the voice of a champion Ice Queen.

"Well, you're—" He paused, searching for the word. "I mean—"

"Look," she cut him off. "Before you say anything else, maybe you should know something."

"What's that?" he asked, sounding amused by what he seemed to consider her presumptuousness.

"Senator Powers is my mother," she said.

He stared at her. "Y-your mother?"

She nodded. "My mother." She pushed off and down the slope again. "Thanks for helping me up."

THAT NIGHT, SHE and her family had dinner at the Trapp Family Lodge, all having gotten through the day without any broken legs or torn ligaments. Right after their salads were served, her father frowned suddenly, glancing at her mother, who followed his gaze across the room and laughed.

"Meg, there's a boy over there who can't take his eyes off you," she said. "Steven, be a nice kid and pass me the salt, will you?"

Meg recognized Dave, sitting at a table with two other preppy-looking guys, and returned to her salad. "He's looking at you, Mom."

"No, he isn't." Her mother checked again. "It's very definitely you."

"Believe me, it isn't." Meg kept eating.

"Yeah, who'd look at Meg?" Steven said, grinning.

"A lot of people would," their mother said. "Your sister is very attractive."

Both Meg and Steven snorted, then Meg frowned at him.

"You're not supposed to agree," she said.

He shrugged. "Hey, except for your face, you're fine."

"If you hadn't been born without a brain, you'd probably be okay, too," Meg said, managing to grab a piece of garlic bread right out from underneath his hand.

"How about a truce?" their father suggested. "At least until after dinner."

"Oh, but we love each other." Steven moved his chair closer to hers, putting his arm around her. "Don't we, Meggie?"

"Oh, yeah." Meg kept eating.

Her father frowned at Dave's table. "I don't like it. He's too old to be staring at you."

"He's only eighteen," Meg said. She glanced up to see the whole family looking at her. "Oh. Guess I shouldn't know that." She shrugged, picking up her knife to cut a piece of lettuce, deciding to start some trouble. "He's a pretty good kisser for an old guy."

Without lifting her eyes, she could feel their heads turning in his direction.

"What's his name?" her mother asked casually.

"Why would I know his name?" Meg asked. "Hey, can I have a martini?"

6

THEY SKIED ALL day Sunday, had dinner at yet another reporter-crowded restaurant, then drove home, not getting in until pretty late. Meg was so tired that next morning that she fumbled her way through school, although she didn't actually fall asleep until her last official class, which was history, and always pretty boring. Her teacher, Mr. Bucknell, was a real pain, always talking about her mother—even though the American History part of the course was only supposed to go up to 1865—and trying to get Meg to drop campaign secrets. Not that she knew any. She wasn't even sure if there *were* any.

"Meghan?" a voice said.

"What?" She jerked awake, and saw Mr. Bucknell scowling near-sightedly, gripping his tie with one hand, which made her uncomfortably suspicious that he might have called on her more than once. The grins on the people sitting near her made her suspect that even more. "I mean, yes, sir?"

"I *do hope*," he stretched the two words out, "that you don't mind my interrupting your little nap."

Well, actually, now that he mentioned it. . . . "I'm awake," she said.

A couple of people laughed.

"Well, I am," she said to the class in general.

"She thinks, therefore she is," Rick Hamilton said, and more people laughed.

Meg blushed, but returned the cocky grin he gave her, deciding that he was probably the sexiest—

"Meghan," Mr. Bucknell said impatiently.

Meg focused towards the front of the room. "Uh, yes, sir?"

"We were discussing the Iowa Caucus, and I thought you might be able to give us some insights on the subject," he said.

What did that have to do with early American history? Oh. Right. Nothing whatsoever. "Um, well." She searched for something to say. "It's a week from tomorrow."

"Does your mother have any specific campaign strategy?" he asked.

The man never quit. She looked at Beth, who scribbled a note that said "Tell him about the bribes." Which wasn't much help.

Christ, this was the only class she had with Rick Hamilton all day, and her teacher seemed to go out of his way to embarrass her. If only he would just give her a break already, and not—Rick really *was* incredibly good-looking. Arrogant grin, wavy hair, really sexy eyebrows. She had a thing for guys with acrobatic eyebrows. Usually, the only way she could ever stay awake in this class was by trying to stare at him without getting caught. Beth and Sarah Weinberger almost always got caught. Meg figured she had about a .500 average. Not that he'd be interested in her, anyway; he always went for the tall, blond—

"Meghan?" Mr. Bucknell sounded very testy, practically choking himself with his tie.

"I'm sorry," Meg said. "I just really don't know anything."

"Oh, come on, she must have mentioned something," he said. "You spent the entire weekend with her."

Nothing like having a private family life. Was every class for the rest of the year going to be like this? She looked at Rick, who obviously thought that—damn it. He caught her that time. Flushing, she looked down at her desk. Now, he would know that she liked him. God, what a day.

"What about the debate?" Mr. Bucknell asked. "Does she have any special strategies for the debate?"

Other than showing up on time? Meg shook her head.

Mr. Bucknell frowned. "Well, what about positions? Like gun control. How is she going to handle gun control?"

All he had to do was check her voting record on *that* one. "I'm kind of not supposed to comment on that," she said quietly.

"What?" He took a step backwards, looking so theatrically stunned that most of the class laughed.

"That's telling him, Meg!" someone shouted.

"Well, class." Mr. Bucknell's eyes made a slow sweep of the room. "What would this school be like if *all* of our students went around saying, 'No comment'?"

The same people laughed again.

"The *next* thing you know, Meghan will be taking the Fifth," he said.

Which was, of course, her right, as guaranteed by the Constitution.

In the meantime, a few people were laughing, but everyone else was giving her sympathetic looks, switching back to her side.

"Maybe you'd feel better having an attorney with you in class," he said, and Meg made herself meet his gaze, not looking away until he did.

Then, she stared down at her books. Why couldn't her mother be a psychologist? Or a writer? Or a nurse? Or a professional tennis player? Only then, her gym teachers would be after her—she could hear it now: "Well, Wimbledon's coming up. Meg, do you think you can give us some insights?"

Would she have to be Catholic to join a convent?

The bell rang, and she gathered up her books, wanting to get out of the room as soon as possible.

"Don't forget," Mr. Bucknell said. "I want the answers to the chapter seventeen questions handed in by tomorrow. And, Meghan, would you mind staying after for a minute?"

Yes. Meg paused, halfway to the door.

"Tell him yes," Beth said, right behind her.

"*Meghan.*" Mr. Bucknell didn't sound as though he was in the mood for any smart answers.

Meg sighed and sat back down. When everyone else was gone, Mr. Bucknell leaned against the table near the front of the room, folding his arms.

"I don't think I asked you anything *too* terrible," he said. "We just want to share the experience. I think we're very fortunate to have a major candidate's daughter in here, and I've been trying to get some good discussions going. We can all learn a lot from this."

Meg moved her jaw. "I'm not supposed to go around talking about things."

"No one is asking you to give away private campaign information," he said mildly.

Yeah. Sure.

He smiled at her. "I was thinking that you might be able to get her to come in one day and speak to the class."

Meg shrugged, wondering when, exactly, her mother would find time to do something like that, when she didn't even have time to come *home*.

"Meg, I really don't mean to put you under any pressure," he said.

Then, how come he kept doing it? Meg didn't say anything.

"If you're having some difficulties with the idea of your mother being a candidate, you should share *that*," he said.

She shrugged. "I'm not."

"It would be perfectly natural," he said.

"But I'm not." She checked the clock. "I'm sorry, but I kind of have to get going."

He sighed, unfolding his arms. "Maybe in the future, we can both try to be a little more cooperative."

Meg nodded, standing up to leave.

"I was very impressed with your paper on the Louisiana Purchase," he said. "You seem to have a real grasp of the material."

Flattery would get him nowhere. "Thank you," she said.

Beth and Sarah were waiting for her in the hall.

"So?" Beth asked.

Meg glanced over her shoulder to make sure she had closed the door on her way out. "He wants me to try and be a little more cooperative. I told him he'd have to speak to my attorney about that."

"Wow." Sarah's eyes widened. "What'd he say?"

Meg and Beth grinned.

"Well, I don't know." Sarah shrugged self-consciously. "Meg might do that."

"I bet you said, 'yes, sir, anything you say, sir,' " Beth guessed.

"I told him I'd get back to him," Meg said.

Beth made her hand into a microphone. "Tell me, Miss Powers. What's your mother's position on gun control?"

"Well." Meg leaned back against a locker, assuming a pseudo-thoughtful, pseudo-intellectual stance—standing like any one of a number of her mother's aides. "The Senator is a little torn on this issue. She carries several guns in her purse, but she doesn't like the idea of just any old person being able to get one. Also, she's sponsored several bills on teacher executions, and—"

"Wow," Sarah said. "Does she *really* carry a gun?"

HER FATHER GOT home later than usual that night, having had to appear at a couple of fund-raisers, in lieu of her mother. On Thursday, he was going to fly out to Iowa to be with her for the last few days before the caucus. Even though a relatively small percentage of eligible voters in the state participated in it, the whole thing was a big deal because it was the first *real* vote of any kind. Iowa was pretty conservative, but Meg figured her mother had a halfway decent chance since she was inclined to be a centrist on non-social issues, and her voting record had always had a distinct pro-agriculture bias. The general consensus seemed to be that a high turnout would be in her favor, because her campaign seemed to be bringing a lot of first-time voters into the process.

"Daddy!" Neal saw him first, as Meg, her brothers, and Trudy sat watching television after dinner. "We missed you!"

Their father bent to hug him. "Well, I missed you, too."

"I've got your dinner warm in the oven, if you're hungry, Russell," Trudy said.

"Thank you, that sounds great." He straightened up, rubbing a tired hand across the back of his neck, and then loosening his tie. "But, don't worry, I can get it myself."

"Don't be silly. It won't take but a minute." She bustled out to the kitchen.

"How'd they go?" Meg asked, opening her math book to make it look as if she'd been doing homework.

"Not bad. Crowded." He yawned, taking off his jacket, making Neal laugh by putting it on Kirby. "Your mother call? I kept getting her voice-mail."

"Yeah." Steven opened his science book, which had also been untouched all evening. "She said hi."

"Don't be a jerk." Meg reached across the couch to hit him. "She said for you to call her back around eleven, Dad."

"Guess what?" Neal climbed onto their father's lap. "She said she had a meeting with the President today and everything! *He* called her up to talk to her!"

"*He* wants her support on that trade bill," Meg said. Not that he was likely to get it.

Her father glanced over. "Been keeping up lately?"

Meg shrugged. At school, she worked just hard enough to get good grades—candidates' children were kind of supposed to, but C-Span and political websites and things like *Meet the Press* were different. She liked knowing what was going on. Sometimes, when Mr. Bucknell actually did manage to get the class into a political discussion, she would have to chew her pen or drum on her desk to keep from joining in. If she said anything, people would probably think she was showing off, or had asked her mother for the answer. Like, instead of running for the school's Senate, she was just a class officer, and she and Beth would sit in the back during meetings, being attitude problems. They never volunteered for anything, although when they were assigned to committees, they did whatever needed to be done quickly and responsibly. Being an attitude problem was one thing; being ill-bred was quite another.

After watching television for a while, she went upstairs to check her email, and maybe even do some homework. Mostly, she got A minuses, with a few solid A's here and there—and, when she screwed up, an occasional A plus. The truth was, getting *straight* A's made people expect too much, and—well, she wasn't one to overachieve. Academically, anyway.

She did some French and chemistry, and then moved over to her bed to read, Vanessa joining her. Lately, she'd gotten pretty hooked on mysteries, and right now she was going through a long-running series about a Boston detective named Spenser.

Hearing her father laughing and talking downstairs, she glanced at the clock and saw that it was just past eleven. Well, so, he hadn't wasted any time calling her mother. The fact that he sounded so cheerful made her feel very warm and safe—her parents hadn't always gotten along so well.

The worst time that she could remember had been before Neal was born. It had been when she was six and seven, so parts of that whole period were kind of blurry, but she remembered the tension. She definitely remembered the tension.

It had started around the time her mother had been elected to the Senate, moving up from the House of Representatives. Her workload and constituency had gotten bigger, and suddenly, she was home even less often than before. Then, when she *was* home, her father did a lot of work at his office, while she and Steven spent most weekends with her mother. And they didn't eat dinner together. She remembered for sure that they all didn't eat dinner together.

In those days, she never understood what was going on if she got up early on a Saturday morning to watch television, and found her father asleep on the couch. It just seemed weird. She remembered how unhappy her parents had been, and the extra-hard hugs she got from them separately. The low angry voices in the kitchen, then the back door slamming and her father not coming back until almost too late to say good night to them. Once, coming into the dining room, she found her mother crying, and had been terrified, because parents weren't supposed to do that. Then, during the week, when her mother wasn't there, her father would be quiet and sad, getting furious if she and Steven did something like spill milk, and then being sad again and grabbing them in the very hard hugs. It had been scary because Meg couldn't understand what was going on, and no one ever talked about it. At any rate, not to her.

Sometimes she heard things, though. Her mother sounding very bitter once and saying to her father, "See you at Christmas," as she left for Washington. Which had completely spooked her, because it was July. "We've done separation," her father had said another time. "Maybe we should have a trial 'togetherness.'" That time, her mother had slammed the back door. Steven was too young to pay much attention, but Meg had friends at school whose parents had gotten divorced, and they would all talk about how their fathers didn't live at their houses anymore, and Meg had worried that that might happen to them, which would mean that she and Steven would be all alone.

One day, her father *did* leave, and Trudy took care of them. He came back after what seemed like years, but was probably only three or four days. He took her and Steven out to this really neat hamburger restaurant, and told them they were all moving to Washington. They went to a little house in Virginia, where about half of the kids in her new elementary school had a parent—usually a father—who worked on Capitol Hill with her mother.

It was kind of funny—funny-strange, as opposed to funny-amusing—because right after they moved down, her mother was getting sick a lot and would go to bed early. She was also getting fat. Her parents explained about this new little brother or sister that neither she nor Steven were too excited about, and sometimes Meg would put her hand on her mother's stomach to feel it kick. It kicked *hard.* And suddenly, her father was helping her mother around, and bringing her special things they never bought, like potato chips.

When the baby came, she and Steven decided that it was very ugly. They began to like it, especially when it smiled, and they got used to calling it Neal. As he got older, he wasn't as red and ugly anymore, and she and Steven decided that he was very beautiful. Her parents had always thought he was beautiful. And Neal was such a damn *happy* baby, that having him around made the house feel much more relaxed.

About a year later, they moved back to Massachusetts, and her father was made a full partner at his law firm. In Washington, he had worked at home mostly, flying back to Boston usually only one day a week. Trudy had lived in a small apartment above the garage while they were in Virginia, and Meg sometimes wondered whether part of the reason they went back to Boston so soon was because *Trudy* had been more homesick than anyone—and her parents couldn't afford to lose her. Meg, personally, was glad to go back, and be at her old school, with her old friends again.

Her parents still fought pretty often—and if she or her brothers ever asked them if they thought they might get divorced, her mother would invariably pause and say something like, "Well, not so far today," and her father would say, "Don't be so hasty, Kate, it's still early." And then—most of the time, luckily—her parents seemed to be amused by that. Anyway, her father was much more cheerful, and her mother's face lost the dark circles under her eyes that even makeup had never really been able to hide. Meg still got all hung up if they argued about *anything,* but now it was usually just squabbling and snapping, instead of outright warfare.

Too tired to read any more, Meg dropped the mystery next to

her bed and turned her light off. It was good to hear her father still talking downstairs—that meant that things were okay. Win or lose, a Presidential campaign couldn't be all that great for a marriage. Especially when the *last* time her mother had tried for a more responsible political position—except, she wouldn't worry about that right now. Not with her father's tone sounding so light and stress-free.

She was pretty sure that if her mother lost the nomination, things would be just fine. And—well, she would never admit it aloud—but, she sort of hoped that it would work out that way.

Okay, she *definitely* hoped that it would work out that way.

7

FRIDAY NIGHT, ONE of the seniors on the tennis team, Monica Jacobs, had a party. Definitely the social event of the season. Meg was glad that her father was in Iowa—he would have asked a lot of questions about whether parents were going to be there, if there would be alcohol, and that kind of stuff. Trudy's questions tended to be less demanding, although she did want to know who was driving, and told Meg to stay out of cars with young men. Meg said she would do her best.

She got a ride with Ann Mason, who was also a senior, and had her license. Beth came too, along with three other juniors they knew. Meg was never sure what she thought about these parties, which were always a lot more wild than she expected. She couldn't decide if her parents let her go because they didn't know what the parties were like, or because they trusted her. Both were possible. One thing, she always made sure she rode with someone like Ann, who she knew wasn't going to get drunk or anything if she had to drive. Massachusetts driving laws were *strict,* and Ann, fortunately, was the responsible type.

"I have to get the car back by one," Ann said, parking in front of Monica's house. "So, don't anyone go off with anyone. Or," she corrected herself, "if you do, be back by twelve-thirty."

"Watch yourself," Beth said out of the corner of her mouth.

"Yeah," Meg said. "You should talk." Meg, always afraid of publicity, had never gone off with anyone, except at a dance once. Beth was more inclined towards the occasional casual fling.

They had arrived fashionably late, and the party was already crowded and very noisy, music blasting. Meg unzipped her ski jacket, looking around at the darkened entrance hall and living room, lots of people shouting, some of them dancing, and a few already making out in corners. She could hear somewhat drunken male laughter, and figured that the football team was out in full force.

"Let's get rid of our coats," Beth said, and Meg followed her.

The coatroom was almost always the parents' bedroom, unless there were siblings. In this case, it was the little sister, and the room was so pink and adorable that it actually seemed to *smell* like bubble gum.

Before dropping her jacket on the bed, Beth took out a package of cigarettes. She always held a cigarette at parties. Marlboro Lights.

"Wow," Meg said. "You are so cool."

"I know." Beth released a slow stream of smoke. "It's a lot for you to live up to."

"It's a lot for me to live *down*," Meg said.

"Ha." Beth glanced in the white plastic mirror to adjust her hat. It was grey felt with a small red feather. Very stylish. Meg would never have the chutzpah to wear a hat.

They went out to the kitchen, each taking a Budweiser from the refrigerator. Usually, Meg had one beer—she had never actually gotten drunk, or even, really, come close to it. Partly because her father trusted her not to, but also because she wasn't sure how it would affect her. Lots of times at these things, people got sick—especially sophomore girls—and Meg couldn't stand the thought of that kind of public humiliation. Besides, paranoid or not, she always worried about the possibility of publicity. If she were getting drunk at parties, it would be bound to show up in the tabloids or on the Internet. At the very least, her mother's *constituents* might find out.

"Oooh," Fred, one of the captains of the wrestling team, said as he came in to get more beer. "Big bad sophomores." He nudged Meg. "What would Mom say?"

Beth shrugged. "That she should have Heineken."

"Yeah, well," Fred took out two beers, draining one of them in one long gulp, "think I'll go call the news stations, get them out here."

"Hell," another guy from the wrestling team said, yanking out his cell phone. "Let's just upload it ourselves."

He was probably kidding, but she put the beer down and got a small bottle of water, instead. Better safe than sorry.

"Give her a break," the boy behind them, Greg Knable, said.

Meg blushed. Greg always intimidated her. Not only was he tall and handsome, but he was president of the South Senate, was on the cross-country, basketball, *and* baseball teams, and participated in about six thousand other extracurricular activities. He also got good grades. The really intimidating part, though, was that his father—a wealthy, successful businessman, in every clichéd sense of the phrase—was vehemently, publicly, *constantly* against everything her mother did or said, and always worked actively for any candidate who tried to run against her. It was even stupider because if she was with either parent, and they ran into Mr. Knable at the club or someplace, everyone would be sickeningly polite. Her mother said it was civilized. Meg thought it was hypocritical.

At any rate, she was never quite sure how to act around Greg. Her friends usually made cracks, but he seemed pretty embarrassed about the whole thing, too. Usually, if she was around him, neither of them brought up politics at all—and, in fact, rarely did more than say hello, and then hurry off in opposite directions.

"So." Greg opened a can of beer. "How's it going?"

She looked around, saw that Beth was giving someone a cigarette, Fred was trying to pick up this girl from her honors English class, and that Greg was definitely talking to her. "Not bad. How's it going with you?"

"It's cool," he said, then gestured towards her water bottle. "You don't have to drink that—Sam was only kidding."

Maybe, maybe not. "I heard you got into Princeton early decision," Meg said. "That's really good."

"Yeah. I was pretty happy. My father went there and everything, so he's"—he stopped—"um, pleased."

Meg nodded. "He must be. It's excellent."

"Yeah." Greg blinked, and concentrated on his beer.

"Hey, everybody, look!" Fred said. "A peace treaty! Historical moment here!" He put a heavy arm around Meg's shoulders. "Think your parents'll ground you for talking to him?"

"Fred, shut up, okay?" Greg said.

"Anything you say, Romeo." Fred winked at him, and opened another beer.

Meg kept her eyes on her hands, too shy to check Greg's expression.

"I, uh, I told someone in the living room that I'd kind of be right back," she said.

He nodded. "Yeah. Good talking to you."

She looked up, saw that he was also red, and hurried out to the living room.

"Hey." Beth caught up to her. "Were they being jerks to you?"

Meg shook her head. "No. Just stupid Fred."

"Don't even listen to him," Beth said.

"Yeah, I know." Meg gestured across the room towards some people from their class. "Sophomores."

"Let's go," Beth said, heading over.

The party got better as the night went along—more crowded, more noisy, and more interesting. She was in the middle of an argument—well, more like a friendly, but intense, discussion—with Isaac Pechman, who didn't like the Patriots, when she caught sight of his watch and realized that it was past eleven-fifteen.

There was a news special on about the Iowa Caucus at eleven-thirty, and she wanted to watch at least the first few minutes. Her mother had done really well in the debate, which had been on Wednesday, and the polls had been going up ever since.

So, when Isaac decided he wanted another beer, Meg went to find Monica, who was pretty drunk and having a marvelous time at her party. After being told that there were two televisions upstairs that Monica was perfectly happy to have her "check" for a minute, Meg decided that she would just tune in for the beginning, and then go back downstairs.

"Where you going?" Some guy who must have crashed the party tried to grab her as she went by. "Keep me company, babe."

"Excuse me," she said, continuing past and hoping that he wasn't drunk enough to follow her. Once upstairs, she found a television in Monica's parents' bedroom and flipped to the right channel.

The door opened as the commentators of the special were introducing each other and outlining the format and content of the show.

"Sorry," a guy said. "I thought this was the bathroom."

"I think it's down to the right." Then Meg blushed, realizing it was Greg.

"Hey, what are you doing?" He came all the way in. "You a television addict or something?"

"Despite Senator Powers' strong performance in Wednesday's debate," the main commentator was saying, "Iowa is expected to go with the more conservative Hawley, or possibly Governor—"

"Oh," Greg said.

Meg nodded sheepishly.

"You, uh," his hands went into his pockets, "want me to leave?"

"I'm only going to watch for a minute," she said. "I just thought I'd, um—"

He shrugged, sitting down on the bed next to her. "Of course you're watching. Hell, I know I would."

A film clip came on showing Senator Hawley earlier that day.

"Do you have any predictions about the outcome of next week's caucus?" a reporter was asking.

"These are serious times, and our nation is facing some real challenges," Senator Hawley—tall, slightly balding, and very tough—said firmly. Or maybe even *grimly.* "I'm confident that the voters will make the right choice."

Naturally, the reporter didn't give up that easily. "Do you think Mrs. Powers' victory in the debate will have an effect—"

"The voters understand what's at stake here," he said. "We need a strong leader, not the flavor-of-the-month. But I know that the voters here in Iowa will rise to the challenge, and vote responsibly."

Ouch. Not exactly subtle.

Senator Hawley was being ushered away by his campaign staff and Secret Service agents—full protection for all Presidential candidates had just started earlier that week, and obviously, there were agents posted at her house, and around the neighborhood, but since she hadn't actually seen her mother in person, Meg hadn't let herself do much thinking about what that actually *meant.*

And she didn't feel like thinking about it right now, either.

A film of her mother flashed onto the screen, and Meg saw her parents—along with her mother's retinue of aides and agents—leaving what appeared be a local ice cream shop, everyone looking quite cheerful and relaxed in comparison with the Hawley contingent.

But, Christ, why was *that* her clip-of-the-day? Senator Hawley had been shown in front of an army ammunition factory—a location almost certainly chosen with very great care by his staff—and even though her mother's daily schedule indicated that, among other things, she'd given a speech to a group of Iowa National Guard members, and made an appearance at a John Deere manufacturing plant, the network had decided to go with the damn *ice cream* excursion? A frivolous snack? By comparison, Hawley might as well have been wearing a pair of six-irons—and a codpiece.

On top of which, Governor Kruger had recently gone pheasant and quail hunting, striding around through the underbrush with a bunch of burly Iowans, and the images had gotten—and were still getting—a lot of air-play, and Internet coverage. And, cynically, she was almost surprised that the news editors hadn't promptly gone out of their way to show lengthy footage of her mother forcefully wielding a blow-dryer, or something.

"Senator Powers, how do you feel about the caucus?" a reporter asked.

Her mother grinned. "Oh, my level of excitement is such that I can scarcely begin to describe it."

Everyone nearby laughed.

"All kidding aside," she said. "I actually think that we're blessed to have the opportunity to watch democracy unfold right in front of our very eyes. It should be a very interesting evening."

"Do you think you're going to win?" someone else asked.

"I wouldn't presume to predict," her mother said. "What do *you* think?"

People laughed again, and the clip ended, going back to the commentators, who were smiling, too.

"Well," one of them said. "Two very different candidates."

And how.

Senator Hawley had been pounding the word "serious" for weeks. Strong. Right. Confident. Responsible. Fun stuff like that. Whereas, her mother usually seemed to be going for inclusiveness, although she might have been sending an "I'm not *quite* as secular as you may fear" message this time by throwing the word "blessed" in there, too.

Meg glanced at Greg to see his reaction.

"She's too funny," he said. "Is she always that funny?"

More often than not. "Not always," she said defensively. "They just *show* it when she is."

He slowly crumpled his beer can, then tossed it into the trash can by the bureau. "I don't know. She should be more serious."

Damn it, maybe Hawley's strategy was working—especially if Greg's opinion was representative. "Maybe it would be *good* for the country to go back to being optimistic again," she said. And fearless. And *friendly*.

Just for a change.

"Yeah." He put his hands in his pockets. "I don't know. I guess my parents kind of like Griffin."

Who was the almost-certain Republican nominee—and the sort of glad-handing, ear-marking politician Meg particularly disliked.

Greg shifted his position. "I'll be eighteen by then."

"I'm not even going to ask," Meg said.

"Don't," he agreed. "Hell, *I* don't even know."

"—can't help wondering whether her nuanced position on trade will play well here in the—" one of the panelists was saying.

Meg changed the channel, stopping on ESPN. "Sports are nice, too."

He grinned, and they watched for a few minutes, companionably silent, Meg having no idea who was playing, or whether the game was important, except that it was two college teams. Villanova and somebody.

"I guess we should go downstairs," she said, as the game switched to a commercial.

"Come here," he said.

She looked at him blankly. "What?"

He leaned over and kissed her, his arm going around her waist, and Meg automatically kissed back, but recovered herself almost as quickly and pulled away.

"Why'd you do that?" she asked.

He kept his arm around her waist. "What do you mean?"

"Because you like me, because I'm a girl, or because you feel sorry for me?" she asked.

He laughed. "All three."

"What?" She moved away from him. "Where do you get off feeling sorry for me? There's no reason to feel sorry for me."

"Okay, then," he said. "Because I like you."

Yeah, right. "Oh, come on," she said. "You mean, because I'm a girl."

"I like girls," he agreed. "What's so bad about me liking girls?"

"Nothing." She swallowed, knowing that she wanted to keep kissing him, that he still wanted to kiss her, and they probably weren't going to do it again. She wouldn't have let him get *much* further, but—considering where they were sitting—it would have been nice to stretch out, and relax, and maybe—

"Oh, sorry," a guy said from the doorway. "Thought this was the bathroom." He shrugged at them, and continued down the hall.

Which definitely broke the mood—although not the tension.

"Well," Greg said, after a minute. "I guess we should go back down."

Damn. Meg nodded. "Yeah."

They got up and walked awkwardly together, a couple of feet apart, not talking.

"You're going to love Princeton," she said finally.

He smiled, touched her hand for a second, and they separated to rejoin the party.

8

ON THE NIGHT of the caucus, her house was filled with people from the campaign, some of her parents' friends, and a small pool of reporters, photographers, and camera people. Originally, Meg and her brothers had been scheduled to go to Iowa, but her parents—mainly her mother—decided that it really wasn't worth their missing school. Meg thought that was too simplistic, and figured that either her mother thought she was going to win and that it would be more important for them to skip school at certain points further on in the campaign, or—and this was what she suspected—because her mother thought she was going to lose, and didn't want all of them to be there to see it.

Whatever the reason was, they stayed home with Trudy. Four televisions had been set up in the living room, with each one tuned to a different cable news station, except for the one set to show C-Span all night. People had brought pizza, and things to drink, and it was more like a party than anything else, although most of the campaign people had their laptops open, and also took turns manning the phones, which never seemed to stop ringing.

After helping Trudy make sure that everyone had everything he or she needed, Meg sat on the rug in front of the televisions with Steven, who was gobbling pizza, Neal, who was looking around with huge eyes, and Beth, who was spending the night. Kirby lay in front of them, wagging his tail every so often and eating the crusts Steven gave him, which he always called "pizza bones." Weird kid. The cats were all closed up in her parents' bedroom, so that no one would let them outside by mistake.

There was a flash, and all four of them jumped.

"Good," the *Globe* photographer said. "Can you all maybe turn a little so I can see everyone's faces?"

"Are we going to be famous?" Neal asked.

Perish the thought. "Come on, Meg," Meg said to Beth. "Aren't you going to smile for him?"

Beth shook her head. "I don't want to. I'm a Republican."

"Yeah, but she's your *mother*," Meg said.

Beth sniffed. "She's a bleeding heart, that's what she is."

"Girls," Steven said sternly, imitating their father.

"We're boys," Meg said.

"No way," Steven said. "You're too ugly to be boys."

Meg laughed. "Yeah, well, *you're* too ugly to—"

"What do you all think of this?" Her mother's best friend, Andrea Peterson, stopped next to them, and they all sat up politely.

"I think it's neat," Steven said, helping himself to more pizza.

"I think it's loud," Neal said, still looking around.

"What about you, Meg? Don't you think?" Mrs. Peterson asked.

"Only twice a day," Meg said, grinning back. "And I used them up already." She liked Mrs. Peterson. They had been friends since college, or, as Mrs. Peterson put it, "back in the days when Kate was a simple political science major." "Simple is right," her mother would usually answer, and they would both laugh. Mrs. Peterson was one of the very few people around whom Meg ever saw her even slightly relax. "Oh, Mrs. Peterson, you know my friend Beth, right?"

They both nodded.

"Do you want some pizza, Mrs. Peterson?" Steven asked, reaching onto the coffee table to get a clean plate.

"No, thank you." She touched her waist. "Not all of us have your mother's infuriating metabolism."

Her mother was, indeed, dependably thin, although after Neal was born, she'd had some trouble losing the last fifteen pounds of her baby weight—much to the delight of the media, and a very snarky columnist actually called her "Senator Chunky" once. Whereupon, her mother—who did not, it went without saying, accept this with good grace—had almost instantly dropped the fifteen pounds, and now generally erred on the side of being *too* thin.

She had also, after being accused of using Botox, said testily, "No, thank you, I enjoy moving my eyebrows," but Meg had noticed that—although she didn't seem to be aware that she did it—she sometimes brushed her hair self-consciously across her forehead.

"My God, I never thought I'd be over here watching her run for President." Mrs. Peterson's smile widened. "I'm invited to the Inaugural Balls, right?"

"Yeah," Meg said. "You can stand in for me."

Beth looked surprised. "You wouldn't go to the Inaugural Balls?"

"No way," Meg said. "Wear some frumpy gown on national television and have a bunch of Senators dance with me because they feel sorry for me standing all alone? You've got to be kidding."

Mrs. Peterson laughed. "What if the gown isn't frumpy?"

"Stand there all alone in some skimpy gown on national television?" Meg said. "Not a chance."

Mrs. Peterson laughed again, and then someone across the room motioned her over, and she gestured "Excuse me" to them and left.

"You really wouldn't go?" Beth asked.

Meg shrugged. "At this point, it isn't exactly an issue."

"Well, yeah," Beth said, "but—"

"Hey, where're the smiles?" Preston sat down next to them. "Candidates' kids have to smile. *Constantly.*"

They all smiled.

"Oh, good, very good," he said, taking a swig of beer and looking terribly handsome in dark brown flannel slacks, ankle-high leather boots, a V-neck tan lamb's wool sweater with no shirt underneath, and a brown fedora. "Some scene we've got here." He tilted the hat over one eye, and then looked at them with the uncovered eye. "You know why your mother's going to win?"

"Because everyone loves her," Neal said happily.

"Not just that, little guy." Preston took the hat off and put it on Steven, who tried to adjust it to the exact same tilt. "Because the lady's got style. People like style."

Neal looked down at himself. "Do I have style?"

"Sure, kid," Preston said. "You've got the makings of one fine-looking dude."

Well, if jeans and beat-up, hand-me-down Lacoste shirts were considered chic, then, on most days, she was in good shape, too.

"What about Steven?" Neal asked.

"Ab-solutely. And Meggo here," he draped an arm around her shoulders, "Meggo's got it, too." He nodded at the grey sweatpants tucked into her hiking boots. "Very nice. All you need is here." He touched the neck of her ragg sweater. "A nice scarf here, and you'll have 'em at your feet."

"Who?" Neal asked.

"The world, kid." He looked at Beth. "Good, the friend has style, too. Only, you might want this up." He adjusted her collar, then studied the result. "Good. Very good."

Neal flipped up his own collar. "Does Daddy have style?"

"Russell?" He shook his head. "No, I think Russell-baby needs some help."

"You call him Russell-baby?" Steven asked from underneath the hat.

Preston shrugged. "Sure. What else? You can call him that, too, kid. Tell him I said it was okay."

Luckily, Preston had a deep sense of irony—or he would be too damn goofy and glib to have any credibility whatsoever. "What's wrong with the way Dad dresses?" Meg asked, amused.

"Well, Meggo, it's like this—bourgeois. Upper bourgeois, maybe, but bourgeois. Moccasins, Oxford *everything*, still wearing the old B-school jackets—" Preston shook his head sadly. "No style whatsoever."

He had a point, although her father had, of course, gone to *L*-school.

"Can you help him get style?" Neal asked, sounding as if he wasn't sure whether he should be worried or giggling.

"Sure," Preston said. "Give me a few weeks of intensive—"

"We're now able to project—" the anchorperson on the third television began.

"Shhh!" half of the room hissed, and Meg felt a sudden tension rippling up her back.

"—Senator Katharine Powers, with an unprecedented—"

The room exploded into thirty or forty different cheers.

"—holding strong with almost thirty-five percent of the vote," the anchorperson went on, "with her nearest competitor, Senator Thomas Hawley, taking away only twenty-seven percent of this—"

Meg stared at the pandemonium in the room, at people jumping and yelling and hugging each other, and then at Steven and Neal and Beth, who all looked as stunned as she felt.

"The early caucus results are in, and tonight, we've had an historic—" a commentator on one of the other televisions was now saying.

"This makes her the front-runner!" someone shouted.

"We're gonna do it!" someone else yelled. "We're gonna go all the way!"

Neal yanked on Meg's arm. "Does this mean she's President?"

"It means she might be," Meg said, looking at the piece of pizza Steven had dropped facedown on the rug. The pizza looked like she felt.

"I thought she wasn't supposed to win," Beth said quietly.

"She wasn't," Meg said, feeling almost dazed. "All the polls said—" She shook her head. Projected—holding strong—unprecedented—*historic*—

"Isn't it great?" someone shouted at them. "Aren't you proud of your mother?"

They all nodded, Meg gulping some Coke to calm her stomach.

"Now, we'll move to the Des Moines Marriott, where Mark Wilson is on the scene," a commentator on yet another one of the televisions said. "Mark?"

"Thank you, Lila," a man holding a microphone in a noisy, crowded hotel lobby said as the camera switched to him. "This is Mark Wilson, and I'm standing in the—"

"Shhh!" several people in the room said, the celebration stopping so everyone could gather around to listen.

"Sources have said that the Senator will be coming down to—yes, there she is," he said. "We'll be moving in to—"

Meg watched as the camera focused on her mother, surrounded by people and flashbulbs, dignified in a deep blue dress. Her father was standing next to her, looking a little shell-shocked, but grinning, regardless. He said something to her, she smiled, and Meg thought she saw their hands touch before her mother turned to face the cameras. She waved briefly with her left arm and most of the hotel lobby, as well as the living room, broke into applause.

"Senator, how do you feel?" a reporter shouted.

"Very happy," her mother said. "Very excited, very—very inarticulate."

The people in the lobby laughed in obvious camaraderie.

"Did you expect to win, Senator?" another reporter asked, managing to get his voice heard over the others.

"I make it a practice never to *expect* anything," her mother said.

"Where do you go from here, Senator?" the same reporter asked.

Her mother's grin got a little bigger. "New Hampshire," she said.

After the caucus, her mother was on the covers of *Time, Newsweek,* and *U.S. News & World Report*—which really freaked Meg out. Everywhere she went, she either saw a picture of her mother, or heard people talking about her, or was otherwise reminded about how odd her family's lives had become. There seemed to be kind of a bandwagon effect, and suddenly, people who had never given her mother a second thought were behaving as though they had been life-long supporters, and had always suspected that she might make a serious run at the Presidency one day.

Since New Hampshire was an easy drive, they all spent the next weekend with her mother, and Meg found herself doing some old-fashioned, retail campaigning—which mostly involved handing out leaflets and buttons. Steven was all set to run around shaking hands, but when asked to concentrate on leafleting, worked with exhausting enthusiasm. At first, Neal helped them, but he was kind of afraid of the crowds and would spend most of his time with their parents, holding on to whichever one—almost always their father—had a free hand, probably winning hundreds of votes with his smile, which was currently missing two front teeth. Steven kept telling people that it was because of a gruesome hockey accident.

On Sunday afternoon, while they were at a shopping mall near Concord, she and Steven ran into Senator Hawley's children—three swaggering and obnoxious boys wearing ties. They surrounded Steven, knocked his box of buttons out of his arms, and told him he'd better get the hell out of there if he knew what was good for him. Meg hurried over to help, and the two older boys—both of whom were bigger than she was, although probably only one of them was her age—made comments that were both chauvinistic and obscene. This infuriated Steven, who was ready to take on all three of them, and Meg was starting to get a little nervous, when one of the boys yanked her leaflets away from her, scattering them on the ground. For some reason, this struck Meg as being funny as hell, and as she stood there laughing, the three Hawleys apparently realized what jerks they were making of themselves and left, an angry Hawley staffer meeting them on the way and escorting them to a different section of the mall.

People who had witnessed the scene helped Meg gather up her leaflets and Steven get his buttons back into his cardboard box, quite a few remarking that they were very well brought-up, and that that said good things for their mother. Meg thanked them, and everyone went off with a button and a leaflet apiece.

And, with luck, mentally eliminated Senator Hawley from the list of candidates they were considering.

The incident got back to her parents, and after that, Meg noticed that there was always an adult campaign worker lurking nearby. Linda pulled them aside, telling them that they were very well politicized and had handled a difficult situation quite gracefully. Meg still thought the whole thing was funny, and after he stopped being mad, Steven agreed with her.

They would ride in an SUV or town car driven by Secret Service agents, with more agents riding in front of and behind them. Because the vehicles were so crowded, Meg almost always got stuck on a jump seat, which made her carsick. The Secret Service didn't want them to open the windows, either. Her mother would be slumped against the backseat the whole time, gulping coffee and wearily reading the information packet her advance team had prepared about the next event, scribbling last minute changes in whatever speech she would be giving, while Glen practically had a heart attack.

"Kate, every time you start ad-libbing, I age three years," he'd groan.

Her mother—who *always* ad-libbed—would just ignore this, and continue editing and rewriting.

When they'd pull into the next town, her mother would get out of the car, suddenly cheerful and refreshed, projecting an air of relaxed, friendly confidence. Usually, the speeches went well—crowds were big, audiences receptive—but, not always. Sometimes, the advance team had over- or under-anticipated the number of people who would attend, and once, no one came at all because the staff had publicized the wrong time.

Standing in the empty auditorium, Meg could tell that her mother was furious, but almost as quickly, she was amused and sent someone out to get hamburgers, which they ate sitting on the stage.

"You gonna fire someone, Mom?" Steven asked, his mouth full of French fries.

Her mother arched an eyebrow at Glen. "That depends on whose mistake it was."

"These things happen," he said.

She nodded. "They happen *once.*" Then, she grinned. "Enough said?"

Seeing Glen nod, Meg glanced over at her mother. Kind of weird to see her being an administrator. And a rather cranky and demanding one, at that.

"Well." Glen finished his hamburger. "Why don't we get out of here and head over to Sunapee."

Meg sighed, and looked down at her barely touched meal. She was kind of enjoying hanging out on the stage.

"Is that really necessary?" her father asked.

"No," her mother said, to Meg's surprise. "Glen, I'm going to take this as a sign that I need a break."

He looked alarmed. "But—"

"Can we really stay here?" Meg asked. "I mean, for a while?"

"Don't make me feel so benevolent," her mother said. "Of course we can. I think we all need it." She yawned. "I know I do."

So, they sat on the stage, and ate hamburgers, and didn't talk about politics once. It was Meg's favorite afternoon of the campaign so far. Of course, right after that, they went out to the motorcade and went to Sunapee, and her mother made two speeches, but still. For a while there, it had been almost as if her mother wasn't running for President at all.

Almost.

9

THE DAY BEFORE the primary, the headline above the lead editorial in the Manchester *Union-Leader*—New Hampshire's biggest, and most influential, newspaper—was: *Katharine Vaughn Powers: Very Open and Very Presidential.* It was a big deal, because just about everyone in the state read it, and the endorsement was also quite a coup, since the paper was traditionally conservative, and her mother—despite a bit of a favorite daughter status, since she represented a neighboring state—wasn't the sort of politician the editorial board normally embraced.

And, indeed, her mother won the primary, with almost forty percent of the vote, the media analysts saying that it would have been higher if the voters hadn't been uneasy about her position on gun control.

After that, primaries became the routine, with her mother doing very well in the Northeast and Pacific Northwest, less well in the South and Midwest—where Senator Hawley talked a lot about Tradition and Family, the concept of Motherhood implicit in this. Funny, that no one ever asked where *his* family was. And when they were there in photos—the three boys standing behind their parents with toothy smiles—Meg couldn't help wishing that everyone knew how rotten those kids were. Governor Kruger picked up most of the Rocky Mountain States, although her mother held her own, and outright won Colorado and Arizona.

But, even though Meg was impressed by how well her mother was doing, and also kind of proud, she got tired of only seeing her on the news, or in articles, and only talking to her when she was alone in some hotel room, or on her way to yet another campaign event.

Somehow, no matter how angry or resentful Meg was feeling at that particular moment, she couldn't quite bring herself to say anything mean, because she kept picturing her mother being lonely and sad, hundreds—and sometimes, thousands—of miles away. So, on days when she knew she might say something rotten—not too often, because her father and Trudy would get suspicious—she managed to be in the shower, or on a walk with Kirby around the time her mother was supposed to call. In a way, Meg thought of it as doing her part to help The Candidate.

When her mother *did* come home, she was always completely worn out. She would try to get up to have breakfast with them, and do normal parent things, but was always so tired that everyone was afraid to ask her. Among other things, Meg wouldn't even *suggest* a game of tennis.

Drifting around late at night, she would go into the kitchen or dining room, find a table covered with papers and graphs, stacks of folders, and cold mugs of coffee—and her mother, sitting up, but asleep, her head propped on one hand. Sometimes, after Meg woke her up, her mother would go to bed, but more often, she would fix herself more coffee and keep working. She got mad fast, too—probably too tired to control her temper—which would erupt unexpectedly, as if she had been holding it in for days, exploding into sudden fights which, as far as Meg could tell, were mostly only with her. She knew she should be understanding, and remember how much pressure her mother was under and how tired she was, but most of the time, her temper would come crashing out to meet her mother's, and the fight would end only when one of them left the room.

More often than not, this involved at least one slammed door.

One night, around quarter of two, Meg found her mother hunched over reams of paper in the sitting room and woke her up as carefully as possible.

"What?" Her mother jerked awake, looking around in confusion. "What's wrong?"

Meg jumped a little at the quick reaction. "Nothing. I just thought you should maybe go up to bed."

"I have work to do." Her mother fumbled for her cup of coffee, tasted it, and shuddered.

"You should go up to bed," Meg said. "It's really late."

"I think I can manage that decision by myself." Her mother wearily pushed up her sleeve to check her watch, then frowned. "What are *you* doing up?"

Meg shrugged. "I always stay up."

Her mother scowled, and lifted up a folder about health care or whatever else it was that she was studying. "Terrific, you always stay up. You wouldn't if I were around."

"Yeah, well," Meg tried—and failed—to keep her own temper under control, "you're not around, are you?"

Her mother's folder slapped down against the table, and Meg couldn't help flinching. "Let's not start that again, okay?"

"Yeah, really," Meg said. "Wasted energy on my part."

Her mother's jaw tightened, and Meg could see the flush of anger starting into her cheeks.

"Well." Meg folded her arms. "Guess I ought to leave—I'd hate to waste any of your valuable time. Maybe we can make an appointment to see each other next week." She paused, knowing that she should just shut up and leave the room. "If you have time, that is."

"I said, cut it out!" Her mother's voice was less controlled this time.

"No." Meg shook her head, still trying to tell herself to shut up—and still not doing it. "You said not to start again. I didn't hear anything about cutting it out—"

"Meg, get out of here!" Her mother jumped up so quickly that she knocked over her coffee. "Just leave me alone. Just—" She saw the liquid spreading across her papers. "There! Are you happy?" She picked up the mug and dumped out the rest. "Does that make you happy?"

Meg backed up towards the door. "Mom, I didn't mean to—"

"Oh, yeah, you did!" her mother said. "You know damn well you—"

"Kate," Meg's father said from the door, and her mother stopped, visibly trembling, taking a slow breath to try and get back under control.

Meg glanced at her father and found an expression of such fury that she took another involuntary step backwards, her heart beating a little harder against her rib cage.

"Go to your room," he said.

"Oh, good," she said, nodding. "As usual, you're going to listen to my side of it, too."

His eyes got colder, and she retreated another step, knowing that it was unreasonable to be scared, but scared, anyway.

"*Now*," he said.

She bolted past him and halfway up the stairs, then stopped to lean against the railing, feeling hot, clumsy tears start down her cheeks.

"Okay," she heard her father saying gently in the sitting room. "It's okay. Come on, take it easy."

She let go of the railing, running the rest of the way upstairs and into her room, crying harder. Vanessa jumped off the bed, scurrying out of the room, and Meg got under the covers, bringing the blankets and her knees up as high as they would go, shaking so hard that the tears wouldn't come out right, feeling angry, and guilty—and very, very alone.

THE NEXT MORNING, she stood in her closet, trying to figure out what to wear to school—and still upset about the night before. She smelled perfume before she heard anything and knew that her mother had come into the room.

"I'm leaving now," her mother said.

Meg nodded, not turning around.

Her mother sighed. "I'm not going to be back for at least a week, Meg. I don't want to leave with us still angry at each other."

"Does that mean you're staying?" Meg grabbed a shirt and a pair of pants, carrying them over to the bed.

"You know I can't," her mother said.

Meg didn't answer, going over to her dresser to get socks and underwear.

"Meg, I'm sorry," her mother said. "I lost my temper. I didn't—well, I really am sorry."

Meg shrugged.

It was quiet for a minute.

"Is that what you're wearing to school?" her mother asked.

Meg frowned, realizing that she'd picked out plaid madras pants and a striped Oxford shirt. "Yes."

"Very attractive." Her mother came over and put a hand on Meg's shoulder, ruffling it up through her hair. "You're not going to break down and smile?"

"It's not funny," Meg said, even as a little grin escaped.

Her mother also grinned, sitting down on the bed, and Meg looked at her, noticing the perfection of the green silk dress and smelling the light, penetrating perfume.

"You look pretty damn beautiful," she said grumpily.

Her mother frowned. "I'm not sure that's a compliment."

"I'm not sure either," Meg said.

"I admire your honesty." Her mother put her arm around her. "It *irritates* me, but I admire it." She brushed a light kiss across Meg's hair. "Let's not be angry, okay?"

Meg shrugged. "You're going to miss your plane."

Her mother nodded, automatically glancing at her watch.

Meg got up to put the striped shirt back in her closet. "You'd better get going."

"It's not always going to be like this," her mother said.

Meg hung up the shirt, selecting a pale yellow one, instead.

"It really isn't," her mother said.

Meg frowned at the yellow shirt and exchanged it for a light blue one.

"You are the most obstinate person I've ever met," her mother said.

Meg turned and looked at her. "I'm not sure that's a compliment."

"I'm not sure, either," her mother agreed.

Well, okay, then. Meg turned back to the closet, pulling out a white shirt.

"Kate?" Meg's father called up the stairs. "It's almost seven!"

"I'm on my way," her mother called back. She glanced at Meg. "I'll see you soon?"

"Whatever." Meg brought the white shirt over to her bed, hearing her mother's small sigh. She listened to her walk out to the hall, then couldn't stand it anymore and went after her. "Mom?"

Her mother stopped at the top of the stairs.

"Be, uh," Meg blushed, avoiding her eyes, "careful, okay?"

"You, too." Her mother smiled at her. "Wear the blue shirt."

Meg looked at the white one, then nodded, and her mother went down the stairs.

WHEN SCHOOL ENDED, the plan was that they would all go on the road with her mother, and her father would take a leave of absence from the firm, so that he could travel with them the entire time, too. They would campaign with her, and when she had to go to Washington and be a Senator—which she did less and less, these days—they would campaign without her. Not only was Meg dreading that part of it, but since she and her mother still weren't getting along most of the time, that meant that she and her father weren't doing very well, either. So, she wasn't looking forward to the concept of all of them spending several weeks together, non-stop.

But, Steven was the one who *really* got upset about the idea, furious that he'd have to quit Little League, and refusing to go with them. With Neal, it was different, because he was little, but Steven was so independent and secretive about things that when he blew up, people paid attention.

It was decided, finally, that Meg and Steven would stay in Massachusetts with Trudy until the Democratic Convention, which was in August. Then, depending upon what happened at the Convention—none of the candidates had locked up quite enough delegates during the primaries to win the nomination—they would all spend the rest of August—which was when Congress recessed—campaigning, or if her mother didn't get the nomination—they would stay in the "home district," where, presumably, her mother would campaign out of force of habit.

It was kind of lonely around the house, but restful—she and Trudy never fought, and Steven seemed to be able to find things to do with himself. Since there hadn't been any trouble, like the police calling and saying he was smashing streetlights, or something otherwise delinquent, Meg didn't worry about him. He had gone through a period of minor vandalism when he was about nine and a half—which had turned out to be kind of an expensive hobby.

Since she wasn't going to be around for the whole summer, she couldn't really try to get a job, so she spent most of her time playing tennis and going to movies with Beth and Sarah. A few guys from school called and asked her out, but since she knew they were asking only because she was related to a certain Presidential candidate, she always politely refused. It was Beth's opinion that at least a *couple* of the guys might have been more interested in Meg than her mother, but Meg didn't even consider the possibility.

It was late July—almost August, almost the convention—and Meg woke up at eight, glanced at the clock, and then fell back onto her pillow. Vanessa, Adlai, and Sidney were all on her bed, and she patted each of them, getting two sleepy purrs and one long, somewhat toothless yawn from Sidney.

Hearing a noise downstairs, she stiffened. Someone was in the kitchen, obviously trying hard to be quiet. At first, she was scared, thinking it might be a burglar—or an assailant who had gotten past the Secret Service posted outside, but then, she relaxed. How many criminals sat down to have bowls of cereal?

It wasn't Trudy, because she could hear her sleeping—Trudy had sinus problems, so she kind of wheezed—which meant that it had to be Steven. Only, what was he doing up so early? It could be some kind of sports thing—he was always putting himself on exercise programs and jogging plans. Definitely his mother's child. But he'd been awfully quiet lately—maybe he and his friends were up to something.

Yawning, she climbed out of bed, and the cats followed her as she went downstairs to check. Steven was sitting at the table in his baseball uniform, bent over a bowl of Cheerios.

"Since when do you have games this early?" she asked.

"God, Meg." He sat up, startled. "You always gotta sneak up on people?"

"We would have been worried if we'd gotten up, and you weren't here," she said.

"I wrote a note." He gestured with his spoon.

Since she was up, she might as well eat. So, she opened the refrigerator and took out the orange juice. "I thought Little League was over."

"It is," he said shortly.

She poured herself a glass of juice, and refilled his, too. "How come they let you keep the uniform?"

"They didn't," he said.

Conversations with Steven were not always easy. "So, is this like, an exhibition?" she asked. It had to be something like that, because she and Beth and Trudy had gone to his last game.

He kept eating. "All-Stars."

Whoa. She lowered her glass. "You made All-Stars? When?"

"Dunno," he said. "Couple weeks ago."

That figured. Steven would probably sign with the Red Sox, and no one in her family would have heard about it. "How come you didn't tell me?" she asked.

He shrugged. "Didn't tell anyone."

Oh. "But, you should have," she said, "we all—"

"Yeah, sure." He hunched over his cereal. "Just leave me alone."

"Are you playing?" she asked.

He nodded.

Good thing this wasn't like pulling teeth. "What position?" she asked.

"Pitcher," he said.

Wow. "Hey, that's really great," she said.

He shrugged, putting what was left of his cereal down on the floor so that Kirby could eat from the bowl.

She noticed how neatly he'd put on his uniform and wondered how long it had taken him. His cleats were scuffed, but well-shined, and his pants were carefully bloused just above his ankles. But, it made her sad that he had done this great thing—and not bothered letting them know about it.

"How come you didn't tell us?" she asked.

He scowled at her. "I've been going to practice every stupid day! You never even asked where I was going! No one did!"

"Well—" She flushed, knowing that he was right. "I figured you were going to play baseball with your friends."

"Yeah, right." He got up and poured his juice out into the sink, not having touched it. "I bet you don't even care I had my picture in the paper."

"When?" she asked.

"Couple days ago," he said.

"Well." She felt even guiltier. "Did you save it? I want to see it."

"Because you feel bad." His voice was as hurt as it was angry. "That's all. I didn't show you, 'cause all you care about is going out with your friends and playing stupid *tennis*. You could care less about me."

"Steven," she said, uneasily, "that's not—"

"Oh, yeah? How come I heard you on the phone that time Trudy went out, saying you couldn't go anywhere because you had to stay home with Stupid Steven?" He mimicked her voice, and Meg flinched at the accuracy of the inflections.

"Well, I—" She twisted in her chair, uncomfortable. "I didn't mean—"

"Yo, save it," he said grimly. "I so totally don't care."

She had definitely screwed this one up, from start to finish. "What time's your game?" she asked.

"I don't care if no one comes," he said. "Like, big deal."

She put her glass in the sink, too. "Do you care if someone *does* come?"

"You have a stupid tennis lesson." He put on his cap, very carefully adjusting it in front of the mirror. Preston's influence.

"Yeah, but"—she coughed—"I'm really not"—she coughed harder—"feeling so well. I kind of thought I'd cancel."

"Yeah, sure," he said.

"I mean, all that running around. And I'm really," she coughed as hard as she could, "very sick." She rested her forehead in her hand. "The doctor says I only have a month to live if I don't rest today. He thinks I should go to a baseball game or something."

"Yeah, well—" But he grinned as she had a long fit of coughing, falling off her chair. "You'd really skip it? To come to the game?"

She nodded. "Of course."

"You don't have to or anything, it's not so big," he said. "I mean, it doesn't matter if no one—"

"I wouldn't miss it." She got up from the floor. "Do you mind waiting until I get dressed, and then I can come watch you warm up?"

He looked so happy that she felt even worse about having paid so little attention to him lately.

"Yeah," he said. "I can wait."

10

AFTER THAT, FEELING like a complete and absolute skunk, Meg made an extra effort to spend time with him every day and include him in things she did. Steven was noticeably happier, and she felt like even more of a jerk for not realizing that just because he didn't advertise, he needed attention, and maybe even needed *her*.

Her parents and Neal came home a few days before the Convention so that everyone would have time to pack, and her mother—who Meg noticed was much too thin—could have a brief rest. Steven's good mood was contagious, and everyone got along very well—the house hadn't felt so relaxed in months. It was ironic, because the most important part of the campaign was still to come—one way or the other—but, it was nice.

With her mother home, the Secret Service seemed to be *everywhere*. They had a sort of command post set up on the porch, and regular shift changes, and guards patrolling, and the whole nine yards. Her mother spent part of each day out on the patio, lying in the sun, and it was kind of amusing to think of the Secret Service having to watch her the whole time. Her father didn't think it was so damn funny.

On the afternoon before they were going to leave for New York, she saw her father in the upstairs hall and went out to intercept him.

"What kind of stuff am I supposed to bring, Dad?" she asked.

"Well, I don't know." He glanced at the battered Radcliffe sweatshirt and tennis shorts she was wearing. "Not that kind of stuff."

She grinned. "You sure?"

"Very." He leaned forward to tousle her hair, keeping his hand there.

The night before, he'd come into her room while she was reading *Fiasco*—she didn't know enough about Iraq, and had also been reading books like *Hubris* and *A Tragic Legacy* all summer—and sat on her bed for a while, which made it pretty hard to read. "How's it going?" he'd asked finally, and she'd said, "Fine." "I missed you," he said, and she said that she'd missed him, too. "Well, I love you," he said. "I wanted to be sure you knew that." She'd blushed and focused on the book cover until he gave her a hug, kissed the top of her head, said it was late, and that she should go to sleep. She didn't argue.

"Ask your mother what to pack." He took his hand away. "She knows those things."

Meg nodded. "Preston said stilettos and mini-skirts."

Her father laughed. "Sounds like a good plan."

Downstairs, the back door slammed as her mother came into the house.

"What's she whistling?" Meg asked.

Her father listened for a second. " 'Rhapsody in Blue.' "

God forbid she pick something less demanding. A Christmas carol, maybe.

Her mother came up the stairs, wearing white shorts and a pale yellow unbuttoned Oxford shirt of her father's over her bathing suit. Meg looked at her, deciding that she must have recessive genes. Three days in the sun—even though she'd been wearing high-SPF sunscreen—and the woman was Rhapsody in Bronze.

"Hi," her mother said, reaching out to move the hair her father had just ruffled back out of her face.

When her parents felt guilty, they always touched her head.

Meg frowned briefly, wondering why that was. "You look pretty good, considering how old you are," she said.

"Thanks a lot." Her mother studied herself with a critical eye. "Do you think I got too much color? I don't want the delegates to think that all I do is lie around the beach."

"*I* think you look great," her father said, and her mother smiled a tiny smile.

Yeah, really. Who was she kidding? She knew how good she looked; she had just wanted someone to say it aloud.

And, looking from one to the other, she had the distinct—and appalling—sense that her parents wanted to be a little romantic.

Which was her cue to leave. Immediately.

"I think I'll go get some watermelon," she said. "Mom, later, will you show me what kind of stuff to bring?"

"What you have on will be fine," her mother said, and Meg wasn't sure if she was distracted, or being funny.

"Well." She shifted her weight, feeling very self-conscious. "Guess I'll see you guys later."

By the time she got to the bottom of the stairs, she heard them laugh softly—and made a point of *not* looking behind herself to see if they were kissing.

Frankly, she would just rather not know.

SHE ENDED UP packing dresses, with skirts for being casual. Oh, yeah, real casual.

The Convention was being held in Manhattan—her mother's hometown—and they took a campaign-chartered flight the next day, then rode in the usual small, security-laden motorcade into midtown. When her mother's father had died, some years before, her mother had immediately put the Fifth Avenue apartment where she had grown up on the market—which, at times like this, she probably regretted. Or, anyway, Meg assumed that she probably did, since she would never have the nerve to come right out and *ask*.

So, they were going to be staying at the Waldorf, instead. Like Preston said, the woman had style.

Judging from the crowds gathering on the street as they drove down Park Avenue, the city was pretty proud of this native New Yorker who was running for President. Meg stared at all of the people, wondering for a swift uneasy second if her mother was actually going to win. The concept of her winning—really *winning*—was something she hadn't let herself think about much. She rubbed her hand across her forehead, the idea very scary.

"Wow." Steven peered out through the tinted windows. "Are they all here for you, Mom?"

"I went to a very large high school," her mother said.

Meg smiled weakly. Her mother had actually attended an exclusive private school on the Upper East Side, but it was the right moment to make a joke.

When they pulled up near what was supposed to be a relatively private entrance to the Walfdorf Towers section of the hotel, there were still what looked like hundreds of people standing and waving from behind police barricades, undaunted by the massive group of NYPD officers and Secret Service agents trying to secure the area.

Her mother was probably supposed to be the first one out, but Meg felt so claustrophobic, that she beat her to it. When the crowd saw someone with shoulder-length dark hair, they cheered—and cameras went off all over the place—and she stopped, horrified.

"Not me," she said quickly.

"They know it's not you," Steven snorted, climbing out of the car right behind her.

"Come on, kids," an agent said. "Hustle it inside."

Her mother was on the sidewalk now—and in no apparent hurry, to the Secret Service's undisguised dismay.

"I've been singing 'New York, New York' all the way over in the car," she said.

People cheered, some of them yelling things like, "Go, Kate!"

"One thing's for sure," her mother was always able to make her voice heard without seeming to be shouting, "it's great to be home!"

There were more cheers.

Meg watched her move along one of the barricades to greet people, flanked by police officers and agents. What a consummate politician.

At least Meg had almost never seen her kiss babies. She'd probably die laughing if she saw her mother kissing babies—although she *had* been known to dandle them, here and there. Once, in New Hampshire, she had shaken hands with Meg and Steven in the middle of a large crowd, then looked appalled at herself and gave them hugs. If the people didn't know who she and Steven were, they probably thought her mother was kind of weird.

"A real pro," Preston said, next to her.

Meg nodded.

"Come on," he said, his hand on Neal's shoulder, gesturing for Steven to come over, too. "Let's get you guys upstairs."

"What about Mommy and Daddy?" Neal asked.

"They'll meet us later." He ushered them into the discreet lobby, which was filled with smiling Waldorf staffers. "Now, let's—"

"Won't they worry?" Steven asked uneasily.

"What, you don't trust me, kid?" He guided them over to a private elevator. "I just talked to Russell-baby."

"Is it going to be like this all week?" Meg asked.

Preston looked around the packed lobby and the chaotic street scene outside. "Kid, this is minor league," he said.

THEY WERE STAYING in the Presidential Suite, which seemed really weird—and more than a little premature. Glen had been kind of crowing about the fact that Senator Hawley had apparently wanted to stay there, but it had been given to her mother, instead, and he was either in the Royal Suite—or at another hotel, entirely; Meg wasn't sure which. Anyway, the suite was so fancy, that the word "opulent" would have been a grotesque understatement.

Neal was completely horrified when they walked in, and asked where they were going to *sleep*—apparently assuming that the hotel was going to fill the elegant living room with roll-away beds. The fact that the suite had four bedrooms, and was bigger than most people's *houses,* seemed to have escaped him. He was also upset that there was no television, until someone pressed a button and a cupboard magically opened to reveal one of the most high-tech screens she had ever seen. When their personal concierge explained that the suite had been stocked with a wide variety of multimedia devices for their entertainment, including dozens of video games and movies, Steven had immediately disappeared in the indicated direction, and she hadn't seen him since. Neal, on the other hand, just stood in the middle of the living room, so afraid that he might break one of the vases or something, that he refused to move at all until Preston sat him down at the antique table in the majestic, formal dining room, and arranged to have some food sent up. Even when very nervous, Neal was usually happy to eat, although he immediately—and politely—asked why there was "funny" cheese on his hamburger, and Meg had to scrape it off for him. Since *she* liked blue cheese, she went ahead and ate it herself, wrapped in a piece of what Neal thought was "too fancy" lettuce.

There were huge flower arrangements everywhere, and baskets with fruit, cheese, candy, and champagne, as well as sliced fruit and vegetable platters, and arrays of freshly-made chocolates on various side tables. A gold plaque on the wall outside the main door listed some of the many world leaders who had stayed in the suite, including every President since Herbert Hoover, the Queen of England, Nikita Krushchev—whose name seemed to be spelled wrong, as far as she could tell—Charles de Gaulle, King Hussein, Menachem Begin—and on, and on. There were famous paintings everywhere—all of them by American artists, the concierge assured her—and Meg wondered whether she had looked as though she suspected otherwise, or even cared one way or the other. Marble fireplaces, huge chandeliers, carefully carved wall moldings, silk draperies, thick and presumably priceless rugs and carpets, Presidential artifacts—including one of John F. Kennedy's actual rocking chairs, a table with gold eagles for legs which had come from Ronald Reagan, sconces provided by Lyndon Johnson—all in all, the place was pretty unbelievable.

Hell, there was even a grand piano. Not that any of them played. But, if she was being honest, she might have admitted that she was also sort of afraid to touch anything. It all seemed way too valuable, and historic.

When her parents finally came in, Meg couldn't help being annoyed that her mother did nothing more than glance around vaguely, pluck a fresh strawberry from one of the fruit plates, and then start making phone calls and reading through the massive stack of messages waiting for her. It had to be difficult to swagger on high heels, but it would be fair to say that her mother's stride did not lack for confidence.

"Aren't you even a *little* impressed?" Meg said, when her mother finally paused long enough to let a campaign minion bring her some espresso.

Her mother shrugged. "I've been here before, Meg," she said, and promptly went back to what she had been doing.

There were so many people around that she didn't feel comfortable making the sort of cut-her-down-to-size response that that remark required—but she glanced at her father, who looked almost exactly as simultaneously irritated and amused as she was, which made her feel better. At least she wasn't the only one who thought the Candidate just might be in danger of tumbling over the edge into rather off-putting arrogance.

Despite the fact that the suite was *huge*, there were so many campaign people and party officials and so forth coming in and out, that she began to feel claustrophobic, and escaped to the ornate bedroom where she was going to be sleeping. They were supposed to attend a formal dinner later, although her father had already said that Steven and Neal didn't have to go—and half-heartedly extended the offer to her, too, although she knew that he—along with the entire campaign staff—wanted her to show up, to help make her mother look like a Good Parent with Well-Adjusted Children. So, it looked as though she was stuck.

Her bed had four plump pillows, plus bedrolls, and she selected one at random and stretched out.

Which got boring after about five minutes, so she decided to call Beth, instead.

"They put us in the *Presidential Suite*," she said, when Beth answered.

Beth laughed. "Playing it safe, hunh?"

That was one way of looking at it. "I've been assigned my own hair and make-up person," she said. Information that had pretty much stunned her, when she was told this by one of Linda's very chic and sleek assistants, Caryn. "My mother has an entire *team*." Just about enough to go up to the Bronx and take on the Yankees, in fact. Whether they would win the game was another question, of course—but Meg would certainly root for them.

"God, I love your life," Beth said. "Hell, I *want* your life."

She was welcome to it. "A bunch of designers are going to be coming by, too," Meg said. "To, you know, try and *outfit* us."

Beth just laughed.

Yes, that was the only rational response. Meg glanced over at the door, to make sure that no one was within listening distance. "The last time I looked, she was sitting at General MacArthur's desk taking notes, for Christ's sakes. She doesn't even think it's *unusual*."

Now, it was silent on the other end.

"No way," Meg said. "It's not going to happen. Not a chance."

"Meg," Beth said quietly.

Nope, she didn't want to hear this. Meg shook her head. "It's only because she's from New York. It's like—professional courtesy, for locals."

There was more silence.

Meg sighed. "And even if it does—" *Yes*, her mother had a lot more delegates than anyone else, but she was still far enough from going over the top that a brokered convention was more likely than not. And Senator Hawley was nothing if not a tough guy, so she assumed he'd be more than willing to let the entire floor—and Democratic Party—turn into a virulent dogfight, in order to come out on top. "She won't get past Griffin in the main election. I mean, no way."

Again, it was quiet for a long time on the other end of the line.

"Just don't forget how cool all of this actually is," Beth said finally. "I mean, God, Meg, try to remember to *enjoy* some of this stuff."

Meg shook her head. "No, it would be cool if I got to watch *your* mother do it. When *my* mother does it, it's just selfish and annoying."

"Yeah, okay, I think I'd be pretty damn annoyed at my mother." Beth paused. "Oh. Wait. I'm almost *always* annoyed at my mother."

Well—yeah. Beth and Mrs. Shulman had been engaged in an epic personality conflict pretty much ever since kindergarten.

They were both quiet for another minute, but this time, it felt more relaxed and companionable.

"It's starting to seem as though it could maybe all turn out to be—well, you know," Meg said. *Real.*

"Has been for a while," Beth said.

Yeah. Meg looked around her incredibly fancy room, including the delicate writing table—complete with a gold pen and pencil set, and stationery that actually had her name engraved on it.

"So, what are you going to wear tonight?" Beth asked.

"You mean, what are they *making* me wear," Meg said grumpily.

Beth laughed. "Even better," she said. "Tell me everything."

THE FIRST COUPLE of days at the convention passed in a blur of shouting crowds and bright flashes from what seemed like thousands of cameras. Her mother mostly stayed back at the hotel, receiving a long stream of party officials and prominent Democrats, who were supposedly just there to pay courtesy calls, but also seemed to be doing a certain amount of plotting and planning. Unlike most of the others—who were swiftly ushered in and out—Governor Kruger stayed for almost two full hours, and Meg was pretty sure that if her mother had a short list for possible running mates, he was at the top of it.

Over at the convention itself, the families of all of the politicians—including Mr. Hawley's sons, who seemed to be on their best behavior—had special reserved seats, and quite a few television cameras and reporters congregating nearby. There were noisy, foot-stamping demonstrations for candidates—complete with chanting and sign-waving—that sometimes went on for as long as half an hour. They were so exciting that Meg wished she didn't know that they were all staged, although maybe "artfully encouraged" was a better phrase. Enthusiastic, intricately choreographed demonstrations were sort of a convention tradition.

On the third night, the night of the balloting, her family stayed in a room overlooking the convention floor. Potential nominees traditionally didn't show up until a candidate had officially been chosen, and Glen and the rest of the campaign brain trust wanted her mother to remain holed up at the Waldorf, but her mother was not only going a little stir-crazy, but also pointed out that she hadn't missed a single Democratic Convention since she was twenty-one years old, and that she definitely wasn't going to start with *this* one. Although, in lieu of having her make a public appearance, they made their way into the building and upstairs through a private underground entrance.

The room was actually a luxury box, during the NBA and NHL seasons, but now that the campaign had invaded the space, it was cluttered, and noisy, and full of confusing activity, like the *Hill Street Blues* station house—an old television show she had started watching when her father bought some of the DVDs, and even though it seemed kind of dated, it had rapidly become one of her all-time favorites. Aides were hurrying in and out, barking at each other, and taking and making phone calls.

Her mother stood in one corner, drinking coffee and nodding a lot, as people talked at her. Her father was pacing around, looking very distracted and uneasy, with Neal trailing behind him. Preston, who had been spending hours on the floor, charming uncommitted delegates, came in every hour or two, and gulped soda and water, so he wouldn't lose his voice. It was easy to tell who the campaign floor workers were, because they were all hoarse.

Meg and Steven hung out near a row of televisions, watching everything that was going on, both down on the floor, as well as on the sets.

Steven yanked at the knot in his tie. "It should like, start soon."

Meg nodded, glancing down at her tally sheet. Listed next to each state and territory were the number of committed delegates her mother had, the number of uncommitted ones who had been persuaded to vote for her, and an empty space to write down the number of votes each state actually cast. She also had a calculator, so she could keep track of the total number of votes as the evening went along. There were at-large delegates, district-level delegates, PLEO—party leader and elected officials—delegates, add-on delegates, unpledged delegates who were known as superdelegates, and—well, as far as Meg was concerned, it all seemed to be more complicated than necessary. Essentially, each state was allocated a certain number of delegates, based upon census figures, and their votes *should* reflect primary and caucus results, but there were also lots of uncommitted delegates, so it was hard to be sure how they would all ultimately cast their ballots.

Her mother had about seventy percent of the number of delegates she would need to win the nomination, and Senator Hawley had more than half of the necessary total locked up. Four other candidates, including Governor Kruger, also had earned some delegates during the primary, but no one was pretending that this contest was between more than two people. At any rate, not on the *first* ballot. Meg closed her eyes, wishing that she could put her mind on autopilot.

"Think we can get some food?" Steven asked.

She opened her eyes. "Are you *hungry*?"

"Well, yeah," he said. "Kind of."

There were food trays all over the room, but most of them had been pretty well picked over by now. She shrugged. "I don't know. See if there are any doughnuts left."

He returned with three. "Sort of stale," he said, taking a bite. "Want one?"

She shook her head. This whole situation was much too nerve-wracking to think of food. The chairman was, unsuccessfully, trying to call the floor to order, and she wished the stupid thing would just *start* already.

"We have to do it on the first ballot," Glen said, for about the tenth time. "Hawley could pick up a lot on the second, and the third would be—" He shrugged, indicating a free-for-all.

"How close are we?" her mother asked, sounding very tense.

"So close." Glen put his thumb and index finger almost together. "So damn close, Kate. *This* close, Kate." He moved them barely apart.

Her mother nodded, her hands fluttering up to straighten the collar of her light beige shirt, her sunburn—and bronzer—very dark in comparison.

"Two more from California!" a man holding a cell phone shouted. "That's a positive!"

Meg scribbled that on her score sheet, hearing other pens writing around her, and keyboard keys clicking, too.

"I can't stand this," her mother said, refilling her coffee cup.

"The great state of Alaska," a voice droned on the television.

Meg glanced up, startled. How had she missed the beginning?

"How many so far?" her mother asked, and Meg could see the hand holding her cup shake slightly.

"Forty-one," several people said.

Meg frowned at her sheet. Forty-one? It should only be forty so far.

"Picked up an extra in Alabama," someone said.

Meg nodded and wrote that down, vaguely aware that her hands were trembling, too.

The balloting went on and on, each state's announcement followed by tremendous applause and cheering, including an abortive, transparently rehearsed Hawley demonstration—complete with a brass band—that the chairman managed to quell. Most of the delegates seemed to be standing around talking, and jumping up and waving their signs every so often, but mainly just waiting for their state's turn to present its votes. The television commentators kept switching to reporters on the floor, who tried to make themselves heard over all of the pandemonium, talking about the mounting tension and excitement among the delegates.

"What do you know about tension?" Meg's father snapped at the nearest television at one point. "I'll give you tension!"

"Dad's losing it," Steven said in a low voice.

Meg had to laugh. "He's not losing it." She looked at her father, who was pacing back and forth over the same five feet of carpet, tie askew, sleeves rolled up, and—she had to look twice to believe it—smoking a cigarette. She had never seen him smoke before. In fact, when she and Beth were in the seventh grade, he caught them puffing away in the backyard, gave them a long lecture about the stupidity and health dangers of the habit, and grounded Meg for a week. "I think you're right," she said to Steven.

"Come on, Idaho!" someone yelled.

Meg wrote down the number Idaho gave, noticing that her mother had picked up ninety-eight extra votes so far. Jesus.

"Two definites in Wisconsin," Preston said, coming in. "And a maybe. The maybe is seventy, eighty percent." His voice was very raspy, and he took the Coke someone offered, gulping half of it.

Meg entered the two votes on her score sheet, next to Wisconsin. Adding the newly-committed votes to her mother's guaranteed votes showed how close they were—and they were very, very close.

Terrifyingly close. So, even though there was a long way to go, Meg knew her mother only needed sixty-three more uncommitted votes to go over the top. Sixty-three, and they were only on—

"Hey, that's another!" someone yelled, as Indiana finished casting its votes.

Sixty-two. And they were only on Indiana. She closed her eyes. Maybe she should go hide in the ladies' room for a while, or—

"Hey," a voice said, right next to her.

She stiffened, then saw that it was only Preston.

"I have to talk to you seriously," he said.

She swallowed nervously. That sounded bad.

"See, kid"—he put his hand on her shoulder—"I don't want you to look in that back corner for a few minutes."

Automatically, she glanced over.

"Hey!" he said. "Thought I told you not to look."

Right. She turned her head in the other direction.

"The thing is," he said, "is that it's very hot out there, and I'm going to go into that corner and change my shirt. I don't want you to lose control or anything."

She stared at him, then realized that he was kidding. "That's a joke?"

He grinned. "Yeah, Meg, it's a joke. Relax, okay?"

He expected her to *relax*?

"What," he said, "I'm not a funny guy?"

She smiled, in spite of the fact that her mother had just gotten three extra votes from Iowa.

"Much better," he said, then aimed several mock boxing punches at Steven before continuing to the back of the room.

Meg looked at the nearest television. Every state had to make a big production out of its announcement, taking as much time as possible, while each delegate struggled to get on camera—which slowed everything down considerably. At this rate, the balloting was going to go on all night.

"Wyoming, here I come!" Preston said, getting smiles from most of the people who heard him. He left the room, buttoning his cuffs.

Meg's father was leaning up against a table, fist-curled hands tight in his pockets. Neal was standing next to him, in imitation that was either unconscious—or not. But, at least neither of them had cigarettes. Steven was twisted up in his chair, his tie and jacket off, his shirt untucked, while her mother stood with a cup of coffee—how many was it now?—very stiff, her face absolutely expressionless as she picked up four extra votes in Louisiana.

This was not, in any way, a fun evening.

"Oh, come on, Fran," her father said, when the Massachusetts delegation finally came on, and a woman with a microphone shouted the votes to the convention chairman. "Give her all of them!"

"You know her, Daddy?" Neal asked.

"Sure. Look, there's Mr. Foster," he said, pointing. "On her right. And remember Mr. Seymour? He's behind the girl with the hat."

When Michigan announced its votes, Meg stiffened. Automatically, she wrote the numbers down, then punched them into her calculator. She added the rest of the guaranteed votes to that number, and the result was—good God. Her mother had just—she was going to be the—she let the calculator slide out of her hand, hearing it drop on the floor from somewhere far inside her head.

Glen, very quiet, was saying something to her mother, who nodded, and there was a brief, noticeable silence as she detached herself from the group around the televisions and went to the back of the room with her coffee. There was something impenetrable about the set of her shoulders as she stood there, staring at the wall, and no one went after her.

That meant that it was true. She glanced at her father, who was hanging on to the table, staring at the televisions, looking as stunned as she felt. Someone yanked on the sleeve of her dress, and she saw Steven, with his tie and jacket back on, his expression very worried.

"What?" she asked, her voice unexpectedly squeaky.

He shook his head, dragging her off to the side.

"Steven, what is it?" she asked impatiently.

He glanced at their mother, who still hadn't moved. "Did she lose?" he whispered. "Everything's different."

"She won," Meg said.

His eyes got huge. "What?"

Meg swallowed. "She got more of the uncommitteds in Michigan than they thought she would, and it gives her enough to win."

"But—" Steven blinked. "What about Mr. Hawley?"

"She *won*, Steven," Meg said.

"Yeah, but—" He looked around, still whispering. "Why's everyone so quiet?"

"It's not official." Meg listened to Missouri shout its votes, her mother getting almost all of the unpledged ones, instead of the two or three that had been predicted.

"Bandwagon," someone said softly, other people nodding.

"You look like you're gonna cry," Steven said.

"I do not!" She almost forgot to keep her voice low.

"I feel like I am," he said.

"Yeah, me, too." Meg glanced at the closest television and saw that her mother had almost enough official votes now—and they were only on New Jersey.

Her mother was still stiff in the back in the room and what, ten minutes earlier, had been eager shouting and kibitzing around the televisions had turned into muttering, nervous voices.

"There's something happening out here," a disheveled reporter was telling the viewing audience, struggling to stay in front of his camera as chanting, excited delegates jostled for position. "You can feel it happening! We're getting close to a nomination here!"

"Glen," her mother said, not turning around.

He hurried to the back of the room and they talked for a few minutes, everyone else watching. Then, he nodded once and returned to the televisions. Without ever seeing how it happened, Meg noticed that people were starting to leave the room, until the family, Glen, and a couple of his top assistants were the only ones left.

"Well." Glen grinned at New Mexico presenting its votes. "I think the three of us'll head out, and stretch our legs. I'll be back later, and we can talk."

Her mother nodded. "Thanks, Glen."

The door closing after them seemed deafening.

"Well." Her mother smiled weakly and came back up to the front of the room, where she poured herself a fresh cup of coffee. Meg's father reached over with his hand, and she took it, holding on very tightly. "Meg, tell me about your tennis lessons. How've they been going?"

Meg stared at her. "*Now?*"

Her mother shrugged. "Why not now? What's wrong with now?"

The woman was cracking up. The pressure had finally gotten to her, and she'd cracked. First her father, now her mother. Glancing back at the televisions, she saw New York shout out a tremendous chunk of votes, her mother's total creeping higher.

Her mother looked over at Steven. "Tell me about your game against Medford again."

"We lost," he said.

"Well, tell me about your home run," her mother said.

Steven frowned at her. "I hit it over the fence."

"You can just feel the tension down here!" a reporter was yelling on one of the sets. "Victory is close, and you can feel the anticipation, feel the—"

"Neal, tell me what you like best about New York," her mother said.

He beamed at her. "The horse."

Okay, it had taken three tries, but she'd finally found a willing victim.

"When you rode in the carriage?" her mother asked.

"I *loved* the horse," he said.

"Well, come over here and tell me about it," she said.

Meg watched as the two of them sat down across the room, her mother holding Neal on her lap while he went on and on about the horse, while North Carolina gave its votes.

"And *then*," Neal was out of breath from the joy of the memory, "then, the man gave me an apple, and I put my arm up"—he demonstrated—"and the horse—the horse put down his head, and—"

She was listening. Her mother was about to get the Democratic nomination for President, and she was sitting there listening to Neal tell her about Central Park—she wasn't even faking it. If Meg had told her about tennis, about how she was working on a new second serve, a sort of derivation of the American Twist—she would have listened to that, too. Paid close attention. Nodded a lot. Asked pointed questions.

Meg looked at her father, who was staring straight ahead, several inches above the televisions. It was kind of funny that they were right *in* the building, but none of them had spent much time looking out the windows at the convention floor. She moved next to him, and he smiled, putting his arm around her. Steven came over, too, and the three of them stood silently, not watching television.

Suddenly, Puerto Rico had presented its votes, and her mother needed only two more to clinch the nomination.

"Kate," her father said.

Her mother straightened with a look of utter terror, and he nodded.

"Let's go watch television for a minute, Neal," she said.

A bulky man in a too-tight, off-the-rack suit was holding the microphone as the cameras moved in on the Rhode Island delegation.

"The distinguished state of Rhode Island"—he bellowed—"yes, Rhode Island and Providence Plantations, the smallest but greatest state in the Union, would like to—"

A woman wearing a bright pink pantsuit got in front of him, waving with both arms. "Hello, Cranston!" she shrieked.

"Would like to," the spokesperson went on. "Is proud to—"

"Say it!" Meg's father yelled.

"—thirty-two votes for the next President of the United States, Senator Katharine Vaughn Powers—"

He never got the rest of it out, as the entire convention went wild, confetti flying, balloons dropping down from the ceiling, as everyone screamed at once, screamed and cheered and jumped up and down, the noise actually rattling the windows of the luxury box.

In the room, no one made a sound for a long second, then Meg burst into tears—which she hadn't planned on doing—and everyone was hugging everyone else.

"The first time ever!" a reporter was saying on one of the televisions. "The first time in the history of the United States! The first time—"

They were all hugging and laughing and crying, and Meg felt an intense wave of victory surging up into her back and neck, into her head and arms, laughing and shouting even as she shivered harder, seeing the faces of women on the convention floor, faces sharing the same electric excitement, faces crying because a *woman* had won, because a woman was going to run for President, because—well, just because.

11

MEG HAD THOUGHT that the primary campaign had been about as intense as a campaign could get—but, she was wrong. Minor league, as Preston had said. There were many more magazine cover stories, and her mother was never *not* on the front page of the newspaper. Every newspaper. She was on all of the national newscasts, night after night, and the Internet seemed to be on the verge of exploding with pages and posts and blogs about her, as well as videos and photos and sound-clips.

As Meg had expected, her mother had chosen Governor Kruger as her running mate, and he and his wife had flown up to Boston and had dinner with her family. The Krugers' children were adults, although Meg had met one of their sons at the convention, and he seemed—like his parents—to be very nice, and polite in that Southern courtly way.

The Republican candidate was Congressman John Jasper Griffin—Jay-Jay, to his friends. He was the kind of person who spent a lot of time talking about "God's Country." He was from New Mexico, a wealthy and flamboyant man, buoyed by the current President's enthusiastic endorsement, support—and considerable fund-raising skills. Mr. Griffin was broad and bulky, and Meg thought he looked like the word "obsequious" personified. Her mother called him "the last and greatest of the big-time Babbitts." Naturally, Meg had laughed intelligently at that, but later had to ask her father what it meant.

"*Babbitt* was a book by Sinclair Lewis," he explained. "He was what you'd call a good old boy."

"Ah," Meg said, with a wise nod.

"Bible-thumper, goes to the country club to drink his lunch, conforms to everything anyone says—you know," her father said. "Your mother thinks he's a sexist, unscrupulous puppet."

Meg laughed. The press would love to hear *that* one. "Is he?"

Her father laughed, too. "Well, let's just say that his principles aren't as high as your mother's."

She probably shouldn't bring this up, but—"How high is that?" Meg asked.

Her father sighed. "Very high, Meg. How many times are we going to have this conversation?"

"I don't know." She blushed. "Probably pretty many."

"Well, why don't you discuss it with *her*?" he asked.

"I can't do that," Meg said quickly. For one thing, it would hurt her mother's feelings; for another, would she really tell Meg the truth? If she weren't honest, that is. How could someone be the Democratic nominee for President without, somewhere along the way, having done a few—

"Meg, look," her father said. "Do you think of *me* as being an honest person?"

Meg nodded. "Well, yeah. Of course."

"Would I respect someone who wasn't?" he asked.

She hesitated.

"Would I, Meg?" he asked, looking right at her.

Not a chance in the world. So, she shook her head.

"All right, then," he said. "I'm much more demanding than you are. Remember that."

She nodded.

THE FIRST DAY of school was terrible. For one thing, Mr. Bucknell turned out to be her AP History teacher. But, worse than that, even people she had met when they were all five years old didn't seem to know how to treat her. When she walked into a room, conversations stopped, and people acted as if she had developed an incredibly contagious disease over the summer. Beth was the only person who treated her like a normal human being—even Sarah seemed to be awed.

"You know," Beth said, as people moved to let them through the hall, "this is kind of like hanging out with Moses."

Meg nodded. "Yeah, I know. I'm having a terrible time taking a shower lately."

"Yes," Beth said, sounding slightly ill. "I noticed."

Thank God *someone* was still acting normal.

"It's a difficult life, sacrificing myself like this," Beth said, and then stopped before going into Mr. Bucknell's room. "Do me a favor, okay? Don't let him harass you—you don't have to put up with that."

Meg sighed. "It's not like I can *stop* him."

Beth shrugged. "Tell him off."

Oh, yeah. Excellent plan.

The bell rang, and they both looked at the door. Mr. Bucknell came over to close it and saw them standing there.

"Meghan," he said, frowning, "regardless of your family situation, you're not entitled to special privileges."

"Yeah, Meg," Beth said, and gave her a shove. "Get in there already."

Mr. Bucknell extended his frown to include her. "The same holds true for you, Elizabeth."

"My parents are divorced," Beth said to Meg. "It's been very hard for me."

Meg nodded. "Decay of the family structure. How *dare* women think that they have any right to be in the workforce?"

Mr. Bucknell was not amused. "Girls, I'll be quite happy to put you on tonight's detention list."

Meg and Beth grinned at each other, and went into the room.

THE THREE PRESIDENTIAL debates were among the most crucial events of the entire campaign season. They were all going to be televised—live—as well as running simultaneously as streaming video and audio on the Internet. Meg, her father, and brothers flew out of Logan Airport on the afternoon of the first debate, to meet her mother at her hotel on Rittenhouse Square in Philadelphia. It was a little bit disconcerting that it had become increasingly less surprising to arrive in a given city and find her casually ensconced in an exclusive hotel's Presidential Suite.

That night, during the last hour or so before it would be time to head over to the University of Pennsylvania, where the debate was being held, they were all in—yes, the latest version of a Presidential Suite—which was, as usual, crowded with campaign staffers, and heavily guarded by the Secret Service and local police. The campaigns had been negotiating the details of the debates for weeks, fighting over just about *everything*, including the moderators, the formats, the question topics, and the height of the podiums—especially since Mr. Griffin was about eight inches taller than her mother was. Glen had even reserved an auditorium at Boston College and held a couple of mock debates recently, during which Jim, the greyest of the campaign greybeards, played Mr. Griffin, and other top campaign advisors fired a stream of complex—and often hostile and insulting—questions at her mother, during two marathon sessions—after which the Candidate had come home and slept for about ten hours straight.

Meg sat on the couch, wearing a dress that even *felt* expensive, with Steven and Neal next to her, decked out in ties and jackets, Steven looking like quite the ruffian with the black eye he'd gotten a few days earlier. Ever since her mother had won the nomination, he had been getting in more fights than usual. Linda had quietly suggested that he use some cover-stick on his eye, but he had said that *no way* would he wear make-up.

Everyone else in the suite was milling around being tense, except for maybe Preston, who was leaning up against a windowsill, resplendent in a dove-grey three-piece suit, along with a silk tie and matching handkerchief. He kept saying that "everyone should just *relax*, because the woman is going to be great," but they all seemed to be too uptight to agree.

If Meg thought about it, she could *really* have a major crush on him.

Unless, just possibly, she already did.

Anyway, she watched him pour her father a drink, along with one for himself. Then he offered the decanter to the three of them—Neal giggling, Steven nodding, and Meg blushing. Preston kind of brought new dimensions to the word sexy. It was funny, though—out of all of the people in the campaign, who would have predicted that her father would hit it off with the young, super-cool guy? Preston still made fun of his B-school jackets, and her father called him "The World According to *GQ*." They had a regular squash game together, and her father would wear grey, cut-off sweatpants, a shapeless Lacoste, and a hooded sweatshirt, while Preston would show up in very white shorts and a collared shirt chosen to coordinate with his warm-up suit. Now, standing by the window making jokes, they both were wearing grey suits, but the resemblance ended there.

"You sure you kids got enough to eat?" her father asked.

They all nodded, just back from going out to get cheese-steaks with Preston—who was a native Philadelphian, and had *very* strong opinions about where to find the best sandwiches in the city—along with a few other campaign people, and three Secret Service agents. Luckily, they had made this trip *before* changing into their debate clothes, because Steven, in particular, had dripped Cheese Whiz all over everything.

"Stuffed their little faces," Preston said. "Except for old Meggo. The kid wants to be as sickly as Madam Prez-to-be over there."

Her mother gave him a saluting wave from across the room, going through her voice warm-ups as two hairdressers and a make-up artist worked on her.

"Are you hungry, Meg?" her father asked.

"I'm fine," she said, blushing more. Meggo. Be nice if everyone called her Meggo. It sounded—sporty. Very sporty.

"Good blood, bad blood, good blood, bad blood," her mother was saying over and over again, having finished her scales and now working on articulation. Early on in the campaign, some of the press had ferreted out the information that before she ran for Congress, she had taken three months of professional voice training, and the opposition had spouted about vanity and such, but her mother's response had pretty much just been a "yeah, so?" shrug, and the story had disappeared after a day or two.

"Why's she doing that?" Neal whispered.

"So her voice'll be warmed up, and she won't fall all over her words during the debate," Meg said.

"Red leather, yellow leather, red leather, yellow leather," her mother was saying now, winking at Neal as he laughed.

"Okay, Kate, now let's go over it one last time." Glen scanned his notes. "Relaxed, but not too relaxed. Pleasant, but not too funny. Friendly, but presidential. If things are going well, you should maybe even sit down while he's talking. Or take notes. You look great when you take notes."

Her mother nodded. "Peter Piper picked a peck of pickled peppers."

"Be serious, but smile. Confident, but not arrogant." He lowered his papers. "Any questions?"

"How many pickled peppers did Peter Piper pick?" her mother asked.

"Very funny." He flipped through another stack of papers. "Just don't let him rattle you—the man is famous for it. His people are going to want to make you look emotional or bitchy."

"Peter Piper picked altogether too many pickled peppers," her mother said.

"Don't blow up if he starts getting sexist," Glen said. "For that matter, if any of them do. Your national security credentials are a lot stronger than his are, so squelch them, but be calm about it."

"Friendly, even?" Meg's father asked.

"Peter Piper perpetuated pickled pepper pandemonium," her mother said, which made her father grin.

"Be serious," Glen said, and motioned towards her hands. "Think we ought to put some slightly darker nail polish on her, Claude?"

Her mother frowned at him—and at the make-up artist, for good measure. "I'm not a 'her,' okay, Glen?"

"I know, I'm sorry." He bent down, checking her profile from each side, and then studying her from the front. "You're too thin, that's what you are."

"The monitor put about ten pounds on her," Claude said.

Since, of course, the mock debates had been taped, to give Glen and the gang a chance to critique them endlessly.

"She still looked emaciated," Glen said. "Try to seem as tall as you can, Kate. Griffin's a big guy."

"Linebacker," Meg's father said disparagingly.

"If Russell-baby thinks that, you *know* the man's big," Preston said to Meg and her brothers.

"Sisters assisting selling seashells at the seashore," her mother said.

"Any way you can fill her cheeks out a little?" Glen asked Claude, gesturing to his own face. "The video picked up some shadows."

"Sisters *resisting* selling seashells at the seashore," her mother said, and glanced at her watch. "We don't have time, anyway. I told you I wanted this half hour completely clear." She squinted at the mirror, frowned, and then picked up a brush to redo her hair. "You may brief me to your heart's content in the car."

Glen looked worried. "But, Linda has a roomful of them in the hospitality suite, waiting for a statement—"

"On my way down," her mother said. "Now, please. I need this."

"All right, but, do me a favor, and take off the damn watch, okay?" he asked. "If you look at it *during* the debate, it'll be—"

Her mother nodded impatiently, and pointed towards the exit.

Preston, who was the last one out, paused at the door. "Moses supposes his toeses are roses."

"Moses supposes erroneously," her mother said.

Preston laughed and joined the others in the hall. After the door closed, it was very, very quiet.

"Well," her mother said.

"Simple Ceasar sipped his snifter, seized his knees, and sneezed," Meg's father said, still standing near one of the windows.

Her mother laughed, checked the mirror one more time, and put down the brush. "Do I look all right?"

"Way pretty," Neal said.

"Not too thin?" her mother asked wryly. She sat down and clicked on a huge flat-screen television, just in time for them all to hear a solemn anchorperson saying, "Well, you have to assume it's Jay-Jay Griffin's election to lose. I'm inclined to believe that the polls don't really reflect—" Her mother turned the set off, before he could go any further.

Meg's father came over to stand behind her, squeezing her shoulders. "Relax."

"I'm fine," she said. "Meg, let me see if I can do something with your hair. It's a little funny on the left side."

Meg stood up just enough to be able to get a quick glimpse in the mirror. "Funny-amusing, or funny-strange?"

"Either way." Her mother picked up the hairbrush, and Meg could see her hands quivering.

"You're going to be great, Mom," she said.

"I-I don't think so." Her mother shook her head. "I just don't—" She stopped brushing, and looked at her hands. "I think you'd better do it. I'm only going to make things worse." She paced across the room, pausing in front of Steven. "How's your eye?"

"Black," he said.

"My macho kid." She gave him a gentle tap on the cheek, then went back to pacing.

When the knock came on the door, they all jumped.

"It's time, Kate," Glen said from the hall.

"Well." Her mother swallowed, and looked at Meg's father, who nodded reassuringly. "Right. Okay."

"Kate?" Glen said, in his we're-off-schedule voice.

"Well." She took one final look in the mirror, then strode across the room, stopping only long enough to give each of them a quick, tense hug. "Are we ready? God, I'm really worried about S's." She opened the door. "Simple Ceasar sipped his snifter, seized his knees, and sneezed. Simple Ceasar sipped his—"

THEY HAD BEEN assigned seats in the front row directly across from Mr. Griffin's family: his wife—Bouffant City, a daughter, a son, and a daughter-in-law, all of them husky people with healthy New Mexico tans and strong, determined voices.

"We look like twerps next to them," Steven whispered.

"Except Dad," Meg said. "They look like—politicians. You think they took lessons?"

He nodded. "Prob'ly. We look like little kids who watch cartoons."

Well, as it happened, the three of them had done precisely that earlier, while they were killing some time in their mother's suite. "We *are*," Meg said.

"Yeah." He leaned in front of her. "Dad, what happens if we forget and clap?"

Since the debate wasn't a town hall format, the live audience was supposed to be completely silent the entire time they were on the air.

"Reform school," their father said.

Steven frowned. "Well, what if Mom says something funny?"

Their father grinned. "Laugh as hard as you can."

Meg looked at him, noticing the tightly clenched right fist. So, he wasn't as relaxed as he wanted them to think.

Stagehands and television technicians were bustling about, testing microphones, filling the glasses of water on each of the two podiums, double- and triple-checking everything. There was more security than she could ever remember seeing, and the fact that there were SWAT officers and bomb-sniffing dogs patrolling made her nervous. Neal, of course, had immediately wanted to pat the first dog he saw, but his handler had politely refused—much to Neal's dismay.

The moderator, and the four reporters who would be asking the questions, came out from backstage to sit down at the semi-circular table facing the two podiums, and everyone in the audience abruptly stopped talking.

"Is it starting?" Neal asked, his voice sounding very loud.

Their father nodded, putting his finger to his lips. As the two candidates walked onto the stage, Neal barely restrained a small squeak of excitement, which almost set Steven off, and Meg had to give them both a quick warning elbow.

Her mother *did* look small up there, but not nervous. Mr. Griffin was more obviously jittery, fiddling around with the microphone, sipping water, and straightening his tie. Her mother looked calm and alert, and maybe a little bit excited, but also cheerful—which couldn't be as effortless as it appeared.

The noisy hush faded to silence as it got closer to airtime. Mr. Griffin was acting very jolly, as though his advisors had told him to come out and be Santa Claus. Her mother looked *a lot* more Presidential by just sitting there looking pleasant. She had won—or lost, depending upon how one looked at it—the coin toss, and would be going first in the debate. She stepped over to shake Representative Griffin's hand, and he accepted with a too-solicitous air.

"You look very nice," he said, sounding like someone who had just met a hideously ugly blind date, but was trying to be polite about it.

Meg imagined her mother saying, "Thank you, you sexist, unscrupulous puppet," and almost laughed.

"Thank you," her mother said, sounding very amused. "I can see that we both primped for hours."

Mr. Griffin's hand went to his carefully groomed head, which looked as if it could survive the most driving rainstorm. This time, Meg did laugh, and was thankful that a lot of other people did, too. She glanced over at the Griffin family, and saw four very tight smiles.

Then, they were on the air. Her mother and Mr. Griffin were being introduced, and Meg could feel her father and brothers sitting as stiffly as she was. A member of the panel was asking his first question—the topic for the evening was foreign affairs—and her mother was answering in a clear, friendly voice. Simple Ceasar sipped his snifter, seized his knees, and sneezed. Mr. Griffin was leaning on a casual elbow, hands folded, as though he was neither concerned by, nor interested in, her answer.

"Thank you, Senator," the reporter said, sounding surprised by the lack of campaign rhetoric in her answer. After he asked his follow-up question, the moderator called "Time" just as her mother was finishing up, and it was Mr. Griffin's turn to respond to the two questions.

"I must say," his voice was jovial, "with such an attractive opponent, one almost wishes that there didn't have to be time limits."

The Griffin supporters in the audience all grinned, and a couple of them actually *whistled*; her mother's supporters sat up straight. Worried, Meg looked at her father, who had *both* fists clenched now, and then at her mother, who appeared to be entirely unruffled. Lots of times, debates could be lost for really stupid reasons—like, just for example, a candidate checking his watch; which reminded her to look at her mother's wrist, where—damn it—she was *still* wearing hers, despite having been strongly advised not to do so. Although Meg suspected that if Glen hadn't made such a big deal of it, she might have taken it off of her own volition. He had also said that

Mr. Griffin was going to come out swinging, playing up every possible suggestion that a woman—or, at any rate, her *mother*, in particular—would be inadequate for the job. "If you can keep your head when all about you are losing theirs," her mother had said, and Glen nodded.

Mr. Griffin ran overtime on the follow-up, and Meg wondered if his campaign managers were backstage committing suicide. Her mother leaned forward, then paused.

"I'm sorry, Representative." She moved back, very gracious, her expression so friendly that even her worst enemies wouldn't—quite—be able to describe her as being bitchy. "Did you get a chance to finish?"

Now, her mother's supporters grinned, and her mother went into her rebuttal, speaking logically and succinctly, finishing with time to spare.

Meg could almost hear her father's unspoken "Good, Katie, good!" as he strained forward in his seat, eyes fixed on the stage.

Her mother was sitting with one leg gracefully crossed over the other, listening with obvious attention as Mr. Griffin fielded the next question. When it was her turn, she responded with clear specifics, providing a casual underlining of the more general answers he was giving. The panel of reporters seemed pleased—not something Meg could pin down exactly, but more like a feeling in the air. She turned enough to locate Preston, two rows behind them, and he nodded, giving her a thumbs-up.

Further on in the debate, her mother absently slipped off her blazer, hanging it over the back of her chair, and Meg pictured Glen fainting backstage—and the rest of the high-level campaign people toppling over right after him. A candidate wasn't supposed to be *too* relaxed. But, her mother always said that blazers were masculine—and boxy—and spent more time taking them off than putting them on. Her action didn't go past Mr. Griffin, who, after finishing up his remarks, glanced over and commented that if he'd known this was going to be casual, he would have worn a sports shirt. Her mother's only reaction was to smile.

"I'm sorry," she said, with just the right note of endearing self-deprecation, gesturing slightly behind her. "A habit of mine."

The moderator and all four reporters smiled back at her, and the simple elegance of her silk dress was suddenly more Presidential than the blazer had ever been. The dignity came across even more as she answered the question as if she had never been flustered in her entire life. As she sat down, quite a few people in the audience clapped, and television crew members frowned at them until they subsided. Her mother's expression was, as it had been throughout, utterly benign, and now Meg wondered how she was managing *not* to grin. Broadly.

Mr. Griffin didn't make any more unnecessary remarks, trying to create his own air of gravitas, but it seemed like too little, too late. When the debate ended, her mother initiated a closing handshake with damn near *majestic* confidence and, interestingly enough, Mr. Griffin didn't seem quite as tall as he had earlier.

Game, set, and match to the Senator.

Meg wasn't sure if the cameras were panning to the candidates' families, and it probably wouldn't look that great to be cocky or overconfident, but she grinned anyway, so proud that she was kind of embarrassed. Then, the lights came up, indicating that they were off the air, and Meg saw her father and brothers grinning, too. Her mother, on her way to shake hands with the moderator and the panel members, looked over, giving them a very, very small wink.

LATE THAT NIGHT, after a noisy and crowded celebration in the living room of her parents' suite, Meg went down the hall to the smaller suite she was sharing with Steven and Neal, and checked several different cable channels to see how the press had reacted—*without* any of the biased spin from her mother's staff. She felt more comfortable watching the coverage privately, anyway.

"The turning point was the blazer incident," a political analyst was saying on CNN. "Not only did Mrs. Powers show a remarkable sense of poise, but in the simple act of taking off her jacket, demonstrated the special quality a woman could bring to the office. Mr. Griffin was outclassed from that moment on. I think we were privy to something very special this evening."

They were already calling it *The Blazer Incident*? She switched to another channel—which was taking a similar approach, and was also showing results from polls taken both before and after the debate—and her mother had jumped eight points. She and Mr. Griffin were almost even.

Almost even.

Meg turned off the television, and went over to the window, looking out at Philadelphia. The city where Rocky ran up the steps.

Almost even.

Good God.

12

HER MOTHER DID very well in the second and third debates, and the pundits decided that the election was too close to call. At school, everyone seemed to be wearing either a Powers button or a Griffin one, and would either grin at her in the halls—or smirk. Teachers weren't supposed to show political bias, so none of them wore buttons, but Meg could tell from their attitudes—and sometimes, her grades—whom they were supporting.

Then, Mr. Bucknell came up with a swell idea. On the Friday before the election, the school would have a mock election and—the idea got even more swell—Meg and David Mason, the South Senate president, could play the parts of the candidates and give speeches at a school-wide assembly.

So, protestations overruled, Meg found herself sitting on the stage in the auditorium, quite certain that she was going to throw up. Her kingdom, for a fire drill.

Her mother, amused by the whole thing, had insisted that Meg borrow her blazer from the first debate, and now that she was sitting up in front of the entire damn school, Meg regretted giving in. People were really going to think she was a jerk. David Mason was wearing a three-piece suit, and had slicked his hair down to look like Griffin. Even wearing the exact blazer and a similar dress, Meg was pretty sure she fell far short of looking like her mother—but, she had done her best.

A faint expensive perfume lingered in the wool, and for a second, Meg fell as if her mother were right up there with her. She sat up straighter, deciding that even if all else failed, she would maintain presidential elegance.

"And now," Mr. Bucknell was saying, from the podium.

Meg closed her eyes, briefly forgetting to be elegant.

"Even though I know they need no introduction," he said, "I'd like to present Representative John Jasper Griffin on my left, and Senator Katharine Vaughn Powers on my right. Mr. Griffin will make the first statement."

Hokum. She had allowed herself to be forced into hokum.

There was great applause, along with some catcalls—terrific—and Meg thought she saw camera flashes. Christ, they were even making it look as though the press was there? She was never, ever—for the rest of high school—going to be able to live this down.

David read his statement, gesticulating and promising that he was going to build up defense, foster democracy aboard, lower taxes, blah, blah, blah. Same old thing. Consciously imitating her mother, she sat with her best posture, her right leg crossed over her left. Relaxed, but not too relaxed. Pleasant, but not too funny. Friendly, but presidential. Maybe she should even sip her snifter, seize her knees, and sneeze.

The bright lights were still there, giving her a headache, and she looked out at the audience, realizing with a deep, sickening thud in her stomach that there *were* reporters out there. Lots of them. Reporters, and what looked like television cameras, and—someone had called the press. She glanced over at Mr. Bucknell, who smiled at her and motioned towards the media.

Jesus, *he* had called the press? Great. Absolutely great.

Panicking, she tried to force herself to take a deep breath. In keeping with her mother's style, she hadn't written her speech down, so she had no idea what she was going to say, and David was almost finished, and—she was going to throw up. It was as simple as that. She was going to throw up, and it would be on television.

And if that happened, she would have to kill herself. Except, if she killed herself, there would be all kinds of publicity, and her mother would lose the election, and it would be all her fault—David was done, and everyone was clapping wildly. Why were they making her run against someone who was so incredibly popular, anyway? It wasn't as though she had *volunteered* for any of this.

"Senator Powers?" Mr. Bucknell asked from the podium.

She nodded, trying to pull her expression under control, reminding herself to be presidential. She stood up, crossing—elegantly? gracefully?—to the front of the stage, blushing as there were quite a few whistles, but making herself keep going. There were some cheers and shouts of encouragement, too—mostly from the juniors, which she, indeed, found encouraging.

"Thank you," she said to Mr. Bucknell. Then, she smiled at the audience, noticing with an inner terror that the television cameras were *filming*. Did her mother feel this scared when she got up to speak? Legs shaking, muscles tight, hands perspiring? "Well." She let out her breath. "I guess I should start off by saying—" She paused, taking off her blazer, then smiled. "I'm sorry, they make me tense."

Everyone laughed, and Meg grinned, draping it over the back of the nearest chair.

"At any rate," she said. At any rate *what*? "I must say that I've enjoyed the campaign—I've gotten to meet so many marvelous people. My opponent, of course," she gave David a dignified nod, "people all over the country, half of Iowa, *all* of New Hampshire—" She smiled when that got a laugh, deciding that maybe this wasn't so bad, after all. It was kind of fun, even. "And I can only say that I've enjoyed it. It's—" She paused. "It's a very special country. I mean, it really is—we should all be proud. There's no other place like it, it's—well, maybe it's why I ran for President. This country is so great, and I really wanted to be able to do something to—to make it better. I have ideas, you have ideas, we all have ideas. What we need is *action*. Cooperative action. We need to forget party differences, racial differences, gender differences, religious differences. In spite of everything, we all have something in common. We're all Americans, every one of us. We need to use it, we need to be proud of it. I know we can do it—I think everyone knows that. But, I want us *to* do it. We can. And we will." She stopped, out of things to say, and for lack of a better idea, smiled. "Thank you very much."

To her surprise, people clapped and cheered, and she stood there uncertainly, not sure if she should sit down, or acknowledge the response, or—sitting down would be the best choice. But then, Mr. Bucknell gestured for her to stand back up, and the school band began—*quel* hokum—playing "Yankee Doodle Dandy." She and David weren't supposed to *sing*, were they? No, they all were supposed to march out. Which wasn't quite as bad as singing—but just barely.

Everyone else filed out first, the band bringing up the rear. As soon as the auditorium had cleared somewhat, and before Meg could get out, the reporters and camera people came hurrying down to the stage. Alice, a woman from Linda's staff, was right there with them.

"Meg, they would like to ask you a few questions," she said.

"Yeah, but—" Meg shifted her weight, very self-conscious. "I mean, I sort of have to go to biology."

Alice gave her a this-is-*very*-important look.

Meg smiled weakly. "Then again," she said.

Alice nodded.

AFTER SCHOOL, SHE jittered around until six o'clock, waiting for the local news to come on.

"What's gotten into you, Meg?" Trudy asked, stirring the spaghetti.

Meg shrugged, looking at the clock. Quarter of six. "I thought Dad was going to be home by now."

Trudy tasted her tomato sauce, and frowned. "All he said was before six-thirty."

"Six-*thirty*?" Meg said. The news would be over by then.

Trudy snipped some basil from the planter on the windowsill above the sink, and began rinsing the leaves. "If you're that hungry, why don't you have an apple or something?"

Meg shook her head. When she got home from school, Trudy had asked how the speech went, and she had said, "Okay." She was too embarrassed to admit that she was probably going to be on the news, but she did kind of want them all to see it. Even though she would probably look stupid. It turned out that Alice had been there because someone at Channel Four had called campaign headquarters to ask if it was true that the Candidate's Daughter was giving a speech. The reporters had asked lots of questions—like had her mother written her remarks for her, and that sort of thing, with Meg trying to be dignified and mature, rather than kicking the floor and blushing a lot. But mostly, she had kicked the floor and blushed.

She wasn't sure if the media presence had influenced the voting, but Senator Powers had won the school election by an overwhelming margin.

"Meg," Trudy said.

She looked up.

Trudy indicated a wedge of Parmesan on the counter, as she chopped the basil and added it to her sauce. "Would you like to grate me some of that?"

Meg checked the clock. Five of six. "Um, if you want." She glanced at the television in the corner. "Can I turn on the news?"

"Sure." Trudy put the set on.

Channel Five. Yeah, Channel Five had been there.

Meg sat down at the table to grate the cheese, watching as the anchorwoman talked about the election—and the top stories included polls, predictions, interviews, and film footage of her mother in Fort Lauderdale and Kansas City.

"And today," the anchorwoman said, "out in Chestnut Hill—"

Meg flushed, as she saw and heard herself on television.

"Meg." Trudy stared at her. "You're on the news."

Meg went back to grating cheese. "Hunh," she said, being as blasé as possible. "How about that."

ON ELECTION DAY, her mother was in a terrible mood. Meg was in a pretty lousy mood herself, but it was nothing compared to her mother, who was positively *fierce*. Her parents had gone over to the polling place at their church early that morning to vote on national television, but except for that, her mother had stayed in the house. Most of the campaign people seemed to be very happy—even overjoyed—about the latest overnight and exit polls, but her mother had snarled something to the effect of "*saying* they're willing to vote for me, and *actually* voting for me are two entirely different things," and they had all exchanged glances, but tempered their enthusiasm accordingly.

Glen wanted the whole family to check into a hotel in Boston and watch the election returns there, so that they would be in a central location when it was time for her mother to make whatever announcement had to be made, but her mother vetoed that idea, in favor of the five of them watching at home, as privately as possible. After a fairly contentious discussion, Glen gave in, and only a few campaign people stayed behind, along with a significant press pool gathered outside, as well as the Secret Service, of course. Even Trudy left, with—as far as Meg could tell—a very relieved look on her face.

Her mother sent someone out to get her "a trashy novel; *any* trashy novel," and then took it into her bedroom, closing the door. Possibly even *locking* it.

Meg didn't see her again until late afternoon, when she and her father were sitting in the den, watching endless reports about more exit polls and predictions—which almost all seemed to be skewing in her mother's direction, although a number of the pundits seemed to doubt the veracity of the voters' responses.

"I suppose I'm losing," her mother said grimly, standing in the doorway.

"The polls haven't even closed yet," her father said.

"Well." Her mother glanced around. "Where are the boys?"

"Outside playing soccer," Meg said.

Her mother frowned at her father. "Isn't it rather dark for them to be out?"

He glanced at the window. "It's barely dusk, and they have three off-duty agents playing *with* them."

One thing Meg had noticed, right from the start, was that almost all of the Secret Service agents seemed to love sports. *All* sports.

Which was in their favor.

Regardless, her mother left the room and reappeared shortly with Steven and Neal, who looked as if the soccer game had deteriorated into a leaf fight.

"Boys, why don't you go up and take showers," their father said, "and then, we'll see about some dinner."

Steven and Neal looked at each other and went upstairs, for once not making any smart remarks. Meg watched them go, kind of wishing that she could think of a plausible excuse to leave the room, too. To go *hide* from the Surly Senator.

"Um, anyone want anything?" she asked. "I'm going to go to the kitchen."

Her parents shook their heads, and she escaped to the kitchen, where she sat alone at the table, drinking orange juice and eating graham crackers.

When she heard her brothers come downstairs, she followed them to the den, where her mother was more uptight than Meg had ever seen her, moving from one chair to another.

"I feel like making dinner," she said, standing up yet again. "Who wants dinner?"

Cooked by her mother? No one with any damn sense.

"Kate," Meg's father said, "we were going to send out—"

"I feel like it," she said, testily. "How about omelets? We all like omelets."

"I hate omelets," Steven muttered.

"You love omelets," their father said, cuffing him.

"Better not have any vegetable crap in them," Steven said, and their father cuffed him again.

So, they all went out to the kitchen, Meg returning to her orange juice and graham crackers, consciously ignoring the sounds of laughter and ring-tones in the living room. And she didn't *actually* smell completely-forbidden cigar smoke; it was a figment of her imagination. The Candidate was glum and cranky and pessimistic, so, by God, she was going to be, too.

"Oh, great." Her mother took the egg carton out of the refrigerator. "We only have two stupid eggs. How can I make omelets with only two stupid eggs?"

"We could go out and get some more stupid eggs," Meg said.

Steven laughed. "Yeah, the smart ones don't get caught."

Their father cuffed them both, then gave Meg some money. "Go find Frank, and have him send someone out for some intelligent eggs."

"If he can catch them!" Steven shouted after her.

Someone dutifully ran out and got eggs, and her mother threw together soggy vegetable omelets. The frenetic burst of cooking only made her more tense, and she didn't eat hers, jittering around the room, instead. Meg wasn't hungry either, but she pretended to eat, and when Steven scraped his vegetables onto her plate, she stuffed them into her omelet so no one would notice.

"Maybe," her mother gulped some coffee, "maybe I'll go brush my teeth. Yes. I think I'll—"

Glen came in and, damn it, he *did* smell like cigars. "Kate. The returns are starting to come in."

Because the Senator had specifically said that she no longer wanted to hear *anything* speculative, or listen to spouting about trends or internal polling numbers.

Her mother rushed out of the kitchen, mug in hand, and they all followed her, leaving the omelets behind.

"Mom's like, flipped out," Steven said.

Meg nodded. It was quite disconcerting, really.

The numbers on the screen gave Mr. Griffin an early lead.

"Well, that's it." Her mother swigged some coffee, very grim. "I knew I didn't have a chance. Who wants to be President, anyway?"

"Katie, you knew you weren't going to do well in South Carolina," Meg's father said.

Her mother nodded. "Terrific. They hate me in South Carolina."

"Katie—" he started.

"Don't call me that! You make me sound like a poodle!" She blinked, as though surprised by the outburst, and put down her coffee. "I'm going to go brush my teeth."

"How long is this going to take, do you think?" Meg asked, once she had left.

Her father looked very tired. "Probably all night."

Official results continued trickling in, none of them too unexpected—especially her mother's early numbers in the Northeast. Every hour or so, the press pool was allowed to come inside to ask questions and take pictures and film the Candidate and Her Happy Family—even though they all started scowling and bickering again as soon as the media left.

Meg sat in a rocking chair by the fireplace, drinking a Coke and wishing she could go upstairs and read *Tennis Magazine* or something. Or play tennis, even better.

"And, with most of the polls still open," a commentator was saying, "it's still too early to—"

"Oh, for God's sake," her mother said. "Someone change the channel."

Her father clicked to one of the networks—which concurred with the first channel. One minute, her mother would be ahead; the next, Mr. Griffin would be in the lead.

"Voter turnout so far has been much higher than predicted," an anchorman remarked, "and we have a live report from outside a polling center in Trenton, New Jersey. Susan?"

"Thank you," a woman with a microphone said. "This is Susan Gaines, and I'm standing outside the—"

"They hate me in Trenton," her mother said, and changed the channel again.

This time, they heard a male voice saying, "—too close to call," and her mother shuddered, and moved on to yet another channel.

"Now, let's go to our correspondent in Chicago," the lead anchor was saying. "Take it, Bill."

"Boring, boring, boring." Her mother gritted her teeth. "They hate me in Chicago."

Someone knocked on the door. "Meghan, you have a telephone call."

Thank God. Meg jumped up. "I'll take it upstairs." She didn't pick up, until she was in her room, with the door closed. "Hello?"

"How's it going?" Beth asked.

Meg groaned.

"I don't know," Beth said. "She's doing pretty well, so far."

Meg sighed. "Everyone's in really bad moods here." Well, with the exception of the campaign staff—about which she was still not permitting herself to think. "Mom, especially."

"Sounds like you are, too," Beth said.

And how.

"Whoa," Beth said. "She just got a whole bunch in Virginia."

"Really?" Meg frowned. The last she'd heard, Griffin was expected to take Virginia by two or three percentage points. "I'm not sure if that's good or not. I mean, some states, she's *supposed* to win."

Beth laughed.

"What's so funny?" Meg asked uneasily.

"I don't know," Beth said. "I guess this is just a pretty weird conversation."

Well, yeah, it probably was, wasn't it?

"If she wins, are you blowing off school tomorrow?" Beth asked.

If her mother won, she would be too busy inhaling smelling salts and lying on the floor with a cool cloth on her forehead. "Either way, I'm blowing off school," Meg said.

Beth laughed again. "No, if she wins, you have to come in and swagger around a lot. That way—"

"Hello?" someone asked, clicking on.

Meg sighed. God forbid she be able to have a private conversation—in her own bedroom. "I'm kind of on the phone."

"Oh. Sorry." The person clicked off.

"Sounds like you have to hang up," Beth said.

Meg nodded. "Yeah. I should probably get downstairs, anyway. My father's heavily into us doing togetherness."

"Sounds fun," Beth said.

Yeah, so far it had been a complete blast.

Back downstairs, she found her family watching some dumb space movie involving lasers and jet-packs and what seemed like a very complicated battle sequence. The Candidate's Family being devil-may-care and embracing pop culture.

Actually, they *did* look somewhat more relaxed.

"You know," her mother said, as one of the characters skillfully blew up several enemy fighters, and then swooped off deeper into the galaxy. "If I could do that, I would have won. People would have been afraid not to vote for me."

"You haven't lost yet," Meg's father said, putting a calming hand on hers.

"You mean, you think I'm going to?" She jerked her hand free. "Thanks a lot. I bet you didn't even vote for me."

"Sorry." He took her hand back. "I probably should have."

Neal was completely mesmerized by the movie, his mouth literally hanging open, but Meg and Steven laughed, and her mother actually cracked a smile.

The mood in the room was sort of happy for a minute, but then Glen stuck his head in.

"Kate, New York's official," he said.

Her mother instantly flicked over to CNN, which made Neal leap out of his chair and shout, "Hey!"

"—and New Jersey also seems to be going with the Senator," one of the anchors was saying, as the huge map graphic on screen added another blue state to the tally.

Meg grinned. "I thought they hated you in Trenton."

Her mother just looked nervous. "I did, too."

As more and more votes came in—and more state polling places closed—her mother started to pull ahead.

"You're winning, Mommy!" Neal bounced delightedly in his chair, no longer upset about missing the end of the space movie. "Look, you're winning!"

She shook her head. "We haven't heard Texas. Texas is going to be big. And California. We won't hear California for hours, and—"

"Improbably," a pundit was saying, "Georgia still seems to be in play. Certainly, none of us ever imagined—"

Her parents exchanged quick nervous looks, and Meg felt her stomach start churning around. Good thing she hadn't eaten dinner. A few more states like Georgia, and her mother might—Meg drank some of her Coke, which was now flat, as well as warm.

There was a knock on the door, and Glen came back in, sitting down next to her mother.

"The internals were right," he said quietly. "You've got Missouri."

Missouri, the notorious bellwether state.

Her mother gulped coffee. "I know, I was watching."

"No way should you have taken Missouri," he said.

Meg had to swallow, hard. This was starting to get serious.

"And the word we're getting is that they're about to call Florida," Glen said.

Florida? Christ almighty.

"Texas is going to be bad," her mother said, a visible shudder jerking through her body. "He'll get me three-to-one in Texas."

Glen just looked at her.

And the electoral map on the television was surprisingly blue. Shockingly blue.

Alarmingly blue.

"It's early," her mother said finally, nervously. "It doesn't mean anything."

Except that the overall trend was in her favor. *Strongly* in her favor.

"—and preliminary returns from Illinois are giving Powers an overwhelming majority of the votes," one of the anchors said. "It's still too early to project a winner, but we're getting closer to—"

Her mother sat down, trembling. "Maybe—maybe running wasn't such a great idea. Maybe," she was watching her hands shake, "maybe I don't want to be—"

Glen changed the channel and they heard "we're now ready to call Wisconsin for Senator Powers, and we're also expecting—"

"Maybe," her mother got up, heading for the door, "maybe I'll just go upstairs for a while."

Glen switched to another station, where someone was saying, "At this point, I think we're just waiting for the polls on the West Coast to close before we—"

Her mother came back and then sat down, hands tight in her lap.

"—truly an unprecedented—" yet another pundit was saying.

Her mother was going to win. She was actually going to win. Meg watched more numbers go up, feeling dizzy.

Glen moved to the door. "I'll let you all have some time alone together. Then, we can head downtown."

Meg concentrated on not listening—to anything. Her *mother* was going to be President. The thing that had never seemed plausible, that she had always dreaded, was now going to—or about to—or had already—

"—tentatively prepared to put Texas in Representative Griffin's column," an anchorperson said, "but Powers continues to run very strongly in urban—"

Her mother clicked channels, stopping at a soccer game. "Ah. My favorite."

Yeah, right. Her mother often seemed to enjoy baseball, and could be convinced to root for the Patriots now and again, but on the whole, she had never particularly been inclined to watch sports.

Gradually, the tentatively relaxed feeling came back as they watched the game, Meg *almost* able to convince herself that this was any old evening—despite the fact that she could hear almost non-stop shouts of excitement coming from the part of the house where Glen and the others had gathered.

She looked around the room, seeing that none of them were really focused on the soccer game. Her father was holding Neal on his lap, being told some long, involved story. Steven was lying on the floor, patting Kirby. Her mother was the only one who seemed to be paying attention to the television, leaning back in her chair, almost—not quite—slouching. Her shoulders were shaking, and Meg realized, horrified, that she was crying.

"Mom?" she asked, not sure what to do.

Her mother looked over, and Meg saw that she was laughing so hard that tears were coming out of her eyes. "Is this possibly the funniest thing ever?" she asked.

Meg stared at her. "*Funny?*"

"I mean, I've been horrible all day, and now we're watching little men in shorts, and—" Her mother broke up completely, covering her eyes with her hand.

Worried, Meg glanced at her father.

"Katharine," he said, smiling.

"Don't call me that," she said, laughing almost too hard to speak. "I hate that name."

"She's flipped," Steven said to Meg. "She's really flipped."

Their mother just laughed, changing the channel back to one of the news stations.

"The trend is obvious now," the commentator was saying, "and it's only a matter of an hour or so before—"

Their mother clicked the television off.

"Well," she said, her voice weak from laughing. She looked at all of them, her expression softening. "I guess—I mean, it looks as though—"

There was a knock on the door and Meg held her breath, knowing that this was it.

"Kate," Glen said. "You have a telephone call."

Griffin, calling to concede. Meg gulped, feeling her stomach tighten with incredible fear. President. Her mother was the President of the country. *Her* mother. Jesus Christ.

"Mr. Griffin," her mother said, sounding stiff and formal.

Glen nodded.

"Well, then," she said, automatically raising her hands to straighten her hair. "I guess I'd better take it."

Her father stood up too, his grin huge. "Think I might come for the walk," he said. Then, his grin widened. "Madam President."

13

MEG NOTICED ONE big change after the election—boys were breaking their backs to ask her out, quite a few of whom she barely knew. It was flattering, in a way. It was tempting, in a big way. But, how could she say yes to a guy she knew was only asking her because she was the President-elect's daughter? Talk about demoralizing. She had a feeling they were going to go out with her, see how far they could get, and then run to the tabloids with the news.

Two days after the election, Linda came over when she knew Meg's mother wasn't home and sat Meg down for a Talk.

"We need to set some ground rules for you," she said. "First of all, is anything I don't know about going to surface?"

What, like the media hadn't *already* completely invaded their lives? And Linda—or one of her little acolytes—had asked her some version of that question at least twice a week since the New Hampshire primary. "You mean like, topless photos, me holding a loaded gun, and smoking pot at a party?" Meg asked.

In her cool and collected way, Linda looked a little bit terrified

"I don't think any of that is going to come *out*," Meg said. "I've been pretty careful."

"It may seem terribly funny to you," Linda said, after a pause, "but the reality is that you have to be more cautious. And that *definitely* includes the shoot-from-the-lip habit. Anything you do from now on, no matter how innocent it may seem at the time, is going to reflect on your mother, more than ever. We can't have you running around with a lot of boys, or coming home drunk. And, as far as sex is concerned—" She closed her eyes.

"Well, you don't have to worry about boys," Meg said, "because I'm very, *very* gay."

Linda pursed her lips.

"*Toujours* gay," Meg said.

Linda looked down at her coffee cup—one of Trudy's special blends; Trudy was very particular, when it came to coffee—and slowly and delicately stirred one-third of a teaspoon of sugar into it. "Well, be that as it may, I have some concerns, and I think it's important for us to address them now, as opposed to down the road."

Yeah, because she was such a total rebel and miscreant, without a single political instinct anywhere in her body. "Shouldn't my mother be the one doing this?" Meg asked stiffly.

"She trusts you," Linda said.

Meg nodded. "But *you're* expecting me to come home pregnant."

"You're sixteen years old, you're moving into a national spotlight, and I think we need to discuss it," Linda said.

Oh, really? Meg resisted the urge to grit her teeth. Clench her fist. All that good stuff. "I didn't know we were discussing. I thought you were telling."

"Meg, come on." Linda made an impatient gesture. "We have to work together on this."

"Then, how come you *tell* me, instead of discussing?" Meg asked.

Linda sucked in a hard breath.

"Well, you are," Meg said defensively.

"Look," Linda said. "I know you're pretty well politicized—"

That word again.

"—no conception of what it's going to be like," Linda went on. "People are going to be watching every move you make. So, your image—"

Meg grinned. Linda just couldn't say "politicized" without saying "image."

"—very important." Linda frowned at her. "Are you listening to me?"

Meg nodded.

"All right, then. On another subject," Linda said, "you also need to stop posting on the Internet from now on."

Yeah, like *that* was going to happen. Meg shook her head.

"We're aware that you don't use your real name," Linda said, "but if my people can trace your footprints without any trouble, so can anyone else with a little initiative."

Whoa, wasn't that against the law? Had they been going behind her back for months now? "You're *tracking* me?" Meg said. "Who the hell gave you permission to do that?" If it turned out to be her mother, she was going to be really pissed off.

Linda hesitated. "Well, I don't mean to suggest that we—that is, it isn't our intent to interfere with—"

Yeah, right. "It's no one's damn business what I say on the Internet—or anywhere else," Meg said.

Linda sighed. "No, but your screen name isn't exactly a state secret, and I'm concerned that you may not be sufficiently restrained, and we're now on a much bigger playing field than you seem to realize."

Make that, her *former* screen name. Besides, it wasn't as though the world was waiting with bated breath to find out what she thought about various television shows, and the Red Sox, and so forth. Just Linda and her cohorts, apparently.

"I'm sorry if you're offended by any of this, but I'm much more worried about you than I am about your brothers," Linda said. "You're sixteen—it's going to be very difficult for you. You have to be prepared for—"

"Is my mother honest?" Meg asked suddenly.

Linda blinked. "What?"

Meg felt her cheeks reddening, but decided that now that she had asked, she really wanted to know. "Is my mother honest?"

Linda looked at her as if she were an extremely odd specimen. "Are you putting me on?"

"I was just—curious," Meg said.

"Shouldn't you and your mother be having this talk?" Linda asked.

Meg laughed. Unexpected humor from the Ice Queen. "I just wondered. What's your opinion?"

"That she is, to a rather ridiculous degree." Linda shook her head. "A difficult woman to work for, your mother."

"You're not just"—Meg put on a serious expression—"fabricating this for the sake of her image, are you?"

"Are you kidding?" Linda obviously wasn't sure. "I'll tell you, honesty isn't as easy to package as you might think. That kind of image, when it's genuine, requires—"

Meg sat back, grinning, knowing that Linda, despite all of her huffing and puffing, would have given her a straight answer.

"—listening to me?" Linda asked.

Meg nodded.

"Well, I hope you're convinced. Now," she looked down at her clipboard, "insofar as you're concerned—"

"Hey," Meg said. "A man from the *Post* asked me what kind of birth control I used, and I told him I was on the Pill, but was thinking about getting one of those implants, instead. Was that okay?"

Linda looked at her with the same expression she'd had at the top of the mountain at Stowe.

"I mean, I figured in the interests of honesty—" Meg let her voice trail off.

"I do not find your humor amusing," Linda said, half-smiling.

Meg grinned.

PEOPLE KEPT ASKING her out. Knowing that Linda was right, albeit something of an alarmist, Meg said no to almost all of them, giving in only to Rick Hamilton, because she still had a wild crush on him and didn't care *what* his motives were.

She was on her way to her biology class one day when Carl

Lehman, a guy she knew from the Ski Club, but almost never saw otherwise, stopped her, wanting to know if she'd go to the movies with him.

She didn't want to be rude to him—necessarily—but—"I'm sorry, I can't. I promised I'd—"

"Yeah, sure." He shoved his hands in his pockets, rocking back on his sneakers. Carl was pretty good-looking, in a scruffy way, but was the kind of guy who took *pride* in underachieving—and also made a point of abusing the school's already fairly liberal open campus policy. "Heard you went snob on us."

"I didn't," Meg said. "I just—"

"Yeah, sure." He opened a piece of gum, putting it in his mouth and crumpling the piece of paper. "Well, see ya."

"Wait a minute," she said after him.

He turned.

She looked him straight in the eye. "How come you never asked me out before my mother won the election?"

"Don't know." He had the grace to blush. "Guess I never thought of it."

"Oh, please, you flatter me," Meg said.

He smiled a little. "You sound like her. *A lot* like her."

"I do not," Meg said. "I sound like *me*."

"Yeah, sure." He opened another piece of gum.

Christ, she was sick of this. Meg scowled at him. "If you want to go out with my mother, don't ask me, okay? And tell your stupid friends! I don't go out with people who don't ask *me*."

"How come you said yes to Rick?" he wanted to know.

"It's none of your business," she said.

Carl shrugged. "Why you think *he* asked you out?"

She held tightly to her biology book, not looking at him.

"You're in AP *everything*, and you can't figure it out?" he said.

There was really no way to respond to that, so she just hunched her shoulders and headed down the hall.

He caught up to her, putting his hand on her arm. "I'm sorry. I didn't mean that. 'Sides, it's not why *I* asked you out."

"Yeah," she said. "Sure."

"Well, think what you want," he said. "Only, I asked you out, 'cause I always thought you were kinda—I don't know—quiet and stuff. Only, you got up and made that speech, and looked really beautiful and everything—you were kinda something else."

Well, at least it was a creative attempt to dig himself out. "I was being my mother," she said.

He shook his head. "Naw, you were just wearing her blazer." He tossed his crumpled ball of gum paper and foil at a wastebasket farther up the hall. "F'you don't want to go out with me, don't go out with me."

"What if you were only telling me that so I'd go?" she asked.

"Hey, think what you want." He went down the hall. "Maybe I'll try again sometime."

"Maybe I'll say yes," she said.

"Hey, don't flatter me." He flipped her back a piece of gum. "See ya."

She was late for class. And when she walked in, everyone stopped working on their experiments and stared at her.

"Sorry I'm late," she said to her teacher, Mr. Collinsworth.

"Uh, no problem," he said, blinking several times. "No problem at all."

Meg frowned. "You're not going to make me go get a pass?"

"No," Mr. Collinsworth said. "That won't be necessary."

She started to go over to her lab bench, where Beth and Sarah had already started setting up their equipment, but changed her mind. "Sir, *everyone* who's late has to go get a pass. It's a rule."

He straightened his glasses. "I told you. It's not necessary."

"Yeah, well, I think it is," she said.

Now, everyone was *really* staring.

"Meghan," Mr. Collinsworth said, "I might remind you that unexcused tardiness to class is an automatic detention."

"So what?" she asked. "I broke a rule."

He sighed. "Meghan—"

She looked at him, stubbornly folding her arms across her chest.

"Very well," he said. "Go get a pass."

"Thank you, sir." She left the room and went down to the office, where no one was very eager to give her a late pass. Finally, a reluctant aide wrote one out.

"Thank you," Meg said. "Where's detention tonight?"

"Well, perhaps your teacher would be willing to overlook—" the woman started.

Meg shook her head. "No, that's okay. I'd rather jump straight to an administrative detention."

"Then, um, please report to your housemaster during J-Block," the woman said uneasily.

Meg nodded. "Thank you."

"Hey, all right," the guy next to her, a senior who had apparently been caught skipping, said. "Way to go."

She gave him a tough-kid grin, which he returned. "See you there."

Back in biology, she handed her teacher the pass. Then, because everyone was watching her, she couldn't resist swaggering a little on her way to her lab bench.

"What a Girl Scout," Beth said, as she sat down.

Meg nodded. "Yup, you know it. Law and order, damn it."

"Your parents are going to *kill* you," Sarah said, her voice horrified.

"No way. Too much publicity." Meg turned up the flame on their Bunsen burner, the contents of the test tube bubbling furiously in response. "Bet we could get *suspended* if we blew the lab up."

Sarah turned the flame down. "That's not funny."

Meg and Beth laughed.

"Meghan, please put on your gloves and your safety glasses," Mr. Collinsworth said from the front of the room.

She grinned and snapped on a pair of heavy-duty sterile gloves, then picked up a pair of plastic goggles. "Yes, sir."

"Know what we ought to do tonight?" Beth dropped some extra powder into the test tube, which almost certainly contaminated their original sample. "Let's knock over a liquor store."

"No." Meg added even more, just to be *sure* that they would have to start from scratch. "Let's rob a bank."

HER MOTHER WASN'T home much, but that wasn't anything new. Her transition team was based in Boston, but between meeting with possible appointees, receiving high-level briefings, and winding down her Senate office, she was in Washington most of the time. Her father flew down for a few days, and her parents went through the White House, deciding what furniture they were going to need and that sort of thing.

The White House. Meg had never even been on one of those White House *tours*. And now, she was going to be living there? How utterly bizarre was *that*?

Her father had taken an indefinite leave of absence from his firm, and was also spending time arranging for the various blind trusts where her parents' money would be kept, during her mother's time in office. He wasn't talking about it, but the press was giving him a pretty hard time, enjoying the idea of a First Gentleman. They kept asking him about his plans for redecorating the White House, his ideas on fashion and entertaining, and what he was going to wear to the Inaugural Balls. Usually, he would pass it all off as a joke, saying things like he was going to do the East Wing in blacks and browns, but whenever he got home after a session with reporters, he would be tense, and they would all have to watch their step. Steven, with his usual tact, had asked him when he was going to start wearing lacy dresses, and he had blown up, yelling at everyone in the house. One of those days when Meg thought about joining the Foreign Legion.

Hearing her parents come home one night in mid-December,

back from a dinner in Boston, Meg went downstairs to find out if they'd had a good time.

"Russ," her mother's voice was low, but warning, "you really have to watch what you say in front of those people. *I* know when you're kidding, but—"

Meg paused in the doorway, seeing that they were having another fight. They'd had a lot of fights lately. Kind of scary.

"My dear Madam President." Her father spun around to face her mother, sounding calm, but furious. "Let's get something straight. I will say whatever the bloody hell I feel like saying."

Her mother nodded. "I know, but—"

"As long as you know." He strode to the door, and then saw Meg. "Hello," he said shortly, moving past her.

"Uh, hi," Meg said, wishing she hadn't come down at all. She glanced at her father going up the stairs, then at her mother, who looked thin and tired in her bright red, very Christmasy dress, and decided to pretend that she hadn't heard anything. "Did you have fun?"

"Lots." Her mother filled a glass with water, drank half of it, then dumped the rest in the sink. "They're not letting your father be a person." She refilled the glass, drinking another half. "He's right to be angry," she added quietly, and then put the empty glass in the dishwasher. "Everything go okay tonight?"

Since the evening had been fine, but not even vaguely interesting, Meg shrugged.

Her mother nodded, heading for the stairs. "Turn off the lights and everything before you come up, okay?"

Right. Meg went over to lock the back door, even though there were plenty of agents posted outside, again feeling as if she really shouldn't have come downstairs at all.

HER MOTHER MADE a huge effort during the next week to try and make the press be nicer to her father, and he got his own full-time press secretary, which helped things considerably. Although Meg was pretty sure her mother wasn't thrilled about losing him, her father chose Preston—which appeared to be a nearly perfect fit. He sat Meg down in the kitchen right after he got the job, looking at her with a stern-but-I'm-just-putting-you-on frown.

"I'm going to say one word to you, Meggo," he said. "Only one word."

"Plastics," Meg said, grinning.

He laughed. "Close. Style, okay? Style."

She had the general idea, but—"In what sense?"

"No grandchildren for the next four years," he said. "No drug busts. Don't join the Nazi party."

Well, okay, that was nice and specific. "Are you going to flip if I say stuff on the Internet?" she asked. Her mother had assured her that she *wasn't* being monitored, but just in case, she had been changing her screen name every few days—which was a big pain.

Preston shrugged. "Not as long as you're hilarious. And make sure you spell everything correctly."

The former might be difficult; the latter was manageable.

"Style, kid," he said. "That's all you have to remember."

Steven and Neal got the same advice, although Meg assumed he was less worried about the prospect of either of them producing grandchildren anytime soon.

With every passing day, there seemed to be more and more publicity, a lot of it focused on the family, and articles with titles like "The Storybook Family" were appearing constantly. Meg was kind of hoping for one called "The Stylish Family," but so far, it hadn't happened.

"Quiet and bookish?" She had been appalled by that description of her in a national magazine, when she happened to pick it up during breakfast with her father and brothers one morning. "How come Steven gets 'a quick grin,' and I have to be 'quiet and bookish'?"

"You were," her father said. "You spent the whole time turning red and muttering things about having to do homework. What was he supposed to think?"

"Daddy, do I have a shy smile?" Neal asked, worried.

"You have a beautiful smile," their father said, lifting him up onto his lap. "You were embarrassed that day, too."

Meg shook her head. "'Quiet and bookish.' Can I skip school today?"

"What are you complaining about?" her father asked. "It also says"—he picked up the magazine—"you 'inherited your mother's beauty with an adolescent charm all your own.'"

Meg had to grin. "Well, okay, I liked *that* part."

HER MOTHER TOOK off ten full days at Christmas, and they spent part of it at home, part of it in New York shopping for what her father called "proper Presidential family clothes," and part of it skiing. Obviously, it went without saying that Meg liked the skiing part the best.

Coming home one day right after school had started again, Meg heard music and laughing in the living room. She went in to see what was going on, not even pausing to take off her coat.

Peeking into the room, she saw most of the furniture pushed back out of the way and the rug rolled up, as the dancing song from *The King and I* played in the background. Her parents—who seemed to be cracking up; literally and figuratively—were dancing around the room in a classic waltz. Her mother was laughing particularly hard, and kept missing steps, which would confuse her father.

"Come on, cut it out," he was saying, eyes on the floor and where he put his feet. "This is serious."

"Oh, right." She changed her footing so that she could lead *him*, and they struggled for control, still laughing.

Clearly, they had gone mad. The pressure had finally gotten to them, and they had lost their minds. Or maybe they had caught that disease that made people dance non-stop until they dropped dead.

All things considered, there were probably worse ways to go.

"Come on, can't you feel it?" her mother asked, letting him lead again. "One, two, three; one, two, three."

"No, I think it's one, two, three, *four*; one, two, three, *four*," he said, dancing intently to *that* rhythm.

"But, it isn't." She tried to slow him down. "It's one, two, three. Listen."

He shook his head. "I don't hear it."

Her family was nothing, if not entirely lacking in musical talent. "You guys do this a lot when we're not home?" Meg asked.

Her parents stopped, startled.

"All the time," her father said, and bent her mother over in a precarious dip.

"Every afternoon," her mother said, letting him sweep her back up.

Meg considered that, shrugged, and turned to go to the kitchen.

"Actually"—her mother crossed the room, to start the song from the beginning—"your father has pointed out, with some rather reasonable concern, I think, that we will be dancing on national television in a couple of weeks, and we thought we might try some practicing while free from the prying eyes of small, pesky children."

Hmmm. Meg shifted her knapsack to her other shoulder. "I'm not sure how to take that."

They both grinned at her.

"Oh. Well." She shifted the knapsack again. "Guess I'm in the way."

"We'll be done in a little while." Her father put his hand on her mother's waist. "Come on, Madam President."

"Now, remember," her mother said, as Meg went towards the kitchen. "It's one, two, three; one, two, three. . . ."

14

IT WAS A couple of nights before they were going to Washington for the pre-Inaugural festivities, and Meg couldn't sleep. In the morning, it was going to be her last day of school, there were suitcases and boxes everywhere—and she couldn't sleep.

Moving Vanessa off her stomach, she got up. It was cold, so she put on an inside-out sweatshirt, and went downstairs. After rummaging around the kitchen, she came up with a ginger ale and some chocolate chip cookies Trudy had helped Steven and Neal make—which were large, misshapen, and delicious. Taking three, she wandered to the den to see what late-night movies might be on, and fumbled for the light switch.

"Before I scare you, I'm here," someone said, and Meg jumped, spilling part of her soda.

"How come the light's off?" she asked, trying to sound as if she hadn't been startled at all.

"I don't know." Her mother's voice was sad. "I was thinking."

"Oh." Meg squinted, barely able to see her in the dark, other than the tall outline of a figure sitting on the couch. Was she crying, maybe? She had never seen her mother cry, except for once when she was little. Cry from laughing, maybe, but that was all. "Should I leave?"

"No, sit down," her mother said.

"Should I turn on the light?" Meg asked.

"I guess so," her mother said.

Meg flipped the switch, her mother blinking in the brightness. There was a half-empty glass of dark amber liquid on the coffee table, with a crumpled napkin beside it.

Maybe her mother *had* been crying. Why else would the napkin be crumpled? Unless she had a cold. If she had a cold, it made sense. Was she sniffling, maybe? Except, crying might have made her sniffle, too. Meg frowned.

"You don't have to look like that." Her mother sounded very defensive. "My God, I just felt like having a drink."

"I wasn't—" Meg stopped. What was she going to say, that she had been studying the napkin to see if she had been crying? Maybe it would be better to have her mother think that she was pushing temperance. "Um, are you upset?"

"I guess, a little," her mother said, her eyes far away.

"Well, is it like, something we did?" Meg asked.

"What?" Her mother glanced away from whatever she was seeing. "No. No, it isn't."

"Oh." Meg shifted on the armchair. "Well, are you worried about your speech and everything?"

"No. I mean, I suppose so, but no." Her mother also moved restlessly, one hand sliding up to massage the back of her neck. Then, she brought the hand down, folding it around the napkin.

That meant that she had been crying. Meg frowned again, wondering what she looked like when she cried. The other time, she had been kind of small and hunched over.

"Actually," her mother looked at the napkin now, "today was my father's birthday, and I guess I've been depressed."

It was? Meg hadn't known that. Her father should have said something. She thought for a second. Only, maybe he had. At breakfast, he had been talking about them being extra-nice to her mother, and Meg had nodded, tuning him out, worrying about having to start saying good-bye to people at school. But, maybe that's why Steven and Neal had behaved so well, because she couldn't remember hearing any fights at all—which almost *never* happened.

"He would have been—sixty-nine?" she asked awkwardly.

“Seventy,” her mother said, somewhat sharply.

Neither of them spoke for a minute.

“Oh, I’m okay.” Her mother was brisk now. “I mean, it’s been almost six years. I’m fine.” Part of her mouth smiled, her eyes staying dark. “I’m lying, of course.”

“He, uh, he would have been really proud,” Meg said.

“I know.” Her mother picked up her glass, holding it in both hands. She looked over. “It makes me feel alone.”

“Well,” Meg twisted in her chair, “you have us.”

“Thank God.” Her mother sipped her drink, and Meg remembered that her grandfather had always had scotch at night—expensive scotch. “It made me think of my mother, too,” she said quietly.

Meg immediately pictured the framed photo on her mother’s dresser of a thin, beautiful woman in her mid-twenties, holding hands with a little girl with dark braids and a very sweet smile. “What was she like?”

“It’s hard to say how much I remember, and how much my father and everyone else told me. After all,” her mother tilted her glass, rolling the scotch around, “I was even younger than Neal.”

Meg nodded, wondering with a sudden cold shudder what it would be like to have her mother die, to be missing that huge part of her life. She looked up, relieved to see her mother’s chest moving with light regularity, her face healthy and alive, not frozen in a photograph.

“What was it like?” she asked tentatively.

Her mother glanced over. “What?”

“Not—” Meg hesitated. “Not having a mother.”

Her mother’s laugh was bitter. “I wouldn’t think you’d have to ask.”

Damn it, she should have seen *that* one coming. “But,” Meg said, “you—”

"It's been the same thing, hasn't it?" Her mother took a very large sip of the scotch. "I haven't been here when you've needed me, I haven't been here when you've wanted me, I haven't been here for any of you." She put the glass down with a slightly clumsy movement, and it occurred to Meg that maybe it wasn't the first one she'd had. "Now, we're going to Washington, and it's going to be—you're all going to end up wishing—" She shook her head, and picked the glass back up.

Meg shook her head. "No, we're not—"

"Don't say things because you feel as though you have to, okay? You've got every right to feel lousy about me, I've certainly never—" She took a sip that was more like a gulp. "Don't ever be alone. Alone is lousy."

"But, you're not alone," Meg said.

"I could be." Her mother finished the drink. "You all might—" She stopped, stared at the empty glass, then put it down with a dull clink. "Well, I guess we've got self-pity talking here. Or, as Humphrey Bogart would say, maybe it's the bourbon. They're a lot alike."

"I thought you were coming right up." Meg's father was unexpectedly in the doorway. Then, he noticed Meg. "Terrific, a whole *family* of insomniacs. How about we all go get some sleep?"

Meg jumped out of her chair, very relieved to see him. She saw her mother hesitate, not getting up. Maybe she was afraid she would look drunk, and didn't want her to see. Meg decided to make it easy and leave.

"Well." She stretched, trying to look tired. "Night, I guess."

"Good night, Meg," her father said, giving her a hug, and she could tell he understood.

She nodded, and then looked at her mother. "Night, Mom. Have, uh, have good dreams and stuff." Then she left, not hearing anything behind her.

She went up to her room, closed the door, and sat on the bed.

Then, she lifted Vanessa onto her lap and stared at the shadowy suitcases and boxes.

Now, she *really* couldn't sleep.

IN THE MORNING, her mother didn't mention their discussion, so Meg didn't bring it up, concentrating on the craziness of their last couple of days at home, what with packing and good-byes. And arrangements. There were lots of arrangements. Like the caretakers who were going to move into the house—while the Secret Service kept it under continuous protection, transferring records to their new schools in Washington, and that kind of stuff.

Probably the saddest thing was having to say good-bye to Trudy, who was going to Florida to live near her son and his family. But, she had promised that she would come to visit them regularly at the White House, where her mother assured her that she would be waited on hand and foot—which Trudy thought sounded great.

On their last afternoon in Chestnut Hill, Beth and Sarah came over, sitting on the bed to watch Meg throw a few last-minute things into the Red Sox duffel bag she was going to carry with her on the plane.

"Wow," Beth said. "Can we like, have your autograph and everything? So people'll believe we know you."

"Maybe," Meg said in an "if-you're-lucky" voice.

Beth looked thoughtful. "Actually, get a couple from your mother, too, so I can throw them up on eBay."

"Beth!" Sarah elbowed her. "That's not funny."

Meg struggled with the zipper on the duffel bag, feeling a lump of homesickness starting before she even got downstairs. The zipper, actually, was quite happy to zip, but she kept fussing around with it, not wanting to look up, afraid that she was going to cry or do something otherwise disastrous.

"You need help?" Beth asked, getting up.

"No. No, I'm—" Meg let the zipper close. "Everything's fine. It's all set."

"Look, it's going to be great," Beth said. "*You're* going to be great."

Not likely.

"Beth's right," Sarah said. "And you get to live in the White House, and I bet your school has thousands of cute guys, and—well, everything!"

Meg sat down at her desk, not sharing Sarah's enthusiasm. She swallowed, wondering if she really was going to cry—and hoping like hell that she wouldn't.

"Are you that scared?" Sarah asked.

Meg shook her head. "No. Just kind of." She smiled weakly. "Kind of a lot." Her smile weakened even more. "Kind of petrified."

"Well," Sarah said awkwardly, "you *look* nice."

Since she had now joined a world where she was supposed to wear dresses and skirts all of the damned time. Meg shook her head and went over to her dresser to check the drawers for the fiftieth time and make sure she hadn't forgotten anything crucial.

"Miss Powers," Beth made her hand into a microphone, "looking nothing if not ravishing, recommends traveling in simple tweeds—"

"I'd call this wool," Meg said, looking at her skirt.

Beth ignored her. "Tweeds, and a single strand of pearls. The President's daughter also likes a shoe with a low heel and favors a thin black vanity case for afternoon outings."

"I prefer a money belt," Meg said to Sarah, who laughed, uncertainly.

"Her makeup is subdued," Beth went on, "in muted blues for winter, accenting her best features."

"Which are?" Meg asked.

"Her best features being, of course, the young woman's knees," Beth said.

"Oh, no," Sarah disagreed. "I think it's her eyes. Meg, you have great eyes."

"Well, maybe," Meg said. "But, have you seen my knees? I have kind of incredible knees."

Sarah frowned. "I never noticed."

"The President's daughter is also a very accomplished girl," Beth said. "She makes Christmas decorations out of egg cartons—"

Meg laughed, picturing the foil-covered monstrosities they had made when they were in junior high—which Trudy had tactfully put on the tree, in the *back*. "Hey, remember that?"

"She does very nice paint-by-numbers, and shyly confesses that she's been known to read four or five romantic novels at a sitting," Beth said. "While most of her conversation is disjointed, if not, in fact, gibberish, she has been known to—"

Sarah shook her head. "Beth, you're terrible. Why don't you say something nice about her?"

"I was about to," Beth assured her. "Anyway, like I was saying, she has been known to make witty comments with biannual regularity."

"I thought it was more like biennial," Meg said.

"She also likes to show off her vocabulary," Beth said to her unseen audience.

"Meg, come on!" Steven shouted up the stairs. "Everyone's waiting!"

Meg swallowed and opened her duffel bag to recheck the contents. "You guys are going to come down during spring break, right?"

Beth nodded. "Definitely. I'm going to bring my camera, and then sell the pictures."

Meg smiled; then, they all looked at each other.

"I, uh," Meg took a deep breath, "I'm not so great at good-byes."

"This is only a see-you-later," Sarah said.

Maybe. "I'm not good at them, either." Meg gave each of them a stiff hug, then stepped back. "I can't cry or anything if I'm going to walk out by all those stupid photographers."

"It would spoil the look," Beth said.

Yeah. "But, I kind of—" Meg had to blink quickly. "I kind of—"

"Meg, come on already!" Steven yelled.

Right. "Okay, I'm coming!" she yelled back, then picked up her suitcase and took one last look around her room.

Beth put a friendly arm around her shoulders as they walked down the stairs. "If it helps, think about how nice you look in your tweeds."

Meg nodded. "They do hang well. Would you believe I've had them since college?"

"You guys are weird," Sarah said. "You really are."

Of this, Meg had little doubt.

"Oh, and remember," Beth said. "It's been a few months, so you're about due for a witty comment. So—choose it wisely."

Meg nodded. "I'll try." Then, she grinned. "Make sure you give Rick"—with whom she had ultimately refused to go out—"my love."

"Oh, you jerk," Beth said sadly. "You wasted it!"

15

THEIR FIRST FEW days in Washington were a blur of honorary breakfasts and dinners, special concerts and theatrical performances—and Secret Service agents. She and Steven and Neal were going to have three rotating shifts, with two primary agents on each one, although others were going to work in various logistical positions, she assumed. In any case, the guards were going to go everywhere with them, including school, the movies, or anyplace else they happened to be. Each of her father's shifts would have six to eight agents assigned to it, while her mother seemed to have hundreds. Steven, who was really bugged about the whole thing, kept asking if the agents were going to stand on the mound with him when he was pitching. It was a stupid question—but Meg couldn't help wondering if, when she was on the tennis court, they were going to make her play *doubles* now. She hated doubles.

Steven had also asked if Kirby and the cats would have to have guards—which she thought was quite funny. Most of their agents were men, although there was one woman on her detail, and two or three on her mother's. They would probably have these agents for no more than a year, and then they would get new ones, because the Secret Service worried about people getting emotionally attached to their protectees and relaxing on the job. Steven and Neal were going to have theirs changed more frequently, because the younger people were, the more likely it was that attachments would form. Meg kind of wondered if the inference there was that she and her parents were too old to like. Anyway, for the next four—or eight; God forbid—years, they would all have official, constant protection. How depressing.

Meg woke up very early on the day of the Inauguration. They

were staying at her mother's Georgetown apartment—instead of the more traditional site, Blair House—because her parents wanted them to have one last chance to be in normal surroundings. One last chance to have some *privacy*. Which was why even Trudy—who hated crowds and attention, anyway—wasn't staying with them this time. In fact, she was hiding out in *Florida*.

She went out to the kitchen, her brothers appearing almost simultaneously.

Neal sat up at the counter in his pajamas. "Where's Mommy?"

"Taking the first shower." Meg got down some cereal bowls. "I think she wants to go over her speech again." The staff was under strict orders not to show up until eight-thirty—and she assumed that Glen, who was going to be her chief of staff, and her other aides were already pacing around nervously outside on the sidewalk, despite the fact that it was barely seven.

Steven took orange juice and a carton of milk out of the almost empty refrigerator. "Want some juice, brat?" he asked Neal.

Neal hit him. "I'm not a brat!"

Steven held the carton over his head. "You want some juice?"

"Steven, don't be a jerk, okay?" Meg tried to get it away from him, and they scuffled for a minute until she finally yanked it free. "Mom and Dad'll be uptight enough without you starting trouble."

"Meggie thinks she can play mother," Steven grumbled to Neal.

She got out a loaf of bread. "Want some toast, brats?"

"Meg!" Neal hit her, too.

She put four slices in the toaster. "Think Mom and Dad'll want cereal, or something better?"

"Why don't you make poached eggs?" Steven asked, and snickered.

"I know how to make them," Meg said. Defensively.

"And *boy,"* he dumped sugar on his cereal, "are they good."

"You're going to get another cavity," she said, watching him. Two days earlier, all three of them had had to pay a visit to their new dentist—who was an Army Lieutenant Colonel—and they had *each* had a cavity. As a result, she was anticipating many "have you flossed yet?" and "did you use your fluoride rinse?" daily questions from her father for the foreseeable future.

"Tastes better this way," Steven said, but—she noticed—pushed the sugar bowl aside.

Their father came into the kitchen in his plaid bathrobe. "You guys all set on breakfast?"

They nodded, and Meg surreptitiously moved the sugar all the way to the end of the counter.

"I'm going to try to get your mother to eat an omelet," he said. "Anyone else want one?"

Steven gagged. "No way. Hey, what time do we have to be at the White House?"

"Who says you're coming?" their father asked, melting butter in a frying pan. He grinned at Steven's expression. "Ten-thirty. The President and the First Lady want to meet our *whole* charming family."

"Toto, too?" Meg asked, scraping the burnt parts off the first batch of toast.

Steven started to reach for the sugar, but then pulled his hand back. "I bet Meggie'll be quiet and bookish."

"I bet you'll chew with your mouth open," Meg said.

"Bet I won't," he said.

Yeah, right. "Bet you will," she said.

"Well." Their mother came into the kitchen, her hair wrapped up in a large blue towel. "If it isn't the Storybook Family."

By ten past ten, they were all dressed and sitting in the limousine that would take them to the White House.

"Well." Her mother looked them over, then smiled. "Very good." She straightened the front of Steven's hair, fixed Neal's—even though he didn't need it—then lifted an eyebrow at Meg. "You look very old."

Meg glanced at herself, worried. "Is that bad?"

"It's just frightening," her father said, looking from her to her mother, and shaking his head.

Meg slouched against the seat. The clothes *did* feel too old. The boots were great, though—high black suede ones that kind of wrinkled at the ankles. Spiffy, her father had said. Her dress was a very basic, but unquestionably elegant, dove grey sweater dress, which reached down to her mid-calf—hiding her knees, too bad—and she was quite certain that it would look better on her mother. She was also wearing a long wool coat Beth had helped her pick out at the Chestnut Hill Bloomingdale's. She had gotten her hair cut so that now it just grazed her shoulders, and it was very full, making her look even more like her mother—except without quite the panache.

Instead of just being adorable, Neal was oddly masculine in grey flannel pants and a blue blazer from Brooks Brothers. Sort of a miniature adult. Steven's jacket was a brown herringbone tweed, and she knew he was going to die when he grew out of it. He'd stubbornly insisted on wearing his Top-Siders, saying he didn't want to be seen in any damn patent leather, and following his example, Neal rebelled, too. There was something appealing about the well-worn leather they'd both tried to shine.

She winked at her brothers, who were sitting in the jump seats, and they gave her shy smiles back.

So, for all his big talk, Steven was nervous. He probably *was* scared he would chew with his mouth open or something. She tilted her head, making a contorted face at him, and he laughed, the tight hands in his lap unfolding a little. She reached forward with her left boot and kicked him—quite hard—in the ankle, and he relaxed more, kicking back.

That taken care of, she studied her father. She didn't think of him as being handsome, but he was, in a craggy sort of way. He looked solid, he looked healthy. His suit was—big surprise—grey, and very distinguished. This wasn't a man who burned omelets and swore, especially when his wife only took one bite of hers and then set it aside; this was a man who was served a silver tray with poached fish, melon in season, light flaky croissants—she liked the man who burned omelets.

There was a myth or something about a person who could hold a bird in his hand, and no matter how hard the hand was crushed, the bird would be safe—there was something so strong and safe about the person that he could always protect the bird, no matter what. Her father was like that, she decided.

And maybe her mother was like the bird. No matter what happened, her mother would pop out without a feather ruffled. She might be little and scared—birds' hearts always beat like crazy when they were held—but then, it would open its mouth, start to sing or whatever, and it would suddenly seem very big. Yeah. Yeah, maybe that was her mother.

Meg grinned. Like, wow, how profound.

It wasn't exactly a shock that the President-elect looked smashing. So smashing, in fact, that Meg was almost positive that she'd heard Glen say quietly to the hair and make-up people, "Don't make her look *too* pretty." Not that the President-to-be was vain or anything, but she had apparently instructed her handlers *not* to follow that advice.

Her dress was bright blue, and very regal, and made her eyes seem even more striking than usual. Behind the scenes, it had taken quite a few weeks for her mother to find an American-designed dress that she genuinely thought would fit the occasion, and Meg knew that, privately, she was still wishing that she could have gotten away with wearing some of the French haute couture she had always—and, often, notoriously—preferred.

And, even though it was barely forty degrees, she had declined to wear a coat, although a minion had been duly assigned to carry gloves and a swingy short coat that looked more like a cape. Apparently, future world leaders *did not get cold.*

They had turned onto Pennsylvania Avenue, and the motorcade

was now stopping to go through one of the White House gates. They drove inside, pulling up in front of the house at the North Portico, where the President and the First Lady were waiting to receive them, with Marines in full dress uniform standing behind them at attention. A huge press pool was gathered in a strategic spot on the North Lawn to capture the moment for posterity.

"Wow," Steven whispered as they went inside, staring at the marble columns across the great hall, a red carpet running down another hall behind the pillars. The floor in the Entrance Hall was incredibly shiny, with a checkerboard pattern, and Meg hoped like hell that she wasn't going to slip in her new boots. There were huge chandeliers, and open doors behind the red carpet revealed what could only be the Green Room, the Blue Room, and the Red Room. On top of all of that, a small Marine Band, in bright red uniforms, was set up over to the right, playing traditional American tunes.

They were introduced to both the Curator and the Chief Usher, and other smiling White House employees seemed to be everywhere. And they were supposed to *live* here, and be at all normal?

"Why don't we go upstairs?" the President said, and they crossed to the left side of the hall, and walked up four red-carpeted steps to a small landing, and then more steps leading to the—also red-carpeted—Grand Staircase.

Dignified paintings of former Presidents hung on the walls, and Meg thought about how much the one of her mother was going to stick out someday. They were escorted upstairs, and through the Center Hall, which was yellow and quite formal, with lots of chairs and several small antique couches and settees, a small piano, and what looked like Chinese screens or something running along one wall. Famous paintings, mostly European, hung on the walls, and there were also built-in white bookcases, filled with historic artifacts—and even some books. There were fresh flowers all over the place—probably because this was such a big day, Meg figured. Having them all the time would be pretty expensive.

The President and the First Lady took them through some mahogany doors and into the Yellow Oval Room, which was where people like Popes and Queens were received. Again, there were priceless paintings, lots of upholstered chairs with dark wooden legs, along with two comfortable couches, and small antique tables covered with fragile china urns, candlesticks, and even more flowers.

After the President and First Lady took seats in the two chairs in front of the fireplace, Meg glanced at her mother for reassurance, and then tentatively sat down at the far end of one of the couches, her brothers immediately taking their places next to her.

Everyone was very friendly, and they were served coffee and cocoa in dainty cups, along with plates of fresh pastries, cookies, and petit-fours. Steven wiped his mouth with his napkin about ten thousand times to make sure he didn't have a moustache, and Neal imitated him, giggling and wiping his mouth, too.

The President and his wife asked the usual questions about school, how they felt about their mother being elected, and if they were looking forward to living in the White House. Meg thought all three of them answered rather quietly and bookishly. Neal dropped a pastry on the rug and looked terrified, but the President just laughed, leaning forward to scoop it up, saying that it happened all the time. It was nice that he hadn't been eligible to run again. If her mother had beaten him, this probably wouldn't be as relaxed.

Before noon, aides came in to say that it was time to go to the Capitol for the ceremony. Downstairs, the Marine quartet played "Hail to the Chief," and everyone shook hands a lot. Her mother and the President got into the limousine with flags on the hood and a Presidential seal and all. The second two were for Secret Service agents, and her father and the First Lady got into the next one. The former Vice-President, Mr. Kruger, and their wives got into the fifth car.

Meg and Steven and Neal sort of stood around, Meg baffled by motorcade protocol.

"This way, kids," an agent said. "We have to get moving, kids."

They were ushered into the seventh car; the President's two children—whom they had met upstairs—and the Vice-Presidents' children were all in other cars.

"Wow." Steven reached for the button to open his window and look at the long line of cars. "I bet this is really expensive."

"Hey." One of the agents in the front seat turned around. "I'm sorry, but you have to keep the windows up, kids."

Guiltily, Steven jerked back his hand.

"It's just a precaution," the man behind the wheel assured them. "We have a lot of rules around here."

They sure did.

AT THE CAPITOL, the Secret Service brought them up to the platform, facing out over the grassy mall that led to the Washington Monument. The theory was that the new President could look west and out over the country that way. Pretty whimsical, but definitely picturesque. They were supposed to sit in the front row, the entire Congress and other invited guests in chairs spreading out behind them. Everyone smiled as they went by, and cameras were going off like crazy.

"Where's Mommy and Daddy?" Neal asked, as they were seated on one side of the podium.

"Back there." Meg gestured with her head. "They have to wait inside until everything's ready to go."

"Do we have to keep smiling, in case the television cameras are pointed at us?" Steven asked, letting his teeth show.

Meg looked around, alarmed. "You think they're pointing at us?"

"They always film the families," Steven said.

Well—yeah. "I don't know." Meg shrugged nervously. "Look happy or something, I guess."

There were hundreds upon hundreds upon thousands of people below the platform, waiting to see the President-elect, hundreds and thousands of blurred faces—with untold millions more tuning in on television.

Neal gulped. "Meggie, I'm scared."

She took her eyes off the winter-clouded sky, afraid to look anywhere else, afraid of all the people. "Why?"

"They're all staring at us," he said.

"No," she said, flat-out lying. "They can't even see up here."

"But, what if they can?" He looked at the massive crowd, and then around the packed platform.

Meg shook her head. "They can't. I swear they can't."

"I don't feel good," he said uneasily.

"Oh, God," Steven groaned. "I'll die if he gets sick."

"He's not going to get sick." Meg closed her eyes, knowing, however, that he was fully capable of doing just that.

"I don't like it, Meggie." Neal's face was very pale. "I really don't like it. I want Mommy and Daddy here."

Jesus. "Steven, trade places with him," Meg said. What if Neal got sick on national television? What if *she* got sick on national television?

Now, Steven looked scared. "I'm not sitting over there."

"All right, all right," she said impatiently. "Trade places with me, then."

His face was now as pale as Neal's. "What if they wonder why we're doing it?"

She shook her head. "Nobody'll notice." Maybe.

He stood up, unsteadily, and she sat down between them. Neal's hand shot over and she took it, praying that he wouldn't get sick.

"Meg, I feel kind of funny, too," Steven said, his voice very small.

Who didn't? "Come on, you're fine." She made her voice hearty, in comparison. "This is going to be fun."

"Are you scared at all?" Neal asked.

"Why would I be? Mom and Dad'll be out here in a minute." She changed the subject. "What do you think they'll have to eat at the luncheon?"

"Squab," Steven said glumly. "And I'll get sick."

Meg had to grin. "You know, I bet everyone watching this on television thinks we have green faces."

"You mean, *you're* scared?" Steven asked.

"Well, sure," she said, without thinking. "I'd be kind of a jerk if I wasn't. Besides, no one's looking at us, anyway."

Neither of her brothers seemed to be convinced, and just as she was starting to feel pretty sick herself, there was a flurry of activity on the platform, everyone standing up and looking behind them towards the Capitol itself.

"What is it? What is it?" Neal asked, sounding petrified as he tried to see over all of the people.

The Marine Band went into "Hail to the Chief."

"I think it's Mom and Dad," Meg said.

16

THE PRESIDENT AND the First Lady came out to the platform with her parents, and the crowd cheered and applauded for several minutes, while they waved, and then finally, took their seats on either side of the podium.

Her mother, cheeks bright with excitement, smiled down the row at them, and her father leaned over, touching each one of their left shoulders for a second. Meg felt her nausea ebbing at the security of having their parents there, and saw her brothers relaxing, too.

The ovation finally died down, fading into near-silence, and it was time for her mother to be sworn in. Her parents looked at them, and Meg felt a strange long privacy in the seconds of eye contact, the people and noise blotted out, as if—for that brief moment—no one except their family existed. The intensity was kind of scary, maybe because it was so powerful, and no one else in the world had been part of it. Her parents were up now, and she saw their fingertips barely touch before they got to the podium, where the Chief Justice of the Supreme Court was waiting with an open Bible.

And it was very quiet.

"Raise your right hand and repeat after me," the Chief Justice said, the sound echoing through the speakers.

Her mother put her left hand on the Bible, lifting her right hand, and Meg could see it shaking slightly.

"I, Katharine Vaughn Powers, do solemnly swear," he said.

"I, Katharine Vaughn Powers, do solemnly swear." Her mother's voice was clear and strong, going out over the people.

The Chief Justice smiled at her. "That I will faithfully execute the office of the President of the United States."

"That I will faithfully execute the office of the President of the United States," her mother said.

"And will, to the best of my ability, preserve, protect, and defend the Constitution of the United States," he went on.

"And will, to the best of my ability, preserve, protect, and defend the Constitution of the United States," she said.

"So help you God," he finished.

"So help me God." Her mother's head tilted up for an instant, and Meg looked up, too, hoping that if there *was* some kind of higher power up there, he or she was listening.

"Thank you, Mr. Chief Justice," her mother said.

"Thank you, Madam President," he said.

The Marine Band started in on "Hail to the Chief" again, and everyone was standing and applauding, the now-former President and other government officials moving to shake her mother's hand. Before any of them could, Meg saw her parents tightly grip right hands, and then her mother turned, giving the three of them a quick, conspiring wink.

President. Her mother was the President of the country. *The Leader of the Free World.* Feeling sick again, Meg wanted to sit down, but everyone would notice.

"Meggie, clap!" Steven hissed, elbowing her.

Meg clapped, everyone clapped, and her mother—the President—stood there, smiling and waving—with the entire country, and probably most of the entire *world*, watching her. She gave her speech, and people went wild, interrupting her with applause about every third sentence. Speaking from only a few note cards, without prepared typescript—nothing new there, although obviously there was a copy of what was supposed to be the final draft of the speech scrolling on the teleprompter—speaking with sincere conviction and strength, it was clear that this was now the President of the United States. A calm, confident, and very hopeful President of the United States. Also, a very funny President of the United States.

After the ceremony ended in a confusion of more handshaking and applause, they went to a Congressional luncheon, then down Pennsylvania Avenue in the motorcade to watch the Inaugural Parade—which was long, and got very dull—from the official viewing stand. Then, finally, they were in the White House, standing in the entrance hall where they had been only a few hours earlier.

Only now, this was their *home*.

"Well." Her mother smiled at the four of them, then at Glen, and Linda, and Preston, and the many other new Presidential aides grouped around them, as well as the Curator and the Chief Usher.

"There are a few matters that need your attention, but the only thing you really need to do is sign those Cabinet appointments," Glen said. Then he grinned, which made him look about ten years younger. "Madam President."

"Quite right." Her mother grinned back, then looked at the family. "What do you all want to do?"

"Can we check this place out?" Steven asked.

"Absolutely." Her mother gave him a one-armed hug, then glanced at various aides. "I'll want to see all of you in the Oval Office at four-thirty, for a few minutes. Linda, why don't you go down to the Briefing Room, and tell them I'll be in to make a statement and take a few questions at five. I think that's all."

"Madam President?" the Curator asked. "Do you want me to accompany—"

"No, thank you, although that's very kind," she said. "I'd like to be alone with my family for a while." She nodded a nod of dismissal, and her aides and the White House permanent staff members dispersed, most of them heading for the West Wing and their new offices, others moving towards the East Wing. Her mother watched them go. "This could really grow on me," she said.

Meg's father laughed. "You're a wonderful President."

"Come on, let's look around already," Steven said impatiently.

"Quite right." Their mother struck out across the marble floor, between two pillars to the red carpet.

A number of Secret Service agents had stayed behind—they all had protection everywhere, except for the family quarters on the second and third floors of the Residence—but, they seemed to be making an effort to melt into the woodwork, and trailed them at a discreet distance.

Neal pointed to a plaque on the floor that said "1817, 1792–1902, 1952." "What's that?"

"Those are the dates for the original building, and the reconstructions," their mother said.

It seemed sort of obscure—but, okay, why not?

They walked down to the East Room, past some guards, who smiled. Neal stopped in the doorway, his mouth open.

"It's beautiful," he said, his voice hushed.

"Wow. Cool." Steven went in first, stepping carefully on the well-polished oak floor, staring up at the gold chandeliers and tall, gold-draped windows, paintings of George and Martha Washington dominating the huge room. He paused by the grand piano, which was held up by gold, carved eagles, instead of regular legs. "Come on, Meg, play 'Greensleeves.' "

"I know other songs," she said.

"Then, how come you never play 'em?" he asked.

Well, he had her there. Meg glanced back at one of the guards, then hesitantly touched middle C on the piano, the sound echoing across the room. "Are we allowed to play this?"

"We live here," her father said.

Oh. Right. She sat down on the gold-and-white upholstered bench. "I bet even 'Greensleeves' sounds professional on this."

"Hey, check it out!" Steven said, from one of the two doors near the fireplace. "What's this one?"

Meg went over to join him. "The Green Room, stupid, can't you tell?"

"Just 'cause it's green, they call it the Green Room? I think *that*'s pretty stupid." He sat down in a green chair, trying to look solemn.

Neal laughed, and promptly stretched out on a stiff green, gold, and white striped couch, pretending to be asleep.

"Cute," Meg said.

"I think it is," her mother said, going over and pretending to tuck him in. Then, she pointed through another door. "Steven, what do you think this room is?"

He got up, looked through the door, and snorted. "The *Blue* Room, right?"

Their mother nodded.

"They've got a wicked lot of imagination, hunh?" he said, and wandered over to the huge windows at the end of the oval room. "Is that like, the backyard?"

Okay, she was officially unimpressed by his powers of recall. "We've *been* there, Steven," Meg said. To Congressional picnics, and a couple of Fourth of July celebrations. He and Neal had even played T-ball out there once.

For some reason, that made both of her parents laugh.

"Been there, seen *that,* right, Meg?" her mother said.

Hey, she'd come by the attitude honestly. She looked up at the ceiling—which had yet another massive chandelier. "Is that yellow room we were in before above this?"

Her father nodded, then went over to join Steven by the windows. "That porch out there is the South Portico."

As far as Meg knew, they had come in through the North Portico. "What's a portico?" she asked.

Her father shrugged. "A porch."

"A porch with a roof supported by columns," her mother elaborated.

"Oh," her father grinned at her, "the woman thinks she's smart because she's President."

"Oh, Christ," Steven said, from yet another doorway. "This's the Red Room, right?"

"Watch it with the Christs," their father said, and Steven saluted.

Next was the State Dining Room, gold and comparatively austere, with a painting of Lincoln frowning down from over the mantelpiece.

"What, is this like, if the Queen or someone comes?" Meg asked.

Her mother nodded. "If the Queen comes." She opened yet another door. "This is the Family Dining Room."

Which was cheerful enough, but large and very formal. Meg stared dubiously at the long mahogany table, a silver antique tray covering most of it. "We *eat* here?"

"Tonight, we will," her mother said. "But, usually, we'll be upstairs. Although it isn't much better."

Meg folded her arms, not wanting to start trouble. "Is the whole house like this?" Namely, chandeliers, antiques, paintings—and nothing that looked at all comfortable.

Her mother looked at her. "Pretty much."

"I figured," Meg said.

Her mother opened her mouth to say something, then stopped. "Well. Would you like to look around downstairs now?"

Meg shrugged and followed her down what seemed to be a private staircase, leaving her father and brothers behind. "Are you mad about tonight?" she asked.

"It's not too late for you to change your mind and come," her mother said.

Meg sighed. She probably shouldn't have brought it up—her not going to the Inaugural Balls had been an issue for weeks now. "I'm sorry, I'm just really not into it. But I don't want you guys to be mad at me."

"'Disappointed' is a better word," her mother said. "I think you'd have a good time."

Or else, die of embarrassment.

Her mother stopped, leaning back against the railing, which looked a little precarious, considering that it was a spiral staircase. "Well, as your father and I have said, we're not going to *make* you come."

"But, you're disappointed," Meg said.

Her mother laughed. "Yes. I may not go myself."

Meg smiled uncertainly. "That's a joke, right?"

Her mother just laughed.

They took a quick tour of the busy kitchen—where chefs and sous chefs and prep cooks and butlers and so forth instantly snapped to attention, when they saw her mother. Then, they went across the hall to the medical area, which included treatment rooms, her mother's new doctor—who was a Navy Rear Admiral—reception areas, and several on-duty nurses—and, once again, everyone sprang to their feet when they saw the President poke her head in.

A reaction her mother did not seem to find at all unsettling. She also seemed to find it routine—already—that Winifred, the new deputy chief of staff, and Frank, who was now officially her personal aide, kept appearing every so often, and saying something quiet to her, and she would nod, shake her head, or murmur something back in response.

The Ground Floor Corridor was actually more cool than the Cross Hall upstairs, because the ceiling curved upwards, and it looked sort of subterranean—and futuristic. They checked out the Map Room, the odd old North Hall, and the Curator's reference-book-cluttered office—and then met back up with her father and brothers in the Diplomatic Reception Room, which was large and oval, dominated by painted wallpaper that showed early American scenes, with a lot of what looked like Pilgrims.

After that, they wandered through the China Room—which bored Meg almost as much as it did her brothers—the Vermeil Room, and the Library. They didn't take the time to visit it, but apparently, there was even a bowling alley on this level, built underneath the

North Portico. None of them had ever particularly bowled—but it was kind of neat to have it right in the house, in case they wanted to or something.

"This place is really cool," Steven said, as they walked upstairs to the second-floor family quarters—although, with those high heels, Meg had a sneaking suspicion that her mother might have preferred taking their private elevator.

"This place is really *big,*" Neal said.

The second floor was connected by three large halls—the East, the Center, and the West. A low ramp led up to the East Sitting Hall, and Neal asked sympathetically if it had been put in to help crippled people, but it turned out that the east end of the floor was raised slightly, because the ceiling in the East Room underneath it was so high.

The East Sitting Hall itself had yellowish-gold walls, and was set up as a small reception area, with a formal couch and chairs, and an impressive half-circle window with decorated panes, which made it look almost like a spiderweb. The Lincoln Bedroom and Sitting Room opened off one side of the hall, the bedroom itself bold and masculine, with lots of mahogany furniture and gold-patterned wallpaper. On the other side of the hall was the Queen's Bedroom, which also included a formal Sitting Room and large bathroom.

Meg looked at the canopy bed, and the undeniably royal surroundings. "Bet you guys want me to sleep in here, right?"

"Yeah," Steven said. "Far away from us."

They went into the Treaty Room, which seemed to be an upstairs office—to the point of being sort of intimidating, although Neal immediately flopped down on a big red hassock and started bouncing.

Meg sat down in the leather executive chair, behind a heavy walnut table—upon which she assumed many treaties had been signed. "Wow." She touched the heavily polished surface. "Bet I could really get homework done in here."

"Yeah, me, too." Steven tried to open the drawers built into the Victorian table, except that they all seemed to be locked. "Will you sign junk in here, Mom?"

Their mother looked slowly around the room, and then grinned. "I don't think I'll be able to resist."

They went through the Center Hall, past the Yellow Oval Room where they'd had coffee that morning, to the West Sitting Hall.

Neal pointed at the couch and two matched armchairs. "Hey, that's our stuff!"

"So you'll remember that this is our house," their father said, ruffling his hair.

"Wow, I'm glad." Neal sat in one of the chairs, looking very pleased.

Their mother pointed through a fancy semi-circular window that seemed to match the one in the East Sitting Hall. "You can see the Oval Office from here."

Steven threw himself onto the couch, taking off his jacket. "Is this like, where we're supposed to hang out?"

Their father nodded. "A lot of the families do, I gather."

Meg explored a little more, finding a kitchen with two butlers and a cook, all of whom smiled and nodded, a fancy dining room, a huge bedroom—which had a lot of her parents' stuff unpacked in it already—and a smaller dressing room next door. The gigantic bedroom connected to a living room—through a door that actually looked like part of the wall, with wallpaper covering it and everything. The living room had some of their furniture from Massachusetts, too, and she walked through it to a small hallway with a master bathroom and a closet on one side, and what seemed to be more closets on the other side.

The hallway opened into the Center Hall, and she crossed over to another hallway that had an elevator, a private staircase, and what looked like a *beauty parlor* at the end. There were also more closets, and two bedroom suites, one of which was very, very *pink*.

"This is *way* ugly," Steven said, standing behind her.

Meg nodded. Had they thought that a female President wouldn't be happy unless there were pink bedrooms around, or something?

As they walked back to the West Sitting Hall, a butler was just coming out of the kitchen.

"Madam President, may we get you or your family anything?" he asked.

"Thank you. I'm perfectly fine, Jason, but I'm not sure about everyone else," her mother said. "Oh. These are my children. My sons, Steven and Neal, and my daughter, Meghan."

"Hi," Meg said, her brothers also sounding quiet and bookish.

"Hey, yo," Steven said suddenly. "Where's Kirby?"

"Yeah, where's Vanessa?" She hadn't seen her cat since they'd left the apartment that morning. Staff people had been instructed to bring the animals to the White House, but they must have forgotten.

"They have been put in kennels downstairs," the butler said, "for the time—"

"Kennels?" Steven said. "They don't live in *kennels*!"

Her mother nodded. "Traditionally, animals—particularly dogs—have—"

"If Vanessa has to live in a kennel, *I'm* living in a kennel," Meg said.

"*But,*" her mother went on, "we just arranged to have them kept downstairs until we got here."

"Oh," Meg said, and saw that Steven now looked as embarrassed as she felt.

"I'll have them sent upstairs right away, Madam President," Jason said, and bowed slightly before stepping out.

"Okay, then," her mother said. "We have more bedrooms upstairs, a billiards room, a solarium—"

"What's that?" Neal asked.

"Oh, you're going to love it," she said. "Lots of windows, plants, a little kitchen, the best television I may have ever seen—you three will probably take it over. At any rate, your father and I figured that you would probably want a bedroom down here, Neal, that you'd take the other one or go up to the third floor, Steven, and you'd be upstairs, Meg."

"I'd rather be down here," Steven said quickly.

Well, *yeah*. "I have to be upstairs by myself?" Meg asked. "I don't want to be by myself." In an historic house that was supposed to have *ghosts*.

"Oh." Her father looked surprised. "Your mother and I just assumed you'd want privacy."

Meg shook her head. Vehemently. "I don't. I'd rather live with you guys." Especially here. At *home,* she'd want privacy.

"But, you haven't even seen it up there yet," he said.

"What, you want me to be away from everyone?" Meg asked, knowing that they had probably meant well, but still hurt.

Her father laughed, putting a calming arm around her. "No, we want you where we can always see your smiling face."

She moved away from his arm. "Now you're making fun of me."

"A little," he said.

Great.

"Meg," her mother said, "I'd prefer that you were down here with us, anyway—I *want* the family to be together. We need to be together. So—" She moved out to the Center Hall and opened the door to the room that looked like a living room. "Neal, how would you like to be in here?"

Neal looked uneasy. "I have to sleep on a couch?"

Their father grinned. "I think we can probably find you a bed. And maybe even a dresser or something."

Now, Neal beamed. "So, I get to be right next to you and Mommy?"

"Absolutely." Their mother gave him a small hug. "Now, you two can fight over the other two rooms."

Meg and Steven looked at each other.

"I don't do pink," he said.

"Neither do I," she said.

"We'll have it redecorated," her mother said, an answer ready for everything. No wonder she was President. "I'm sure they can do it in blue or green, or whatever you want. We can get them started on it tomorrow." She glanced at her watch. "And now, if you'll excuse me, I think it's time to go to work for a while."

"Can we come, too?" Neal asked.

"I think maybe I have to be by myself. Dinner at six-thirty?" She smiled at all of them, then headed towards the elevator, her walk much slower in this house than it was at home. A very dignified walk.

"There goes the President," Meg said.

Her father shuddered. "The mind boggles."

17

HER FAMILY DIDN'T really have many relatives—her father's sister and her husband, and their two sons, who were in their late twenties, then two great-aunts, both of them Vaughns, very old and proper and kind of disturbed by the idea of a Vaughn being elected President—so, a lot of her parents' friends had dinner at the White House before the Inaugural Balls. Meg felt like a little bit of a jerk because she wasn't going, but she had this very sharp image of herself sitting alone in some corner, the wallflower of all-time, and people like the Speaker of the House—who was notoriously conservative, but still a really good friend of her mother's—asking her to dance, because they felt sorry for her.

Dinner was a major production, with roast beef and Yorkshire pudding—which just happened to be the President's favorite meal. Only, people were too excited to eat and kept jumping up to make toasts and everything. Whenever someone shouted, "Toast!" Meg wanted to play *Rocky Horror Picture Show* and throw bread at them.

At one point, Steven leaned over and said that the painting of Lincoln—they were in the State Dining Room—was frowning because he was disgusted by Meg's table manners, and they laughed so hard that their father had to frown at them. Decorum. *Toujours* decorum.

When her parents left for the Balls, they looked about as good as Meg had ever seen them. Her father, very formal in white tie, was wearing gloves and carrying a silk hat that he was too embarrassed to put on. Her mother's dress—once again, designed by an American, albeit one of French descent—was a smooth, simple black with immeasurably flattering lines. She didn't look over forty. She didn't look over *thirty.*

Which was going to charm part of the country—and terrify the rest of them.

The neckline on the dress was a thin, sort of oval, V-neck that would probably become a wildly popular fashion. The Presidential Look, it would be called. Her father was right—the mind had to boggle.

Her mother had put her hair up, and soft tendrils curled around her very high cheekbones. She wore elbow-length gloves, and a short, elegant jacket, which matched the dress. Her father had an evening cape—which made Steven laugh his head off. They were both flushed with excitement and, standing together, made a pretty incredible picture. They also made Meg glad that she wasn't going—she really would have felt in the way.

Alone in the house, Meg and her brothers wandered for a while, met more butlers and maids and stewards, and unpacked a little. They ended up in the solarium—which *was* a great room, all couches and windows—and incredible views of the Washington Monument and Jefferson Memorial, watching their parents on television at the Balls. Kirby stayed with them, the cats came in and out, and a butler named Felix brought up some food.

Steven took a cookie and leaned back on his couch. "This is pretty excellent. I didn't know they waited on us and everything."

If she were taking bets about which one of them was the most likely to let the White House go to his or her head, Steven and her mother would tie for first place. She looked over at Neal, and saw that Kirby had climbed up next to him, and now, the two of them were asleep next to each other.

"The kid practices being cute," Steven said.

Quite possibly. Meg helped herself to a cookie. "Kirby's probably not supposed to be up there."

"It's a *couch,*" Steven said. "Not like, antique."

Maybe. "Well, I guess it's okay," Meg said uneasily.

The television was focusing on her parents dancing together, and they looked very happy. Earlier, one of the bands had played a tango—which clearly amused her mother, and frightened her father. Dancing wasn't his best skill. Probably, most people were watching her mother, anyway. The woman looked good. Very good.

Meg watched as she whispered something to her father, he whispered back, and they both laughed, still dancing.

And she was almost *sure* that they weren't paying any attention to the cameras. Especially when the song ended, and he brushed his lips across her hair for a second. Usually, they were too reserved to do anything like that in public.

After a while, Steven fell asleep, too, and Meg got them both downstairs and into bed—a bed and dresser and small desk having magically appeared in Neal's new bedroom while they were at dinner.

The cats' main litter box was in the Presidential bathroom—which they probably weren't going to advertise to the country—and she had one for Vanessa in her bathroom, too. She carried Humphrey and Vanessa down from the solarium, and put them each inside one of the boxes, to remind them. Sidney and Adlai were asleep on her parents' bed, and she decided to assume that they were well aware of where their box was.

When she was standing in the middle of the Center Hall, trying to figure out what to do with herself, Felix appeared. He was an older African-American man, and seemed to be very kind.

"Miss Powers, would you like me to arrange to have your dog taken out?" he asked.

Hmmm. She thought about that. "Do I need Secret Service, if I do it?"

He nodded.

She wasn't really in the mood to be guarded right now. "Is it a pain if you guys do it? I mean, like, just this once?"

He shook his head. "Not at all, Miss Powers."

Which was a relief, but she still felt kind of funny about it. Then, she remembered something else. "Um, sir?" she asked. "Is it all right if I make a phone call? I mean, are there rules?"

He shook his head, smiling at her. "No rules. Would you like me to get a number for you?"

She wasn't even going to *ask* if it was okay to use anything other than a secure land-line. "Are you supposed to?"

"It's no trouble," he said.

Okay, he was just being helpful. "That's okay, sir," she said. "I mean, thank you, but I'm fine."

There were telephones all over the place, but she decided to use the one in her room. Her very pink room.

Beth answered on the third ring.

"Hi," Meg said.

Beth sighed. "Oh, God. Thought I'd heard the last of you."

No such luck. "Guess not," Meg said.

"I can't believe you didn't break down and go," Beth said. "What a jerk."

That was probably a fair description. Meg sat down on the bed, which had four posters and a very high mattress. "Yeah, I know. What's going on?"

"Same old whirlwind of activities," Beth said. "You know. What's it like there?"

"I don't know." Meg looked around at the stiff and unfamiliar bedroom, which had its own fireplace, bathroom, two built-in bookcases, and a view of the North Lawn and Lafayette Square. "Scary. I don't like it much."

"You haven't even been there overnight," Beth said.

Good point.

"What," Beth said, "you called me just to grouch?"

Something like that, yeah. "I just—I don't know." She let out her breath. "Steven says he heard the White House has a self-destruct button somewhere." Which had been giving her the creeps ever since he'd mentioned it. Along with the notion of the other security secrets she didn't know.

Beth laughed. "Well, you'd better hope he doesn't *find* it."

True enough. Although she liked to think that if he did, he would have the good sense to run in the other direction. "I don't want to start school, either," Meg said.

"My God, Meg, they're going to be afraid of *you*," Beth said.

Not likely. Meg shook her head. "But, I'm just normal."

"Well," Beth said, "let's not get carried away."

Now, it was Meg's turn to laugh. "And you call *me* a jerk."

They talked for a while longer, mostly about stuff going on in Massachusetts, but a little about Washington. It was Beth's opinion that Meg and her brothers had been, as Meg suspected, distinctly pale green during the Inauguration before her parents came out. Chartreuse, even.

"Oh, I forgot," Beth said, as they were hanging up. "Is it okay if I recorded this conversation? Bucknell wants me to keep in touch with you, so the class can like, share your experiences and everything."

"You know what Bucknell can do?" Meg asked.

"I *am* taping this," Beth reminded her.

"You'll be hearing from my lawyer," Meg said.

After they finished talking, Meg felt very lonely again. For a place that was full of people—guards and aides and personal staff and everything—the White House was about as quiet as any place she had ever been. She went back up to the third floor, watched some more coverage of the Inaugural Balls, and looked around at the massive entertainment collection in the main hallway. As far as she knew, film and music companies donated copies of their movies and CDs and all on a regular basis. Not a bad fringe benefit.

She returned to the second floor and played around for a while, sitting in the Yellow Oval Room and the Treaty Room, then remembered that Lincoln's ghost was supposed to come out at night, and ran—quietly—back down towards the west end of the floor. If worse came to worst, she could always wake Steven up—and pretend that she had done it by accident.

She went into her very pink room, looked at the books some unknown stranger had unpacked and put on the shelves for her, and took out a copy of *Living History*—which she had appropriated from her mother's collection, long ago. Kind of a fun book to read in the White House. She carried it out to the West Sitting Hall, deciding to wait there until her parents got home.

It was pretty comfortable, sitting on the couch from home with her feet resting on Kirby's back, and she must have fallen asleep, because suddenly she smelled perfume and saw her mother sitting next to her.

She tried to wake up, wondering who had covered her with a light blanket. "What time is it?"

"Almost three," her mother said, reaching over to smooth her hair back.

"Oh." Meg yawned. "You guys have a good time?"

Her mother nodded. "We had a marvelous time."

"Your mother was the belle of the ball," her father said, taking off his gloves.

Felix came out of the kitchen. "Is there anything we can do for you, Madam President, Mr. Powers?"

"No, thank you," her mother said. "And please—much as I appreciate it—I don't want you all to think you need to stay late like this."

Felix nodded politely, and returned to his post.

The staff probably wasn't going to be thrilled when they found out that her family tended to be night owls on a regular basis.

"Steven and Neal asleep?" her mother asked.

Meg yawned again. "Yeah. They were pretty tired."

"Maybe you ought to get some sleep yourself," her father said.

"Yeah, I guess." She glanced around, remembering all of the guests who were supposed to be spending the night, mostly up on the third floor. "Where is everyone?"

"Downstairs celebrating," her mother said. "If tonight is any indication, I'm afraid my administration is going to be known for drunken revelry."

Meg grinned. "Does that mean you guys, too?"

"Nope." Her father stumbled and fell on the couch.

Her mother laughed. "Will you stop?"

"Melly, I ain't so very drunk," he said. Slurred, really.

Her mother laughed again, and Meg put on an intelligent smile, almost sure that he was referring to a scene in *Gone with the Wind*. She hated it when she didn't get her parents' references.

Last of the big-time Babbitts.

Damn it.

"Take your hands off me, woman!" her father was mumbling.

"You're very silly, but you're awfully cute," her mother said, and looked at Meg. "I love this man very much, in spite of himself."

"Should I, uh—" Meg edged towards her room—"maybe leave on that note?"

Her father got up, no longer drunk. "Sleep well, kid."

"Night, First Gentleman." She shook hands with him, then with her mother. "Night, Madam President."

Her mother smiled. "Good night. Do you need any—"

Meg shook her head. "No, thanks. Think I can deal with it. I'm glad you guys had a good time."

"The revelry hasn't even *started*," her father said, drunk again.

Meg grinned back at them and went to her room, noticing that someone had turned down her bed and laid out a nightgown—although there were no chocolates, because, frankly, she *looked*. Usually, she slept in old, very large t-shirts.

There was a scratch on the door, and she quickly let Vanessa in, before she could do any damage, then started to get undressed.

This room was extremely pink. The sooner she turned the lights off, the better.

SHE WAS UP and dressed by eight the next morning, deciding to wear a skirt—just in case, but hoping she'd be able to go back to regular clothes soon. The plan was for her family to have a private breakfast in the Presidential Dining Room, while everyone else slept late.

The dining room had deep blue draperies, a blue, gold, and white rug, and its antique wallpaper was covered with scenes from the Revolutionary War. Battle scenes. The table was already set beneath the huge chandelier, with an arrangement of fresh flowers—mostly yellow roses—as a centerpiece. As she hesitated on the threshold, yet another butler came out to greet her. How many *were* there?

"Good morning, Miss Powers," he said, and bowed a little, the way most of them seemed to do. "What would you like for breakfast?"

Meg resisted the urge to curtsy back. "You mean, I can choose?"

He nodded.

"Wow, not bad." She thought for a minute. "What do you have?"

"Just about everything," he said.

"Okay. Um, orange juice?" she asked.

He nodded, and she could tell that he wanted to smile.

"And—cereal?" she asked.

"Certainly," he said. "What kind would you like?"

"Hmmm." She shot a glance at the door. "Do you have Captain Crunch?"

He nodded again. "We weren't sure what you and your brothers liked."

"Oh, wow, great," Meg said, impressed. "All we get at home is boring junk. Mom and Dad always say—" She stopped, deciding not to mention that her parents thought cereal with added sugar would rot their teeth out—and make them hyper and annoying, to boot. "Yeah, that sounds good. I'd like some Captain Crunch, please."

"Anything else?" he asked. "Toast? English muffins? Doughnuts?"

Meg grinned. "Sure. Oh, and could you bring the box, please?"

He looked confused.

"I like to read the cereal box," she said. "It's kind of a habit."

"I'll bring the box." The butler left the room, smiling.

Meg glanced around, finding the bold Revolutionary scenes somewhat intimidating. She'd read somewhere that a few previous Administrations had taken the wallpaper down and painted the walls yellow or light green, depending. Why would anyone have wanted to put the war back up? It was going to be like eating in Cyclorama.

She studied the five place settings, and the ornate silverware, then touched one of the glasses, which was very thin and delicate. Boy, the staff was going to hate Steven. He was always breaking things. She sat down, deciding on the chair that corresponded to her position at home. This wasn't a table where a person could lean her elbows. It also probably wouldn't be appropriate to throw mashed potatoes, either. In spite of age and maturity and all those things, she and Steven generally threw mashed potatoes. It had gotten so that Trudy refused to make them anymore.

She heard tentative footsteps, and Steven peeked into the room.

"Hi," she said.

"Hi." He came in, subdued in neat flannel slacks, a dark blue sweater, and a white Oxford shirt.

"Where's your tie?" she asked.

"What?" He stopped, looking down at himself. "Do I have to wear a bloody tie just to have *breakfast*?"

"Hey, watch your mouth!" she hissed, checking the door.

"Yeah, well, I'm not wearing a stupid tie," he hissed back. "Mom won't make me!"

The butler came in, carrying a silver tray. "Good morning, Master Powers," he said, pouring juice from a crystal pitcher into Meg's glass.

"Uh, hi," Steven said.

"What would you like for breakfast?" The butler set a pitcher of milk on the table, along with a basket of hot muffins. Then he lifted the box of Captain Crunch, filling Meg's bowl.

"What she has looks pretty good," Steven said. "We never get to have decent cereal."

The butler smiled, and brought the box over.

"Would you like anything else?" he asked, after pouring Steven some juice as well, and making sure that they both had muffins.

"No, thank you," Meg said.

"No, thank you," Steven said. Then, as soon as the butler was gone, he put down his spoon. "Some room."

Meg nodded. "That's for sure. Don't the walls make you nervous?"

"Yeah." He looked up at the chandelier. "If that thing falls, we're in trouble."

"Good morning," their mother said, striding into the room.

Apparently, being the President agreed with her, because after no more than a couple of hours of sleep, she still looked cheerful and refreshed.

"You look nice, Mom," she said.

"You think?" Her mother checked her outfit, adjusting the cuff of her dress—which was dark red—and pushing her gold bracelet down. She lifted an eyebrow at Steven's bowl. "Captain Crunch?"

"Want some?" he asked.

"Why not," she said, and reached for the box.

The butler hurried in. "Madam President? What may I bring you?"

"Good morning," she said, smiling at him. "Just some coffee, please."

"The President of the United States should have some protein," Meg said.

Her mother shrugged. "So should the President's daughter."

Which Meg took as a cue to drop the subject. Immediately.

Neal and her father came in with Kirby, who went under the table the same way he did at home, presumably expecting people to sneak him food.

Neal stopped when he saw Steven, and scowled at their father. "He's not wearing a tie—how come I have to?"

"Can't make me wear a bloody tie," Steven said.

Neal yanked his off. "Then, *I'm* not wearing a bloody tie!"

"You two looking for trouble?" their father asked.

"Ground them," Meg said, reading the nutritional information on the box. "Ground them for *months*."

Their mother shook her head, putting half an English muffin on her plate. "Ah, another joyful morning with the Storybook Family." She smiled pleasantly at the butler as he brought milk and sugar for her coffee. "That's skim, right?"

The butler nodded. "Yes, Madam President. Unless you would prefer fresh cream, or—?"

"No, this is perfect, thanks," she said.

Well, okay, that made sense. The staff would have been briefed extensively about the incoming President's likes and dislikes. Quirks. Habits. Pet peeves, even.

"You're going to try and be President without a decent breakfast?" Meg's father asked.

Her mother waved that off, flipping through the stack of folders and papers to the left of her plate and skimming the top page of the morning news summary some aide must have prepared.

"Kate, make me happy," he said. "Have a poached egg or something."

She laughed, spooning up some cereal.

"Wow, Captain Crunch!" Neal grabbed the box. "Do we get to have this all the time now?"

"Yes," Steven and Meg said.

"No," their father said.

Neal looked at their mother. "Mom?"

"No comment," she said, picking up the *Washington Post*—which had banner headlines about the Inauguration above the fold.

The butler came in with a beautiful platter of sliced fresh fruit, which he put within easy reach of her mother. He refilled her barely touched coffee cup, then held up the silver pot inquiringly, and her father nodded. "What else may I bring you, Mr. Powers?" he asked.

He gave the entire family a pointed look. "Could I have a couple of poached eggs, please?"

"Right away, sir." The butler turned to Neal. "Master Powers?"

Neal giggled.

"Would you like some eggs?" the butler asked. "Or some French toast, or—"

Neal shook his head, giggling.

"How about 'no, thank you'?" their father suggested.

"No, thank you," Neal said.

Steven grabbed another muffin. "Robot."

"Sexist unscrupulous puppet," Meg said, taking one, too.

"Bad-mannered children," their father said.

The butler waited until they were finished—and Meg was pretty sure he felt like laughing. "Would anyone else like anything? Madam President?"

"Yes, actually. Thank you." Her mother lowered her newspaper, her eyes terribly amused. "You wouldn't happen to have a box of Frosted Flakes back there, would you?"

18

MEG AND STEVEN kept trying to count all of the White House employees, but there were so many people like laundresses, switchboard operators, doormen, electricians, and carpenters—to say nothing of the butlers, cooks, maids, and gardeners—that they gave up after a while, deciding to just call it the Cast of Thousands. Weird place, the White House.

For the next few days, her mother held near-constant receptions—and teas, and breakfasts, and luncheons, and dinners—for members of Congress, for new staff members and their spouses, for government civil service employees, for the permanent White House staff and their families, for the press, for various branches of the military, for prominent donors, and so forth. When Meg and her brothers didn't have to make appearances, they continued checking out the house and the grounds, trying to get used to everything.

Whenever they went outside, agents would accompany them, and—almost always—tourists beyond the cast-iron fences would point and wave and aim cameras at them. Between ten and twelve in the morning, they were supposed to try and stay away from the State Floor, because small tours were usually being given. Steven thought it would be funny to go down to the East Room some morning, and bang on the piano for them or something, but her parents made a point of strongly discouraging this idea.

There were lots of special gardens outside: the Rose Garden, the Jacqueline Kennedy Garden, and the Children's Garden. It turned out that there was even a fully functioning greenhouse up on the roof of the Residence, which they found when they were walking around the Promenade, outside the solarium. The Children's Garden was near the tennis court—where Meg planned to spend every moment of her free time, once the snow melted. There was also an outdoor heated pool, south of the Oval Office, well hidden by foliage, a small basketball court, a putting green, and a jogging track—as well as a full gym and work-out room, up on the third floor. And they had already gotten to watch a just-released movie in the Family Theater, on the first floor in the East Wing.

Most of the trees and shrubs on the grounds were marked with little signs, and Steven got a kick out of taking Kirby over to the Jimmy Carter Cedar of Lebanon or the Franklin D. Roosevelt Small-leaved Linden. It was possible that the gardeners and horticulturists were less amused by this.

On Saturday, her parents were going to be gone most of the day and early evening, attending thank-you events for campaign workers and donors, a special mass at the National Cathedral, and a reception at the British Embassy. Her mother suggested that the three of them spend the afternoon exploring the city a little, and having nothing better to do, Meg and her brothers agreed.

After her parents had left, and Steven was in the kitchen getting more to eat, Meg went to find out what was taking Neal so long. She found him in his room, on his bed with his shoulders slouched, looking close to tears.

"What's wrong?" she asked. "Come on, we're ready to go."

He shook his head.

He had seemed fine during brunch, although maybe a little quiet. She had just assumed he was feeling shy, because they ate downstairs with about four hundred Congressional staffers, as opposed to their bosses—the second in a series of three get-togethers that had been one of Preston's brainstorms, and would almost certainly pay off down the road, when it came to passing difficult legislation.

"Come on, it's going to be fun," she said. "We can go to the museum with all the rockets and everything. Remember that one? With the planes?" She sat next to him. "What is it? Don't you feel good?"

He looked up at her with very worried eyes. "Are Mommy and Daddy safe?"

"Well—yeah," she said. Especially considering that, at this very moment, she was pretty sure they were inside a *church*. "They're just doing regular political stuff."

"Rob told me," he gulped, quoting his best friend in Massachusetts, "he said we have to have guards because people want to hurt us. Like—like with *guns*. Especially Mommy. He said—"

She put his arm around him. "No one's going to get hurt. It's just a rule that we have to have agents. Kind of—a tradition."

He shook his head. "Rob says his brother told him—"

Rob's brother was a couple of years younger than she was—and had always been obnoxious. "Who do you believe, me or Rob's brother?" she asked. "The agents are part of it, that's all. Like, does it bother you that people bring dinner into the room for us? And clear the table and all?"

"No," he said slowly.

"Well, the security is the same thing," she said. "They're there to take care of us when we're outside the White House, and the butlers and everyone take care of us when we're inside."

He still didn't look convinced.

Not that she was going to boot this one upstairs, but—"Look, talk to Mom and Dad about it, okay? They can explain it better." She fixed the knot in his tie. "Come on, let's go find Steven, and—"

He pulled the tie off completely. "I'm not wearing this. I don't like it."

Yeah, but did they have a choice? "I know, but we're not supposed to—" She stopped, considering the fact that he would *never* have to wear a tie to go around Boston on a Saturday afternoon. Why should he have to here? "You're right." She threw it up on top of the Victorian dresser—another incongruous touch in this room where stiff, formal furniture and little boy possessions were fighting for control. "You don't have to."

"Will I get in trouble?" he asked.

He had better not get in trouble for something so basic. She shook her head.

"But *you* look nice," he said.

Unfortunately, yeah. She looked down at the dress she had worn to the brunch—which she figured must look okay on her, because several young male congressional aides had flirted with her. In fact, one of the House Majority Whip's Deputy Directors of Floor Operations—a hot-shot just out of the Fletcher School of Law and Diplomacy—made a point of easing next to her in line at one of the buffet tables and had asked, with a sly wink, if there was a chance she was actually over eighteen, and therefore, fair game, and she'd said that yes, she was, but the family was trying to cover up the fact that she'd been held back four out of the last five years. Luckily—or, unluckily—Maureen, who was one of Preston's top assistants, had suddenly appeared and began chatting about Meg's upcoming first day of school until the guy finally grinned, took the hint, and went over to try and charm a blond policy analyst instead.

"Do me a favor, and wait here, okay? Don't move." She started for the door, hearing him get off the bed. "Hey! I said not to move."

Neal laughed, and got back up.

"That's better." She opened the door, waiting for his second attempt, turning when she heard it. "I thought I told you not to move."

He laughed harder and climbed onto the mattress again.

"I'll be right back." She went down to her room, changing into a Lowell Spinners sweatshirt, a button-down shirt, and jeans. Shoes. What was she going to wear for shoes? She looked out the window at the grey winter slush, and pulled on her L.L. Bean hiking boots. Then, she went back down the hall, feeling normal for the first time since they'd come to Washington.

Neal was still sitting on his bed. "Wow," he pointed at her jeans, "can I, too?"

"Sure," she said, gesturing expansively.

"Are we allowed?" he asked.

"Sure," she said, in a less certain voice, but with a more expansive gesture.

He put on jeans and sneakers, traded his cashmere V-neck for one of Steven's outgrown crewnecks, then turned and smiled at her. "Can we go to the place with the rockets, first?"

"Sure. Hey, Steven," she called, as they went out to the West Sitting Hall. "Come on, let's go."

He came out of the kitchen, holding a chocolate doughnut and grinning when he saw their outfits.

"Hot damn," he said, and pulled his tie off.

ON THEIR WAY downstairs, they ran into Preston in the Ground Floor Corridor.

He frowned at them. "Hmmm."

"Hi," Steven said in one of his most arrogant and defiant voices.

"The cats didn't drag in anything very stylish today, did they?" Preston said, flashily dignified in a dark blue pinstriped suit, his shirt and handkerchief a lighter blue, the tie *white*—as though he might be on his way to audition for *Guys and Dolls*.

Neal and Steven looked at Meg.

"No, guess they didn't," she said.

Preston nodded, with almost no expression on his face.

"Meggie told us it was okay," Neal said defensively.

If she weren't such a nice person, she might be annoyed at him for throwing her to the wolves like that.

"Oh, did she now," Preston said.

"Sure did," Meg said, in *her* most arrogant and defiant voice.

He motioned towards her boots. "Tying them might help the look."

Meg shrugged. "I like them this way."

"Well, whatever. But, if you break your ankle, I'm not going to have any sympathy for you." He grinned and gestured towards the South Grounds. "You know how many reporters are hanging around out there?"

They looked guilty.

"Oh, don't worry about it—you're kids; *of course* you dress this way." He straightened Neal's collar and adjusted Steven's Red Sox cap more rakishly. "Have a good time, and don't talk to too many strangers. And go to the National Gallery, if you have time. You'll learn something."

"I'm not going to any stupid art museums," Steven said. "Mom always makes us go to art museums. We're going to the FBI."

Since when? Meg took her sunglasses off. "The FBI? We're not going to the FBI."

"Yeah, we are," Steven said. "I'm not going to any stupid—"

Neal looked anxious. "I thought we were going to see the planes."

Preston patted him on the head. "Good idea. Take the kid to see the planes."

They ended up going to see the planes. That is, after the photographers outside took their pictures and reporters asked a few questions—like where they were going, and if they were dressed casually to avoid getting spoiled by the glitter and glamour of the White House. Meg repressed the urge—mostly because Preston was standing right there, monitoring the press encounter, and she didn't want to bug him—to say that they were dressed that way because the cats hadn't dragged in anything very stylish. Actually, Vanessa was probably fully capable of foraging through the closets of fashion-savy Washingtonians—and hauling home the spoils.

They got into a huge black SUV—about which, Meg was really going to have to talk to her mother, given the environmental implications—with a lead security car, and two follow cars. As they drove through one of the gates and out onto 17th Street, tourists who were gathered outside watched the cars go by, and most of them took pictures.

"We should, like, charge 'em for those," Steven said.

Meg hit him. "Don't be a jerk."

"Don't hit me," he said, and punched her in the arm so hard that she would have yelped if she hadn't been quite so cool.

"Don't be a jerk, then," she said. She wasn't even going to rub her arm, because it didn't hurt even a tiny, miniscule bit at all.

"The Air and Space Museum, kids?" Barry, one of the agents in the front seat, asked, and they nodded.

The Air and Space Museum was part of the Smithsonian Institution. There were art museums—like the National Gallery, and the Natural History Museum, the American History Museum, and a bunch of others Meg couldn't remember. The museum buildings ran along either side of a long grassy mall about a mile long, which stretched from the Capitol Building all the way to the Washington Monument, with the Reflecting Pool and Lincoln Memorial just beyond that. Over the years, the Mall had been the scene of lots of protests and marches, but more often than not, people just walked around, and snapped photos, or jogged along it.

Their agents parked in front of the Air and Space Museum, and they went inside while everyone they passed stared and nudged companions. Meg could kind of take planes or leave them—mostly leave them—but Steven and Neal loved the exhibits, standing open-mouthed in front of World War II fighter planes, one of the Wright Brothers' original flyers, and the Spirit of St. Louis. They looked at some moon rocks, a couple of Apollo Command Modules, missiles, and Hubble telescopes—and her brothers probably would have spent the next *year* in the flight simulators, if other people hadn't been waiting in line. Meg kind of thought that the space program was a waste of time, when there were starving people in Appalachia and that sort of thing, but she generally tried to keep potentially controversial political opinions to herself. It was easier that way.

They walked across the Mall to the Natural History Museum—delighting still more tourists—and Meg kind of wished she could have a copy of one of the many pictures being taken, since the image of nervous-looking, well-dressed men walking along with three kids in ski jackets and jeans was probably an hysterically funny sight. She had been told that their agents were going to try to dress more casually, to fit in better, but so far, she hadn't seen that in action.

The Natural History Museum was more to Meg's tastes, although taxidermy always made her think of the movie *Psycho*. Steven and Neal made a bit of a ruckus, calling each other wombats and ring-tailed lemurs and that sort of thing, Steven yelling, "Yo, it's Meg!" in front of the Dogs of the World exhibit. None of them was too enthralled by rocks, but they went to the mineral and gem section to look at the Hope Diamond, Steven making a lot of loud remarks about how they were going to steal it, and that the agents were their gang. Meg thought he was pretty funny, but most of the people around them didn't seem to be sure that he was kidding.

In the Museum of American History, they looked at some old trains and automobiles, but then went to the part devoted to the history of the political process—*definitely* Meg's scene. She wasn't into the idea of running for office—probably—but, she kind of had a feeling she would probably end up going into the family business in *some* form. Maybe she could be a learned pundit or, at least, an *opinionated* and very verbal one. It might be fun to be a pundit.

There was a special exhibit focusing on the President, mostly a pictorial history of her life and career—including a photo Meg had never seen of her mother riding a tricycle in what appeared to be Central Park. There was lots of campaign memorabilia, dating back to her first Congressional campaign, with buttons, bumper stickers, and posters, and lots of more recent shots, including a huge blow-up of her accepting the Democratic nomination. Meg was surprised to see *herself* in two of them—toddling around on the floor of the House in one, and then, with the whole family at Stowe, which was the same picture the *Times Magazine* had used, and made them look incredibly tanned, All-American—and a tiny bit elitist. She and

Steven both had snow in their hair, and she vaguely remembered their having had a fight right before the photograph was taken.

The only thing funnier than that section of the museum was the area devoted to First Ladies. This part had reproductions of rooms in the White House during various points of history—like the Red Room, as it was in 1870—and mannequins of all of the First Ladies in their Inaugural gowns. In the room that had all of the most recent First Ladies, starting with Mrs. Reagan, there was a little empty space at the end, and a white card that said: "COMING SOON: RUSSELL JAMES POWERS." They laughed for about ten minutes, attracting many stares, as Meg pictured a tall, broad-shouldered model of their father in white tie and tails. She only hoped that they would remember to include his silk hat. Oh, and the cape. It wouldn't be the same without his cape.

Since nothing could top "COMING SOON: RUSSELL JAMES POWERS," they left the museum, fighting about where they were going to go next. The FBI Building was closed for tours, so Steven said they should go to the Pentagon, an idea Meg immediately rejected—even as Neal was saying, "Yeah! Cool!" They ended up going to get ice cream at a place in Foggy Bottom that one of their agents recommended, although they had to get back into the car with their cones, because so many people were looking at them. It was completely weird to be recognized, but the agents were a dead giveaway.

It was starting to get dark, and they drove over to the Vietnam Veterans Memorial—which was quiet and solemn in the dusk, and then walked up to the Lincoln Memorial from there. It was large and square, supported by marble columns, and as stately and dignified as a piece of architecture could be. The kind of place where people automatically spoke in hushed voices. They walked up the long flights of stone steps, where the massive statue of a serious, but benevolent, Lincoln was framed between the two middle columns. Meg felt sort of as though she were approaching the gates of heaven, the statue lit up in the darkness, looking as if it were sitting in judgment. She could have stayed there all night, but Neal decided that he was scared, Steven was getting hungry again, and their agents pointed out that they should probably go home—*home?*—for dinner.

They took the scenic route back, swinging out past the Tidal Basin and the Jefferson Memorial, and then Jeff, who was driving, slowed down near the Washington Monument so that they could stare up at the Mall, at the Capitol Dome, all of the monuments lit up and looking golden against the winter sky.

"Wow," Steven said.

"Wow," Neal said, also whispering, and Meg felt the same mingled pride and fear, thinking about how incredibly important—how utterly vital to the entire *world*—it was to be the President.

They drove around the outside of the South Lawn of the White House, which was also bright with spotlights, the fountain spraying into the night. Once they had pulled up in front of the South Entrance, they got out of the car, thanked their agents, and went upstairs, none of them talking much.

"That was really something," Meg said, finally.

"*All* of this is really something," Steven said, and Meg and Neal nodded; the three of them stepping very carefully and quietly on the marble stairs.

19

BY SUNDAY NIGHT, all of the company was gone, and her mother had come upstairs from the West Wing, and they spent the evening together in the nest in the West Sitting Hall, sprawling on the couch and chairs from home. Meg had been trying to read *The Making of the President: 1960*, but gave up, taking a cream puff from the coffee table—First Family refreshments—and killing a little time by trying to eat it without making a mess.

Finished with that, she looked around the room. Her mother was sitting with Neal on her lap, the two of them smiling and talking softly. Neal was lucky to be young—it seemed to make everything so much less complicated. At any rate, except for his very occasional flurries of tears, he and her mother rarely argued at all, as far as she knew. But, she couldn't help thinking of the military aide nearby—probably on the Stair Landing outside the Center Hall, who was holding the notorious black bag—known as "the football"—which had to be close to the President twenty-four hours a day, in case she needed to make an immediate decision about nuclear war. Meg didn't quite understand the logistics of it all, but the controls and authorizations were supposed to be inside that briefcase. Walking to breakfast that morning, she had seen one of the other aides sitting in a straight chair, silent and expressionless in his uniform. There were five aides, one from each branch of the military, who rotated shifts carrying the bag, and she had only seen one female one, so far. Even though nuclear war didn't seem to be the biggest threat facing the country right now, the potential that it *might* be someday was pretty scary.

Steven was sitting on the floor with Kirby, stuffing his face with pastries. Did he think about stuff like war? Other than in video games? Probably not. But, it was hard to tell—he was always so reserved. No, "restrained" might be a better word. *Con*strained. Controlled. Very, very controlled. As always, his mother's child.

Sometimes—sometimes, she just felt like grabbing him when he walked by, giving him a big hug, and saying, "You know what? I love you." But, he would probably hit her. Or pretend to throw up. There wasn't a single member of her family—except for Neal, maybe—who wouldn't think she was really weird if she walked up and hugged them. She was maybe a little on the constrained side herself.

She leaned forward to get another pastry, and Steven grinned up at her, showing her a mouthful of mashed cupcake. Nice. Definite charm school graduate. She sat back, eating the raspberry tart she'd chosen. But, when he glanced up a minute later, she opened her mouth for an equally disgusting demonstration of masticated raspberry tart. They both laughed, and she had to grab her Coke and gulp down half of it to keep from choking. Her father looked over his reading glasses at them, and they gave him angelic smiles. Proper Presidential children. Yeah, right.

Her father had been sitting at the other end of the couch reading First Gentleman briefing and protocol books all night. Hard to believe there was such a thing. He was going to have to give speeches and do good works and all of that, and Meg figured he would concentrate on global warming and building affordable housing, since they were two of his top political interests. As far as she could tell, the idea that he could accomplish things, too, made him feel better about being the First Gentleman. At least, he seemed pretty secure lately.

Neal went to bed early, her mother disappearing with him; then Steven went in around ten, and her mother left again so that she could say good-night to him—and probably to make sure he turned his computer *off*. It was strange to have her mother home, and able to say good-night in person. In spite of the fact that she was

President, they were seeing more of her than they ever had. Kind of ironic.

Alone with her father, Meg put her book down. "Dad?"

He took off his glasses, blinking to focus. "What?"

"I'm kind of"—she kept her hand in the book so she wouldn't lose her place, then just closed it altogether—"scared about school tomorrow."

"Well, that's normal," he said.

She brought her knees up, wrapping her arms around them. "What if they hate me? They'll all already have friends, so no one'll talk to me, and because of the Secret Service, they won't talk to me even more."

"Of course they will." He moved over next to her. "Just be nice and friendly."

Neither of which necessarily came naturally to her.

"Say hello to people, to break the ice," he said. "And don't worry about your agents—they'll stay out of your way. Besides, a lot of people at your school will be government kids, so it won't seem strange to them. Just be yourself."

"What if they hate myself?" she asked.

He smiled. "They won't."

Yeah, right.

"You're going to end up being the most popular person there," he said.

Not bloody likely. She shook her head. "You're only saying that because you're my father."

He lifted his eyebrows. "You accuse the First Gentleman of lying?"

Meg nodded.

"Not only," he said, "are you going to be the most popular, but every boy in that school is going to ask you out—I guarantee it."

Would it upset the country to find out that the First Gentleman was severely delusional? "What about reporters?" she asked.

"Well, I'm hoping *none* of them ask you out," he said, "but given what I heard from Maureen about the brunch yesterday, yes, I'm a little concerned about the possibility."

That was funny—but, she had actually been asking a serious question.

"I'm afraid there *will* be some interest, because it's your first day," he admitted. "But, once you're inside, they won't be able to bother you. I have Preston and the others working very hard to try and figure out ways to help the three of you keep as much privacy as possible."

In a world where total strangers asked them what flavors of *ice cream* they had just ordered?

"Look," her father said. "It's not too late for me to come with you—you can just go in a little later, after I take Neal and Steven."

It was a tempting offer, but Meg shook her head. "Thanks, but I can do it myself."

"I know you *can,*" he said, "but—"

But, it would make her look like a kid—which would suck. "I'd really rather go by myself," she said. "I'll be fine."

"Well, just don't forget that the offer's there." He turned over her book, reading the title. "Don't you ever read anything for fun anymore?"

"Well—" Meg grinned sheepishly. "It's sort of interesting. I mean, like, we're supposed to know stuff."

He grinned back. "You don't enjoy it or anything, right?"

Hell, no.

Her mother was coming back, and she stood up, figuring that her parents might want to be alone for a while. "Well, back later maybe." She passed her mother on her way to her still-pink room. "Hi."

Her mother nodded. "Hi. Was it something I said?"

"What?" Meg tilted her head, not getting it. "Oh. No, it wasn't."

"Going to bed?" her mother asked.

"Not yet," Meg said. "I'm just—you know."

Her mother nodded, and Meg continued to her room. Once inside, she opened the closet, trying to figure out what she was going to wear. She'd asked Beth on the phone earlier, who had suggested that she go with her tweeds—which was lots of help. She should probably pick out a skirt, though. But, if she looked too dressy, they would all think she was some rich jerk. And if she dressed down, she would look like a rich jerk who didn't give a damn.

Instead of being considered just an *ordinary* jerk, which was probably closer to the truth.

Although she definitely had to allow for the press. Pictures of her first day of school could show up anywhere—television, newspapers, magazines, the Internet. So, she had to be smart and avoid controversy.

Maybe she could arrange to be tutored at home.

"Having trouble deciding what to wear?" her mother asked.

"Hunh?" She turned and flushed, putting the clothes on her bed aside as if she were just doing inventory. "No. No, I'm all set."

"Oh." Her mother leaned against the doorjamb. "What are you wearing?"

Meg shrugged, and began putting things back in the closet.

"A skirt might be a good idea," her mother said.

Yeah, yeah, yeah. Meg hung up an armload of shirts more violently than necessary. "Don't worry. I'm not going to embarrass you or anything."

Her mother sighed. "I didn't say that."

Maybe not directly. Meg shut the closet door, hard. "You were going to."

Her mother's gaze sharpened, but she came all the way into the room. "Are you nervous about tomorrow?"

Meg shook her head.

"Not at all?" her mother asked.

"Nope," Meg said.

"Oh." Her mother leaned against the Early American desk, which was still empty, other than Meg's computer. "Well, I would be."

Meg was going to say, "Yeah, well, I'm not you," but that seemed unnecessarily provocative. "I don't know, maybe I am. It's not important."

"I think it is," her mother said.

Yeah. Sure. Meg shrugged and patted Vanessa, who was lying on her pillow.

It was quiet for a minute. Painfully so.

"You know," her mother said, "I feel as if we haven't talked to each other for months."

Well, that was probably because, for the most part, they *hadn't.*

"Are you still angry at me because of that night before we came down here?" her mother asked.

It certainly didn't rank as her favorite conversation of all time. "I'm not angry at you." Or, anyway, not *much.* Meg looked at her. "I'm just—I don't know."

Her mother came over to the bed, sitting somewhat hesitantly at the bottom. "I gather you and Beth had a pretty long talk today."

Information which must have come from her father. Meg shrugged again. "Yeah, kind of." A rather mopey conversation, in fact.

"She and Sarah can come down here during their vacation," her mother said.

Meg nodded, and then, it was quiet again.

"Are you sure you aren't angry at me?" her mother asked.

Meg shook her head. "I said I wasn't."

Her mother moved her jaw. "Okay. Maybe it's my imagination. But, you seem a little—brusque."

"Good word," Meg said.

"Thank you." Her mother reached out, tentatively, to pat Vanessa—who hissed at her, and leapt off the bed.

A pretty clear statement on Vanessa's part, at least.

"You know, you make me hate myself," her mother said.

Were they doomed to have nothing *but* nightmare conversations from now on? "Why?" Meg asked, stiffly. "For bringing me into the world?"

Her mother shook her head. "Because you're such a nice kid, and you have this defensive chip on your shoulder all the time."

"I do not!" Meg said.

"What would you call that reaction?" her mother asked.

Hmmm. Meg frowned.

"Exactly." Her mother leaned over to squeeze her shoulder. "I keep trying to take it off, and you put it back on, and I take it off, and you put it back on—" She paused. "Having a laugh at my expense, are you?"

Meg just grinned.

"I rather thought so." Her mother smiled, too. "Could you do me a favor?"

"What?" Meg asked, not committing herself, just in case.

"Tell me how you feel about something," her mother said.

Meg looked at her blankly. "About what?"

"About anything," her mother said. "Just tell me how you *really* feel about something."

"I'm in favor of the separation between church and state," Meg said.

Her mother smiled, but in a faintly exasperated way. "How about something a little more personal?"

"I don't like olives," Meg said.

Her mother shook her head. "Even more personal than that."

"Yeah?" Meg glanced at her. "Can I say what I really think?"

Her mother nodded. "I'd like that very much."

"Okay." Meg folded her arms across her chest. "I don't like reporters, paparazzi, Secret Service agents, or starting school tomorrow."

"No argument there," her mother agreed.

"I wish we lived in Massachusetts," Meg said. "I wish our lives were completely private, I wish you were an English teacher, I wish—"

"My God"—her mother fumbled around on the floor—"where's the chip?"

Okay, that was funny. Meg grinned. "I was only going to wish for world peace."

Her mother laughed, hugging her even though Meg's arms were still folded. "Do you really think it would be better if I'd been an English teacher?" she asked, her face pressed against Meg's hair.

God, yes. "I don't know," Meg said.

Her mother nodded. "Just anything but President."

Well, that was certainly up near the top of the list. "It could be worse," Meg said, and paused. "You could be *Pope*."

Her mother laughed again, kissing her on the top of the head before releasing her. "Do you really hate my being President?" she asked.

Were they going to go over and over this, non-stop, for the next four—or eight—years? Jesus. "I don't know," Meg said.

Her mother looked worried. "Well, do you—"

"Mom, don't push me, okay?" Meg asked. "We haven't even been here a week."

Her mother nodded. "I know. I'm sorry."

Oh, for God's sakes. Meg sighed. "You don't have to say you're sorry. I'm just not sure how I feel. I mean, you wanted the truth, right?"

Her mother nodded.

All right, it was *way* past time to change the subject. "You know what I wish?" Meg asked.

Her mother shook her head.

"I wish Cary Grant would ride up and carry me off," she said.

Her mother grinned. "That sounds exciting."

Hell, yeah. She had never been one for the latest pretty boys—give her the real thing, any day. Meg nodded. "Carry me off to the frozen tundra, and—"

"I get the picture," her mother said quickly.

"And we'd go skiing together," Meg said.

"Oh, well, that sounds like a nice time," her mother agreed.

"I thought so," Meg said.

Her mother smiled, and kissed her on the forehead. "It's late. You ought to get some sleep."

Had her mother still never noticed that she *absolutely hated* being told what to do? "I always stay up this late," Meg said.

"I'm sorry, I forgot." Her mother stood up. "You know, Meg, I think all of this is going to be okay. We're all going to be together a lot more, spend some time with each other, find out a great deal about our family. I think you're going to end up feeling better about it, I really do."

One could only hope.

"I honestly think you are. That all of us are." Her mother paused at the door. "Come out and say good-night before you go to bed, okay?"

"Maybe," Meg said, in her if-you're-lucky voice.

Her mother drew her breath in between her teeth. "Did I ever tell you that you can be an extremely irksome child?"

Many times. Meg nodded cheerfully. "SAT word."

Her mother tried, but wasn't able to keep her smile back. "Perpetually impudent. Unabashedly churlish."

"Some applause for the woman who swallowed a thesaurus," Meg said.

Her mother narrowed her eyes. "Incessantly obstreperous."

"Oh, very good," Meg said, impressed.

"Thank you." Her mother opened the door. "Come out and say good night before you go to bed."

Meg nodded.

20

AFTER AGONIZING AGAIN the next morning, Meg decided to wear a pleated wool skirt and a white Oxford shirt with a sweater over it. She felt a little evangelical, but surely, that would be casual enough, yet dignified enough, to please everyone. Or, anyway, not *offend* anyone. She solved the shoe problem by selecting—God help her—knee socks and Top-Siders. How very girlish of her. She would reflect well upon the Administration.

She rode in the backseat of the car, with Barry and Jeff in the front, two other agents following them in another car.

"Nervous?" Jeff—who was a stocky, African-American former Army Ranger—asked, slowing for a red light, not very casual in his blue suit and tie.

"Nope," she lied. Then, she leaned forward. "You think someone who walks into school with two pens and a brand-new notebook looks like an idiot?"

"The person looks prepared," Barry—who was Caucasian, slightly balding, and had once been a third-round pick for the Miami Dolphins—said, even less casual in his grey suit.

"The person looks quiet and bookish." And, inevitably, unpopular. Meg sat back. "I don't want to go."

"I think you're stuck," Jeff said, turning off Wisconsin Avenue and driving toward the main administration building, where she could see a press pool and what seemed to be a bunch of school officials waiting. Maureen, who was one of Preston's assistants, was hanging around, too—even though Meg *really* hadn't wanted anyone to accompany her. She liked Maureen well enough, so far, but the fact that her parents apparently didn't think she was capable of going to school by herself, despite her express insistence otherwise, was very god-damn annoying.

There were also several other Secret Service agents there, either for crowd control—or possibly to make sure there were no crazed gunmen or whatever around.

The latter, being a less than comforting thought.

"Do I have to get out of the car?" she asked, her throat feeling very tight.

"I think it might be a good idea," Barry said, both agents scanning the waiting group.

"Should I swagger, or slink?" she asked.

"Stroll," Jeff said.

Marcy, from the follow car, opened her door for her, and as she stepped out, she saw cameras go off and flinched—even though she had been planning not to do so.

A man in a tie and jacket moved forward, his right hand out. "Good morning, Miss Powers. I'm Thomas Lyons, the headmaster."

Meg shook his hand. "Hello, Dr. Lyons."

Then, she was introduced to the Assistant Head of School, the Upper School principal, the Dean of Students, the Director of Community Service—the school was big on community service, she'd been told—and the Head of Security.

Her mother had gotten some grief for not sending them to public schools, but she had used the excuse that there were security concerns, instead of harping on the more-obvious reality that the D.C. school system was not the world's best. Her parents had seriously considered sending Neal to public school, since the elementary schools were better than the high schools, but in the end, he had been enrolled in the same school where Steven was going.

"Miss Powers, how do you feel about starting school?" a reporter asked.

"Nervous," Meg said without thinking, and everyone laughed.

She had to answer a few more harmless questions, but finally, someone asked the predictable "why are you attending this exclusive private school, when the President is such a strong proponent of public education?" one.

Maureen quickly stepped forward. She was in her late-twenties and very tall, with black hair and skin so pale that it looked as though she had never let a single ultra-violet ray ever touch her face. As far as Meg knew, Preston had poached her from the DLC—Democratic Leadership Council—staff. "I'm afraid that's a matter of policy, and not something Meg needs to address."

Which didn't change the fact that it was a proverbial gun on the wall—and really *should* be addressed. "It *isn't* fair," Meg said—and Maureen looked aghast. "I'm very lucky to be in a position where my parents can send me to the best school they can find, and I wish the same held true for everyone."

"So, you're advocating school vouchers?" someone asked.

Aw, hell, she'd sauntered right into that one, hadn't she. Damn.

Maureen shook her head firmly. "I'm sorry, but classes have already begun for the day, and Meg—"

"No, I don't support them," Meg said—and it was possible that Maureen gasped. Although, luckily, she didn't actually topple over. "Public education hasn't gotten enough funding for *years,* and it makes a lot more sense to me to do everything possible to improve the entire system, and bring everyone back into it, instead of the other way around. Vouchers are only going to perpetuate the problem that already exists."

Which was actually quite close to her mother's position.

The reporters were all grinning, and taking notes like crazy, and she realized that she was being filmed, too.

"So," a print person said, "you're saying that your mother will definitely—"

Meg shook her head. "I can't speak for the Administration. I'm just giving you my personal opinion."

"How about social issues, in general?" a television reporter asked, with a very sly look in her eyes. "Would you care to weigh in on any of those?"

She could tell that Maureen was about to drag her away forcibly—but that she was also sort of mesmerized by all of this, and wondering exactly how far the President's obnoxious child might be going to go.

"I don't think this is the right time for that," Meg said, "but thank you for asking."

Now, Maureen pulled herself together and actually stepped in front of her. "I think we really need to let Meg go to class now," she said. "If you have any further questions, though, I will be happy to respond later, or you can go directly through Mr. Fielding's office."

Mr. Fielding was Preston, although she had never once called him that, or thought of him that way.

She was ushered into the main administration building, away from the media, and Maureen promptly pulled her aside. *Dragged* her, in fact.

"That was actually pretty good, Meg, but—gosh," she said. "Please don't ever do it again."

Meg grinned sheepishly. "Yeah, I know." Christ, Linda was probably going to *kill* her. "But, it's not like my parents can pretend that my being here is anything other than what it is." Which was, namely, a function of them being rich and powerful—and their children receiving extra advantages, as a direct result.

Maureen moved her jaw. "You handled the situation at brunch the other day very well, too."

Her prospective, smarmy suitor.

"But—gosh," Maureen said. "Okay?"

That was a whole lot better than the "*everything* you say must be vetted through our people" lecture she was likely to get from Linda later today. But, it maybe wasn't a good sign that as soon as they separated, Maureen was immediately on her cell phone.

Once she was inside the Upper School itself, Barry went off with the Head of Security to whatever area had been set aside for the Secret Service command center. She was pretty sure that there were going to be at least three agents on the campus with her every day, and one of their duties would be taking turns sitting outside each of her classrooms, or the cafeteria, or wherever she happened to be. Fun job. The White House had to keep track of where everyone was twenty-four hours a day, and they even all had code names—she was Sandpiper. She couldn't help wondering what they called her behind her back. Steven was Snapper and Neal was Snowflake. Her mother was Shamrock, her father Sunflower. What a team. The Secret Service liked to keep things innocuous and neat, and it was a tradition to have everything begin with the same letter. Barry was probably already contacting the PPD—Presidential Protective Division—communications center: "Sandpiper safe and sound. Mission successful." They talked like a bunch of astronauts.

As she walked down the hall with Jeff, Dr. Lyons, and Mr. Haigwood, the Upper School principal, various teachers came up and introduced themselves, while passing students just stared—upon which, Meg remembered to start being nervous again.

"Everyone's very excited about having you here," Mr. Haigwood said.

Meg blushed. "I hope they're not going to be disappointed."

After going through some red tape, including signing various forms and getting her official schedule, as well as meeting the entire office staff, Dr. Lyons and Mr. Haigwood took her down to the last half of her first-period class, Literature of the United States, with a Mrs. Simpson.

"Your grades from your old school are excellent," Mr. Haigwood said.

Actually, Meg considered them subpar, since she had never put out anything genuinely approaching full effort, but she nodded politely.

Dr. Lyons smiled at her. "We're looking forward to having you as part of our student body, and obviously, if you run into any problems at all, you should just come to one of us directly."

Would being shunned by her classmates count as a serious problem? Certainly, that was what she was anticipating.

Once they were outside her classroom, Jeff sat down in a chair outside. "Do it up, kid."

Meg smiled weakly, then followed Dr. Lyons and Mr. Haigwood into the room. All work stopped, and what seemed like hundreds of faces looked up.

It took some effort, but she ordered herself to focus on something else. *Anything* else. They were hostile, she could tell they were all hostile.

"This is Meghan Powers," Dr. Lyons said. "As you all know, she's going to be a student here."

Meg nodded stiffly, afraid to look at anyone. The room was very quiet, and she could hear her heart up in her ears.

"Do you like to be called Meghan?" Mrs. Simpson, a short woman with greying hair and a very friendly smile, asked.

"Just Meg." Her voice squeaked a little. Way to go, Sandpiper.

"Well, it's wonderful to have you here, and I know you're going to be a great addition to the class." Mrs. Simpson handed her a thick anthology and several paperbacks. "These are the texts we're using right now. Why don't you choose a seat?" She gestured towards two empty desks in the front row.

No way. She couldn't sit in front. She'd be sure that people were looking at her. Not that she was paranoid or anything.

"Meg?" Mrs. Simpson asked pleasantly.

Seeing a place in the back, she made her way to it, her face painfully hot as everyone watched her. She stumbled a little as she pulled out her chair, but managed to sit down, pretending that she wasn't aware that every single head was turned in her direction.

"I think we're all set here," Mrs. Simpson said to Dr. Lyons and Mr. Haigwood, who nodded, and left the room. "Now. Why don't we pick up our discussion where we left off?"

Meg took mechanical, obedient notes, knowing that she couldn't concentrate—not that anyone else in the room seemed to be paying much attention, either. People kept looking at her, and she would stare down at her desk, embarrassed. There were about ten guys in the class, some of whom—on quick glance—looked as if they might be handsome.

She caught eyes with one of the best-looking boys she had ever seen, a guy sitting diagonally across from her. In fact, he was *so* attractive, that she almost dropped her pen. She glanced back and saw him grinning at her. Redder than she had been so far, she focused on the board, where Mrs. Simpson was writing something about class and social conflicts in the early 1900s. One of the books she had been handed was by Edith Wharton, so she assumed that's what they had been reading.

A hand flashed over to her desk and away, leaving behind a small wad of paper. She unfolded it and saw "You blush more than anyone I've ever seen" in masculine handwriting. She—naturally—blushed again, and heard him laugh.

But, it was entirely possible that she was in love. He was *really* sexy. Forget Rick Hamilton, he of the clay feet. She looked at him, admiring the blond hair and charm-school smile. He dressed right, too. Most of the other guys were wearing sweatshirts, but he had on faded, not too faded jeans, and a blue and white rugby shirt, and she had a sudden desire to touch his arm, wanting to feel the material.

Although he was so handsome that he *had* to have a girlfriend already.

She watched him from behind, eyeing the wide shoulders and the muscles that showed through his shirt. Very, very handsome. A 9.3. No higher, because she had never given a 10, and she wanted to leave the possibility open. He was a strong 9, though.

She squinted at the board, scribbling down the diagram of wealthy New York societal structure Mrs. Simpson had drawn on a clean, neatly dated page in her notebook. Soon, there would be drawings of cats, concentric circles, and small figures running or skiing, but right now, it looked pristine and far too well-organized. Which made her nervous, and she scrawled a fast cat curled up on a rug. It was out of proportion and very ugly, but relieved the perfection of the page.

Sometimes—she drew a skier slaloming down a steep slope—sometimes, she had extremely graphic thoughts. Not too often—she tried not to encourage them, but sometimes—like, if she saw someone really, really handsome—and, well, she had the feeling that she was about to have some good ones. Very detailed. Although it was kind of funny that people could have graphic thoughts without really having a frame of reference. She had seen an old movie once where this character was going on and on about sex and passion and that sort of thing, and another character said, "How do you know?" "Well," the first character admitted shyly, "I read a lot."

Once, when she was about twelve, she was in her parents' room—putting on make-up because no one else was home—and she found an old paperback called *The Sensuous Woman*, which she hid in her room and studied at great length. It was more confusing than informative, and late one night, when her mother was home and they were alone in the den, she asked her if she was a sensuous woman. Her mother, who was drinking iced tea, choked, and then laughed for about ten minutes.

"What do you think?" she'd asked, finally.

Meg wasn't sure how to answer.

Then, her mother had gotten serious, and they discussed Sex in much more detail than the time her mother had explained that there was going to be a little sister or brother because she and Meg's father loved each other so much. She was given one of those *A Doctor Talks to Kids* books, which was kind of clinical, and equally obscure, and she mostly forgot about all of it until the night she got her period, and her father had to deal with it because Trudy had gone home and her mother was in Washington. He was very calm, seemed proud, but kept turning red. He'd hurried out to the store, returning with several brands of pads and tampons, so she could choose. In retrospect, it was pretty funny to imagine what the clerk in the store must have thought of the man who was buying out the feminine protection department. Meg hadn't been able to decide which was best, and called her mother for suggestions. Tampons weren't as easy as the directions led her to believe, and she'd had to practice for a few months before catching on. Until then, she had been convinced that she was deformed, although her mother assured her she wasn't, finally offering to take her to a gynecologist so she could get an expert opinion. The idea of *that* was so mortifying that Meg immediately learned how to use them, and never mentioned the problem again.

It had taken a very long time to go through all of the boxes her father had gotten.

She heard Mrs. Simpson asking a question and looked up, realizing that she had been in school for about twenty minutes—and was already having trouble paying attention. Junior year was the most important one for her transcripts—at least, according to guidance counselors—and she needed to make sure to keep up her average. Of course, being the President's daughter, she would undoubtedly get in anywhere she applied to college, but it would be nice to be accepted—or not—on her own merits. Since Harvard was a Vaughn tradition and they would be sixth generation, either she or one of her brothers was going to have to go there. Maybe she would make Steven do it. She would rather be at some little school in the mountains where no one would know who she was. She glanced around the room, seeing almost everyone else still sneaking looks at her. She would rather go *anyplace* where no one knew who she was.

"Hard to concentrate the first day," Mrs. Simpson said, smiling at her.

Meg realized that the bell had just rung, and flushed—again. "Kind of, yeah."

"Well, we're very happy to have you with us," Mrs. Simpson said.

For now, maybe—but probably not once they got to know her. "Thank you," Meg said. She gathered up her books and put them in her knapsack—at least the knapsack felt familiar. Her next class was History of the United States, and she was glad that Jeff was out in the hall, so at least she wouldn't have to worry about walking alone, while everyone else in the school walked with their many friends.

"Hi," a chubby blond girl said. "I'm Gail. Do we call you Meg?"

Meg shrugged affirmatively, albeit shyly.

"What's it like living in the White House?" another girl asked, most of the class still in the room.

"Uh, I don't know." Meg shifted her knapsack to her other shoulder, flustered. "Big. Very big."

"Do you get to go wherever you want?" someone else asked.

"I thought you were supposed to have Secret Service agents," someone else said.

"Do you get waited on?" another person asked.

This was like reporters. Worse, even. She gripped her knapsack strap, too intimidated to answer right away.

"Told ya the kid'd be a snob," she heard a guy say, heading for the door.

"It's, um"—her voice still wasn't coming out right—"it's kind of weird, I guess." Oh, yeah. Nice and articulate. She was *definitely* headed for a top college.

"Hadn't all of you better get along to your next classes?" Mrs. Simpson said from the front of the room.

People started for the door, and Meg let a small, relieved sigh escape, relaxing slightly.

"Hi." The guy with the rugby shirt came over, holding out a confident hand. "Adam Miller."

"Hi." She tried to return the handshake perfectly, not holding on too long, not letting go too quickly. What a production. So, she let go. "I'm Meg Powers."

In case he hadn't gotten the word.

"Oh, yeah? How do you feel about being called Meghan?" he asked.

She was completely in love.

He held the door for her. "Must be something, living in the White House."

"I guess. It doesn't seem very real yet." She smiled nervously at Jeff, as he stood up from his chair. "Um, Adam, this is Jeff. Jeff, this is Adam."

"Hi." Adam glanced at her. "Friend of yours?"

She nodded. "My husband. He's very possessive."

Adam looked surprised, maybe not expecting her to have a sense of humor, then laughed. "Where are you going now?"

"History," she said.

"So'm I." He held out his hand. "Let me see your schedule."

She handed him her official schedule grid, and he ran down the list, nodding.

"You're going to have the same kids from English in most of your classes." He gave her back the card. "What, were you a brain at your old school?" He grinned. "Or, do your parents have pull?"

"Um, well—" Meg wasn't quite sure how to answer that.

"Come on, it's down here." He started down the hall, then turned left, with Jeff trailing behind them. "He always follow you around?"

Meg nodded. Not that it would necessarily always be Jeff, but there would unquestionably be agents nearby whenever she was out in public. She had asked her father if it would be possible, once school started, for them to give her more space—and his immediate response was a very open-minded "Absolutely not."

"What happens if you go out or something?" Adam asked.

"I don't know," Meg said. But, did that mean he maybe wanted to ask her out sometime? She would probably die. She was going to have to figure out a way to take a surreptitious picture of him with her cell phone, and email it to Beth and Sarah—who were bound to approve.

"This is it up here." He pointed down the crowded corridor. "Patterson—he's the teacher—he's been looking forward to having you come for days."

Which made it sound like he'd been marking them off on a little calendar—which seemed unlikely. "Oh, yeah?" she said.

Adam nodded, smiling at her as he opened the door.

She smiled back. He had nice teeth. Very nice, white teeth. And a nice mouth, too. He'd probably never had chapped lips in his life, or—she should stop looking at his mouth, already. She should look at his eyes; it was always more appropriate to look at someone's eyes. He had a great mouth, though.

"Hope you're ready to tell everyone about 'your experiences,'" Adam said. "He's really into it."

Meg forgot about his mouth. "My experiences?"

Adam nodded. "Yeah. He can't wait."

She made an effort to keep her sigh inaudible.

21

MR. PATTERSON *DID* WANT to share her experiences—it was almost like being home again. As usual, she stuttered a lot and couldn't think of anything to say. Why did they always do that? On the first day, even.

Of course, if he'd wanted to hear about the efficacy of school vouchers, she could probably have given him a nifty little speech about *that*.

Barry and Jeff switched assignments at lunchtime, with Barry taking a position along one of the cafeteria walls. She had to say that she didn't envy them this particular duty—they were going to be bored out of their skulls.

Adam brought her over to his table and spent a couple of minutes introducing her to everyone: Gail, the girl who had said hello at the end of English class; Matt, curly, dark hair, wearing a Georgetown sweatshirt; Phyllis, who had suspicious eyes and kept her arm locked through the arm of a tall, very good-looking black guy named Nathan; Zachary, almost as good-looking, but with a goofy quality, too; Alison, who was wearing a long white button-down shirt, with a striped, fitted vest and filmy long scarf—reminding Meg very much of Annie Hall; and Josh, a boy with brown hair and glasses, who ate with quick motions, either tense because she was there—probably *not*—or just generally tense. But, his sweater was pretty nice, argyle and all.

She took a seat at the far end of the table, wishing that she had her mother's ability to remember names.

"What's the matter, Josh?" the boy in the Georgetown hoodie—Mike? Mark? Matt?—asked. "Where're the jokes?"

Josh—the one with glasses—concentrated on his sandwich. "What jokes?"

"Usually, we can never get him to shut up," Adam said, taking a napkin out of the holder in the middle of the table, brushing his arm against hers.

Wow. Had he done that on purpose? What a nice arm. She wanted to grab him, throw him down, and kiss him. Hell, do a lot more than kiss him. *That* would attract attention. She glanced at Josh to take her mind off what might be turning into graphic thoughts, and he flushed and dropped his sandwich, both of them immediately looking away.

Christ, with her luck, *he* would be the one who ended up liking her.

Then, Gail motioned toward her brown paper bag. "Hey, who packed your lunch?"

"Your mother?" Adam asked, and they all laughed.

"No, um, I did," Meg said.

"You mean, a chef did," Phyllis said.

"No, I did. See, I always figure—" She stopped, wishing that she could just crumple herself up, along with the bag, and get rid of this whole conversation.

"What?" Matt or Mike or Mark asked, when she didn't go on.

"It doesn't matter, it's pretty stupid." Looking around, she could see that they wanted her to tell them, anyway. "See, the thing is, I guess I'm neurotic or something, I don't know, but I can't stand tomato seeds." Which Trudy, of course, knew, and so, she *trusted* Trudy's sandwiches. "And just about everyone puts tomatoes on sandwiches, so I almost always make my own, so I can take the seeds out."

"How do you do that?" Gail asked dubiously.

Very, very special sleight of hand. "You cut off the top, and—" Meg pantomimed squeezing a tomato, then turned red, realizing that they were all going to think that she was a maniac.

"Like this one here." Zachary pointed at Josh with a half-eaten apple. "He won't eat hot dogs or bologna or anything."

"Are you kosher?" Meg asked him.

"N-no, only at Passover." He didn't meet her eyes. "I saw a film about how they make all that stuff, and I haven't been able to eat it since."

Matt-Mike-Mark laughed. "That film was probably fifty years old."

"Beef lips?" Josh looked up with sudden animation. "You like to eat beef lips? And hearts? And—"

"Enough already," Nathan said. "I got a sandwich to finish here." He frowned at his bologna sandwich, then bit off about a third of it.

He wasn't quite in Adam's league, but Nathan was pretty damn cute himself. No wonder Phyllis was hanging on to him. But—okay, if looks could kill, she had just barely escaped a very painful death. Meg Powers, femme fatale. What a joke.

"What's that?" Matt-Mark-Mike asked.

Meg looked down at the small plastic bag of delicate cookies in her hand. "What do you mean?"

"Did someone bake them, or do they buy them, or what?" he asked.

Oh. Meg frowned. "Well, they were, uh, left over."

Gail looked very curious. "Left over?"

"There were receptions all weekend, and there was stuff left-over." Meg put the bag down, too self-conscious to eat now.

"Did the chefs bake them?" Zachary asked.

No, her mother had—slaving away for hours, more pressing professional responsibilities entirely ignored. "I guess so. Or, you know, the pastry people." She held out the bag. "You want some?"

He nodded. "If it's okay, yeah."

Well, whatever floated his little boat. "Sure." She looked around uncertainly. "Anyone else want a cookie?"

Just about everyone did, so she put the plastic bag in the center of the table. Even Phyllis helped herself to one. When they had all finished, Meg took a bite out of one of the two that were left.

Hell, they weren't even all that *good*—she'd take a regular old Oreo, any day.

IT WAS A relief when school ended, and she could escape. She'd spent the entire day feeling like a tiny deer at the zoo, having everyone come up to the fence, then say nervously, "Does it bite?" Some guy had held the door for her and exchanged a few pleasantries as she left her French class—and two girls had given her incredible scowls. Being the President's daughter was a royal pain. Why couldn't her parents own a hardware store or a coffeehouse or something?

When she got back to the White House and ducked through the vestibule and into the Diplomatic Reception Room to head upstairs, she saw Preston lounging in one of the upholstered yellow armchairs by the fireplace, clearly waiting for her.

"Well," he said. "If it isn't Meghan Winslow Powers, her very own self."

Oh, swell. "No, I'm the doppelgänger," she said.

He motioned towards the chair across from his, with a quick jerk of his head. "Have a seat."

She was almost sure that these two particular chairs were generally reserved for heads of state—but that probably didn't mean that she and Preston would be imprisoned for sitting in them. Not indefinitely, anyway.

"Did you know," he said conversationally, "that the President recently appointed a Secretary of Education?"

She might have heard something about that, yeah. "Well, actually, she has to undergo confirmation hearings," Meg said.

Preston nodded. "So, you're hoping you still have a shot?"

"Yeah," Meg said. "Which would be good, because I think it would put me sixteenth in the line of succession."

"Actually, you'd be fourteenth, because Morales and Kimura"—two of the other Cabinet members-to-be—"weren't born in the United States," he said.

So much the better.

"But, maybe you should aim for Interior or Agriculture," he said, "because then, you would be in the top ten."

Good advice.

He straightened his tie—red silk with a gold paisley pattern—even though it was already perfectly aligned. "Of course, since you're not thirty-five, the line would skip over you, and everyone else would move up another slot."

Damn. Meg frowned. "That means it'll be years before *you* can assume office, either."

He nodded. "I know. It's a great disappointment."

They looked at each other, and she gave him her very most winning smile—which he returned with a half-grin.

"Living here doesn't mean that we're going to abrogate your First Amendment rights, Meg," he said, "but common sense should still trump intellect every so often, don't you think?"

For a hip guy, he could talk the talk with the best of them. And since that was an absolutely fair and reasonable argument, she nodded. "Is Linda going to come and yell at me, and say I need a full-time handler, and I'm not allowed to talk about policy, and all of that?"

Preston shook his head. "No, I promised I'd do it for her."

Oh. "Has that already happened?" she asked. Since it was kind of hard to tell.

He nodded.

Okay. Good. "You know, I *could* go to public school," Meg said. In fact, she had offered to do so, back when her parents had started discussing which schools she and her brothers would probably attend in the city. "I mean, if it would take some heat off her."

He shook his head again.

"It's hypocritical," she said. "Saying there are 'security issues' doesn't quite do it."

Preston sighed. "There *are* security issues."

Yeah, whatever. It was still hypocritical.

"They're not going to send you to a halfway decent public school, when they can send you to a *great* private school," he said.

Meg nodded. "Some animals are more equal than other animals."

He just shrugged. "And maybe you wouldn't be able to snap off a quote like that if you hadn't gone to *excellent* schools your entire life."

They had all been public schools—but, okay, public schools in an affluent suburb.

"Give her a chance to try and fix a few things," Preston said. "If everything's still exactly the same four years from now, *then* you can hammer her."

Which didn't allow for the probability that Congress would not be entirely cooperative about passing her legislation, of course. She looked around the room—an extremely *pretty*, and intimidating, room, feeling as though someone should come and serve them nectar, at once. And bow and scrape, too, maybe.

"Do you think we're both a *little* bit too comfortable in the world leaders' chairs?" she asked.

He grinned at her. "I won't tell, if you won't."

AFTER HE HAD gone back to his office in the East Wing, she wasn't quite sure what to do with herself. She talked to Barbara, who worked in the flower shop, for a few minutes, and then went up to the First Floor to goof around on the piano in the East Room for a while. She played "Greensleeves"—which really was just about the only song she knew, then part of "My Favorite Things," the first nine bars of "Deck the Halls," and the introduction to "No Business Like Show Business." Her repertoire exhausted—except for the last part of the "Mapleleaf Rag," which she quickly played—she got up from the piano and went to sit in the Green Room. She slouched in a Sheraton mahogany armchair, resting her feet on an undoubtedly priceless New York sofa table. After a few minutes of that, she got bored—and very briefly considered going down to the Oval Office to say hello—but, her mother would be busy, and she would be in the way.

The Oval Office was very impressive. Her mother had taken them in there on the second day, and it was the kind of room that made Meg want to stand up straight. The room had been—swiftly—redecorated, her mother giving the room a soft blue emphasis, and there were quiet hints of gold and yellow, too, which coordinated nicely with the Presidential Seal rug. There were two darker blue couches, and then, two formal armchairs on either side of the fireplace. A plant that had been growing for *decades*—being reproduced by countless cuttings, no doubt—covered most of the mantelpiece, and there were busts of Franklin Delano Roosevelt and Thomas Jefferson. Although there was usually a slight Western influence in the Oval Office, since her mother despised horses, she had had all of that removed. She had also added many more books to the built-in bookcases than Presidents usually displayed—because, she said, shelves covered with tchotchkes—even ones with historical significance—made her nervous.

There was a huge, mostly blue, impressionistic painting of Fifth Avenue on a rainy day by Childe Hassam in the White House collection, and her mother had had it hung over the fireplace. A Monet was on the wall to the right of her desk, and there was also a John Singer Sargent and a disturbing Margaret Bourke-White photograph that had been taken at a concentration camp at the end of World War II—both of which were on loan. The other art she had chosen was more traditional—although she had mostly stayed away from the predictable portraits of stern male statesmen.

The desk was the famous *HMS Resolute*—the same desk John F. Kennedy Jr. had played inside in a photo she'd seen about a million times—and it was made of dark, gleaming oak. Her mother had a complicated telephone system on it, a leather blotter and fountain pen set that had belonged to her father, a primitive clay paperweight—it was supposed to be a cat—that Meg had made when she was nine, and an ashtray that Steven had done as an art project—not that anyone in the family smoked—except for Trudy, who generally only did it furtively. Her mother used the ashtray for paper clips and things like that.

"What about me?" Neal had asked, and she had shown him the framed drawing that was going up on the wall to the left of her desk.

"What about me?" Meg's father asked, and her mother had grinned at him. Her parents might be under a lot of pressure lately, but other than a few snappish exchanges here and there, they sure seemed to be getting a kick out of each other. Thank God.

There were photos of everyone—including Kirby and the cats—on the table behind the desk and the tall, black executive chair. It was Meg's opinion that the school pictures of her brothers and the one of her were absolutely horrendous. Her mother liked them.

"How come there's one of everyone but you?" Steven asked her, studying the pictures and laughing uproariously at the one of Meg with prominent braces.

"I know what I look like," her mother said. "I want to feel as if you all are keeping me company all day."

Which was probably true, but her mother almost certainly meant figurative company, not literal companionship, so Meg decided to go upstairs. She found Steven and Neal in the solarium, drinking Coke, eating brownies, and watching a *Brady Bunch* DVD. Their aunt had given them the entire *series*, because she had said that it was one of her favorites when she was growing up, and even though the clothes were really stupid and mod, Meg and her brothers loved it, too, and had seen every episode at least twice.

Anyway, it was so refreshingly normal to see them lying around like that—despite the soaring view out the windows—that Meg flopped down on the couch next to them.

"How was school for you guys?" she asked.

Steven belched.

Meg nodded. "Me, too. How about you, Neal?"

Neal tried to burp, and made a noise that was more like a squeak.

"Absolutely," Meg said. "Same for me." She looked at the television. "Which one is this?"

"Jan gets glasses," Neal said.

Oh, good. Jan-centric episodes were always a goof.

Steven held out the back of his right hand for her to examine.

She frowned. "What am I looking at?"

He sighed deeply, and indicated the bruised knuckle.

What, and she had gotten a lecture just for pointing out the inequities of the American education system? "Oh, God, Steven," she said, "what did you do?"

"Some guy said I looked totally retarded in my tie." Steven grinned. "Guess *he* won't be bugging me anymore."

Great. "Steven, you can't go around hitting everyone who makes you mad," she said.

"Why not?" he asked. "Gets 'em off me."

"Yeah, but—" Meg stopped, not having any good way to contradict that. "What did your agents do?"

Steven shrugged. "Broke it up and yelled at us."

"Did you get in trouble?" she asked.

"Nah, no teachers around." He put most of a brownie in his mouth. "Kid's a nice guy. Said he plays baseball, and can probably get me hooked up with his team and all."

Meg looked at Neal. "What about you? Did you hit anyone?"

Neal laughed, and shook his head.

"Girl tried to kiss him," Steven said.

"Really?" Meg looked at her little brother—possibly in an entirely new, post-latency period, light. "What did you do?"

"Let her," Steven said. "What else?"

Neal giggled. "On the lips."

"Said she was pretty." Steven gave Kirby half a brownie, Kirby thumping his tail and going under the coffee table to eat it.

Neal nodded, giggling some more.

Great. She was sitting with a brawler—and a heart-breaker.

"The guys at your school all think you were ugly and stuff?" Steven asked.

With her luck, yeah.

"But, you're not," Neal said.

So speaketh the Heart-Breaker. Meg smiled at him. "Is that an expert opinion?" Then, she gestured towards the television. "Which one are we watching next?"

Steven pulled over the box, and looked at the list of episodes. "Maybe when Peter's voice changes?"

"Great," Meg said, took a brownie, and put her legs up on the coffee table. "I love that one."

DURING THE NEXT week or so, it began to seem as though school wasn't working out to be quite as bad as she had anticipated. She didn't *love* it—but, she wasn't miserable, either. In a couple of classes, like French and chemistry, she was ahead; in the others, she was just about even. Her computer programming class was incredibly boring, but she had to take an elective, and it fit into her schedule. She had some catch-up reading to do in English, and her new Calculus and Linear Algebra book was sort of confusing, but she figured she would just put extra time into those two subjects for a while.

Most of the people in her classes were either still intimidated, or asking constant questions. And girls were being very possessive with their boyfriends. It didn't look as though she was going to be making any female friends anytime soon.

Adam, on the other hand, was very attentive. Sometimes, she had the uneasy feeling that he had staked her out, and that it was more of a prestige thing than anything else, but since she had a pretty irreversible crush on him, she pushed away any suspicions, easily convincing herself that they would be a perfect couple.

Now, all she had to do was convince *him.*

Then, finally, he asked her out. It was a Tuesday, and he wanted to know if she could go to a movie or something on Friday.

"Um, yeah," she said, trying not to sound as delighted as she felt. "That would be nice."

"How's it work?" He glanced back at Barry, who was just down the hall.

"I'm not sure," she said. "I think they have to follow me in other cars."

Adam frowned. "Do they come inside the movie theater and everything?"

Well, *yeah,* presumably. "I think they have to," she said. "I mean—well, you know." Security issues, and all.

"What happens if we go somewhere after?" he asked.

She shrugged, since she hadn't exactly spent a lot of time talking to the agents on her detail about *dating.* "Um, I guess they have to sit at another table, maybe."

Adam didn't say anything.

Swell. "Hey, we don't have to go at all, if you don't want to," she said.

"It's not that." He shifted his weight. "I don't know. It's just kind of weird."

Yeah, but it wasn't like she had any *choice* in the matter. "I can't help it," she said.

"Yeah, yeah, I know." He kicked at the floor with one Nike, hands sulkly moving into his pockets.

He wasn't going to turn out to be a jerk. No way.

"It's just—" He touched her shoulder, moving his hand down her arm, and she felt a warm tremor of excitement in her back, trying to suppress an instant stream of potentially graphic thoughts, and making an effort *not* to move closer to him. "I wanted to be alone with you."

He wasn't a jerk—she knew he wasn't a jerk. He *did* like her.

"Well, how do I pick you up?" he asked. "Will they let me in?"

She hadn't had any visitors yet, but that didn't mean that she couldn't—as far as she knew. "I think I just have to tell them what time you're coming."

He nodded. "Okay. Seven-thirty sound good?"

Six in the morning would sound good. "Yeah," she said. "It sounds fine."

22

HER PARENTS DIDN'T react the way she expected. Her father—disappointingly—acted as though he wasn't sure that anyone was good enough to take out *his* daughter, and her mother looked worried, saying that she wasn't very happy about the idea, either. Meg found this incomprehensibly infuriating. She had been talking about him for days—where had they been?

"So, what am I supposed to do?" she asked her mother in the West Sitting Hall that night, after Steven and Neal had gone to bed. "Tell him I'm sorry, but my parents are prehistoric and won't let me go?"

Her mother lowered the papers she was studying. "I didn't say you couldn't go. I said that your father and I didn't like the idea of your going out with some boy we haven't met."

Yeah, because her mother was *always* so hands-on. "What, like it's my fault you aren't going to be home?" Meg asked.

"The last I heard, you were coming to the play *with* us," her mother said calmly.

"But, Adam asked me out. God." Meg shook her head. "Don't you understand anything?"

Her mother nodded. "Probably more than you think."

Yeah, right. Meg felt her teeth clench. "I didn't say I was definitely going to the play, I said maybe. Then, when he asked me, I forgot. Is that why you're mad?"

Her mother put the papers down. "There's a very simple solution to all of this. As I said before, invite him to dinner on Thursday, and that way, your father and I will get a chance to meet him before you go out."

"I can't do that." Meg sat down on the couch, very discouraged. She had expected her parents to be pleased and send her off with their blessing. It had never occurred to her that they might not let her go.

"Why not?" her mother asked.

"That might scare him off," Meg said. "To have to come here and sit through dinner and everything."

Her mother smiled. "What's wrong with us?"

And Beth complained about *her* mother? The next time they spoke, Meg was definitely going to offer to *swap*. Permanently. "Oh, forget it," she said. "You don't understand anything."

Now, her mother sighed. "Meg, I'm sure he's a perfectly nice boy, but there are a lot of strange people out there, you're in a very high-profile position, and can't you see why your father and I might be a little concerned?"

"I'm going to have a bunch of stupid agents with me," Meg said. "How much safer can I get?"

"Granted, but—" Her mother rubbed her hand across her eyes, looking as though she had just gotten a very bad headache. "What can you tell me about him? The only thing we've heard is that he's handsome."

Which was absolutely accurate. "I don't know," Meg said. "He plays football."

"That's it?" her mother said. "That's all you know? Where does he live? What do his parents do? Is he a good driver?"

"I, um, think his father works for the FCC," Meg said uncertainly.

Her mother frowned.

What, was that an agency she disliked or something? "We don't talk about that kind of stuff," Meg said, aware that she wasn't making a very good case for herself.

"What *do* you talk about?" her mother asked.

Hmmm. Well, okay, they didn't talk all that much; mostly, they just *looked* at each other. Meg shrugged. "Sex, drugs, liquor. You know how it is."

Her mother's eyes narrowed. "If you're trying to reassure me, it's not working."

Had the Senator had a better sense of humor than the President did? Surely, she must have. Whereas, the President was a damn grouch. "What do you want to hear?" Meg asked. "My God, we're only going to a movie. I'm even going to have armed guards. How much trouble can I get into?"

"Probably not very much." Her mother sighed again. "I'm afraid I still don't like the idea."

Which meant that her position was starting to move, finally. "But, I can go?" Meg asked.

"I suppose so. I mean, I guess," her mother picked up a delicate silver pen, toying with it, "that I should trust your judgment."

Hell, yeah. Meg nodded. "Absolutely. And don't worry, he really is nice."

"And handsome?" her mother asked wryly.

"*Very* handsome," Meg said.

HER FATHER WASN'T happy that her mother had given in, saying that if Adam was really all right, he wouldn't mind putting it off until they could meet him, but Meg won him over with the agents-as-strict-chaperones logic. Needless to say, she didn't tell Adam how concerned they were about the whole thing.

Friday, in the locker-room after gym class, Alison MacGregor, the girl who reminded her of Annie Hall, came over to talk to her, both her expression and her voice hesitant.

"Hi," she said, very distinctive in baggy pants, cowboy boots with skinny heels, and an oversized shirt with a man's tie for a belt.

"Hi," Meg said, hoping that—for once—someone was going to treat her normally.

They looked at each other.

"I hate gym," Alison said. "Don't you?"

Okay, so they would establish some common ground. "Yeah, really," Meg said. And it was even true, since she only engaged in sports involving racquets or downhill skis. "How many times can you play volleyball?"

"Last fall, we did square dancing," Alison said.

Oy vey. Meg managed not to shudder. "Sorry I missed it."

"That's what you think." Alison started to say something, then stopped. "I, uh—you look a lot like your mother."

Yeah, so what else was new? Meg shrugged, pretty much losing interest in wherever this conversation was now going. "A little, I guess."

"It's just—" Alison stopped again. "I mean—"

The bell rang, and they both automatically looked up at the clock.

"We'd better get to French," Alison said.

Where a vocabulary quiz awaited them. "It's just what?" Meg asked.

Alison shook her head. "Nothing."

Naturally. Meg adjusted her knapsack on her shoulder and started for the door.

Alison caught up to her. "Wait a minute."

Meg paused.

"I was new last year," Alison said.

Okay, that was potentially interesting—and certainly common ground. Meg looked over. "Oh, yeah?"

Alison nodded. "It takes people a while to loosen up."

"How long?" Meg asked.

Alison laughed. "Is it really that bad?"

Unless one enjoyed being unpopular.

"I just meant that it would probably be easier if you looked like your father, instead," Alison said.

"What—you mean, masculine?" Meg asked.

Alison grinned. "If you think that would work for you, sure."

Well, it would certainly be a good way to torment Linda.

As they went out into the hall, she saw Adam coming towards them and moved her hair back over her shoulders, hoping that she looked fairly presentable. Unlike certain Leaders of the Free World, she didn't always remember to check mirrors whenever they were handy.

"Do you like him that much?" Alison asked.

Meg blushed. "He seems like a nice guy," she said, trying not to stare as he ambled along in their direction. How could any human being be that incredibly good-looking? She glanced at Alison. "Don't you think so?"

"Yeah," Alison said, although her voice sounded kind of—flat. "Sure."

"Hi," Adam said, nodding slightly at Alison and then grinning at her.

"Hi," Meg said, flushing as he slid his arm around her waist. "Adam, come on." She pushed at his hand. "Don't."

He kept his arm right where it was. "Why not?"

"I guess I'll see you guys later," Alison said, edging away.

"Well, wait—" Meg started, but Alison had already joined some other people from their gym class and was heading down the hall. She turned back to Adam, and he put his other hand on her shoulder. "Come on, don't," she said, knowing that her arms wanted very much to go around his neck, and for him to kiss her—no matter *what* anyone else thought.

"How come?" he asked, leaning closer.

"Everyone's looking," she said. Including, she assumed, the Secret Service.

He glanced around, grinning. "Yeah. So?"

"Just don't, okay?" She pulled free, very embarrassed.

He shrugged, put his arm back around her waist, and walked her towards their next class.

RIGHT BEFORE HER parents and brothers went off to the play that night—Steven complaining that there was *no way* he should have to go, if Meg got to skip it—her mother told her to be careful, still not looking happy about the situation, and her father warned her not to give her agents any trouble, and to be home by midnight. Steven had been doing things like trying to lose his agents lately, and her parents were really mad about it.

To say nothing of the agents.

She took a shower, then paced around her bedroom, trying to decide what to wear. Adam was the type who would show up in a jacket, maybe even a tie, so she ended up going with a skirt and the grey cashmere sweater she'd gotten for Christmas. She put on some perfume—too much?—grabbed her Bloomingdale's coat from the closet, and went downstairs to wait for him. He was supposed to be coming to the South Entrance, and she decided to wait in the Red Room, sitting on the American Empire sofa, which had legs in the shape of what Meg thought were very unattractive gold dolphins. She checked the clock above the mantelpiece several times, drumming on the red damask arm of the sofa with her right hand, getting more and more nervous about this date as it got closer.

She *didn't* really know him. They *hadn't* talked much. She had no idea what, if anything, they had in common—other than the fact that they went to the same school. And, worst of all, what if her parents were—*right*?

Which made her feel a little better, because there was *no way* that they were right; they were just being overprotective.

Promptly at seven-thirty, a butler appeared.

"Mr. Miller has arrived, Miss Powers," he said. "Shall I show him upstairs?"

"Oh." She stopped drumming. "No, thank you, I'll go right down."

She took the elevator instead of the stairs, staring briefly at the mirror and deciding that she looked—not so hot. Maybe she should have worn something else. Beth had been full of suggestions—none of which she had taken, and now, that seemed like a really big mistake.

Adam was standing just inside the Diplomatic Reception Room, wearing, indeed, a jacket, with a tie underneath his sweater.

"Hi," he said. "I mean, hello." His eyes went down her outfit. "You look nice."

And if she were less stubborn, she could probably have looked *nicer*. Damn it. "Thank you," she said. "So do you."

"Is your family here?" he asked, looking around.

She shook her head. "They went to the Kennedy Center."

They stood awkwardly for a minute, not looking at each other.

"Guess we should probably be going," he said.

Meg nodded, relieved that he hadn't asked her to take him on a tour or something. She'd feel like a jerk doing that, even though she could tell from his expression that he wanted one. "Uh, my parents are going to be home around eleven or so. Maybe after, you can come up and meet them. They were sorry they had to miss you."

"Sounds good," he said, immediately.

They didn't say anything else until they were in his car, with her agents in two other cars. He glanced over, now not shy about letting his eyes move.

"You look great," he said.

She blushed, focusing out through the windshield.

"You sure this movie is okay with you?" he asked.

"Oh, yeah," she said. Lied, actually. When they had made the plans, he'd suggested going to one of those serial murderer movies Hollywood was always churning out. Since it had seemed like he wanted to see it, she had agreed without blinking, even though she would have been much happier going to almost *anything* else. At dinner, her father had asked what movie they were going to see, and when she told him, he had frowned and exchanged glances with her mother, who asked if it had been her idea or Adam's. Meg feigned confusion and changed the subject by asking her to pass the salt.

A big, dumb comedy was opening that night; maybe she should ask him if he wanted to go to that, instead. Or, in retrospect, they could have watched absolutely any movie they wanted in the White House private theater—and he probably would have been really into the idea.

Too late now, though.

"Why you sitting way over there?" he asked.

Because she was shy, maybe? "Am I?" she said.

"Yeah. Come on, move over." He patted the seat next to him.

She wasn't really comfortable taking off her seatbelt, and she looked behind them at one of her agents' cars, and didn't move.

"What," he gestured with his head towards the rear window, "you uptight about them?"

"Kind of." She looked through the windshield at the city streets, ignoring the battle the emotional and intellectual parts of her head were having. The emotional part was insisting that he was really nice, really handsome, really everything—while the intellectual side was saying, very quietly, that he was kind of a jerk, and she ought to face up to it.

"You okay?" he asked.

"What?" She blinked. "Oh. Sure."

"You look good tonight." He reached over and touched her face with his right hand. "I wasn't kidding."

Yes, flattery would get him everywhere. "Thank you," she said, feeling her intellectual arguments weakening.

The theater was mostly empty, so they had no trouble finding seats, and only one person seemed to notice them, although he promptly nudged his companions, who all turned around and stared.

Great. The guy probably hadn't recognized *her,* but even when her agents dressed down, they were still pretty obvious.

Adam chose seats far over on one side, letting her go into the row first. One of her agents sat up near the front, and two others were up behind them somewhere.

"You want popcorn or anything?" he asked, taking off his jacket.

"If you do," she said.

He looked around. "Am I allowed to leave you to go get some?"

"Yeah, they're right there," she said.

He nodded, a little grimly, and then headed for the concessions stand.

While he was gone, two of the people who had recognized her started to come over—but one of her agents instantly took such a subtle, but threatening, position that the guys stopped in their tracks and then went straight back to their seats.

When Adam returned, he settled into his chair, putting his arm around her as soon as the lights went down. She spent the first few minutes of the movie thinking about how much she liked the opposite sex and how great their arms were. She felt warm, she felt safe, she felt very female—and she felt like throwing him down and kissing him.

Yeah, the emotional argument was gaining ground.

He pulled her closer. "You still here?"

"What?" she asked. "I mean, yeah."

"You like it?" he asked.

She nodded, looking up at the screen, seeing that the movie was in the middle of another embarrassing sex scene, which, if the plot stuck to its current course, would end with the beautiful girl lying on the floor in a pool of blood, while the camera lingered on her. She closed her eyes.

His hand was creeping down over the front of her shoulder and she moved, avoiding it. He tried again, then got the hint, and kept his hand where it was.

The fourth murder was particularly offensive, and even Adam seemed uncomfortable.

"I didn't know it was going to be this bad," he whispered.

"It's not that bad," she said bravely.

"It's awful." He glanced behind them, then at her, sliding closer. "You really do look good tonight."

"Well, so do you." She also looked over her shoulder, sensing that he was about to kiss her, and wondering if her agents—and the people who had recognized her before—were all going to be able to see him do it.

At least, they were way over on the side. Did she really want him to kiss her so much that she was willing to do it in public? The answer was very easy, and she blushed in the darkness. Better to have him kiss her here, where her agents could pretend to be paying attention to the movie.

"Come here," he said, and turned her face to him. Then, he kissed her, one hand on her cheek.

She couldn't keep back a quick, shuddering sigh of relief, having wanted him to do that ever since she'd met him, but then she pulled her head away, embarrassed—and startled—by the intensity of her reaction.

"You okay?" he asked.

She nodded, blushing, and as he kissed her again, she let a tentative hand move up into his hair, feeling very—new—at all of this. She opened her eyes, and saw that his were closed, then checked to see if her agents were watching—which they weren't, thank God.

His breathing was faster, and she hoped that it was something *she* had done, and not just puberty. His arms were warm around her, and she noticed how good he smelled; he was wearing some kind of really sexy aftershave. And—his hand was not only already under her sweater, but also under her *bra*. She flinched, surprised that it felt so good—and that he had managed it so deftly. But, this was the first time they'd ever—and they were sitting in a movie, and—she really couldn't let him—

"Adam, don't," she said in a very low voice.

He looked confused. "Hunh?"

"Come on, don't." She pushed his hand down, hoping—again—that no one was watching or listening.

"Why not?" he asked.

"Because I don't want you to," she said.

He tried to get his hand back underneath her sweater, and she dodged it. "Why not?"

"Because it's—I mean, because we're—" She tried to think of a way to explain it. Especially since the answer seemed so damn *obvious*. "I just don't."

"I don't believe it." He sat back in his seat, scowling up at the screen, and Meg sat back, too, folding her arms defensively across her chest.

"We didn't see you as a tease," he said quietly.

What? She stared at him. "I'm not!"

"You led me on," he said.

How? By *sitting* next to him? "I did not," she said.

"Yeah, well, guess we didn't see you as being frigid, either." He watched the fifth murder.

"I'm not—" She stopped, shoulders crumpling. "You said 'we.' "

He shrugged. "So what?"

"Oh, God." She lowered her head, not trusting her expression, and fumbled for her coat.

"What are you doing?" he asked.

She got up, walking—almost running—up the aisle, as her agents jumped up to follow her.

"Meg?" One of them caught up to her in the lobby. "What's wrong?"

"I don't feel very good." She didn't look at him, fighting back a strong urge to burst into tears. "I think I'd better go home."

Adam hurried out after them. "Meg, what's going on?"

"I need to go home," she said. "I don't feel very good."

He stared at her. "You're gonna leave? Just like that?"

Damn straight. Luckily, the lobby was almost empty, and she was able to make her way to the main doors almost completely unrecognized.

"You're not even going to let me drive you?" he asked.

"I have a ride," she said, and kept walking.

"Meg, come on." He touched her arm. "Look, let me drive you, okay? I'm sorry."

She shook his hand off. "I have a ride."

"Okay, okay, look," he said. "Just get in my car for a second. I have to talk to you, okay?"

She hesitated.

"Just for a second, okay?" he asked.

She thought about that, then nodded and got in, staying close to the passenger's door.

"Look, uh—" He put his keys in the ignition, then turned to face her. "I'm sorry. What did I do?"

She was supposed to believe that he didn't know *precisely* what he had done? She stared back at him. "Did you ask me out because of *who* I am?"

"No, I—" He shifted uneasily. "I mean, it's not that you're not—"

She nodded stiffly, and opened the door.

"Meg, wait." He put his hand on her arm again. "I didn't mean it that way—it was before you even came. Everyone figured you might go with me, and then we could—"

"Figure out how far I went?" she asked.

"No, I—" He stopped. "Well, sort of."

"Terrific." She knocked his hand away. "Make sure you tell them."

"Meg, come on." He tried to touch her shoulder, and she shrugged him off. "I really am sorry. I like you. I didn't know I was going to—I thought you'd be—I don't know. *Famous*. But, I like you. When we started fooling around, I didn't even think about those guys. I kissed you because I wanted to. Really."

She nodded, pushing the door all the way open.

"Can we try again sometime?" he asked. "I'd like to."

"Well, I wouldn't." She got out of the car. "Tell your friends that, too."

He sighed. "Meg, at least let me—"

She slammed the door, ran over to one of her agents' cars, and jumped into the back.

"Is everything—?" one of them started.

"Just take me home, okay?" She folded her arms. "I mean, please."

Both agents nodded, and the one behind the wheel, Ned, started the engine.

23

AT THE WHITE House, she went straight upstairs to her room, ripping off her coat and throwing it on the bed. Luckily, her family wasn't home yet. Of course, why would they be? It was only ten. She took off her sweater and skirt, slamming them onto her closet floor, and then changed into a battered, huge chamois shirt, a pair of old navy blue sweatpants, and her hiking boots.

She went out to the hall, where Felix was just coming out of the kitchen.

"Did you have a nice time?" he asked, smiling.

None of this was his fault, so she definitely wasn't going to snap at him.

No matter how much she wished she could.

"Yeah, I did." With a great effort, she smiled back. "Do you think I could have a Coke, please?"

When he came back out, carrying her glass on a silver tray, along with a crisply pressed napkin, and a plate of cookies—which she didn't want—she thanked him, and carried the glass up to the solarium, where she could be alone for a while.

She sat down on one of the couches, knowing that she was going to cry, but afraid to start. To distract herself, she turned on the television, and slumped down, watching *SportsCenter* for a few minutes. She was going to call Beth, but it was Friday night, and any *normal* person her age had friends and was out with them. She sipped her soda, occasional tears sliding out and down her cheeks, not bothering to wipe them away.

At around eleven-thirty, by which point she had given up on television and was just plain crying, she heard footsteps in the hall and dragged her sleeve across her face to get rid of any traces of tears.

"Hi," her mother said.

Meg didn't look at her. "When'd you come home?"

"Just a little while ago," she said. "Felix told me you came in, but I wasn't sure where you were."

Meg didn't answer, drinking her Coke.

"Do you want to tell me about it?" her mother asked.

"About what?" Meg looked up at her mother, who was, naturally, ravishing in a slim red velvet dress. So beautiful, in fact, that Meg felt a strong flash of hatred, hating her for always looking, and being, so perfect.

Her mother must have felt something, because she paused on her way across the room. "May I keep you company?"

"Why?" Meg asked. "So you can gloat?"

"I don't think you meant that," her mother said.

Well, maybe the President wasn't quite as god-damn smart as she thought she was. Meg didn't say anything, her arms tight across her chest as her mother moved Kirby off the couch and sat down. They sat there in complete silence, Meg scowling and her mother brushing at an invisible piece of lint on her sleeve.

"Well," Meg said finally. "Aren't you going to say I told you so?"

Her mother shook her head. "No. What happened?"

Meg clenched her fist, very close to crying again. "He only asked me out because of you, okay? You were right, are you happy?"

"I'm sorry," her mother said, and put her arm around her.

"Don't!" Meg moved away. "Please don't touch me."

Her mother slowly withdrew her arm. "I want to help you. What can I do?"

Meg shook her head, bringing her left hand up to cover her eyes, the tears starting again.

"I really am sorry." Her mother reached over to rub her back. "I wish I could—"

"I just want to be by myself," Meg said, feeling the tears come harder, not wanting anyone to see them. "Please?"

"Oh, Meg." Her mother kept rubbing her back. "I don't want to leave you alone."

"You have been for sixteen years," Meg said. "Why stop now?"

There was a silence so silent that Meg was sure she could hear both of their hearts beating, especially hers.

Why had she said that? She never should have said that. She swallowed. "Mom, I'm sorry, I didn't mean to say that. I don't know why I said that."

Her mother sat back, looking suddenly smaller, her face expressionless.

"I'm sorry," Meg said. "I didn't mean it."

"I expect you must have," her mother said, so softly that Meg almost couldn't hear her. She stood up, her eyes as distant as a *Time* magazine photograph. "Excuse me."

As she started towards the door, Meg knew she didn't want to let her leave first, since she'd be afraid to go downstairs, if she did. So, she jumped up and hurried past her, running downstairs to her room and slamming the door, leaning against it, too out of breath to cry.

Why had she said that? She shouldn't have said that. She should have just told her that she hated her, or something. Lots of people said they hated their parents when they were angry, and her mother would know that she hadn't meant it. And she hadn't.

Well, okay, she *had,* but not really. It just came out. But how come, when she felt terrible, she had had to turn around and immediately hurt someone *else?* A hell of a thing to know about herself.

Slowly, she pushed away from the door, realizing that she was crying again. She hadn't even shouted it in anger—she had said it calmly. Maliciously. *Vindictively.* Somehow, that made it worse. Anyone could get mad and yell things. Nothing like going for someone's weak spot, though.

She sat down on her bed, taking off her hiking boots and

sweatpants, then getting under the covers and reaching up to turn the light off. She stared up at the chandelier in the darkness, tears sliding down her cheeks and into the pillow. She lay there, feeling a lot of tired hatred—almost all of it directed towards herself.

SHE DIDN'T SLEEP much, and the next morning, she was afraid to go to breakfast. Only, she would have to face her sooner or later. So, she got up, took a shower, put on jeans and a thick ragg sweater, and went out to the Presidential Dining Room with its stupid wallpaper. She hesitated in the doorway, seeing her parents at the table, eating silently. They glanced up, neither of them looking very happy to see her.

Her father. She had forgotten about her father. He was probably ten times angrier than her mother was. She backed up toward the hall, figuring that she would just skip breakfast.

"Meggie, come on!" Neal shoved her from behind, trying to get into the room, so she took a deep breath and went over to sit in her usual place.

"Morning." Neal hugged their father. "Hi, Mommy." He went over to the other end of the table, fastening his arms around their mother's waist.

"Hi, Neal." She hugged him back, her face hidden by her hair as she kissed the top of his head.

Meg tentatively checked her father's eyes, found them very cold, and focused on her place setting.

"What would you like for breakfast?" a butler asked.

"Just cereal, please," she said, not looking up.

"What kind?" he asked.

"Uh," she tried to think of a brand, "Rice Krispies."

Once he had served her, she tried to eat, but her stomach felt like lead. Neal kept up a high-pitched running conversation about the play they had seen the night before, which he had apparently loved.

"And then," he bounced in his chair, "when the man came out

and danced, and his friend, his friend came out, and *he* started dancing—"

"Hi." Steven came in, wearing sweatpants and a cut-off compression shirt, which meant that he had a new athletic conditioning plan to get ready for baseball. He took a boxer's stance and gave their father several light, quick punches on the arm. "Hi, Pop," he said breezily. Then, he saluted the other end of the table. "Hey, Prez." He sat down, slapping Neal on the head. "How ya doin', brat?" He grinned across the table at Meg. "Betcha looked pretty ugly last night. D'ja have to pay him to take you?"

Something snapped somewhere inside, and Meg threw her cereal and milk at him, then put the bowl down, running out of the room. She saw the surprise on the butler's face, and heard her father's furious "Meg, get back here!" but she didn't stop, even though she wasn't sure where to go. She kept running, and then ducked into the Lincoln Bedroom, lying down on the antique bed and wishing that Lincoln's ghost would come along and carry her off.

She knew they wouldn't follow her, and no one did, so she stayed there for what seemed like a very long time, hands folded behind her hair, staring up at the chandelier, which she decided that she hated. She hated all of the chandeliers in the house. In fact, she hated every chandelier in the *world.* They didn't have chandeliers at home; they had lamps. She liked lamps. She lay there, hating chandeliers, sitting up when she heard a gasp.

"Glory, and you startled me, Miss Powers," the housekeeper in the doorway said, holding a dust cloth. "I'm sorry, I didn't expect—I'll just come back later."

"No, I'm finished." Meg got off the bed, smoothing the wrinkles. "Sorry."

She moved out into the East Sitting Hall, trying to decide where to go next. But, the longer she put it off, the more time her father would have to simmer. Maybe she should just go back to her room, and if she ran into him on the way, she could at least find out how angry he was.

He was in one of the chairs in the Center Hall, holding the morning *Post*, obviously waiting for her, and she wondered what time it was. Seeing her, he stood up, folded the paper under his arm, and indicated the Presidential Bedroom with one sharp point of his hand.

"I-I don't feel good," she said. "I have to sleep."

He just looked at her, and she swallowed, and went down to her parents' room. He followed her, closing the door behind him.

He couldn't actually *kill* her. It would be all over the news.

She sat in a rocking chair, and he sat across from her on a small sofa. He put the paper down, folding his hands, and she wondered if he was going to crack his knuckles. Sometimes he did, although it drove her mother crazy. He looked at her, cracking them halfway.

Yeah, he was mad, all right.

"I didn't mean it," she said, making an effort not to sound nervous, holding onto the worn wooden arms of the chair.

He frowned at her. "Why did you say it, then?"

Good question. She avoided his eyes. "I was mad."

"A little below the belt, don't you think?" His voice was very calm. Almost casual. People in her family didn't yell much.

"Does she, uh, hate me?" she asked, not looking up.

"What do you think?" he asked.

Meg shrugged, running her hand along the right arm of the chair.

"Do you hate her?" he asked.

She shook her head. "You know I don't."

"I'm not always convinced," he said.

She nodded, watching the bones and muscles of her hand move as she tightened and loosened her grip on the chair. "As usual. Taking my side."

"Hey!" He grabbed her arms, holding them just above the elbows so she would have to look at him. "Let's get something clear. I don't want any more fresh remarks out of you. Not to your mother, not to me, not to your brothers. Is that clear?"

She looked right back at him. "You're hurting my arms."

"You know I'm not," he said, but loosened his grip. "Is that quite clear?"

She jerked free, folding her arms so it would be hard for him to grab them again.

"Well, it had better be," he said.

Yeah, fine, whatever. "What happens now?" she asked.

"First of all, you're grounded," he said. "More because of what you did to your brother than anything else. For two weeks, and if you don't shape up by then, I'll add on more time."

Big deal. "Just moving here grounded me," she said, standing up.

He glared at her. "Where are you going?"

"I thought we were finished," she said.

"We aren't," he said.

Oh. She sat back down.

"Look, Meg," he said. "I know you were upset last night. Neither your mother nor I is even exactly sure what happened, but we know how upset you were. Do you want to tell me about it?"

She shook her head.

"Are you sure?" he asked.

Very god-damn sure. She nodded.

"You might feel better," he said.

She shook her head again.

"Well, all right, but I think it might help." He sighed, pulling absent-mindedly at his tie—which he normally wouldn't be wearing on a Saturday morning. "I know how difficult it's been for you—it's been difficult for all of us. What it means is that we all have to try harder, especially with each other, okay?"

"I'm sorry," she said stiffly.

"Neal and I aren't the ones who deserve apologies," he said.

No, probably not. Meg got up. "How angry *is* she?"

"She's more hurt than anything else." He let out his breath. "You and I both hit below the belt, Meg. It's something we need to work on."

"Yeah, I guess." She opened the door. "I'll be in my room."

The hall was empty, although she could hear a vacuum cleaner going somewhere on the east end of the floor. Inside her room, Vanessa—who had fallen asleep on her chamois shirt—woke up and stretched out a front paw, flexing her claws.

"I wish it was this time yesterday," Meg said, Vanessa purring in response—and then swiping at her.

She was going to check her email, but took an Anne Tyler novel out of her bookcase and stretched out on her bed to read for a while. To read something *fun*, instead of stupid homework.

Sometimes, she wished she had a sister. Having a sister would probably have made it easier. Being a son of the first female President meant having a successful, courageous mother. Being the only daughter meant having something to live up to. Her mother was beautiful, a phenomenal tennis player, *President*—Meg could never do anything *as* well. It was like she was defeated before she even tried.

She flipped over onto her stomach—which annoyed Vanessa—since all she wanted to do was read for the rest of the day. Take a vacation from real life.

For weeks, if possible.

At twelve-thirty, there was a knock on the door.

"Do you want lunch?" Neal asked.

She hesitated, but then opted for cowardice. "No, thanks, I'm not hungry."

"It's onion soup, and hamburgers, and stuff," he said through the door.

"Thanks, but I'm not hungry," she said.

"Are you sure?" he asked.

Fratricide. She got up and opened the door. "Neal, I'm just not hungry. Thanks, anyway."

When the next knock came, she was reading a Laura Lippman mystery.

"May I come in?" her father asked.

"Uh, yeah." She turned over, so she would be facing him.

He opened the door, dressed to go out in a dinner jacket and black tie.

"Where are you going?" she asked.

"The French Embassy," he said.

Oh. Right. There was a big dinner there tonight.

"They'll have supper ready for the three of you in about fifteen minutes," he said. "I think we'll be home fairly late, so I'd like it if you spent some time with your brothers, instead of holing up in here all night."

Meg nodded.

"It might be a nice idea for you to go in and say good-bye to your mother," he said.

It was hard not to groan. "Now?" she asked.

"I think it would be a very good idea," he said.

If she tried to argue, she wasn't going to win, so she just nodded and went down the hall. The door was open, but Meg knocked, anyway.

"Come in," her mother said.

Meg put her hands uneasily in her pockets. "Uh, hi."

Her mother nodded, not turning from the mirror.

"You, uh, you look nice," Meg said.

Her mother shrugged, putting on her earrings.

This conversation definitely wasn't going very well. "I'm sorry," Meg said.

Now, her mother turned, looking less than convinced. "Oh?"

Meg sighed. "I really am. I was upset, so I wanted to make someone else upset. I'm sorry, and I didn't mean it."

"Okay." Her mother picked up her brush, but lowered it. "I'm sorry I haven't always been there."

"I told you I didn't mean that," Meg said.

Her mother turned away, brushing her hair.

Great. One slip of the tongue—and apparently, they were never going to like each other again. She eased back towards the door, very uncomfortable. "Uh, have a good time."

"Thank you," her mother said. "Please keep an eye on your brothers."

Meg nodded, they looked at each other for a very short, uneasy second—and then, Meg left the room.

24

SHE SPENT MOST of Sunday in her room, sometimes doing homework, but mostly reading and wasting time on the Internet. She had apologized to Steven, who thought that getting hit with cereal was funny, but her mother was still distant. It didn't seem to be blatant, or calculated, but it was definitely uncomfortable. So, Meg stayed in her room.

Going back to school was going to be terrible, too. Adam was sure to have gone around telling everyone. She wasn't sure what was worse—having people laugh behind her back, or laugh in *front* of her. Both were sure to happen.

Getting dressed on Monday morning, she thought about Scarlett O'Hara. Scarlett had been caught with Ashley once in what looked like an affair, but wasn't, and she had to go to a party that night to face all of Atlanta's society, a society that had never liked her much in the first place. So, she went looking her best, her attitude a damn-the-torpedoes sort of defiance.

Accordingly, Meg decided to attempt to look *her* best, an outfit that included her black boots, her Inaugural Day skirt, and a black velvet blazer that Beth had always insisted made her look *très chic.* Dashing, even. She also spent a long time blow-drying her hair so that it would be thick, full, and dramatic, sweeping back from her face. She even went with some mascara and lip gloss. What did she care if Adam had spread rumors all over the place.

Okay, she cared a lot—but no one else was going to know it.

She was at her locker, getting her books before her first two classes, when Josh Feldman walked by, eyes nervous behind his glasses, but smiling at her.

"H-hi," he said, reddening at the stutter. "How was your weekend?"

Meg stiffened and concentrated on her books, not answering. What was he trying to do—get her off the rebound? See if he could burnish his reputation by tricking her into a date and making his way *past* second base? What a creep.

Josh hesitated, saw that she wasn't going to respond, and reddened more, backing away through the morning crush of students.

Except for that beginning lapse, she was careful not to be rude to anyone, but she didn't go out of her way to be friendly, either. Adam never spoke to her, and none of his male friends would make eye contact with her, either. She made a point of avoiding the opposite sex in general—which, stupidly, got her quite a few smiles from girls in her classes.

She was staring down at her math homework, most of which she was sure was wrong, since she was having some trouble grasping the correct polar coordinates, when someone sat next to her.

"Hi," Alison said cheerfully, wearing tapered pants and a cropped wool blazer, layered on top of a slim-cut t-shirt.

Meg smiled briefly. "Hi," she said, and looked back down at her notebook.

"What's with you and Adam?" Alison gestured up a few rows to where Adam was sitting and laughing with his friends. "I thought you guys went out on Friday."

Meg shrugged.

"How'd it go?" Alison asked.

What, like it was any of her business? They were complete strangers, for Christ's sakes. "It was fine," Meg said, her hands tightening on her notebook.

"Did you have a good time?" Alison asked, sounding much less sure of herself.

Yes. It was swell. Meg nodded, not looking at her.

"If you say so." Alison flipped her own book open, rather forcefully. "Sorry I asked."

Meg shrugged. Yeah, this was the only person at the whole damn school who had been making a genuine effort to try and get to know her—but, so what? Who needed friends, right? Everything she'd ever read said that most Presidential children had trouble fitting in; why should she be any different?

"How come you make it so hard for people?" Alison asked.

She made it hard for people? But, points for Alison, for being a bit of a pit bull.

"Up until now, the only person you really talked to was Adam," Alison said. "Now, you aren't talking to anyone. No wonder they think you're obnoxious."

Whoa. "Who thinks I'm obnoxious?" Meg asked, carefully expressionless.

"It doesn't even bother you, does it," Alison said.

Maybe it did—and maybe it didn't.

Alison nodded, and turned away with what appeared to be disgust. "Yeah, that's what I figured."

She didn't consider herself obnoxious, but she maybe didn't consider herself to be particularly friendly, either. "It bothers me," she said quietly. "It bothers me a lot."

Alison slapped her book shut. "Can I tell you something?"

Meg shrugged and nodded at the same time, her hands tightly clasped together under her desk.

"Adam is just a big, conceited—well, you name it." Alison glared at the back of his head as he said something to the group of guys around him, and they all laughed. "If the rest of us weren't scared of you, someone would have told you. I almost did after gym on Friday."

"Why would anyone be scared of *me*?" Meg asked.

Alison looked at her, rather pityingly.

"I'm just, like, normal," Meg said, feeling grumpy, fretful, and irritated—all at the same time. "You guys are the ones who are intimidating."

"*We* are. Look at you today." Alison motioned towards her outfit. "My God, you look like the cover of *Vogue*."

Meg blushed, wishing that she'd worn sweatpants, instead. But, even if she put out a hundred percent effort, she was never going to come anywhere close to being *Vogue*-worthy. "More like *Town & Country*, probably," she said.

Alison laughed. "Actually, yeah. Good call."

Not that *Town & Country* had been her intent. Meg ran her pen slowly down the spiral of her notebook. "At home, I used to wear just jeans and sneakers and all."

"No shirts?" Alison asked, grinning.

Meg shook her head. "No, I don't like shirts much."

"Come on now, settle down, everyone," their teacher was saying, sounding very annoyed.

Alison shot a note over, and Meg picked it up, unfolding the paper.

"Are you really quiet and bookish?" it asked.

Meg thought about that, then scribbled, "Sometimes," and flicked the paper back.

It returned almost immediately.

"Me, too," it said.

SO, AT LUNCH, she sat at the same table where she had been all along. Adam was across the room with a bunch of football players, and she found herself with a group that was mostly female, and—mostly—friendly. Nathan was there, too, his girlfriend, Phyllis, keeping her arm through his, and Josh Feldman sat at the far end of the table with Zachary.

Meg watched him eat, wondering if maybe he wasn't one of Adam's friends, after all. Maybe he was just a bundle of nerves. She shouldn't have been so—well—*obnoxious* to him.

He looked up and met eyes with her, his left hand promptly knocking over his milk. He flushed, blotting it up with some napkins.

"But, no one's scared of you," Alison muttered next to her.

"He's not scared of me," Meg said.

Although she kind of had a feeling that he *was*.

When the bell rang, she managed to get over next to him as he threw away his lunch bag.

"I'm sorry about this morning," she said. "You just caught me at a bad time."

"No, I'm sorry," he said, not looking at her. "I didn't mean to—"

She shook her head. "You didn't. *I* did. Please don't take it personally."

"Oh, I-I didn't," he said, his gaze a little to her left. "I mean, it's okay."

"Well, I'm really sorry," she said, and they both nodded, and went their separate ways.

After school, she walked with Alison down the hall towards the section of junior lockers, with Marcy—today's trail agent—behind them.

"Do you play tennis or run or anything?" Alison asked.

"Yeah," Meg said. "I, uh, play some tennis." And it had been almost nine months, so she *wasn't* still pissed off that she'd lost in the semi-finals of the MIAA Tournament.

"Oh, right." Alison grinned. "Guess I read that somewhere. Anyway, I'm not that good, but do you maybe want to play sometime this week?"

She *always* wanted to play tennis. "Yeah—" Meg stopped, sighing. "I mean, I'm sorry, but I can't."

"Oh." Alison looked embarrassed. "Well, okay. It was just an—"

"I kind of got grounded," Meg said. "I was a jerk this weekend, and I got slammed with two weeks."

"Wow." Alison mulled that over. "I never would have thought that they—two weeks, hunh?"

Meg nodded. "Unless I can talk him down."

"Do you think you can?" Alison asked.

Probably not. "Maybe. But—" Meg hesitated, not sure if this was going to be too forward. "Well, it's still mostly too cold to play, but maybe you'd like to come over sometime, anyway. I'm going to be like, *trapped* there, for a while."

"Would that be okay?" Alison asked. "I mean, are you allowed?"

"Sure," Meg said. "And if you come with me after school, you won't even have to go through a big production at the gate or anything." She didn't *think.*

Alison nodded. "Okay, that sounds good. Let's do it later this week, maybe. Although we have this junior class community service thing coming up, and Gail said for me to ask you, if you maybe wanted to help out with the planning committee."

The school was really big on community service, and everyone in the student body was required to volunteer for a certain number of hours regularly. "Sure," Meg said, definitely interested. "How come she didn't ask me herself?"

Alison just grinned and shook her head.

SO, THINGS AT school were getting much better. She was mortified every time Adam walked by, but he made a point of avoiding her, too. Which meant that her main problem switched from school—to her mother. It wasn't even that they weren't speaking, or anything obvious, but it was like those months during the campaign when they had gotten into so many fights and had to concentrate on being careful with each other. Conversations were a major effort.

Of course, being President meant that Meg didn't see her all that much, anyway. The first few months of any President's term were considered the honeymoon, so that the new President could get used to the job, and that meant that it was a great time to get a lot of policy ideas through Congress quickly. Plus, there was a state dinner coming up, a summit meeting with world leaders in Geneva in about a month, Cabinet members and aides all over the place advising and briefing—there was a lot going on.

On the nights when her parents didn't have to make any appearances, and didn't have company, her mother usually worked straight through dinner—or just came upstairs briefly, and then hurried back down to the Oval Office or her private study to put in a few more hours. Meg hated to look out the West Sitting Hall window at the lights on in the Oval Office late at night, and think of her mother bent over her desk, practically killing herself to run the country. They were all supposed to be going up to Camp David soon, so that she could get a short break, but so far, it seemed to be an idea that her father kept suggesting—and her mother just ignored.

But, it was more than the fact that she was so damned busy. The only time she ever seemed to come near Meg's room was when she thought Meg was asleep. Twice, Meg had been awake, but hadn't moved, afraid to start anything. She couldn't stand the idea that it was going to be like this for the rest of their lives, but it was certainly starting to seem that way.

It was Sunday, and she was watching a movie in the solarium with Steven, when it occurred to her that if her mother was down in the Oval Office, her father was probably alone, and she could talk to him.

"Where you going?" Steven asked, as she got up. "You're going to miss like, the most excellent part."

"I'll be right back," she said.

She went down to the second floor, where she found her father in the Yellow Oval Room, deep in a book.

"Uh, Dad?" she asked.

He lowered the book.

"Are you busy, or can I talk to you for a minute?" she asked.

He gestured towards the couch. "I bet I know what this is about."

Probably, yeah. She sat down next to him. "It's like it was during the primaries. I don't know what to do about it."

"It's also for a lot of the same reasons," he said. "She pushes herself too hard, and then doesn't have enough energy left for anything else. It's not that she's mad at you—or at any of us, for that matter—but, when she gets this exhausted, she knows she has a tendency to start arguments, so she makes an effort to avoid controversial situations."

In other words, avoid *her*.

"Give her some time, Meg," he said. "She has so much going on that she—I think the best thing we can all do right now is give her as much room as she needs."

Did that mean that her parents were fighting, too? They were so incredibly private, that she sometimes couldn't tell. Meg slouched into her turtleneck. "Why's she always so quick to think I hate her?"

Her father sighed, and put his book down on the coffee table, out of reach. "Why do you ask such complicated questions?"

"Well," she frowned, "is it my fault?"

"Sure, sometimes. There are a lot of reasons, though." He fingered the gold ring on his left hand, and she wondered if he even knew that he was doing it. "A lot of it is that she hates *her* mother."

Which made no sense at all. "But, she never really had one," Meg said.

"That's why she hates her." He let his hand fall. "Oh, hate's a strong word—it's not that simple. But, her feelings toward her mother have a lot to do with the way she sees yours."

Did that mean that they weren't ever going to be able to resolve it? "But—" Meg said.

"I know you don't." He half-smiled. "I just can't always convince her."

"What am I supposed to do," Meg asked, "tell her I love her or something?"

Her father nodded. "It might be nice."

"But," she twisted uncomfortably, "I don't tell *you*."

"I don't need to hear it," he said.

She slouched lower, folding her arms across her chest.

He picked his book back up, but after reading for a minute, he stopped. "Meg?"

She kept slouching. "What."

"Do you?" he asked.

She tilted her head, not sure what he meant. "Do I what?"

"I don't know," he said. "Like me?"

She shrugged, blushed, and then nodded.

"Do you," he carefully smoothed the binding of his book, "like me a lot?"

She blushed more, but nodded.

"Do you," he put the book down again, "maybe even love me?"

She blew out an irritated and embarrassed breath. "Yes, okay?"

"Just wanted to make sure." He picked up his book and cheerfully resumed reading.

Hell, *that* wasn't fair. She looked at him accusingly. "Well?"

"Well, what?" he asked.

Did he really need a road map? "Aren't you going to say that you like me?" she asked.

He shrugged. "Are you sure I do?"

Mostly, she thought he was funny—but, not always.

He laughed, reaching over to hug her. "Yes, I like you." He kissed the top of her head three times. "And yes, I even love you."

Hmmm. Maybe she should press her advantage, then. "Does that mean I'm not grounded?" she asked.

He shook his head.

"Okay." She pulled out of the hug, arms going back across her chest. "Maybe I don't love you after all."

"God, you're a brat." He ruffled up her hair. "Okay, you're paroled."

She grinned, leaning up to give him a kiss on the cheek.

"This is not a precedent," he said.

She just grinned.

IT WAS PAST midnight, and she was in bed, scrunched up on her side, patting Vanessa and trying to fall asleep. The door slid open, and she smelled perfume, but she stayed huddled on her side, not sure whether she should pretend to be asleep. The gentle perfume was closer, and she felt her blankets being adjusted, then the soft warmth of the quilt from the bottom of the bed being spread out over her. There was a tiny sound—maybe just a breath, maybe a light sigh—and she felt a different kind of warmth, that of her mother's hand on her forehead, then on her cheek, before pulling away, the perfume fading.

"Mom?" she said. "Um, I'm awake."

"So, I gather," her mother said, her voice over near the door.

Meg sat up and turned on the light, Vanessa giving her a good paw smack in protest. "Um, did you get a lot of work done?"

"I don't know." Her mother dragged a tired hand through her hair—which, for once, *wasn't* perfectly combed. "Not really, I guess."

"You've been working really hard lately," Meg said.

"I know." Her mother sighed. "The harder I work, the more there seems to be to do."

She already knew the answer, but– "Are you tired?" Meg asked.

"I think it's a permanent condition," her mother said.

"Oh." Meg idly tugged at a loose piece of wool in her quilt—which she was going to have to have Trudy fix, as soon as she came to visit. "I thought we could maybe talk for a minute."

Her mother promptly sat down on the bottom of the bed.

"You're so tired you fall down?" Meg said.

"It only feels that way," her mother said, and Meg could hear the laugh in her voice. "How are you liking the drama club?"

Which wasn't really her thing, but she had joined, because—well, there was nothing wrong with trying something new. Meg shrugged. "It's okay. They mostly just have me working on the sets, a little."

"I'm looking forward to meeting your friend Alison," her mother said.

Who had come over two days earlier, and even though Steven had been grumping around for some reason or other, and being pretty annoying, she had seemed to have a nice time just hanging out. "Yeah," Meg said. "Beth wants to come down during spring break, and maybe by then I'll know enough people to invite some over."

Her mother nodded. "I would expect so. Is Sarah going to come, too?"

Unlike Beth, Sarah seemed to be having some trouble taking the notion of having a friend who lived in the White House in stride, so they weren't in touch as often these days. Emails, mostly—and not even many of those. "I don't know. I hope so." Meg stopped pulling at her quilt, since she didn't want to unravel it completely. "Um, anyway, I wanted to ask you if you're still speaking at the women's leadership conference this week."

Her mother nodded.

"Be, uh, kind of a big deal if you sold them on the humanitarian deployment," Meg said. Which had been all over the news, because even though it was potentially fraught with far too many perils, the President had made it very clear that she thought that the situation was gravely deteriorating and bordering on genocide—and that they were *compelled* to respond, swiftly, with something more than financial aid.

Her mother glanced over, Meg grinning shyly at her.

"Indeed it would," her mother said.

"Can I come watch?" Meg asked. "I'd like to."

"Really?" Her mother looked very pleased. "It's not going to be very exciting, I'm afraid."

"I'd still like to," Meg said. "Can you write me a note to get dismissed early?"

"Sure." Her mother frowned. "That is, if you think you can miss class."

Obviously, there were few things she enjoyed more than missing classes. "It's only gym. But, um"—somehow, she felt shy again—"can you write the note yourself? I mean, you know, in handwriting?"

"Sure," her mother said. "I'd like that."

25

"HI," JOSH SAID, when he passed her locker the next morning. "H-how was your weekend?"

He really was kind of cute. Shy as hell, but at least with enough nerve to be persistent. *Con*sistent, anyway. "Not bad," she said. "How was yours?"

"Fine." He nodded. "Yeah. Fine."

Jesus. "Are you always so nervous?" she asked.

"Who, me?" He coughed. "No, not always."

"When *aren't* you?" she asked.

"Um, well," he coughed again, "sometimes I sleep."

She laughed, and he allowed himself a small grin.

"You have a very nice smile," he said.

Upon which, she felt herself turn into the shy one.

"You really do," he said.

"Oh, I don't think—" She noticed Adam swaggering down the hall with some of his friends, and pretended to be busy with something inside her locker.

"You might as well give up, Feldman," Adam said. "She doesn't talk to guys."

"Look, Miller," Josh said. "Why don't you—"

"Watch out for your glasses," Adam said, shoving him and continuing down the hall.

Josh recovered his balance, very red, and took off his glasses, shining them with his shirt. He looked different without them. Younger? Less anxious?

"He's really a jerk," she said.

"Yeah." He cleaned his glasses harder.

"If you hate them so much, why don't you get contacts?" she asked. Or that eye surgery, even.

"I don't know. Guess I should." He studied his frames. "Guess these are kind of a turn-off, hunh?"

"Some people look good in them." Meg noticed that he was taller than she'd thought, and that she had to look up to see his eyes.

"Yeah." He put them on. "Men with greying temples. Or women who wear them on top of their heads." He paused. "You really do have a nice smile."

"Thank you." She went back to feeling shy. "But, I don't think—"

They both looked up as the warning bell rang.

"May I carry your books?" he asked. "Or were you brought up to carry boys' books?"

She grinned, and took his knapsack—which was actually heavy as hell.

"Thanks, they weigh a lot." He put his hands in his pockets. "And I'm very weak."

"You don't look it," she said, and he really *didn't*, she decided, studying his deceptively muscled build. Alison had told her that he was on the baseball team, and he also looked like the kind of guy who maybe played lacrosse or something.

"Brought up to be a diplomat, too, hunh?" He took his knapsack—and hers. "Come on."

He was cute. She wasn't interested—no *way* was she interested—but, he was cute. Very cute.

SCHOOL FELT MUCH better. Or else, *she* felt better, maybe. The novelty of being the President's daughter was wearing off, and she could open her lunch bag without everyone wanting to see what she had in there. She could make a joke without people either staring—or laughing much harder than necessary. Best of all, she bumped into some guy in the hall—a senior, she thought—and he said, "Christ, will you look where you're going?" instead of falling all over himself apologizing. Sure, some people were still treating her like a being from Oz, but life was unquestionably improving. She was going to play tennis on Thursday with Alison—whose parents belonged to an indoor club—a couple of people had wanted to see her homework before class, she got reprimanded in French for talking—it was almost like being at home. And Josh was turning out to be very nice. She wasn't interested in him—but, he was nice. One of these days, she might even have a couple of graphic thoughts.

Maybe.

"Are you still coming tomorrow?" her mother asked, the night before the leadership conference speech.

"Maybe," Meg said in her if-you're-lucky voice. "Are you still thinking of writing me a note?"

"Maybe." Her mother had an even better if-you're-lucky voice, and Meg laughed.

So, the next morning, Meg carried in her little note on official White House stationery. It was in two envelopes and everything—her mother was being pretty funny, signing the polite request for her to be dismissed early with a large, dramatic "Katharine Vaughn Powers."

Josh noticed the envelope when he paused by her locker before home-room, an action that had become a habit. "What's that?"

She put her knapsack and the note in his arms, and stuffed her jacket into her locker. "I have to get out early today, so my mother wrote me a note."

"Yeah?" He touched the envelope with an exaggeratedly reverent hand. "Is this kind of like kissing the Pope's ring?"

"Skip right past the Pope, and go straight up to *God,*" Meg said.

Josh laughed—quite hard—and then bowed in front of her. "May I have the honor of escorting you to homeroom, Miss Powers?"

"Well, I don't know." She looked him over. "Jeffrey, darling?"

Her Secret Service agent, who was standing just down the hall, grinned. "What?"

"Do something with this young man, will you?" She brushed Josh away as if he were a small, annoying fly. "I cawn't seem to get rid of him."

"Talk about Boston accents," Josh said.

She shrugged. "I can only assume that you're jealous."

"In your dreams, kid," he said.

"No," she shook her head, "I have to have my dreams screened before I can have them."

Jeff laughed, but Josh just looked at her, his expression—what? Intent? Interested? Attracted. Very, very attracted. *So* attracted, that she blushed in confusion, adjusting the collar of her shirt, which didn't need it.

The warning bell rang, and she headed down the hall, Josh next to her, neither of them speaking.

"Um, here you go," he said, at the door of her homeroom, handing her her knapsack.

"Thank you," she said, keeping her eyes down.

He started to walk away, and then came back. "Meg?"

She stopped, too. "What?"

"I, uh—" He seemed to change his mind about whatever he had been going to say. "S-see you in English."

She nodded. "See you there."

AT ONE-THIRTY, SHE was driven back to the White House to go to the speech with her mother. She changed into a skirt and sweater, then they went out to the motorcade that was waiting on the South Grounds, her mother pausing to banter with the clearly delighted press for a couple of minutes.

Once they were inside the limousine, Meg looked around.

"I almost never get to ride up here," she said. "How come Winnie or Glen isn't in here briefing you?"

"Because I sometimes get tired of being treated as though I'm scarcely capable of speaking my native language," her mother said, flipping through a small stack of index cards covered with handwritten notes.

Woe to anyone who tried to tell the not-ego-free President what to do.

Meg leaned over to try and read the notes, but her mother pointed sternly at her seatbelt, and she sat back, putting it on.

"What are you going to say?" she asked.

Her mother shrugged. "I don't know. I'd like to do a good job, though—I always feel as though I owe women's groups something extra."

Which didn't seem fair. "Haven't you done enough?" Meg asked.

"It just makes them expect more," her mother said.

At the hotel where the convention was being held, she and her mother sat quietly in the holding room for a few minutes. Then, after taking a couple of calls from the White House, her mother drank three shots of espresso in rapid succession, then used some breath spray, and one of Linda's aides walked Meg out to the huge reception hall to her seat in the front row.

She looked over her shoulder at the packed room. Christ, she would be petrified to speak in front of that many people—how did her mother do it? The audience was very excited. In fact, they had even been excited to see *her*. Indicating—to Meg, anyway—that they were pretty hard up.

Everyone turned to watch the door suddenly, and Meg saw her mother, surrounded by Secret Service agents, being ushered to the stage.

After being introduced to great applause, her mother stepped up to the podium, and the applause turned into a standing ovation.

Which the President seemed to enjoy, frankly.

The audience was very receptive, laughing and/or cheering at almost everything her mother said. Including—to some degree—the artfully phrased news-bite about the upcoming military deployment she was proposing, which seemed to be given some cautious acceptance, although not outright *enthusiasm*. But, the entire press pool instantly perked up, and she saw notebooks fly open and pens start writing like crazy. So, at the very worst, her mother had accomplished the lesser goal of feeding the press a nice tasty morsel—a tactic that was almost always beneficial in the long run.

At one point, her mother took off her blazer, which she dryly described as "abandoning male trappings," and got the biggest laugh of all. She winked at Meg, throwing the blazer out to her, and Meg caught it, wondering how the hell her mother even managed to make *being goofy* seem Presidential.

She held the blazer in her lap, smelling the vitality and elegance of the perfume, and it occurred to her that the Leader of the Free World almost *never* wore blazers—but must have specifically chosen to do so today, just to get the big laugh. Which was cocky as hell, but also pretty funny.

She didn't really listen to the speech, just watched the audience's reactions: clapping, laughing, communal nodding. Meg kind of got the feeling that they all thought that her mother really *had* met God. Of course, knowing her mother, that was probably the case. Maybe she'd spent a weekend in Heaven campaigning.

She watched her finish the speech, wondering if her mother ever actually relaxed. Sometimes, Meg thought she looked much happier holding Neal on her lap or sitting with Steven, than she ever did doing political stuff. And lots of times with her father. She had probably never seen her mother as happy as the day she caught the two of them dancing.

Now, the applause was another standing ovation, and her mother looked pleasant enough, but maybe it was the difference between happiness—and joy. Her mother didn't seem to get any *joy* out of this. But, she was winking again, and—only a little embarrassed—Meg winked back.

Sometimes, she thought the President was a pretty soft touch.

WHEN THE APPLAUSE finally died down, there was a reception in one of the hotel ballrooms. No one could say that her mother wasn't a friendly President—nor could they accuse her of ducking out after speaking engagements, although Meg saw Winnie, the deputy chief of staff, whisper into her ear a couple of times, and a tiny look of concern flash across her mother's face once.

Meg made a half-hearted attempt to go over to her, but the crowd was so big, that she decided it wasn't worth the trouble. But, her mother was clearly looking for *her,* and Meg waved, her mother smiling and waving back, most of the women gathered around her smiling, too.

That taken care of, Meg wandered over to one of the tables to check out the food. Steven and Neal were going to be mad that they hadn't come—there were platters of frosted pastries, whipped cream puffing up all over the place. Maybe she could steal them some.

Feeling a little bored and a little bratty, she decided to make her agents nervous and eat a few. They had a poison fixation, always watching everything she put into her mouth. It was enough to make her want to stuff her face.

She ate a couple, then got a paper plate to take some home. The chairwoman of the conference, who was coming over to say hello, saw the pastry-laden plate and looked very surprised—perhaps at the thought that she had such a monster appetite.

Meg blushed. "I was sort of taking them for my brothers. Is that okay? If you want, I can put them back."

The woman laughed. "That's great. That's really great."

Meg reddened more, and covered the plate with a napkin. A lot of other people started coming up to talk to her, which was awkward, when she was standing there with a bunch of stolen pastries.

"Barry, can you hold these?" she whispered.

He shook his head. "Meg, you know I can't—"

Yeah, yeah, yeah. Strict Secret Service rule. "Can you give them to Frank, maybe?" she asked. Since he was her mother's personal aide, and always got stuck carrying *everything*, like a well-dressed little pack mule. "So I can go to the ladies' room?"

Barry sighed and took the plate, gesturing for Jeff to escort her.

It was a serious drag to be followed over to the *ladies' room.* It would have been better if Marcy had been assigned to this shift—but, she wasn't. It was a real reminder, though, of why Steven kept trying to escape from his agents. Sometimes, it would just be nice to be left *alone.*

Jeff knocked on the door, said, "Secret Service," and went inside with her to make sure everything was okay. The two women who were standing by the sinks made a very quick exit.

"Please don't take too long, okay?" he said, looking at his watch.

Meg nodded grumpily, and he went out to the hall to wait for her. She sat down on the couch in the lounge section, realizing that it was the first time she had been by herself in public for weeks. It felt *great.* She glanced around, one idle foot tapping on the floor. Jeff would keep everyone out, being paranoid as usual, so she could stay in here all day, if she wanted.

Tapping her other foot to make a little rhythm, she noticed that there was another door across the room. Did Jeff know that? Probably. Only, what if he had forgotten? It would be pretty funny to go out the wrong way, and then come up behind him. She had never tried anything like that before, and—well, no time like the present.

She opened the door, seeing a long corridor with a door at the far left. There was no one in sight, so she went out there, walking down to the other door. She opened it, finding herself in another hallway, with some boxes stacked along the walls. Maybe this was a storage area, or something. She turned left, figuring that she would make a full circle that way, and end up in the lobby.

It was really weird to be by herself in public. To feel *normal.* And it suddenly made perfect sense that her mother had a tendency to stroll right on over to rope-lines and shake hands, even when her detail was strongly against the idea. There was something to be said for a little independence.

As she walked down the hall, she kind of hoped someone would come out and yell at her, thinking she was just some kid off the street. A janitor or a cook or a bellhop, maybe.

She found another hall, only it led to the right, which wouldn't take her to the lobby. She didn't think.

Hmmm. She looked around uncertainly, then headed in that direction. She would just try to find her way out for another minute, and then give up and go back to the ladies' room, and exit the normal way. She made a couple more turns, realized that she was completely lost, and stopped. So, she went back to the door she had just come through and opened it, but the hall there didn't look right at all. Maybe she had come through one of the other three doors. Except that two of them were locked, and the other opened on to a flight of stairs.

Okay. She was officially lost—and Jeff was going to *kill* her. Christ, she was in the middle of a large city, in a four-star hotel—and she might as well be in the freakin' *Yukon.* How stupid was that?

She went into the one hallway she could still access, not sure if she had originally come from the left or the right. All of the doors on the right side were locked, and when she went down to the left, she found another stairway. Since stairways were now her only option, she went down, finding herself in a pipe-crowded basement. She could hear a steady dripping from somewhere, and an irrational fear skipped up her back when she heard a loud crash that was maybe a machine starting up, or something falling over, or some*one*—she wasn't waiting around to find out. She ran up the stairs and back into whichever hall she had been in, and tried doors until she finally found an open one—which led to another staircase, and an ominously empty storage room.

Okay. Maybe deciding to surprise Jeff hadn't been such a great idea.

She came across another unlocked door and stepped into a grey, uncarpeted hallway. It looked like the set for every rape scene she had ever seen on television, and she came to the conclusion that this had definitely been a lousy idea.

She felt a draft behind her, and spun around, scared. What if someone was after her, or—no, that was paranoid. But, why else did she have Secret Service agents? Because people were afraid that *someone might go after her*.

This had been a terrible, awful idea.

She followed the draft, tentatively opened the heavy metal door from underneath which it was coming, and saw a dimly-lit, car-crowded parking garage.

No way was she going in *there.* Everyone knew that people got kidnapped in parking garages.

Damn.

Damn.

Damn.

She thought about pushing the little panic button they always made her carry, but that would be too embarrassing, so she hurried through open doors and grey corridors, up some more stairs, and finally arrived at a red and gold hall. Okay, that meant that she was back up on the first floor. There was a God.

She had no idea where she was, but she opened a door and saw one of the extra agents assigned to the event striding down the hall, with his radio out.

"Uh, hi," she said guiltily.

"Where have you been?" he asked, sounding furious.

"Well, I, uh, I sort of took a wrong turn," she said.

He was already on the transmitter, relaying the information that Sandpiper was secured.

"Come on," he said, when he was finished. "The President is waiting for you."

"Am I, uh," Meg cleared her throat, "in trouble?"

He nodded.

Great.

26

THE AGENT KNEW his way, and after only two doors, they were out in the very crowded lobby, other agents swarming around her, everyone else staring. The word "mortified" took on a whole new dimension. She let the agents hustle her to the motorcade, noticing how particularly angry Jeff and Barry were. There were camera flashes everywhere, and she could already picture the news reports about the President's klutzy daughter who had gotten lost on her way out of the ladies' room.

She looked down at the red carpet leading to the President's limousine, feeling as if she were being taken to her execution. Her mother, in spite of very nervous agents, jumped out of the car, looking as furious as Meg had ever seen her.

"Where have you been?" she demanded.

"Uh, well." Meg put her hands into blazer pockets that didn't even belong to her. "I sort of—"

"Why do you think you have agents?" her mother asked. "Didn't it occur to you that everyone might be—"

"I'm sorry," Meg said, flushing more as she realized exactly how many cameras—and eyes—were currently focused on them.

Her mother nodded. "Terrific. You're sorry. Glad to hear it. Get in the car!"

"Kate," Linda muttered, lurking nearby. "Not in front of—"

"I can't be angry?" Her mother whirled around to confront the cameras and reporters—and *civilians* with cameras—her posture challenging. "I am absolutely furious at my daughter, I think I'm quite within my rights—and you may quote me! I'm certain that any one of you who is a parent will understand." She shook an agent's hand from her arm. "Will you please get *off* me?"

Wow. The President was completely losing it—on national television. Meg grinned, suddenly not minding the attention at all.

"I thought I told you to get in the car!" her mother said. Or, more accurately, *barked.*

Meg climbed into the limo, still grinning, and her mother followed a few seconds later, the motorcade immediately pulling away.

"Meg," her mother said, very grimly, "I thought we made it very clear—"

That word again. Her parents loved to be clear.

"—that you weren't to give your agents any trouble," her mother said. "Do you know what could have—"

Meg nodded.

"I don't think you *do,*" her mother said. "I was afraid you—"

Meg grinned. "You're yelling at me."

"Damn right I'm yelling at you!" her mother said. "You're grounded, got that?"

Meg felt her grin get bigger. "Again?"

"Yes, again. And get that smile off your face!" her mother ordered. "It's not—"

"I love you," Meg said, and reached over to hug her, hanging on, feeling the hard thumping of her mother's heart.

Her mother tried to move away. "Don't pull that."

"But, I love you." Meg held on more tightly. "I really do." She leaned up to kiss her mother's cheek, still hugging her. "I love you a lot." Tired from saying all of that, as well as embarrassed, she let go, afraid to meet her mother's eyes. "Even though you're President, I love you," she said quietly.

She didn't hear anything on the seat next to her and finally looked over. Her mother was sitting very still, her face averted, and Meg recognized Steven and herself in the slight slouch of her mother's shoulders.

"Mom?" she asked.

Her mother reached out a tentative left hand, and Meg took it, seeing a small braceleted wrist, and older, but very familiar, fingers. She had always thought of her mother's hand as being much bigger than hers, but they were the same size. Her mother was really holding on, as if she needed to, or something.

"Do you look like this when you cry?" Meg asked.

"No." Her mother turned, and Meg saw the brightness in her eyes. "I look like this when I'm trying not to." She took Meg into her arms for a quick, hard hug. "Can I ask you something?"

Meg shrugged.

"Did you mean that?" her mother asked.

Meg tilted her head to see her mother's face. "Could I ask *you* something?"

Her mother laughed. "I might have guessed. Okay. What?"

"Are you insecure?" Meg asked.

"Yes." Her mother laughed again. "Yes, I am very insecure."

Yep. Meg grinned at her. "Did it feel good to yell?"

Her mother nodded. "Yes. I have to admit that it did."

"Are you going to do it all the time now?" Meg asked.

"I just might." Her mother leaned back, leaving her arm around Meg's shoulders. "Are you ever going to pull an idiot stunt like that again?"

"No." Meg slouched down. "I'm sorry."

"Okay. Because—okay." Her mother looked at her for a long minute, and then nodded. "Okay, we'll leave it at that." Then, unexpectedly, she grinned. "Hey, would you like a martini?"

Meg sat up straight. "What?"

Her mother opened the tiny refrigerator built into the back of the front seat. "They keep this thing stocked."

"Very dry?" Meg asked.

Her mother nodded. "Absolutely."

"With an olive?" Meg asked.

Her mother nodded again. "You bet."

Hmmm. Meg looked at her thoughtfully. "Are you kidding?"

"Yes," her mother said.

FILMED REPORTS OF the President yelling at her daughter made every newscast that night, and damn near *flooded* the Internet. Everyone on her mother's staff was having heart attacks—except for Preston, who she heard had laughed for about ten minutes straight. Steven thought it was hysterical, Neal was worried that Meg was in big trouble, and her father groaned a lot. After her mother finally came upstairs—there were, after all, pressing national and world events for her to handle—she and Meg both grinned a lot, as the whole family sat in her parents' bedroom, watching some of the coverage.

"Boy, Meg," Steven said, as one of the cable news shows ran the clip yet again. "They're gonna make fun of *you* at school tomorrow."

No doubt.

"I think they're probably going to make fun of me, too," her mother said.

Shoot, judging from the quick spin she had taken on the Internet earlier, hundreds and thousands of people already *were*.

"Is Meggie grounded again?" Neal asked.

"Meggie is grounded until she's thirty," their father said.

Their mother shook her head. "No, Meggie is grounded until she's *fifty*."

"Oh, right," Meg said, in a yeah-sure-anything-you-say voice.

Her mother didn't even flinch. "Malapert. Recalcitrant. Overweening."

"You forgot 'a joy to be around,' " Meg said.

Her mother smiled. "No, I didn't."

STEVEN WAS RIGHT, and people did give her grief about getting blasted by the President—on film—but it didn't really bother her.

She had apologized to her agents, who laughed and said they would forgive her—as long as it never, *ever* happened again.

"You're pretty chipper," Josh said after school, as he leaned against the locker next to hers. "I mean, for having been chastised."

"You mean, chaste, right?" Meg said.

He lifted her knapsack onto his shoulder. "Whatever you say."

Someone, somewhere, had definitely taught this guy to be a gentleman—she wasn't sure if she had *ever* met someone who treated her quite so respectfully.

"You know, I could probably carry that myself," she said.

"Probably," he agreed. "How about you hold the door?"

"Fair enough." She moved ahead of him, and opened the nearest exit with a flourish.

"Thank you, young lady," he said.

"Young *woman*," she said.

"Sorry," he said, the attraction she'd noticed before suddenly strong in his eyes. "You—you look good happy, Meg."

"What?" she asked, that particular remark unexpected.

"I'm just glad you're happy." He walked her to her car, and they stood there for a minute. "Guess you, uh, have to get going."

"Yeah." She took the knapsack from him. "Um, you need a ride anywhere?"

He shook his head. "I'm all set."

They both nodded.

"Uh," he coughed once. "Hypothetical question."

She nodded.

He looked everywhere *but* at her. "If I were to ask you out—to a, a movie, say, how do you think you'd feel about that?"

"This is just hypothetical, right?" she said.

He nodded, still not looking at her.

"I think I'd feel good," she said. "Can you wait until I'm fifty?"

He glanced up. "What?"

"I kind of got grounded until I'm fifty," she said, then shifted her knapsack to her other shoulder. "Do you like *The African Queen*?"

He shrugged. "Sure. I guess so."

"They're showing it at the house tonight—it's one of my mother's favorites. Would you," she blinked a couple of times, "uh, maybe like to come over and see it?"

His eyes got very wide. "T-to your house?"

She nodded.

"Big white job?" he asked. "Pennsylvania Avenue?"

"That's the one," she said.

"Wow." He took his glasses off, absently wiping them on his sweater, then put them back on, squinting as if he'd only made them worse. Then, he grinned, his whole face brightening. "What time?"

"Um, eight?" she said. "They usually start running them around eight-thirty, nine."

"Black tie?" he asked.

"Wear what you have on," she said.

He glanced dubiously at his sweatshirt and jeans. "Really?"

"Yeah." Then, she remembered something. "What kind of car will be you driving?"

He frowned. "Would it make a difference?"

Well—*yeah*. "If I don't let them know at the gate, they won't let you in," she said.

"Oh." He looked relieved. "Toyota, dark green, pretty ugly."

She laughed. "Okay. Great."

Adam Miller and a group of his friends came laughing out of the school, and without thinking, Meg leaned forward and kissed Josh.

"You just used me," he said quietly.

Yeah. "I know." She turned very red, regretting the impulse. "I'm sorry."

"Don't be." He rested his hands lightly on her shoulders. "Now it's my turn."

He kissed her, and they moved closer together, forgetting about

Adam, forgetting about his friends, and forgetting about agents who might be watching. Remembering, they quickly pulled apart.

"Wow," he said. Awkwardly, he touched her face, then dropped his hand. "I'm sorry."

Adam and his friends had walked past them now, no longer laughing.

"I'm not," Meg said. "Eight?"

AT THE WHITE House, she got off at the South Portico, and cut around underneath one of the ancient Andrew Jackson magnolia trees and straight across the Rose Garden, to the Oval Office.

Her mother's longtime secretary, Mrs. Berger, was sitting at her desk in the outer office, looking—as was typical—as though working for the President was as relaxing and undemanding a job as had ever existed. Which, given the chaos that generally reigned, had to be very soothing for her mother.

"Hi," Meg said. "Is she busy?"

Mrs. Berger laughed.

Good point. "Well," Meg amended that. "Is she *really* busy?"

Mrs. Berger smiled, and looked down at the schedule on her desk. "Actually, if you want to wait, Meg, she has a small window in about twenty minutes."

That didn't sound too long, so Meg sat down, and talked to Frank—whose desk was also in the office—for a while, until some Congressional leaders left the office, all of them looking a bit surly, and she was buzzed in. She found her mother frowning at her reflection in the window, straightening her hair.

"Maybe they should hang a wall-sized mirror up for you," Meg said, "and then you can just sit and stare into it all day long."

Her mother turned, looking a little sheepish. "Hi." Then, she looked worried. "There's nothing wrong, is there?"

"Nope." Meg sat down behind the desk, putting her feet up, enjoying the feeling of power. Maybe there *was* something to public office. Something that went well beyond the simple concept of *service*.

"How was school?" her mother asked.

"Not bad." Meg picked up her mother's phone without pushing any buttons down. "God-damn it," she said into the receiver, "I told you that I wasn't to be disturbed. I'm entertaining." She listened for a second. "Yeah, well, get on the stick, or I know someone who's going to be increasing my unemployment figures. Yes, they are *my* figures. *Everything* is mine. *I* am in charge."

"Having a nice time?" her mother asked.

Meg sighed impatiently. "Miss, please. I'm really terribly busy. If you'll just—oh!" She let her eyes dawn with recognition. Lots of recognition. "The interview—of course. Good God, I'm sorry." She studied her mother, then leaned forward to scan imaginary papers on the desk and nodded. "Yes, you're in luck. We *do* have an opening for an exotic dancer. If you wouldn't mind—"

"You're invading my space, small, pesky child," her mother said.

"Well," Meg said, huffily, "we *are* a mite presumptuous, aren't we?"

Her mother laughed. "We are, indeed." She motioned abruptly for Meg to get out of the chair.

"Boy," Meg said, standing up. "Some Presidents sure are grumpy."

"I'm not grumpy." Her mother sat down, swung her own feet onto the desk, and then grinned. "I'm possessive."

Meg nodded. "That's for sure."

Now, her mother got up, too. "I hate to do this to you, brat, but I have to ask you to leave, okay?"

"Boy," Meg said, kicking at the carpet. "You don't even want to talk to me."

"Perhaps we can find a more opportune time," her mother said. The phone on her desk rang, and she picked it up. "Thank you, I'll be right in." She hung up, glancing into the silver stand of her engraved pen and pencil set, checking her hair again.

"You look fine," Meg said. "I mean, considering how old you are."

"Thank you." Her mother frowned at the phone, as it rang again. "Do you still hate being the President's daughter?"

"Maybe," Meg said, in a bet-you-wish-you-knew voice.

Her mother nodded. "That's what I figured."

Meg grinned and moved in to give her a hard, reassuring hug before leaving. "Are you coming to dinner tonight?"

"*Maybe,*" her mother said.

Meg shook her head. "No, really, I mean it."

"Sure," her mother said, her smile bright with far more joy than happiness. "I'll be there."

Thank you for reading

this FEIWEL AND FRIENDS book.

The Friends who made

THE PRESIDENT'S DAUGHTER

possible are:

JEAN FEIWEL
publisher

LIZ SZABLA
editor-in-chief

RICH DEAS
creative director

ELIZABETH FITHIAN
marketing director

ELIZABETH USURIELLO
assistant to the publisher

DAVE BARRETT
managing editor

NICOLE LIEBOWITZ MOULAISON
production manager

JESSICA TEDDER
associate editor

ALLISON REMCHECK
editorial assistant

KSENIA WINNICKI
marketing assistant